Praise for *Double Bluff*

"Michael Hawley has made an impressive debut with *Double Bluff*. The story benefits from his obvious experience in law enforcement as well as his ability to create an intriguing cast of characters and craft a great page-turner. This is an author with a unique blend of experience and talent. *Double Bluff* is a roller coaster of a read. It will keep you guessing until the very end."
—*New York Times* bestselling author Steve Martini

"A fascinating police thriller starring two great protagonists who deserve their own series. Michael A. Hawley gives the reader an insider's look about what confronts a police officer on a recurring basis. The story line is multilayered so that when the reader peels one subplot off, there is something ever darker and more shocking underneath it. This crime thriller is great escapist reading."
—*Midwest Book Review*

"[Hawley's] background brings gritty detail to the gripping page-turner, evoking vivid scenes from the point of view of those who serve on the thin blue line."
—*The Oregonian*

"Hawley knows the mechanics of both police work and mystery writing."
—*The Herald* (Everett, WA)

"A superb police procedural, marvelously detailed, with believable characters . . . first rate."
—*I Love a Mystery*

"*Double Bluff* is filled with suspense and an amazing plot. Hawley—a former sheriff—pulls together the different story lines simply and expertly. The authenticity of his words rings throughout, and I can't wait for his next book in the series."
—*Romantic Times*

Also by Michael A. Hawley

Double Bluff

SILENT PROOF

Michael A. Hawley

AN ONYX BOOK

ONYX
Published by New American Library, a division of
Penguin Group (USA) Inc., 375 Hudson Street,
New York, New York 10014, U.S.A.
Penguin Books Ltd, 80 Strand,
London WC2R 0RL, England
Penguin Books Australia Ltd, 250 Camberwell Road,
Camberwell, Victoria 3124, Australia
Penguin Books Canada Ltd, 10 Alcorn Avenue,
Toronto, Ontario, Canada M4V 3B2
Penguin Books (N.Z.) Ltd, Cnr Rosedale and Airborne Roads,
Albany, Auckland 1310, New Zealand

Penguin Books Ltd, Registered Offices:
80 Strand, London WC2R 0RL, England

First published by Onyx, an imprint of New American Library,
a division of Penguin Group (USA) Inc.

First Printing, September 2003
10 9 8 7 6 5 4 3 2 1

PUBLISHER'S NOTE
This is a work of fiction. Names, characters, places, and incidents either are the product
of the author's imagination or are used fictitiously, and any resemblance to actual
persons, living or dead, business establishments, events, or locales is entirely
coincidental.

BOOKS ARE AVAILABLE AT QUANTITY DISCOUNTS WHEN USED TO
PROMOTE PRODUCTS OR SERVICES. FOR INFORMATION PLEASE WRITE TO
PREMIUM MARKETING DIVISION, PENGUIN GROUP (USA) INC., 375 HUDSON
STREET, NEW YORK, NEW YORK 10014.

When asked where he got his inspiration, Sir Arthur Conan Doyle is said to have replied, "One needs only to visit his local constabulary for a day to obtain all the details necessary to paint a lifetime of characters." I couldn't agree more. This book is therefore dedicated to my friends and coworkers at the Island County Sheriff's Office, for their quirks, passions, humor, and bravery, but most important, for their unbending sense of duty to the citizens of Island County, Washington.

1

All was quiet on the treelined street of working-class homes. Lights were off except for a sprinkling of porch lamps, their pale glow casting long shadows along the otherwise deserted avenue. This was a safe kind of place. Neighbors knew neighbors, their pets and children. Lawns were mowed every Saturday, and on Sunday, local churches were full.

His vehicle rested curbside, in an eddy of darkness. From here he had a clear view to the next block, and the route that she would soon take. He knew it was only a matter of minutes. He had watched before.

A bead of sweat rolled down his flushed face, past unblinking eyes, and dropped to his pant leg. This was his kind of place also—untouched and unsuspecting.

Without breaking his gaze, he reached to a shirt pocket and withdrew a package of cigarettes. He shook it and lipped a butt, then fumbled for a matchbook. With one in hand, he flipped the cover open, and using only his left forefinger and thumb, bent a match down, and swept its head across the strike board. Meanwhile, his mind raced.

For months, his every spare hour had been spent winnowing prospects, watching, and patiently waiting. Tonight, though, the gathering storm within him could no longer be contained.

He took a long drag off the cigarette and exhaled slowly. The smoke swirled and drifted out the open window into the still night air. He was justified, wasn't he? God had chosen her, not him.

He took another puff while his free hand eased down to the canvas satchel resting on the floorboards. He unzipped the top and tipped the bag his way. It was all in there. Everything he would need. A hunting knife honed razor sharp, a roll of duct tape, a cotton sock for a gag, and a dog-eared Bible to pray for her sins when his work was done.

Suddenly a distant movement caught his eye. He stubbed his cigarette and leaned forward so that his chest bearhugged the steering wheel. His heartbeat surged. She was right on schedule. He craned his head farther, then eased back into his seat. *Take it slowly*, he cautioned himself. *Don't rush.*

Leaning sideways, he reached for his knife and unsheathed it. In the dim light, it still glimmered from the hours he had spent polishing it. With reverence, he fondled the blade, then brought it to his lips for a ceremonial kiss. He was ready.

Sliding over to the passenger side, he grabbed the door handle and pulled. Catlike, he slipped out, using the adjacent trunk of an old maple to conceal his movements. From here he would spring, just as he had practiced. She would never know until . . .

A moment later he was in position, crouched low, his ear cocked to detect her arrival. *This is the best part. The last few seconds.*

He drew a deep breath and held it as his blood pulsed with adrenaline.

Seconds ticked by.

She was nearing. He could sense her presence. But should he chance a peek? He did, but instantly snapped his head back. She was less than fifty paces away and closing. He gulped another breath, his last before he would spring. But suddenly from behind, a car turned from the cross street, its headlights backlighting his lair.

Son of a fucking bitch, his mind screamed.

Instantly, he dived for darkness, rolling beneath his vehicle and wriggling inward in a frenzied search for cover. With his back wedged against the drive shaft, he froze. The car was clearly slowing and coming to a stop—and only feet from where he lay pinned.

He gnashed his teeth and buried his face in his arms. *Who is this intruder?*

Suddenly, above the muffled exhaust of the idling engine, there was the sound of her voice, soft and innocent. He listened hard and heard her say to the unknown driver, "Yeah, she got off early tonight. . . . No, I'm not sure . . . Uh-huh . . . Right . . ."

Cautiously, he twisted his head so that he could peer towards the street. She was so close he had to look. What he saw made his heart skip. Her slim ankles were nearly within his grasp.

"I'll tell her tomorrow, okay?" she went on. "Yeah, Donna and I are both on the late shift again. . . ."

He desperately wanted to reach out, to snatch his prize, but he knew he would have to wait. He was a cautious man. She would be back. She always came back. He drew a deep silent breath, and calmness descended over his being. It was time to go home. The demons had departed, at least temporarily. They would return and so would he. He closed his eyes and waited.

There was more talking and then giggling. She shifted on her feet and finally said, "Naw, I just live down the block. Thanks, anyway . . ."

The car eased away, and the ankles he so longingly desired turned and stepped lightly down the center of the empty street. Seconds later both were gone.

2

"Your Honor," the young defense attorney protested, leaning forward in her chair. She glanced briefly at the stooped middle-aged man, handcuffed and seated beside her, and then glared at the prosecutor at the adjacent table. "I've just been assigned this case. I haven't had ten minutes with my client. I—"

Opposing counsel was at least thirty years her senior and a foot taller, and reeked of experience and connections. "Ms. Quinn," he cut in. "This is only a preliminary hearing. I don't see—"

"But you want my client held without bail."

"Under the circumstances—"

"What circumstances, Mr. Collins? I've seen no offer of proof. In fact, I've seen no evidence. This whole situation is outrageous. Mr. Bakerman was about to walk out of the prison gate. He was literally a week away from being a free man. Instead, he was slapped back into shackles and delivered here. He's done his time, over a decade's worth."

"This is a new allegation."

"New? Clifford Bakerman has been in prison for ten

years. How could he have committed any new crimes requiring detainment without bail?"

Ignoring her pleas, Richard Collins rose and motioned the bailiff to take custody of a legal document he held in his hand. He glanced back into the near empty courtroom towards several reporters scribbling notes. Seeing their heads bob up, he returned his attention to the judge and announced in a melodramatic tone, "There is no statute of limitations for murder."

The uniformed officer reached his side.

"Let me see that," Tessla Quinn demanded.

"I'll be the first, Ms. Quinn," the judge enjoined.

It was early in the day, the middle of another weary week of routine hearings. Apathy seemed to be weighing heavily upon the graying magistrate—at least until now. The sixty-eight-year-old woman had straightened, sharpness returning to her eyes.

"There are copies for everyone," Collins said with satisfaction. He surrendered one set to the bailiff and the other to Quinn's outstretched hand.

She immediately began speed-reading the papers. Meanwhile, her client remained still and emotionless, seemingly detached from the whole proceeding. His hands were neatly folded in his lap as though he were about to say grace before his evening meal.

"Give me a moment to examine this," the judge said. Collins settled into his chair, leaned back, and waited, his smug smile growing suspiciously wider.

In addition to the media scribes, the court clerk, and the two bored jailers stationed at arm's length from Bakerman, Detective Sergeant Leah Harris watched the hearing. She was seated alone in the public area, neatly dressed in a wool skirt, sweater, and comfortable pumps. The thirty-something muddy blonde looked on with intense professional interest—her attention shifting like a watchtower guard's between the two attorneys, the judge, and the lone prisoner. At her side were a small leather briefcase, a raincoat, and a folded umbrella—all ubiquitous equipment for a damp October day in Seattle.

Leah Harris knew both Judge Helen Stromberg and King County prosecutor Richard Collins from prior cases. Both had served multiple terms in their elected positions; both were highly respected, both professionals at the peak of their careers. The young wisp of a defense attorney, though, was a stranger. Harris eyed her suspiciously, cringing at the ankle tattoo showing through her nylons, and the multiple pierced rings protruding from both earlobes. Harris could easily visualize the ink still drying on her newly awarded law degree. Yet the young woman was standing her ground without any outward sign of intimidation or fear, challenging one of the leading legal minds in the area. And while to this point Harris had remained stone-faced, suddenly she too felt a slight smile crease her lips. This was not going to be the cakewalk testimony she had been promised.

Judge Stromberg looked up. "I see that Sergeant Harris is in the courtroom. Under the circumstances, perhaps it would be best if we swear her in and allow opposing counsel the opportunity to question her. Any objection to that, Mr. Collins?"

He shrugged his shoulders.

"Good." The judge motioned to the Seattle detective. "Please come forward, Sergeant Harris, and be sworn in."

Leah nodded, withdrew a file from her portfolio, and made her way to the witness stand, taking a seat as the bailiff came about.

"Would you raise your right hand, please."

Harris complied.

"Do you solemnly swear to tell the truth, the whole truth, and nothing but the truth, so help you, God?"

"I do."

Stromberg leaned her way. "For the record, would you state your full name and the city you reside in."

"Leah . . . Rae . . . Harris. I am a resident of Seattle, Washington."

"Thank you—Mr. Collins, you may proceed."

The prosecutor straightened. "Sergeant Harris, for the record, would you mind stating the name of your employer, the nature of your position, and your background qualification for it."

Harris nodded and began. "I have been employed by the Seattle Police Department for over seventeen years, and currently am a supervisor in the Robbery-Homicide unit. I have been in this position for three years, and in Homicide as a detective for a total of nine years."

"How many murders have you investigated?"

"We prefer to call them death investigations. A suspicious death can sometimes turn out to be accidental, or even a suicide—or vice versa. We wouldn't want to prejudge."

"Certainly—but how many?"

Harris paused and reflected. "In the last nine years, I've probably investigated, or have been a part of a team that investigated, at least four hundred deaths."

"That's quite a few."

Harris nodded with pride.

"And what special training do you have for this job?"

Harris shifted in her seat. "I believe I've completed every investigator course the State Police Academy has offered over the years as well as those through the FBI. I have a bachelor of science degree from the University of Washington in abnormal psychology. I am also a graduate of the

basic and advanced FBI Academy programs and their pro-
filers' school."

"I also believe you are certified in numerous disciplines
as an instructor and have also been an adjunct member of the
FBI's serial killer unit?"

"Your Honor," Quinn broke in, "the defense is well
aware of Sergeant Harris's qualifications as a homicide investigator, and I have the highest regard for her talents—"

"Something we agree on," Collins sniped.

She ignored him. "For the sake of time, the defense will
stipulate to Sergeant Harris's being an acknowledged expert
in her field, so let's stop with the fluff and get on with this."

"I am laying foundation."

"You're laying a smoke screen."

"That's enough," Stromberg admonished.

Quinn bristled. "Your Honor, this whole proceeding
reeks of self-promotion. As you well know, Mr. Collins is up
for reelection, and I believe he is using my client for his own
ends. Why else would he be personally handling this preliminary appearance instead of some junior deputy, as would
be normal?"

Collins's jaw cracked. Tessla Quinn had struck a nerve.
Even Harris winced.

"Your Honor!" he boomed.

"Save the objection," Judge Stromberg snapped. Her face
had gone scarlet also. She glared down at Quinn. "We'll
have no more of that in my courtroom, young lady. Do you
understand me?"

For a moment, Quinn remained unmoved, but then she
nodded silently and retreated. She had made her point. The
seeds of doubt had been planted and for several seconds, the
only sound heard in the room was the frantic scribbling
of the two print reporters trying to capture every word she
had just uttered.

Collins recovered. He turned back to Harris. "Defense counsel has been gracious enough to acknowledge your expertise in the field of homicide investigations. Therefore, let us proceed to one particular death occurring some three decades ago, the rape and murder of a young teenage girl by the name of Cindy Jo Sellinzski."

Harris slowly opened the file that rested on her lap. As she did, her pager, set on vibrate, triggered.

Harris jumped, then caught herself. She quickly looked to Collins for direction.

"Your Honor, a moment, please?"

The jurist gave a popelike wave, granting permission, and Harris reached to her belt loop and scanned the digital readout.

The prosecutor closed in. "Well?" he whispered.

Harris didn't reply immediately. She scrolled though the short communication, sighed, and shook her head, a disappointed no. It wasn't the message they had been waiting for.

3

Lieutenant Frank Milkovich glanced at his watch and then at the diverse faces crowded into the small conference room on the thirteenth floor of the Seattle Police Department. There were African-Americans, Asian-Americans, Hispanics, and several gay and lesbian activists, in addition to a number of opinionated retirees and one fat middle-aged white guy. Meanwhile, a lone administrative assistant sat quietly in a corner taking minutes.

It was the initial meeting of the mayor's Citizens' Advisory Board on Law Enforcement, a forum established for community leaders to address police issues in an informal setting with the goal of improving the delivery of law enforcement services in the city. Milkovich had drawn the short straw and was the police representative.

"A welcome addition," both the mayor and the new chief were quoted as saying.

"A pain in the ass," Milkovich was known to mumble— not that Frank Milkovich was against public scrutiny of cops. To the contrary, he was all for it. As the acting, albeit reluctant, head of Internal Affairs, he knew that many problems could be averted if there were only better communications between officers and all civilians. However, this board and its members, all appointed by the mayor, and all for political reasons, left Milkovich little hope that anything of substance would be accomplished. The pontificating had begun the moment he had opened the meeting—an hour earlier. Each participant had an ax to grind and was not shy in voicing disapproval over every aspect of the department's operation.

Milkovich knotted his hands behind his head and leaned back in his chair. His eyes glazed and mind drifted as yet another thirdhand story of police abuse was related to ravenous ears.

Lieutenant Frank Milkovich was a twenty-five-year veteran of the department and had the scars to prove it: an ex-wife, two trips to rehab, and a chronic back pain providing a daily reminder of the bullet that had put him behind a desk. A decade prior, he had led the department four years running in narcotics arrests—had single-handedly broken up a sophisticated drug-importing scheme employing hundreds of criminals distributing millions of dollars of Chinese heroin throughout the Pacific Northwest. He had twice been awarded the department's highest award for bravery. But there had been a price. Like the criminals he pursued, he too had been hooked on a high—an investigative euphoria as powerful as that peddled on the street. His addiction went untreated and grew, along with his tunnel vision. He barely noticed his wife's departure or anything else unconnected with his work world. It gave him more time to hunt, and drink. Thus, on the night he was making yet another arrest, in yet another trash-filled rental, his senses were dulled, his caution gone. He never saw the kid who shot him, nor did he remember it hurting all that much. It was only during the weeks of recovery that the real pain began, not the physical kind, but the mental anguish that came from drying out and seeing the world clearly for the first time in years. He came to realize he had been a fool, but words said at the height of his obsession now returned to haunt him. His superiors had not forgotten certain righteous pronouncements made over the years, deriding their intelligence, competency, and heredity. Now it was their turn. Given light duty to aid in his convalescence, Milkovich had been temporarily assigned to Internal Affairs. It was a message said loud and clear. He was being banished, exiled to the furthest post in the organization. A place for the unclean, a leper colony where old friends and fellow officers gave him wide berth.

That was four years ago. A temporary assignment had become permanent; a supervisor's retirement had paved the way for his advancement. But to what? He hated the job, hated hunting cops rather than criminals, yet he endured quietly in a sober routine on the fringes of a world where he had once been king—that was, until Leah Harris had entered his life.

"Lieutenant Milkovich?"

It was the fat guy, the lone member who was fervently pro-police.

"What do you think about that, eh?"

Milkovich straightened. "I'm sorry; what did you say?"

The room went silent.

"Didn't you hear what that—that *woman* said?"

Milkovich cringed. The man had almost said *dyke*. His eyes darted to the lady whose arms were now defiantly folded. He couldn't read her name tag and couldn't remember if she went by Alice or Alesha.

"Ah, Christ," Milkovich murmured beneath his breath. He shot a glance to his administrative assistant. She smirked.

"I was merely wondering," the woman began with dag-

gers in her eyes, "why you must all carry guns? I think a lot
of senseless killing could be averted if the police simply dis-
armed, and took the time to negotiate with criminals. People
are reasonable. You just have to take the time to understand
them."

A majority of heads bobbed in agreement.

"Excuse my French, but that's bull," the fat guy blus-
tered. "Isn't that right, Lieutenant?"

Milkovich glanced at his watch again. *Damn*, he wondered, *why didn't I leave word with Leah to give me a rescue
page?*

"Well, Lieutenant?"

Milkovich sighed. "It's a little more complicated than
that." He was careful with his words. He knew every one of
them would be reported to the chief. In addition, while he
was not one to veil his thoughts, he knew a positive reaction
from those in attendance could be his ticket out of IA and
back into a coveted field assignment. He was already planning the lobbying effort.

"How so, Lieutenant?" the woman pressed. "English police do not carry guns."

"But there, possession of any firearm is illegal."

"So why don't we do that here?"

"Aw, for crying out loud, lady," the fat guy interrupted in
a huff. "Haven't you ever heard about the Second Amend-
ment to the Constitution?"

Now it was her turn to roll her eyes and mutter an ob-
scenity.

"Okay," Milkovich quickly wedged in. "I think it's time
for a break. Rest rooms are down the hall, and there's plenty
of coffee and tea over there on the credenza. And help yourself to the donuts."

"I think the lieutenant is right," another member commented. "This has been great dialogue. Everyone is thinking out of the box, but I could use a stretch."

"Yeah," several others agreed, and group members began to rise and amble about while Milkovich made for the door. He didn't get far. His lone, rabid supporter was already there and blocking his retreat.

"Got a minute, Frank?"

Milkovich sighed. "What's up?"

"Can we step out into the hallway?"

Milkovich shrugged nonchalantly, masking his trepidation. The pair then distanced themselves from the rest of the group. After twenty paces, the fat guy stopped, and in a secretive tone said, "Anytime you need help, Frank, just let me know. I got connections. And on the street, I'll back up any of the guys." He patted his waistband. "I always pack and I know how to use it."

Milkovich eyed the obvious bulge.

There was a nervous silence.

"Hey, Frank, what do you carry?"

Milkovich hesitated, then said, "A nine-millimeter."

"Oh, yeah? How big a magazine?"

"Eighteen."

"Why all the ammo?"

"Because," Milkovich sighed, "I'm a lousy shot. I need twice as many bullets as the average cop to hit anything."

The fat guy laughed. "You're funny."

"It's the truth. Say, I've got to make a phone call."

Milkovich was lying.

The portly, middle-aged man gave a thumbs-up and patted his waist again. "Just remember, Frank, ya need me, just call. And don't you worry about all those wackos back in there. I'll take care of 'em. God, where'd the mayor come up with all those losers, huh?" He gave Milkovich a friendly jab in the ribs and waddled off to the lavatory.

Milkovich glanced at his watch again as an ominous feeling overtook him. For the past two weeks, he and Leah Harris had seen little of each other. Except for a few lunches, every attempt at spending a weekend or evening together had been rudely interrupted by a suspicious death. Of all people, he understood, yet being on the receiving end of these disappointments was beginning to gnaw at him.

"Hey, boss."

Milkovich whirled around—it was his administrative assistant.

"What a group you drew."

Milkovich slumped. "You can stop with the funny faces when we get back in there. You're killing me."

"I'm trying to keep a straight face."

"So am I," Milkovich chuckled.

"By the way," she continued, "Leah called just before we got started. Said she'd be over at super-court doing a prelim and probably wouldn't be free until noon. She said lunch was still on."

"Well, that salvages the day."

"Oh, and the chief also wants a call after we're done."

Milkovich raised a suspicious brow. "What now?"

His assistant shrugged. "Wouldn't say exactly, just something about needing you to look into something. I kinda got the feeling it was important, though."

Milkovich didn't have time to ponder the point or guess who had screwed up this time; from the corner of his eye, he saw several group members heading his way. "Oh, great," he murmured, and he braced for their arrival.

4

"Okay, Sergeant Harris," Prosecutor Richard Collins sighed. He had just completed yet after another heated exchange with his young opponent. "We're back on the record. Now let me ask you, are you familiar with a murder investigation that occurred in 1975—Seattle Police case number 75-9568?"

Leah Harris gave a hesitant, "I am."

She was, but not nearly enough for her liking. Especially now, having to testify to its elements from the hot seat of a witness stand. Case 75-9568 was still open; all homicides were until someone was brought to justice. And while open cases were routinely reviewed on a yearly basis, this particular one had escaped Harris's scrutiny until yesterday. From that point, she had had less than twenty-four hours to skim over the volumes of faded notes, statements, and related documents. A length of time far too short when someone's freedom might be hanging in the balance.

"Good," Collins said, clasping his hands together with eagerness. "Could you give the court a brief overview of the circumstances?"

Harris nodded, shifting on the hard, unpadded seat. "On August 16, 1975, at oh six ten hours, officers from the Seattle Police Department responded with paramedics to a wooded area just inside the Woodland Park Zoo, near the North Fiftieth and Phinney Avenue entrance. An early-morning walker, strolling in the area with his dog, observed a bloodied, unclothed leg protruding from thick undergrowth, just off a pathway leading to the footbridge over Aurora Avenue. He immediately went to a nearby pay phone and reported it."

"What happened next?"

"Law enforcement arrived first. An officer checked the victim's vital signs and, to his surprise, found the victim, an eighteen-year-old female, to be still alive. Though just barely."

"What were her obvious signs of injury?"

Harris paused and visualized the photos she had recently studied. The attack had been particularly savage, with multiple knife wounds about the neck, breasts, and vaginal area. Further, her face had been beaten beyond recognition, the deep bruising swelling her eyes shut. The images were horrific, but for Harris, the stomach-turning content was routine. The detective drew a deep breath and relayed this information in a dry, clinical manner. Collins nodded knowingly. "Oh, I almost forgot," Harris added. "There was one other significant injury. The victim's left ring finger had been completely severed."

"Severed?" Collins's tone was rhetorical.

Harris grimly dipped her head. "At the second joint."

"I see, and what about the knife wounds? They were unusual in themselves, were they not?"

"Yes."

"As an acknowledged expert in the field, how would you characterize them?"

Harris fingered an armrest and said, "Several ways. The incisions on her neck were nonfatal, only shallow cuts. They were meant to simulate a throat cutting—apparently part of the perpetrator's fantasy."

"Objection!" Quinn fumed. "The witness is offering pure conjecture. There's no foundation for this."

"You laid the foundation," Collins snapped back as he spun towards her. "You stipulated that Sergeant Harris is an acknowledged expert in her field."

"But—"

"Objection overruled." Judge Stromberg intervened. "Mr. Collins is correct, Ms. Quinn—you opened the door. Sergeant Harris is allowed to walk through it. Go on, Mr. Collins; please continue."

The prosecutor grinned. He stepped close to the witness stand and casually leaned on the thick oak rail, worn smooth from decades of hearings. "Now, where were we? Ah, yes, the wounds. What about the other ones?"

Harris eased back in her seat. "As I said, most were shallow."

"By design?"

"I would have to believe so. Any one of them could have been fatal if they had been a hair deeper. Besides, if you plot their locations and connect the cuts, they formed a cross."

Collins stepped back. "A cross or, perhaps more accurately, a crucifix?"

Harris thought for a moment, glanced about the near empty courtroom, and said, "Yes, the latter would be a better characterization."

"I see."

Collins turned and cast his gaze towards the defendant. Continuing his examination, he said, "We'll get into the significance of that later. Now, Sergeant Harris, what about the missing finger—was it found?"

"No."

"In your opinion, why not?"

"It was a trophy. The perpetrator severed it as his last act before departing. A memento, so to speak."

"Quite a grisly one."

"But typical. It's been my experience in cases like these that the killer tends to collect something from the victim—an earring, perhaps a button, lock of hair, or—"

"A finger."

"Correct."

"Hmmm. By the way, had Cindy Jo Sellinzski been raped?"

"Yes. There was deep vaginal bruising."

"Then there was semen present and other trace evidence?"

"Yes."

Collins paused and drew a deep breath. He had hoped to detect some sort of reaction from Bakerman, but the man had not batted an eye. The accused was near catatonic in his stiffness, seemingly detached from the entire proceeding.

Harris also noted this. From where she now sat, she had a good view of the man. For her, he was extraordinary in his ordinariness. Dressed in ill-fitting street clothes the prison had issued him, he had a bookish look, like a low-level accountant or government bureaucrat who had been tucked away, for an entire career, in an anonymous cubicle. Perhaps it was his thick glasses, Harris thought, or the weak chin and balding hair, but she was having a hard time imagining a killer lurking beneath this bland veneer—even as a young man.

"Sergeant Harris—"

The detective's focus returned.

"You stated," Collins said as he returned to the prosecutor's table and twisted about, "that the victim was still alive when she was found, isn't that right?"

"Yes, just barely."

"Was she conscious?"

"No."

"Did she ever regain consciousness?"

"No. She remained in a coma for a number of months. Then, according to the autopsy report, she died of a brain hemorrhage."

"As a result of her attack."

"That's what the autopsy report concluded."

"Very good. Now let's move on to Mr. Bakerman and how he's come to be our guest here." As Collins said this, Harris reflected. At noon the prior day, Richard Collins had telephoned. He had received an unsolicited letter, from a man named Carl Eckler. Such letters were common to both the prosecutor's office and the police department. Composed by unstable but literate minds, they generally warned of ongoing government conspiracies or pending catastrophes. Their hallmark was their length, long and rambling, with a heavy dose of polysyllabic words. But this had not been the case with Mr. Eckler's communication. It had been short and to the point, with details that could be verified.

"Sergeant," Collins went on, "would you relate to the court the essence of a conversation I had with you yesterday around lunchtime, and what you did thereafter."

Harris cleared her throat and continued in her professionally distant tone. "You asked if I or one of my detectives would come to your office, take custody of a letter, and attempt to locate and interview its author. The rest of my staff was tied up on other assignments, so I volunteered myself."

"And did you find Mr. Eckler?"

"Yes, shortly after we met."

"That was quick work, Sergeant."

Harris smirked. "The letter was postmarked from the King County Jail. A quick call to that facility confirmed that Mr. Eckler was still a guest there."

"I see; then what happened?"

"You made arrangements to have him brought to your office. His attorney, a Mr. Stuart Malconni, accompanied him. And after setting some ground rules, he agreed to speak with us on the matter."

"In exchange for what?" Quinn sneered.

"That is enough, Ms. Quinn," Judge Stromberg ordered. "I don't want to hear another word out of you until cross."

Quinn tweaked her nose—but only after the judge had glanced away.

"Proceed."

"So what did Mr. Eckler have to say?"

"He told us he had been convicted a number of times in the past for various felonies and had recently completed a three-year sentence in the Monroe State Reformatory for burglary. He had become an acquaintance of Mr. Bakerman's while there, owing to the proximity of their cells. They were next-door neighbors for six months."

"I see."

"And during a recent overcrowding situation, they bunked together for several weeks."

"In the same cell?"

"Yes."

"So he had access to all of Mr. Bakerman's possessions?"

"Correct, there's not much that can be kept secret in close quarters like that."

"Understood. Now let's move to the point of all of this. In the letter my office received, Mr. Eckler wrote he had discovered something while he was housed with his new cell mate—right?"

Harris nodded. "According to Eckler, Bakerman was a voracious reader and also fancied himself a writer. Over time, he had accumulated quite a dusty collection of books and papers that the guards left untouched. One day recently,

Bakerman was in the prison hospital undergoing tests. Left alone, Eckler, out of curiosity, glanced through some of the handwritten documents, and came across one old legal pad that contained some sort of journal, or diary."

"And what was in this journal or diary?"

"Lengthy and detailed descriptions of sadistic sex acts involving young girls and women."

"Fantasies?"

"At first, Eckler thought so. They read like something out of a bad porn magazine. But the account of one sparked a memory—a thirty-year-old one."

"How so?"

"In 1975, Eckler was a high school student and working part-time at Woodland Park Zoo with the groundskeeping crew. He was on duty the morning of the Sellinzski murder and was questioned by police as a potential witness. The elements contained in Bakerman's narrative were so chillingly accurate, from what Eckler remembered, that he came to believe that Bakerman had, in fact, committed the act."

"I see." Collins thought for a moment, then asked, "Besides this rather old recollection, was there anything else that made Mr. Eckler believe his cell mate was responsible for Cindy Jo's brutal murder?"

"Yes. In the narrative penned by Bakerman, he not only severed the finger as a trophy, but later, when Bakerman returned to his van, he found the victim's purse still on the floorboards. Instead of discarding it immediately, he took it back to his residence and went through its contents, keeping one more item."

"Which was?"

"A small religious card in a plastic holder. It was of the Virgin Mary at Fátima."

"A religious article, eh?" Collins again glanced at Bakerman. Not a muscle twitched on the prisoner's face.

"Your Honor!" Tessla Quinn vaulted upward. "Enough is enough. Where is this stroll through ancient history going to end? We're not at trial. There is no jury here. This is a preliminary hearing. Where are their facts? Let's see the letter and this so-called diary. If there isn't anything more than this, then let's all go home, including Mr. Bakerman. He's paid his debt; it's time to let him resume his life."

The judge raised an eyebrow and was about to speak when Collins whirled around and faced his opponent. "My dear Ms. Quinn, would you mind not interrupting me while I am examining *my* witness? Or don't they teach proper courtroom decorum in *night* law schools these days?"

A reporter giggled.

"Enough of this petty bickering," Stromberg ordered. "Proceed, Mr. Collins. I would like to hear more about this diary. Is it in your possession? I do trust you have more than the word of a convicted felon for your probable cause."

Collins nodded. "The state does, Your Honor. I can assure you of that."

Suddenly, Harris's pager went off a second time. Instantly, her right hand slid to her waistband and she twisted the device so she could read the text of the newly arrived message. It was just one word and a first name: CONFIRMED—PHIL.

Harris looked up and winked at Collins. He understood. He clasped his hands together and with a wide, satisfied grin said, "Now, where were we? Ah, yes, the religious card."

5

Evidence technician Roy Stoddard leaned up against one of the many floor-to-ceiling storage racks that filled the industrial-sized warehouse. "Look at all this worthless crap," he sighed as he surveyed the maze of evidence storage bins before him. The cribs were overflowing with all manner of items: bowling balls, barbells, and beer bottles—wallets, mallets, and crowbars—all bagged, tagged, and collecting decades of dust. All awaiting the unlikely event they might be produced in a court of law. Thinking he was temporarily alone, Roy pulled out a pack of cigarettes and lit one up. However, as he did, his coworker Jane Fenton unexpectedly appeared from an adjacent walk-in freezer.

Fenton was the best laboratory technician the department had, skillful in her collection and processing techniques and possessing an encyclopedic brain for details. But more importantly, she thought like a cop. Given a hundred pieces of evidence gathered at a crime scene, in short order, she knew exactly which one would cinch the probable cause for an arrest warrant, and which were simply background noise cluttering the way to the truth. Because of this, she was afforded the status of near equal to the

sworn staff. A notable achievement in an organization rife
with pecking orders.

On the other hand, Roy Stoddard's skill and dedication
were negligible. He was a medically retired cop. Six years
before, he had been partially disabled in an on-duty traffic
accident that he had caused. He had been drunk at the time,
but had pulled in all his markers, and the review board
levied no action. Then, because of his disability—his left
foot had been crushed, amputated, but fitted with a high-
tech prosthesis—the department was forced to accommo-
date him and provided this job. Much to Jane's frustration,
he took it. He had to. His pension checks were not enough
to cover his alimony and monthly bar tab.

"Jesus Christ, Roy," Fenton whispered loudly as she
rubbed herself to warm up. "They catch you smoking in here
again, your butt will be out on the pavement for a couple of
weeks."

He shrugged and continued to inhale.

"Come on, Roy, can't you just go out onto the loading
dock like everyone else? You'll get us both in trouble."

Stoddard winced. "Why the hell should I have to go out
there and freeze my ass off? Christ, back in the old days, no
one would have batted an eye, me smoking in here. Now,
just because a bunch of goddamn faggot health nuts are running this country, I've got to suffer."

"Didn't you get written up last year for the same thing?
Didn't Captain Varna catch you? A second offense will get
you suspended—as if I really care."

Stoddard grinned. "That was three hundred and sixty-six
days ago. The pull date on that little ol' piece of disciplinary
paper expired yesterday. Ergo, my dear partner, even if I
were written up today, by the terms and conditions of our
labor contract this instance would have to be considered a

first offense, punishable at most by a written reprimand—so screw 'em."

Fenton sighed. There was no changing the man—and little reason to try. The effort expended would far exceed any measurable result.

"So, where did that little twerp of a clerk go?" Stoddard continued. "That lazy SOB couldn't find his ass from a hole in the ground." He puffed again and exhaled with a series of satisfied smoke rings.

"George went back up to his office. He's going to try to run it through the computer again. He thinks it has to be in the first freezer we tried."

"Computers. You know, we used to do pretty good police work when all we had was paper and pencils."

"That's because you never wrote any reports," Fenton retorted. "You'd catch a kid trying to jack a car, and simply bust his jaw. Then take him back home so his ol' man could finish what you started."

"Your point?"

"Things are different."

"Things are screwed." Stoddard drew one more puff, then flicked the butt to the ground. With his right foot, he quashed it, then kicked the debris beneath the bottom shelf. "Come on, let's move over a couple of rows. That way no one will be able to prove it was mine."

"Christ, Roy, we're in a fifty-thousand-square-foot warehouse. Except for George and that other clerk, we're the only ones in here right now."

"You never know who's watching you." He pointed to a security camera directed away from where they stood. "Lousy gold badges."

Roy began walking. After a few steps, he suddenly paused. A green evidence tag dangling from the handle of an old toolbox had caught his attention. He stepped closer to the item and read the markings. Fenton sidled up to him. "Who was 481?" she asked. The securing officer's initials and badge number were clearly inked on the metal box.

Stoddard let go of the tag and replied, "An old partner of mine from years ago, Eddy Merlock."

Fenton stepped back. "That name rings a bell."

Stoddard sighed wistfully. "He ate his gun 'bout ten years back, after he got fired."

Fenton thought for a moment, then suddenly straightened. "The guy who nearly killed his wife?"

"It wasn't his fault," Stoddard quickly countered.

Fenton raised a questioning brow. Compassion for other people was not one of Stoddard's attributes. In fact, Jane couldn't recall the man ever speaking about anyone except in disparaging tones. She was about to press the issue, but the sound of approaching feet echoing off the smooth concrete floor caused her to hold her tongue. A moment later, a compact, middle-aged man of Philippine descent emerged from the cross aisle. He was carrying a file folder in his right hand.

"Well?" Roy challenged.

Jane elbowed her partner. "Give him a chance."

The man affected a weak smile. "Sorry," he said in a low tone. "The audit trail stops in 1987."

"Let me see that." Roy scowled. "I don't want to spend all fuckin' day here."

The warehouseman hesitated.

"Damn it, George, give it to me."

The warehouseman's hand rose. Midway, Stoddard snatched the paperwork and took a step backward into better light. Opening the folder, the lab tech scrolled down the entries with his forefinger until he halted midway. "Wouldn't you fuckin' know it?"

Jane's ears perked.

"That bastard Dellhanney was the last supervisor to sign it off." Stoddard looked up. "Toss me your cell phone. I'm gonna call that fucker and light a fire under his ass. Ten to one, he's the reason we can't find this shit."

6

Judge Stromberg leaned forward. Richard Collins had paused, taking a moment to study his notes before continuing with his examination of Sergeant Harris. Simultaneously, the doors to the courtroom discreetly opened, admitting several new spectators. Like late arrivers to a church service, they quietly took seats at the rear of the courtroom. They were not, however, random members of the public. Harris immediately recognized their faces; both were female reporters from competing television stations. Their well-coiffed, model-like figures were in sharp contrast to everyone else present.

Collins swiveled around and nodded recognition to them. Turning back, he resumed his questioning, his voice dropping an octave. "Now, Sergeant," he said. "In Bakerman's journal, he described how he obtained the religious card from Cindy Jo's purse after he had left her for dead. Let me ask you, was there anything unique about this card?"

Tessla Quinn had been sitting silently for the last five minutes, her lips clenched tight, her fingers manhandling her pen. Suddenly she bolted up. "Objection. This is all hearsay. There is nothing to establish there ever was a journal, that Mr. Bakerman was its author, or that the victim alluded to was Cindy Jo Sellinzski."

Stromberg straightened. "Well, Mr. Collins?"

"Sergeant Harris is simply relating a conversation she had with Mr. Eckler yesterday," Collins confidently replied. "At this juncture, I am not asserting that the contents of the conversation are fact. Simply that the conversation occurred and that it prompted Sergeant Harris to delve deeper into the situation."

"Okay, Mr. Collins, I'll buy that for the moment—objection overruled. Get back in your seat, Ms. Quinn."

Quinn reluctantly complied.

"Thank you, Your Honor," Collins said smugly. "We're getting close to the heart of the matter."

"Proceed."

"All right, Sergeant, Mr. Eckler found something else in that cell, correct?"

"Yes. He told us that as he flipped through the pages of the journal, a small, tattered card fell out. It was partially encased in a yellowing plastic cover. Eckler examined it and found that the object he now held in his hand matched the one Bakerman had described in his writings as belonging to his victim, Cindy Jo Sellinzski."

"Quite coincidental, wouldn't you say, Sergeant Harris?"

"I would."

"Then you were skeptical of what you were being told?"

"Under the circumstances—of course."

"So what did you do?"

"I discussed the situation with you."

"And?"

"Well, due to the fact that Mr. Bakerman was scheduled to be released from prison next week, in order to detain him any further we were going to need something more substantial than this unconfirmed story from Mr. Eckler. Some type of independent facts were needed."

"And I agreed. Let me stop here for a moment and talk about the letter."

Like an actor working the entire stage, Collins strode pensively to the now empty jury box. He looked it over, then spun on his heels. "Sergeant Harris," he resumed, "doesn't it seem rather self-serving, and thus suspicious on Mr. Eckler's part, to suddenly come forth with this information, since he is currently a resident in our county jail?"

Harris shrugged agreement. "At first I thought so. But Mr. Eckler swore that he had gone to a prison official and reported his suspicions about Bakerman. He said initially there was interest, but after several weeks, nothing was done. He attempted once more, this time stealing the card in question, to back up his words. Unfortunately, the official he had disclosed to was called away on a family emergency and couldn't meet with him. However, for Eckler's protection, this official had already arranged for him to be transferred to a different cellblock. Hence, Eckler never had an opportunity to return the card to where he had found it."

"So where is the card now?" Collins asked.

"It was recovered earlier today by one of my detectives. Right where Mr. Eckler told us, tucked in a Bible in the glove box of his pickup. Ironically, the card has been in police custody since his most recent arrest. His vehicle was impounded after he was stopped for a minor traffic violation and found to have drugs in his possession."

"Very good. Now let's get to the heart of the matter. The card in itself is interesting and unique. Something that ties this whole matter together, isn't that right, Sergeant?"

"Yes," Harris replied. "Stamped on the back is the name of a Catholic church and the name of the nun who awarded it."

"And why is this so important?"

Harris's eyes narrowed. "One of my detectives has just confirmed that our victim, Cindy Jo Sellinzski, attended the Catholic school there, and that the nun on the card was her sixth-grade teacher."

"Very good, Sergeant. We therefore have a nexus."

"Indeed."

Collins turned towards his young opponent. "*Indeed.*" The prosecutor allowed the courtroom to go silent for one last time. As he did, Harris looked again at the defendant. He remained unmoved, although his eyes suddenly swung her way, and his pupils locked on hers. For others, it would have been unnerving, the eyes of a killer upon yours, but the years had steeled Sergeant Harris to the worst of humankind. Blood-spattered bodies and tattooed murderers were the company she routinely kept. Not only did she not blink, but the intensity of her own gaze caused Bakerman to quickly disengage. She looked back to Collins. He was stealing a glance towards the two television reporters.

"Okay," he said, turning back. "I have just a few more questions."

Harris cracked a relieved smile.

"What happens to evidence collected in cases where there has been no resolution—specifically, homicide cases?"

"It is all retained."

"Even thirty-year-old cases?"

"Certainly."

"Therefore, a semen sample collected from the victim would still be available for matching against Mr. Bakerman's DNA?"

"It should be available. I have evidence techs retrieving it right now."

"Good," Collins said. He then looked up to the judge. "Your Honor, I believe the state has established probable cause to have Mr. Bakerman held in connection with the 1975 cold-blooded murder of Cindy Jo Sellinzski. Further, because of Mr. Bakerman's prior criminal history, he is a danger to the public and should therefore be held without bail. Lastly, the state requests the court direct the defendant to immediately surrender a sample of his blood, so that a DNA comparison can be made with those samples in the custody of the Seattle Police Department."

"Objection!"

"Save your breath, Ms. Quinn."

"But—"

Ignoring the young attorney, Judge Stromberg continued. "Although the evidence is somewhat slim, I find the state has established grounds for detaining Mr. Bakerman, at least temporarily."

Collins beamed.

"However—"

His head jerked toward the bench.

"However, I think it imperative that the state confirm its possession of the DNA sample." She turned to Sergeant Harris. "How long should that take, at least to verify you still have the evidence?"

The Seattle detective bit at her lip.

"By Friday, perhaps? That would give you forty-eight hours."

Harris thought for another moment. "That should be sufficient."

"Very well," Judge Stromberg said, returning to Collins. "To hold an individual without bail requires extraordinary circumstances, and thus, I am leery of making a final ruling without confirmation that a decades-old biological specimen is still intact. Therefore, I would like to continue this hearing at nine o'clock Friday morning, at which time, Mr. Collins, we shall reassess the matter."

"And the blood draw?" Collins reminded.

"So ordered. However, as you are well aware, since Mr. Bakerman is a convicted sex offender, under our state law, a mandatory DNA blood draw will be done pro forma on the day prior to his release, with a subsequent database check."

"We are aware of that, Your Honor. But it is in everyone's interest to resolve the identification question as early as possible. If Mr. Bakerman is innocent, he deserves to go free. If we obtain a positive identification, well—"

"Understood."

"Thank you, Your Honor. . . . By the way, may I add just one more thing for the record?"

Stromberg frowned. "I suppose, if you must."

Collins turned to the reporters, and cleared his throat.

All looked his way.

"Sergeant Harris," he began, "a little earlier, defense counsel made a rather unflattering remark about my motivations in this case. Something to the effect that I was grandstanding, so to speak, for political purposes. Do you recall that?"

Harris hesitated for a moment and replied, "Yes."

"And do you believe that?"

"Ah—"

"Don't bother answering. Instead, I believe you have the original case report from 1975 in front of you—do you not?"

"I do."

"Does the detective's report make note of who the police officers on the scene were?"

Harris nodded. Collins shifted on his feet and looked directly at Quinn. "Would you mind telling the court one of those names listed on the report? The one with badge number 1038."

Harris drew a deep breath. Without looking at the file, she said with irony, "Badge 1038 was you, sir, Officer Richard C. Collins."

7

Detective Philip Gilroy set aside the tattered holy card of the Virgin Mary and rose from his cluttered desk. *It's good evidence*, he thought, *real good*. But he knew they needed more. As he stretched, he gazed absently at all the empty desks in the Homicide squad room. The preceding two weeks had been relatively quiet. Every suspicious death had been cleared as noncriminal. It was nearing a record. A chalkboard on the far wall kept the box score. The interlude had given his colleagues an opportunity to catch up on the reams of paperwork that every death generated. Even the cold cases had been given their yearly review. Then, with the lull, many of the detectives had taken the next few days off, leaving only a skeleton crew for the remainder of the week.

Philip Gilroy was young to be in Homicide, only thirty-two. His boyish charm and good looks mattered little here. Instead, his quick advancement had come from technical prowess, especially in the area of computer applications. He had recently solved a murder without ever leaving the squad room. He had simply sifted through the thousands of databases available on the Web to disprove a suspect's once solid alibi.

Beep.

Gilroy bent over and punched ENTER on his computer keyboard. Simultaneously, he muttered a string of mild oaths. His home machine was state-of-the-art, twenty times faster than this ancient government-issue.

Another beep.

Gilroy pressed ENTER once more, but this time his wait was short. His screen lit up with a long series of tangential information on Clifford Bakerman: credit report, driving and military records, marriage information, as well as names of people who may have resided near the suspect over the past twenty-five years—the outward boundary of the database.

Gilroy clicked his mouse, and the records spooled to the network printer located on a counter some fifteen feet away. However, instead of retrieving the printout, he grabbed his jacket and proceeded out of the squad room to the elevator at the end of the hallway.

Five minutes prior, he had received a call from the Medical Examiner's Office indicating that a fresh copy of Cindy Jo Sellinzski's autopsy report was ready for pickup. He had ordered it earlier because the old-style Photostats in the original case file had faded and were now unreadable.

As he waited for the lift his eyes drifted upward to the floor indicator. It was stalled on the top story. Seeing this, he opted for the adjacent stairwell. He popped through the fireproof door and began a rapid descent to the basement floor, finally traversing an underground parking lot to emerge onto the crowded sidewalks of Third Avenue. Here he paused, drew a deep breath of the moist autumn air, and started the four-block journey to the King County Administration Building.

As he neared his destination, Gilroy slowed from his brisk pace. He strode through the entrance and flashed his department identification at the security officers standing guard. He was recognized immediately and waved around the slow-moving queue of visitors crowded in front of the walk-through metal detector.

From here he bypassed another large group standing at the elevators and proceeded to the back of the building, to an unmarked stairwell. He went down a flight of steps, exiting into a brightly lit but sterile reception area. A young woman staffed the counter. She looked up and smiled.

"Hey," Gilroy said, taking quick note of her buxom figure. "How's it going?"

The receptionist was about to reply when her telephone rang. She waved the detective off and slid him the packet he had come for. Gilroy ripped open the thick envelope and poured the contents out. Inside was a fifty-page document, and a dozen eight-by-ten glossy photographs he had not seen before. There was a small yellow sticky note attached to the top one. It read, "These turned up in another old file that I recently went through. Thought you'd like copies."

Shifting on his feet, he began to peruse the report. Ironically, he had done the last review of the case only eight weeks prior, and was therefore familiar with many of the details. He immediately recalled its unusual circumstances, a young woman beaten, raped, and knifed to within an inch of her life only to die months later, having never regained consciousness. *Too bad*, Gilroy thought. If the same situation had occurred today, the killer would have been easily identified via DNA, given all of the biological evidence left at the scene.

Switching to the photographs, he spread them out over the counter while the receptionist continued her telephone conversation.

Most of the bodies Gilroy dealt with were bloodied and maimed, ripped apart by bullets or knives, internal organs exposed like roadkill. However, because Cindy Jo Sellinzski had temporarily survived her attack, her broken body had begun to heal. The bruising and swelling that had caused her brain to enlarge and nearly explode her skull had long since faded, leaving only slight disfigurements about her cheeks and forehead. So, too, the cuts and puncture marks about her neck and plump torso. They had knitted back together leaving only deep red lines. Even the hand with the missing finger had mended—enough so that the violence wrought seemed distant. Gilroy's cursory inspection suddenly came to a halt on the second-to-last picture. He dropped the others he was holding and brought this one close. "What the—?" His gaze was now focused on a still sutured wound, different from the rest. He grabbed the autopsy report to see the pathologist's comments regarding this seemingly fresh cut but could find no mention of it.

A look of puzzlement creased the young detective's brow.

"Something wrong?" It was the receptionist. She had finished her call.

Gilroy didn't respond. Instead, he continued to scrutinize the image. A moment later, still puzzled, he asked, "Is Dr. Reid around?" She was the deputy medical examiner he had worked with the most.

The young staffer nodded but added, "She just started on one of this morning's deliveries. You want to leave a message?"

"Sure."

The receptionist retrieved her handset and dialed in a short number. "Here's her voice mail," and she handed the telephone over to Gilroy. Moments later a recorded voice said, *"Hello, you have reached the desk of Dr. Phyllis Reid with the King County Medical Examiner's Office. I am either on the telephone or away from my desk. If you would like to leave a message, I will get back to you as soon as possible."*

There was a beep.

"Hey, Dr. Reid, it's Phil Gilroy. When you got a sec, give me a call, extension 7382. Better yet, pull out our case file number 75-9568, Cindy Jo Sellinzski. Can you tell me what that incision on photo number nineteen is all about? I can't find anything in the report about its origin. Thanks—talk to ya later."

8

"What do you mean, you can't find the samples?" Sergeant Harris groaned as she clutched her cell phone in an alcove outside the courtroom. She was only twenty feet away from where Richard Collins was preening before a group of eager television reporters. The rising noise of their collective shouts and the glare of the spotlights forced her to turn away.

"We've got to find them, or this guy walks on Friday."

"I know, Leah," Jane Fenton replied. "We're working on it, but God, after thirty years, stuff does get lost or tossed."

"That bastard."

"Huh?"

"Nothing, not you. I'm just pissed Collins rushed us into this. Damn him. Before he opened his friggin' big mouth, we should have confirmed that the samples still existed and were testable. Bakerman still had another week to go before he was to be released."

"What'd ya say? I can barely hear you."

"I'll call you back," Harris spat. She disconnected and spun towards the media as one reporter's voice surfaced out of the din. "Mr. Collins . . . Mr. Collins . . . what about the other murders?"

Harris stiffened.

"Can you confirm that Mr. Bakerman is also a suspect in a number of other unsolved homicides, here and in other states?"

Collins grinned widely. His teeth sparkled. "He is certainly a person of interest."

"Then he's a suspect for, say, the Wendy Rose killing?"

"Rose?"

"In 1982, she disappeared in Discovery Park. A credit report shows that Bakerman lived near her parents' home."

"Is that right? Boy, you're ahead of me on that one, but I'm sure the police are aware of it."

Collins flashed a questioning look towards Harris but resumed before she could respond. "Look, ladies and gentlemen, it's way too early to tell just exactly what we have here with Clifford Bakerman. Let's try not to speculate. The facts will soon speak for themselves."

"Mr. Collins?"

A perky female reporter had pushed her way to the front of the pack. She jabbed her microphone into the prosecutor's face. "Your opponent in next Tuesday's election claimed this morning that your office has routinely practiced discrimination against minorities by charging them at higher levels than you would for nonminorities, under the same circumstances. Further, your office is less likely to grant minorities deferred prosecution or dismissal of charges than nonminorities. What is your comment on this?"

Collins's grin evaporated.

There was a long awkward silence. Finally, the lean prosecutor cleared his throat and clasped his hands in a gentle, thoughtful way. He glared directly at the reporter. "Madam, we are standing in a courthouse—a temple of justice. The most sacred institution, outside a church, in this great land of ours. Look over there at Lady Justice." He pointed towards the statuette on display just to the right of them. "She is blindfolded. Only the weight of evidence tips the scales. Skin color, gender, or national origin mean nothing here, nor in my office ten floors above."

"But your opponent, Mr. Bernhardt, says he can show statistical evidence to the contrary."

"I stand proudly on my record," Collins angrily proclaimed. "And I'll tell you right now, these unfounded, outrageous, eleventh-hour charges by Mr. Bernhardt only serve to demonstrate his unfitness for office."

"Mr. Collins . . ." Another reporter jumped into the melee.

Collins turned. He recognized a familiar face. His voice calmed. "Yes, Fred?"

"I have a copy of the press release Mr. Bernhardt passed out a short while ago. On it, he says minorities are three times more likely to be prosecuted for cocaine possession than nonminorities."

"Let me see that!"

The reporter handed Collins the single sheet of paper. Harris could see his face grow crimson as he read it.

"Well, sir?"

The prosecutor looked to Harris once more, then back to the reporters. "Listen," he said in a slow, controlled tone. "I've got work to do. A girl has been murdered. Be it yesterday or thirty years ago, Cindy Jo Sellinzski deserves to have her killer brought to justice. Politics pale in comparison to the duties I am entrusted with. These charges about discrimination are just politics and must take a backseat to seeing Cindy Jo finally rest in peace."

"But Mr. Collins—"

"No *buts,* ladies and gentlemen. Tonight, I am meeting my opponent in a debate on our local public television station. You all have your invites. I'll be happy to respond to any of your *political* questions then, but for now, I expect to be spending the next ten hours doing what the citizens of this fine county elected me to do in the first place, and that's keeping a vicious killer behind bars."

Collins gave a Nixon-like wave, hunkered down, and spun away.

"Mr. Collins, Mr. Collins," the chorus continued.

He did not reply. He made straight for the employee elevator, pausing midway only to grab Sergeant Harris's arm as though it were a brass ring on a merry-go-round. "Let's get the hell outta here," he whispered without breaking his politician's smile. Meanwhile the cameras continued to roll and the wire photographers snapped away.

9

Tessla Quinn leaned up against the cold concrete wall of the attorney's waiting room inside the King County Jail and shook her head in despair. Two years ago, graduating summa cum laude from Seattle University law school, she had chosen public defense, in part because of her initial belief that police were inept, and routinely arresting the wrong people. Two years of working in this gutter, defending wife beaters, drug addicts, and con men, had completely reversed that view. Not only were the area's police excellent at what they did, but the clients she routinely represented were obviously guilty—and usually of many more crimes than the police knew about. Clifford Bakerman was no exception. She had tried to interview him prior to his hearing, to get some ammunition, but he had remained nearly silent, his only words rambling disconnects, useless for anything except an insanity plea. This second attempt had ended before it had even started. Right as the old con was being led into the interview room after court, he had become faint and was immediately taken to the jail's infirmary.

Quinn debated whether she should wait for word on her client's condition or return to her nearby office. That decision, however, was immediately tabled by the sound of the

outer sally port door opening. She spun and groaned.
Through the inch-thick, bulletproof glass, she saw another
attorney entering the secure area, her late-arriving cocounsel, Paul Anders. He had been detained by another
matter and had been unable to attend the preliminary hearing—much to Quinn's relief. It was standard procedure to
assign two lawyers to a case like this, but Tessla was certain
that this gangly jeans-and-flannel-clad peer, despite his impressive Yale Law School pedigree, would be more hin-
drance than help. She had worked with him before. And
while on a personal level they had some things in common,
on a professional plane, Anders was inept. Not because of
his legal work. He penned the best briefs in the firm. It was
his courtroom demeanor. Once on stage, he quickly poi-
soned every jury with his whining arrogance.

One other detail bothered Tessla about her associate. He
was constantly hitting on her.

Quinn forced a smile as Anders passed through the inner
door. Under his right arm, he carried a thick inmate file.

"Hey, sorry I'm late," Anders said as the heavy metal
door clanged shut. He returned the smile and gazed about.
"So, where is he?"

Before Quinn could reply, a voice on an intercom spoke
up. "Ah, Ms. Quinn?"

It was a control room guard speaking from several floors
away.

Both lawyers looked up to the small surveillance camera
suspended from the ceiling.

The voice continued. "The nurse in the infirmary wanted
to let you know that Bakerman is okay. His blood sugar is a
little out of whack. He'll be fine; just give him half an hour."

Quinn waved acknowledgment and added, "Thanks."
Turning back to Anders, she said, "Guess we wait."

He shrugged and motioned to a nearby table and chairs.

"It'll give us a chance to go through this." He held up Bakerman's record. "And you can fill me in on what happened at the hearing. God, I wish I had been there. There was just no way I could get out of that other hearing. My guy jumped bail and the judge was really pissed. I'm sorry I wasn't there to help."

Quinn shrugged and the pair proceeded to the table. As they settled in, Quinn nonchalantly remarked, "I was up against Richard Collins. . . ."

She knew that would give her colleague a rise.

"Collins? Oh, man, now I'm really jealous. How'd you do? I mean, I've heard he's a pompous ass, but whip smart on examination."

"Watch the six o'clock news—you'll see."

Anders frowned. "Like, when do I watch TV—really, Tess."

Quinn rolled her eyes while Anders opened the bulky folder and split its contents in two. "Here's your half," he said, handing the documents over. "You've got from 1968 to 1981; I've got from then on." He leaned forward and cupped his chin on his hands. He began to peruse the paperwork, but a moment later he straightened. "I wonder why Stuart isn't taking this case?" Stuart Malconni was their boss. "Did he know Collins was personally handling the prelim?"

Irritated by the interruption, Quinn glanced up from her stack and replied blandly, "He said he had a conflict of interest." Her head bobbed back down.

"How so?" Anders pressed.

Quinn sighed and sat up. "The guy who snitched off Bakerman, Carl Eckler. I guess Stuart has defended him a couple of times—dope charges, I think."

Anders smirked. "Figures Stuart would handle that. I wonder what his fee was? How he ever got to be managing partner, I'll never know."

"Stop that."

"Hey, look, Stuart's a cool guy—but he smokes too much dope. I mean a little's okay. Like, who am I to judge, but I think he's doing more than just weed. Did you see his eyeballs at that last bar training? They were bouncing like ball bearings in a pinball machine."

Quinn winced.

"Now what's the matter?"

"Nothing."

"Ah, come on, we're friends. You can tell me. You look bothered by something."

"It's your ponytail," Quinn joked to defuse the inquiry. "You ever going to cut it off? It's kinda out of style."

"I will if you go out with me."

"Forget that."

"You're hurting my feelings."

Quinn grinned.

"Okay, I get the message—back to work."

Silence followed as both attorneys scoured the pages in front of them. However, after ten minutes of quiet, Anders shifted in his seat and shook his head in disgust. "How they ever thought . . . ," he mumbled to himself.

"Thought what?" Quinn said without looking up.

"That Bakerman would make it in a halfway house."

Quinn straightened. "Huh?"

"Says here that he was going to be transferred to Hope House down in Pioneer Square when he was released from prison. Christ, the guy is bipolar, suffers from bouts of dementia, and is a severe diabetic to boot. He belongs in a hospital, not a halfway house."

"That explains it."

"Explains what?"

"This morning, in the courtroom, Bakerman was zonked out. I bet he was having an insulin reaction."

Anders leaned forward. "Why do you say that?"

"My dad suffered from diabetes too. Late in life, if he missed an insulin shot, he'd lose touch real quick. Of course, part of it was his own damn fault; he was a chain-smoker. He puffed away, right up to the day he keeled over from a stroke."

Anders cringed.

Quinn continued. "God, I hated how our house smelled while I was growing up."

"Didn't your mom complain?"

Quinn shook her head. "She was the dutiful banker's wife. Never had a bad word about anything, even when she was the one who got throat cancer. She died two years after my dad."

There was an uncomfortable silence.

Quinn twisted in her seat and filled the void. "Hey, I still have my little brother, Bill. He's three years younger than I am—we're close. He's in med school right now at Johns Hopkins."

"That's cool."

Quinn smiled and asked, "So what's your family like?"

Now it was Anders's turn to roll his eyes. "Oh, boy, the opposite of yours, it sounds like. Give my mom a cause and look out. When she was our age, she was the classic sixties bra burner, and she still is. Of course, that worked out real well cuz my dad was into burning his draft card—it was love at first ignite."

Quinn chuckled.

"Changing the subject," Anders went on, "is there anything you see in these documents?"

Quinn shrugged her shoulders. "Zero."

"You think he's guilty?"

"Does it matter?"

Anders didn't bother to reply.

10

Detective Sergeant Harris stepped out of the elevator and paused as the doors behind her slid shut. Ahead, down the long hallway, was her squad room. She was in no hurry to get there. Her meeting with Richard Collins had gone poorly. In a heated exchange, she had made clear her agitation at being used for his political purposes. "One of the first officers on the scene," she had scoffed. "Christ, all you did was carry the lab tech's equipment into the zoo. And that was hours after Sellinzski had been transported. Christ, gimme a break." That was rapidly followed by, "Listen to me, Collins. Don't you ever drag me into court again before I have all the evidence nailed down." She had then stormed out. However, by the time she had reached street level, her anger had been replaced by second thoughts. Had she been out of line? It wouldn't have been the first time. She was known throughout the department for being blunt, but was she really just tactless or, worse, arrogant?

That last thought troubled her. She prided herself in always being in control, yet there were times—and more so lately—when she just lost it. She sighed and, with effort, forced the notion from her mind. She had work to do, and personal feelings had no place on her plate today. She had less than forty-eight hours to develop enough evidence to keep Bakerman held. That's what was important. All the rest could be worried about later. Especially the inevitable trip upstairs when she'd have to stand tall in front of her superiors and explain how she had the gall to dress down the King County prosecutor, deserving or not.

She proceeded on, her pace picking up, her confidence returning. As she crossed the threshold of the Homicide squad room, her loud footsteps caused Detective Gilroy to swivel in his seat. "Hey, boss."

"Where is everybody?" Harris asked.

"You gave 'em the day off, remember?"

Harris sagged.

"Want me to call a couple of the boys back in?"

Harris thought for a moment and replied, "Naw, let's wait a bit. I want to look the case file over once more and maybe go out to the original scene. Besides, if Jane and Roy can somehow come up with the semen sample or the pubic hair that was recovered—and if we get a match—we're home free."

"That's a big if. Say, I understand they haven't been able to find 'em yet."

Harris nodded grimly.

Gilroy remained upbeat. "By the way, I got a clean copy of the ME's report. Oh, and some Dr. something or another left a message for you. Said he had treated Bakerman out at Monroe and would like to talk to you when you had some free time. The number is on your desk."

Harris ignored the part about the doctor and focused in on the report. "Anything in it?"

"Nothing we didn't already know. "

Harris frowned, shifted a bit, and said, "Right after the hearing, at the press conference, I heard a reporter ask Collins about other victims."

"Others—who?"

"I missed the name."

Gilroy whipped back around. He immediately began typing on his keyboard as Harris continued. "I'll bet Collins leaked the information beforehand. I'd sure like to know how he came up with it."

A moment later Gilroy straightened. "Here ya go."

Harris leaned inward so she could read the computer screen. She recognized the Web site immediately. It was the state's Homicide Investigative Tracking System, or HITS. Within the relational database, operated by the attorney general's office, were the details of every homicide, suspicious death, and still missing person from the last four decades. Bits and pieces of seemingly unrelated information could be entered by investigators, and with a press of a button, a victim could be identified, a suspect discovered, or new leads uncovered in an otherwise dead-end case.

"I was just in the process of entering Bakerman's profile and stats from all these reports when you came in. Look, boss, there're two potential hits right there."

Gilroy beamed.

Harris leaned even closer and shook her head in disgust. "Son of a bitch, Bakerman did live in the area of that other rape-kill victim."

"Yeah, but he moved out a year before the attack."

"Still?"

"Looks like a county case."

"What about the other one—Julie Alexander, 1978?"

Both speed-read the information on the display.

"Hey, this isn't good," Gilroy mumbled. "Bakerman and this Alexander girl worked at the same nursing home on the Eastside a couple years before she was killed."

Harris snatched up a legal pad and pencil from Gilroy's desk and scribbled down the case numbers. She then reached for the nearby telephone. Before she could dial, the squad room door popped open, and in walked her most senior detective, Ed Jennings. Under his right arm, he was carrying a manila folder.

Harris straightened. "I thought you were taking the day off?" She was slightly miffed. She had been trying for weeks to get Jennings to take more vacation time. He had months of unused leave on the books—like her.

The middle-aged detective shrugged. "I am, but my wife was having her women's group over for lunch, so I thought I'd come down here and hang out for a while. Besides, I've got a lot of paperwork to do."

"Whatcha got there?" Gilroy asked.

Jennings stepped over and handed the younger detective the folder he was carrying. "Ran into Stan from DOC on the way up. Said you were looking for this. It's a copy of Bakerman's prison record."

Gilroy took the envelope as Jennings turned his attention to his supervisor. "Say, how'd it go in court this morning?"

"Long story," Harris sighed. "But since you're here, you mind going over to County Records and ordering up these case files?" She handed Jennings the page she had scribbled on. He took the scrap as Gilroy ripped open the Department of Corrections file.

Meanwhile, Harris fingered through the pile of documents next to her and sifted out Bakerman's rap sheet. It was a long one.

Jennings edged close. "What's his history like?"

For the moment, Harris ignored her subordinate. Then she uttered, "Look, he was arrested for disorderly conduct in 1969, and indecent exposure in 1970."

"A weenie waver?" Gilroy joked as he fingered the enclosed DOC booking photo. "He looks like the trench coat type. I bet he spent the better part of his life camped out in a public rest room."

"So?" Jennings pressed.

Harris continued. "He was arrested again in 1972—indecent liberties with a minor."

"Convicted?"

"There's no disposition. Must've beat it."

"What else?"

"Another disorderly in '73, a second DUI in '75, a prostitution arrest in '76, and another in '80."

"How much time did he do?"

"Never more than sixty days in the county can."

"Anything more current?"

"A trespassing in 1980. Another in 1982 and, here, a soliciting-a-child-prostitute rap in 1986. That got him almost a year in County."

"What got him the prison time?"

"The two counts of child rape in 1993. He got the max on that—ten years." Harris paused, thought for a moment, and suddenly slumped.

"What's the matter?"

"That goddamn Collins. He rushed me into this thing and look at this." Harris waved the rap sheet. "This guy doesn't profile out at all. He's a kiddie fuck . . ." Her voice trailed off.

"But what about these other victims," Gilroy said, "Alexander and Rose? Maybe he's a switch-hitter? Boss, do you know what the odds are that this guy is associated with three rape-kills and he's not involved? I'd say a hundred to one—no, make that a thousand to one. It's way too much of a coincidence."

"And what about the holy card?" Jennings pointed out. "Seems to me that cinches it."

Harris glanced at Gilroy. "Let me see that booking picture."

He handed it over.

Harris gazed at it while rubbing the back of her neck. A reflective moment passed; then she said philosophically, "If you are our boy, where are the rest of them?"

"Rest of what?" Jennings spoke up.

"Bodies," Harris deadpanned. "There have to be more bodies. That's the one pattern I'm sure of. Once you've killed for gratification, nothing else will satisfy. We got Sellinzski in '75, maybe Alexander in '78 and Rose in '82. Bakerman wasn't put on ice until 1993. There's got to be more."

Jennings suddenly headed for his desk.

Harris looked up. "Where ya going?"

"Just letting the wife know I'll be late tonight."

Puzzled, Harris asked, "Why do you say that?"

"Cuz, boss, you got the look." Jennings winked at Gilroy.

The younger detective leaned back in his chair, grinned, and nodded agreement.

Harris blushed—they were all too right.

11

Frank Milkovich plunked down into his office chair and gazed nervously at the telephone resting squarely in front of him. He had survived the Citizens' Advisory Board meeting without any major incidents and had managed to schedule more meetings for the months to come. But now he had to report in. And the chief had something for him to look into. This was not good. When a complaint originated from that high up, guilty or not, heads were bound to roll.

But there was another aspect to Milkovich's uncertainty—his minimal contact with the new Seattle police chief, Thomas Logan. Most of the rank and file possessed this same uneasiness. Logan was a credentialed East Coaster, with a ticket full of punches. A former deputy chief of police in Philadelphia, he had been an FBI agent and a Clinton-era Justice Department appointee. This alone would have made him unwelcome, but he was also an academic, serving as an adjunct professor of public policy for the Kennedy School of Government at Harvard University.

Milkovich reached for his handset and punched in the direct interoffice number. There was one ring, and the call was picked up. "Chief Logan." The Boston accent was unmistakable.

Milkovich gulped. He knew the man on the other end of the line was the only person on the planet who could approve his transfer out of IA. He straightened in his seat and firmly replied, "Good morning, sir, it's Lieutenant Milkovich."

There was a moment's pause.

"Internal Affairs," Frank added as a memory jogger.

"Right—Frank, isn't it?"

"That's right, sir."

"So, how did it go this morning? I've already heard you had some interesting discussions." The chief chuckled.

Milkovich sagged.

"Don't worry, Frank. These things take time. I know you did a good job, but that's not what I wanted to talk to you about."

Milkovich's stomach rumbled.

"I got a curious telephone call first thing this morning," the chief continued. "Do you happen to know a former captain by the name of Patrick Dellhanney? I believe he retired from here about seven years ago."

Milkovich held his reply for a moment. He knew Dellhanney well, but not because he was a friend. Dellhanney had been Milkovich's first sergeant. When the man wasn't drunk, he was always trying to get there. Yet he had managed to rise in the ranks, thanks mainly to his brother-in-law's being on the city council for two decades. That was the way the system had worked. And while blatant favoritism and blackballing had faded over the years, outright mistrust of the administration, and anyone over the rank of sergeant, still hovered like an ever-present ground fog.

"So?" the chief prodded.

"Yeah, I know Dellhanney."

"What kind of man is he?"

"Ah—"

"I got the impression he was rather old school, if you know what I mean. But he appears to have an interesting story he wants to tell."

"About what?"

"Something he would only give details about in person. How's your afternoon look? I'm tied up until at least three, maybe four. Would you be available to get together with him in my office sometime around then?"

"Sure," Milkovich was quick to reply. "Whatever you need. Just give me a call, or if I'm away from my desk, have my assistant page me."

"Appreciate it. I'll be in touch." The chief hung up.

Milkovich settled back into his chair. "Dellhanney," he mumbled with disgust. "I wonder what that asshole is into now?" He drew a deep breath and let it go slowly. As he did, his mind drifted. Without thinking, he reached down and pulled a side drawer open. Inside, he had taped a small snapshot he had taken of Leah. He had caught her smiling as they had walked together on a driftwood-strewn beach. That weekend was crisp with memories—a quaint waterfront B and B near Port Townsend, rustic shops, and moonlight walks. The squabbling seagulls and salty odors still permeated the recollection.

Milkovich sighed and shoved the drawer back in. For nearly a year now, he and Harris had been a department "item," although a discreet one. Both were well aware of the gossip mill they inhabited, and all the written, and unwritten, rules constricting their personal lives. Nevertheless, both were content to navigate this relationship under these conditions. It made the limited time they spent together that much more precious.

Yet Frank Milkovich felt an uneasiness growing in the pit of his stomach. One with no specific cause, simply a growing dread that his feelings for Harris had evolved beyond hers for him. It was a recent development. No more than a week old, but the signs were there. His bellyache suddenly rippled through the rest of his body as his next thought morphed into pure paranoia. Had Leah sensed the imbalance and was she now planning to terminate their ties? His mind fixated on that thought as his eyes bored off into space.

Ring . . . ring.

Milkovich groaned. He drew a deep breath and grabbed for his telephone again. "Internal Affairs, Lieutenant Milkovich speaking."

"Hey, Frank."

His heart skipped—it was Leah. It took a moment for him to reply. "Wh-where ya at?"

"My desk."

Milkovich glanced at the clock. It was half past noon. With trepidation he asked, "Are we still doing lunch?"

"Sure, but—"

His heart sank. Now what?

"Instead of Jake's, how about the zoo?" Leah suggested.

"The zoo?"

"Yeah, I'll buy. Can you meet me there in thirty minutes? South gate by the children's section—you know the petting area?"

Milkovich leaned back in his chair and thought for a moment. "I guess so." There was disappointment in his voice. It was obvious to him that this was going to be a working lunch. Worse, it was likely part of her team would also be there—so much for a chance to be alone.

12

Richard Collins leaned back in his thickly padded office chair and knotted his arms tight. Despite his attempt to look confident and relaxed, his body language said otherwise. Before him was another man, about his own age. The similarities, however, ended there. Whereas the prosecutor possessed an athletic physique, dressed well, and maintained neatness in all public aspects of his life, Patrick Dellhanney was a short, ruddy-faced man with a truculent demeanor and complete disregard for social niceties. From his viselike handshake, cocked eye, and bellicose voice to his natty but out-of-date attire, the man exuded roosterlike self-assurance. And while Collins spoke with an attorney's smoothness, Dellhanney was blunt and usually quick to a point—except now.

"So, Patrick," Collins said with forced friendliness, "long time, no see. What can I do for you today?"

Dellhanney let go a toothy grin, ignored the inquiry, and eased over to the entryway he had just passed through. He shut the door and turned. "I hear your campaign has hit a snag—losing your *touch?*"

Collins said nothing.

Dellhanney's impish grin remained. "Say," he continued.

"I also heard a rumor that the party's going to put you up for that opening on the state supreme court next year. In fact, it's a sure thing if you get reelected."

"What's it to you?" Collins said in a suspicious tone.

Dellhanney shrugged coyly and looked about. He stepped to one side of the spacious office to a wall covered in framed photos and awards.

He looked them all over, then focused on the two center ones. The first was a simple walnut memorial, a Marine Corps eagle, globe, and anchor emblem, attached above a tarnished brass plate. The engraved words were sparse. It simply read 1ST LT. RICHARD C. COLLINS, 3/1 KILO CO. 1ST PLT, CHU LAI, VIETNAM, SEPT. 7, 1970, TO OCT. 15, 1971— SEMPER FI. Right below it was a shadow box containing numerous medals and ribbons from that era. A Silver Star and Purple Heart were among them.

He turned back.

Their eyes met.

"So, Rich, I understand you've been getting some big contributions from the building PACs. Guess the last thing they need is some liberal, tree hugger type like Bernhardt sitting in here and interpreting the county's zoning and rent control codes differently, hmmm?"

Again, Collins chose not to reply.

"Why, I was just downstairs in the Elections Department looking over the public disclosure forms, and my-oh-my, they're putting some real money where their mouths are. Too bad that bastard Bernhardt pulled the race card on ya. That can be tough to beat."

Their eyes remained locked. Collins suddenly growled, "Look, Dellhanney, get to the point."

The retired police captain parted his coat and withdrew a tattered old photograph. He eased close to the outsize mahogany desk. "I was cleaning out some things the other day and found this. I thought you might like it." He tossed it Collins's way. "Mickey sent it to me in one of his letters. Right after he convinced me to give you a job on the force."

Collins fingered the photo. Mickey Dellhanney was Patrick's kid brother, whom Collins had served with in Vietnam. Suddenly, the prosecutor's face became grimly distant. Meanwhile, Dellhanney stepped back from the desk and turned to admire a series of seascapes hanging on the opposite wall. They were views from a family cabin that the Collins family owned on nearby Whidbey Island.

"So, how you doing in the polls?" Dellhanney continued while keeping Collins in constant view from the corner of his eye. "Last one I saw it was neck and neck."

The prosecutor remained focused on the old photo.

"Well?"

Collins finally looked up. His face had gone pale. But not because of the photo. He had guessed Dellhanney's true purpose for being here. "Well, what?" he weakly replied.

Dellhanney turned to him. "The polls, Rich. The polls."

Collins opened a side drawer and deposited the image. He gritted his teeth and replied, "I'll get a bounce with this Bakerman case. And tonight, I'll rip Bernhardt a new ass during our debate."

"Maybe, maybe not," Dellhanney purred.

Collins's face flamed. He clenched both his fists and blurted, "You can cut the fucking games. What the hell is it you want—this time?"

13

Leaning on the split rail fence inside the crowded petting zoo, Frank Milkovich judged the distance from his position to an old maple standing like a giant umbrella over the many sheep, goats, and toddlers.

"So, how far do you think?" Harris asked. She was next to him, although her attention, unlike his, was centered on a small spiral notebook she held in her hand.

"Thirty feet," Milkovich suggested. He shifted his stance and gazed back towards the parking lot they had come from. "The streets in this neighborhood are gridded on magnetic north. I say we take fifty paces—"

"That way," Harris finished. She spun and started off.

Milkovich tossed the remains of a soda he had been sipping into an adjacent trash bin, but instead of stepping quickly after Leah, he paused and listened to the distant sound of an elephant trumpeting, a reply to an equally distant lion's roar.

His thoughts drifted into a debate.

Ya got to ask her, he said to himself. *Just be up front and ask . . .*

But what if—?

You'd rather have the truth, right?

It can wait . . .

No, it can't—chicken.

"Excuse me."

Milkovich was oblivious.

"Sir?"

The trance broke. Embarrassed, Milkovich moved sideways, clearing the way for a young woman with twins in a stroller. "Sorry," he mumbled. Refocusing, he saw Harris now standing in front of a shoulder-high wall of mortared stone. It enclosed the mock barnyard from the hundreds of acres of main zoo. She was waiting impatiently for him.

"Coming," he mumbled, and commenced stepping off the distance, keeping track of every footfall. When he arrived at her side, his count was at forty-four.

Harris gazed up at the dense canopy of mature rhododendrons looming beyond the bulwark. "I'd say ten or fifteen more feet."

Milkovich nodded tentative agreement. "What's the measurement again?"

"Due east, one hundred and eighty feet from the maple, there should be a large boulder on the other side of this wall. That's the actual monument that was used as the reference point."

"Odds are it was moved or pulled out altogether when they built this new section."

"When was that?"

Milkovich thought for a moment. "Must have been around 'eighty-two. Maybe a year later."

"God, I was still in high school."

Milkovich chuckled.

"What?"

"Nothing."

"Aw, come on. You got that look on your face. What are you thinking?"

"It's nothing."

"Frank—"

"It was nothing, really. I was just thinking you probably hated high school."

"Why do you say that?"

"Really, it's nothing." Milkovich turned away.

"Frank—"

Milkovich ignored her. "We can use the gate over there and circle round to the other side."

Harris sighed and proceeded with her partner. After a short walk, they passed out of the children's area and into the thickly landscaped general zoo. Wide paths disappeared into multiacre habitats of savanna and forests, while others branched off towards the many enclosed exhibits.

After a few steps, they paused.

"Looks like we go cross-country from here."

Harris nodded.

Milkovich took her hand, and they both gingerly stepped over the flower bed, up a berm, and through an opening in the hedgerow. Once through, they entered a deeply shaded, overgrown area, screened from the general public. They were now alone, the sounds of the park muted by the thick foliage. Ahead was a sofa-sized rock resting at the apex of a small incline, its base paralleling an abandoned trail that once wove through the grove.

Milkovich was first to speak. "So what is it exactly you want me to do?"

Harris reached into her coat pocket and pulled out a steel tape measure. She tossed it to Milkovich. "You take the dumb end. Come on."

Reaching the rock, Harris knelt down and brushed away several inches of humus. Not content, she dug further.

"Want a glove?" Milkovich asked.

"You got some?"

"Not with me. I can go back to the car."

"Never mind. I think—"

Harris suddenly stopped. With a pleased grin, she looked up. "Bingo." She pointed to a faded spot of red spray paint, placed an inch above the spot where a metal survey marker had been driven into the ground.

"The original baseline?"

"Yep." Harris straightened and consulted her notebook. Satisfied, she said, "Eighteen feet, right out from here—down in the dip."

Milkovich pulled out two feet of the tape and handed the smart end to Harris. He then knelt where she had been and placed the tip of the ruler squarely on top of the monument. "It's your show."

Harris smiled and eased down the slope, playing out the tape as she went. When she judged she had gone far enough, she stooped and pulled the line taut. "Right about here." She reached for a dead branch and planted it on the spot.

"Was that where she was found?"

Harris nodded grimly. "She was transported alive, so the measurements were based on witness statements, but they should be near exact given that we had officers on scene soon after the attack."

"How long after?"

"Maybe an hour."

Milkovich straightened and moved to the edge of the depression. "Okay, so now that I have helped, is that all you need?"

Harris ignored his snappishness. "What's the scene tell you, Frank?"

Milkovich's eyes narrowed. He knew what Leah was asking, but his thoughts were still focused on his own personal dilemma. He played dumb and shrugged.

"Come on, you know what I mean. Think, twenty-eight

years ago, a teenage girl was knifed, raped, and for all intents murdered on this very spot." Harris pointed at the twig. "Right here. What does the scene tell you? Except for the bushes having grown, this place hasn't changed a bit since then."

Milkovich gazed down. "The beer cans have."

Harris raised a questioning brow.

"Behind you, to your left. There's an old can with a pull tab. I think they stopped making them about the time they built the kiddie zoo."

She twisted and saw what Milkovich was referring to. It was the remnants of a rusted steel container, barely visible among the dead leaves. She looked back. "Okay, besides the litter, what else?"

Milkovich sighed.

"Ah, what's the matter? You've been acting weird since we got here."

"Us," Milkovich blurted.

Harris reared back. "Us?"

"I've been wanting to talk to you for the last week, but God, every time I've tried, you're either too busy or too tired. What's up?"

A look of innocence flashed across Harris's face. "Nothing," she replied weakly.

"Oh, that sounded real convincing."

She dropped the pretense and frowned. "Can we do this later? Christ, Frank, I've got forty-eight hours to come up with something, anything, to keep a killer behind bars. I need your help now, not—"

"Not what?"

"We'll talk about it later, okay?"

"When?"

"Later. Seriously, I do need your help. Come on, humor me. You have the best sixth sense I've ever seen in a person.

It's like you can see right into the past and see it in real time. Besides—"

"What?"

"You know what—tonight." Harris winked and grinned.

"Oh, now you're trying to bribe me."

"Maybe," Harris said slyly.

Milkovich folded his arms, drew a deep breath, and looked about. "Okay, you win. Our discussion is tabled for the time being. Besides"—he unlocked his arms—"you got me curious now."

Harris's grin widened. She knew that once Milkovich got a taste of an interesting case, everything else would become secondary until its resolution. Food, friends, and family were all forgotten. It was a trait she couldn't explain or excuse. And she possessed it too. It was an obsession—the only antidote the sound of handcuffs ratcheting down on a suspect's wrist.

"So tell me more. What do we know about the victim?"

Harris let go the steel tape. Looking south, she said, "Sellinzski lived about a mile from here, with her mom. She had just graduated from high school two months prior, and was flipping burgers at Dick's, part-time."

"Her dad?"

"Died when she was twelve—commercial fishing accident in Alaska."

"Any other family?"

"Nothing that was noted."

"What about suspects at the time—anyone of interest?"

"Not really. She was the studious type, average looks, no boyfriends. Had a full-ride scholarship, and was set to start college fall quarter."

"Who was the last to see her alive?"

"The night manager at Dick's. According to his statement, the two of them closed up at midnight, and about fifteen minutes later, she left on foot. Her house was only eight blocks from there. She should have gotten home in under ten minutes—she never made it."

"The night manager, did he report seeing anything odd? Seems to me that a killer like this didn't just swoop down and scoop her up on her way home. She would've been stalked first, for weeks, maybe months."

Harris nodded agreement. "You're absolutely right about that, and that's the primary problem with this case, and practically every other old serial investigation I've reviewed over the years. Back then, the detectives always asked the same stupid question—was there anything odd or out of place? The hallmark of a serial killer is exactly the opposite."

"How so?"

"There isn't going to be anything odd or out of place. The killer always blends in. That's how he gets away with multiple murders. Christ, I could solve every old serial case in a couple of minutes if the witnesses had provided a full description of everything that was *in* place—who drove by regularly, who was always at the café at the same time every day, who was out walking their dog. It drives me crazy that that one simple question was never asked—ever."

Milkovich broke a slight smile. "I like it when you go crazy."

"Stop that."

The smile grew larger.

Harris ignored him and looked the other direction. She said, "There's not too much else to tell. From the moment she left the drive-in until six in the morning when she was found, we have a blank, and not one thing to fill it in with."

"Any idea how she got here, to this particular spot, I mean? Was she carried, or led here?"

"Good question. I think the original investigators had it

right. Based on the grass stains and scratches on her legs as well as a couple of footprints they found at the head of the trail, it looks like she was running away from the guy. She certainly wasn't carried here."

"Then why this spot?"

"Probably ran out of steam. She had already been cut up pretty bad and been bleeding."

"No footprints of the killer?"

"Nothing usable. The medics and cops were so frantic to save her life, they made a mess of the scene. Any usable prints were mixed with the rescuers'. No way to tell whose were whose."

"So tell me about Bakerman. How does he fit in besides having that religious card of hers? That seems kind of slim."

"He's a convicted sex offender."

"Yeah, I heard that on the news, but a child molester. That doesn't seem right."

"I know, but—well, there is more."

"Like what?"

"At the time, he lived in the area. Two blocks away from the Sellinzskis. Plus we may have two other victims. He lived a block away from another girl, although he moved out eleven months prior to her death. And he worked at the same place as the other. She turned up dead a few years later. It may sound slim, but in this business that's way too many co-incidences."

Milkovich rubbed his chin and said, "So what you are actually telling me is you've placed all your chips on the DNA match."

Harris stiffened. "Collins has—not me. But if we don't have Sellinzski's, odds are County has samples intact from other, more recent victims. I'll get this bastard one way or the other."

Milkovich hunched down to one knee and scanned the vicinity where Harris stood.

Seeing his mind focusing, she went silent. This was what she was waiting for. It was nearly a minute before he stirred. When he did, Harris was quick to ask, "So, Frank, what does the scene tell you?"

He didn't reply. Rather, his eyes began shifting from one sector to another, his ears listening, his nose dissecting the odors in the air. After he had completed his sweep, Milkovich picked up a small pebble and fingered it in his palm. He suddenly said, "Do you hear it?"

"Hear what?"

"Listen."

Harris turned her head, then shrugged her shoulders.

"It's the traffic on Fifty-fifth. You can hear it from here."

"So?"

Milkovich tossed the pebble and rose. "You think the killer ever came back?"

"What, to here?"

"Yeah, you know, returning to the scene of the crime."

"Could have. This place isn't exactly inaccessible."

Milkovich nodded, then eased down the slope to join Harris. However, instead of stopping by her side, he proceeded past her to the spot where the old beer can lay. With care, he picked it up. "Hmmm, Rainier Ale. I use to drink a lot of this."

Impatience was beginning to gnaw at Harris. "So, what are you thinking, Frank?"

Milkovich continued to examine the can.

"Frank—?"

He glanced up. "Think about it, Leah. The killer could have come back here and had a beer, weeks, months, even years later. He might have sat up there on that rock and reveled again in the last moments of his pursuit."

"You think—?"

"What, the can?"

"Yeah."

"Who knows? You asked me what the scene said to me. Heck, a worker could've simply tossed the can here when they were building the wall over there."

Harris's cell phone suddenly rang. She groaned. "Now what?" She fumbled for the device as Milkovich tossed the piece of trash into a thicket. "Hello," she answered. "Yeah, hi. . . . What? Ah, Christ . . ."

Milkovich alerted.

"So the prison doesn't have a record of it. Goddamn it. What'd I tell you, Phil? I knew Collins was rushing things. Right . . . yeah, that's a good idea. Give their evidence people a call. . . . Right . . . okay . . . oh, that doctor called again? Did he say what he wanted? Right, I'll get to him when I can. . . . Okay—bye."

Harris disconnected and slid the phone back into her pocket. She was obviously upset.

"What's the matter?"

"That damn Collins," Harris fumed. "He rushed us into this without verifying a thing. We're screwed."

"Now what?"

Harris's face clouded. "Eckler claimed he reported Bakerman and his diaries to prison officials. Phil finally got a call back from them. They've got no record whatsoever of Eckler doing this. Shit—there goes our witness's veracity."

Milkovich stepped forward and was about to give her a comforting hug when his eyes were drawn to a slight glimmer among the dead leaves and twigs. It was just beyond where Leah stood.

"What the—?" He brushed past Harris and knelt. From there, he lowered himself down until his nose was almost ground level.

"What do you see, Frank?" His back blocked Harris's view of the object.

Milkovich didn't reply. However, a moment later he knew that any plans for a quiet evening with Leah were now done for. His eyes were focused on a small metallic object—not a beer can this time but a woman's ring. It lay barely visible beneath a layer of old vegetation.

"Frank?"

Milkovich eased back up and looked to Harris's anticipating face. He said, "You better get an evidence recovery team out here right away. It's a ring. I think it says 'Lincoln High School, Class of 1975.'"

14

"Thanks for letting me eat while we talk," Clifford Baker-man said as he shoved the plastic tray aside. "I shouldn't have gone so long without food or having a shot. I was nearly in a reaction back in the courtroom."

The old convict was still dressed in the street clothes he had been issued at Monroe State Reformatory and was seated across from Tessla Quinn and a restless Paul Anders. He appeared to have recovered from his earlier ailments. His cheeks had color, his eyes were clear, and what little hair he had left was now neatly combed.

Quinn suddenly felt a discreet nudge from her cocoun-sel's knee. She glanced sideways, but Anders remained mo-tionless. His gaze was fixed on a point beyond Bakerman's shoulder. Quinn resisted the urge to elbow him. He had been constantly interrupting her questioning, despite having agreed to let her take the lead on this first round of inter-views. She turned back and forced a reassuring smile on her face. "Mr. Bakerman, you've got to let me know right away if you need medical care, or anything else, for that matter."

"Cliff. Please just call me Cliff."

Quinn nodded with hesitation. Despite the man's out-wardly friendly demeanor, she felt uncomfortable being this near to him. She could feel the heat of his breath. The young attorney shifted in her seat and replied, "Okay, Cliff, but please, in the future—I've seen your medical file—you have to let me know if you are feeling ill. I'm your advocate and I can't do my job without your absolute trust and cooperation."

Bakerman leaned back and patted his stomach. "Jail food has improved since I was here last. That wasn't a bad chicken-fried steak—not bad at all. Wonder what's for supper tonight?"

Quinn felt the nudge again. This time, though, she ignored it.

"Say, how long you been a lawyer, Miss Quinn? I mean, I don't want to be disrespectful, but you seem kinda young. Not that that matters. You did a real fine job in court today— real fine. You had that ol' prosecutor all red-faced. I really enjoyed that."

"But I thought—"

"Say, Cliff?"

Bakerman turned to Anders.

"How long have you been a diabetic?"

The older man gazed upward. As he did, he massaged the nape of his neck. "Hard to say," he replied. "Pretty near most my life, I guess. At least that's what the docs have told me. Of course, I didn't know it for a long time. I just thought it was normal to pass out after drinking a couple of beers— well, not really pass out, I just kinda—"

"Lost touch with reality?"

"Yeah, that's right. I'd have a reaction and dang it, next thing I'd know, I'd wake up, and it'd be the next day, and I'd have no idea what or where I'd been."

"You're a convicted child molester," Anders deadpanned. "Tell us about that."

Bakerman blushed.

Quinn glared at her partner. Quickly she said, "You don't need to answer that right now, Mr. Bakerman."

"It's okay," the old con replied. "If you all are going to defend me right and proper, you need to know the real truth. Not just what the cops say, and all those other people."

"Other?" Anders probed. "Who do you mean, *others?*"

"Damn it, Paul," Quinn burst. "Would you . . ." Her voice trailed off as she caught sight of Bakerman's eyes beginning to cloud. Tears suddenly welled up and one began to roll down his cheek. Embarrassed, the man quickly used his shirtsleeve to wipe it away. "Sorry," he sniffled. "I've gotten kinda emotional in my old age. Especially when I think about the past."

Quinn reached for her briefcase and withdrew a small packet of Kleenex. She was still simmering over Anders's intrusions. "Here," she said and offered several tissues.

"No, thank you, Miss Quinn. I'll be fine. Really, I'll be just fine."

Quinn retracted her offering but kept a careful eye on her client. He sniffled once more and said, "I know you're here to talk about this girl I'm supposed to have killed, but I need to tell you about how I got here in the first place. That's so you'll know when I say I haven't the slightest idea how I could be responsible for something so horrible—well, maybe you'll believe me then."

Anders quickly spoke up. "We believe you."

"Oh, you're just being nice. I can tell that right now. Neither one of you have much faith in the words coming outta my mouth—heck, I don't blame you. I wouldn't trust me neither, especially if I was sitting where you're sitting."

"It's not my job to believe you," Quinn replied while tilting towards her briefcase again. "My job is to defend you, guilty or not."

She returned the packet of tissue and pulled out a fresh

legal pad. Setting it squarely before her, she was about to resume her questioning when Bakerman shook his head and muttered, "It's the same darn system. Folks like me don't stand a chance."

"What do you mean?" Quinn asked.

"Heck, even if you are innocent, they tell ya to plead guilty cuz if ya don't, ya get twice the sentence. The two children I supposedly molested, the Nikklesen girls—it never happened."

Quinn's eyes narrowed on her client's.

Bakerman sighed. "Oh, I bet you've heard that before. Heck, I'll bet everybody you defend says that. Isn't that right?"

Neither counsel replied.

"See, I can tell just by looking at you. But that doesn't matter. Like I said before, if I was on the other side of this table and lookin' at me, well, I'd be pretty skeptical. You got to be; there's so many liars in this world."

"Who was your attorney on that case?"

"Oh, gosh, he was a young one, like you two. Ummm, it'll come to me. Just give me a second."

"If you were innocent," Quinn asked, "why'd you plead guilty?"

"It's like this," Bakerman voiced earnestly. "I had a good job driving bus back then. Gots lots of overtime and was making real money. Anyway, I'm a churchgoin' man. And the Good Book says to be charitable to others. Well, that's how it all started. Her name was Judy. Cute little gal. Poor thing—her husband had run off, and she was having a real hard time making it, what with two little girls and all. See, she belonged to the same church as me. And every Sunday, rain or shine, she'd be there, right smack in the front row with her girls—and both of 'em in pretty dresses and polished shoes."

"So what happened?" Quinn's interest was now piqued.

"Like I said, Judy was having a real hard time making it, and our reverend got wind of this, and so he gave me a call and asked if I could put the family up at my place for a while."

Both attorneys raised skeptical brows.

"Oh, before you start thinking bad things, let me explain. The house I owned at the time had lots of extra space—I had built a mother-in-law apartment onto it and was planning on renting it out, but seems there was always someone in need—good Christian folks that were just down on their luck. The reverend was always finding someone who needed shelter, and I was more than happy to do the good work."

"Where was this house?" Anders asked.

"Wallingford. I got the place cheap, before prices went sky-high. I think I paid twenty thousand for it way back in 'seventy-seven. In a couple of years, I had the place fixed up real nice."

"Bet it's worth half a mil now," Anders sighed.

"So what happened?" Quinn pressed. She was growing impatient. Her legal pad was still blank.

Bakerman turned to her. "Well, Miss Quinn, I took the Nikklesens in—Judy, Jody, and Jana—and everything was fine the first couple of weeks. In fact, it was just like having a real family in my home. We started to do things together. On my days off I'd take the kids to the zoo, I'd cook dinner, and even help with their laundry. And believe me, I didn't expect anything in return—nothing."

"But how did you get from there to here?"

The old con's eyes hardened with bitterness. He drew a deep breath and let it go through clenched teeth. "They tried to make me into some kind of monster. Like I was someone who hid in bushes waiting for some innocent child to walk by."

Quinn picked up her pen.

"It was all lies."

"Then you never molested those two girls?" Quinn asked.

Bakerman raised his hands in earnest. "I swear, never touched them—never."

There was a moment of silence as the con lowered his hands. He gulped and continued. "See, Judy had a problem with drugs and alcohol that I didn't know about at the time. She kept it hidden real well. And with me now kinda looking after her kids, she was free to stay out later and later. Six weeks after she and the girls had moved in, she got fired from her job. That put her over the edge. She went on a binge and started bringing home these men that I didn't want on my property."

Bakerman paused and shifted uncomfortably in his seat. "For a while, I tolerated it. Those poor girls needed a place to live, but it got worse and worse, so finally I had to confront Judy, and let her know this had to stop, or else."

"Were you planning on throwing her out?" Quinn asked.

Bakerman nodded guiltily. "Even the neighbors were complaining about the late-night noise and cars coming by at all hours."

"So, did you confront her?"

Bakerman nodded again.

"What'd she do?"

"Next afternoon when I was home alone, two police detectives came to my house. They asked me a lot of really awful questions. You can't imagine. I tried to tell them the truth—time and again, but it was like they didn't believe a word I said."

"What happened next?"

"Oh, my . . . after about an hour, they asked me if they could have permission to search my home."

"Did you let them?"

"Of course, I had nothing to hide."

Anders cringed.

Bakerman worried a look. "What's the matter?"

"Cops," Anders sniped. "That's what. But go on—this is getting real interesting. Did they find anything?"

"Well, ah—" Bakerman blushed again and slumped.

"Come on, Cliff," Anders urged. "You can tell us."

With a chest heave, he reluctantly continued. "There was this picture," he said, his voice quivering. "And honest to God—and may I be struck by lighting right here, right now—I don't know how it got there. It could only have been her doings."

"What kind of picture?" Quinn questioned.

"It was all innocent—really."

"You can tell us."

The old man slumped farther. "It was in my nightstand. That's where they found it. Just a picture of Jody and Jana in a bathtub."

"Naked?"

"Of course—it was no big deal. Their mom had taken it a couple weeks back. They were just little girls—really, it was no big deal. Moms are always taking pictures like that."

"How'd it get in your nightstand?" Quinn asked.

Bakerman straightened and scowled. "She put it there. It's the only way it could've happened."

"Why would she do something like that?"

"Cuz she and her druggy boyfriends were getting desperate for cash, so they thought they could blackmail me. She knew I had money stashed away. I saved everything. Yeah, I think that was their original plan. Use the cops to scare me, then cut a deal with me to drop the allegation in exchange for cash. Yeah, I'm sure that's exactly what they were planning."

"Did the cops find anything else?" Anders inquired.

There was a long silence. Bakerman's head suddenly drooped in shame.

"What?" Quinn softly asked.

Bakerman glanced up and with hesitation replied, "The sheets on my bed. There were fresh semen stains."

"Yours?"

"No, they couldn't be."

"Then how—?"

"They weren't my sheets," Bakerman pleaded. "It had to have been sometime earlier that morning while I was out—they musta made a switch."

"A switch?"

"Yeah. The sheets those detectives found on my bed belonged to the one in the mother-in-law apartment that Judy had been using."

"But you told the cops that—right?"

"I tried."

"And they didn't believe a word you said," Anders uttered with disgust. "Not one word, huh?"

Bakerman shook his head no.

Anders bolted upright. "My god," he gasped. "We could get a DNA test done on those sheets and prove your innocence." He turned to his colleague. "Right, Tess? We could . . ." His voice trailed off as he saw the uneasy look in her eyes. She didn't reply to her cocounsel. Instead, she fingered her pen and focused her eyes on the still pristine legal pad. Her pangs had not subsided. Bakerman reeked of simple sincerity. The kind a jury easily fell for. In all her previous cases, she would've been glad for this, but not now. She continued to sense something askew, an undercurrent beneath the man's facade. It unnerved her.

Quinn felt Anders's knee again. Her head bobbed up. She cleared her throat and she forced herself to focus. She said, "Tell me, Cliff, you say you pleaded guilty. Why did you do that if you were innocent?"

"They had me," he replied matter-of-factly. "That's why."

"Probable cause, perhaps, but beyond reasonable doubt—hardly. Those detectives, did they take you into custody right then and there?"

"Yes."

"Do you know if they had already taken statements from the kids?"

"I think so."

"Wait a second," Anders mumbled. "If they had already taken statements, they should have Mirandized you before you were ever questioned—Cliff, when did they read you your rights?"

Bakerman shrugged unknowingly. Simultaneously, his stomach rumbled loudly. "Uh-oh." He flinched. "That ol' chicken-fried steak is coming home to roost."

"You okay?" Anders and Quinn asked in unison.

He nodded.

"You're sure?"

He nodded again.

"Okay," Quinn continued. "But please, if you aren't, just give the word and we'll stop. . . . Anyway, they took you in custody, and you were assigned counsel, right?"

"No, I had to pay for my own. Like I told you, I had money put away, so I wasn't eligible for a public defender."

"I see. So your attorney didn't think he could beat this?"

"Not with the kids' statements and, well, that other stuff."

"What were in the statements?"

"Lies. And to think I treated them just like my own. But

I don't blame 'em. Their mom was a scammer. They were only doing as they were told."

Bakerman stopped there and turned to Anders. "I bet if you did a little research into the records, you'd find other fellows, just like me, who got used by her. Look, and you'll see what I mean."

The young attorney nodded knowingly. As he did, Bakerman's stomach growled again and his eyes began to glaze.

"Mr. Bakerman?"

His stomach growled a third time.

"Cliff?"

Perspiration began to form on his brow.

"Mr. Bakerman?"

He went pale. "I'm not feeling so good," he mumbled. "I think I—I think I need to lie down. You mind?"

Anders jumped up and pressed the intercom button. Quinn remained seated, barely able to conceal her frustration. Nevertheless, she forced herself to reach out and pat the sixty-year-old man on his wrist. "It's okay, Mr. Bakerman; we can talk later." Her tone was unconvincing.

Bakerman returned a weak smile as a guard popped the interior door and came over to help the ailing inmate to his feet. "I can make it myself," Bakerman growled. He shook the guard off, rose, and shuffled slowly out the door. When he had disappeared, Quinn suddenly began rubbing her hands uncontrollably.

"Something wrong?" Anders asked.

Quinn didn't reply. She had already risen from her seat and was heading to the nearest rest room to scrub her fingers with whatever disinfectant she could find.

15

"You want the tuna or the egg salad?" Ed Jennings offered as he nestled into his desk opposite Phil Gilroy's. He had with him an old cardboard file box marked COUNTY RECORDS DEPT. He set it on the floor beside him.

"Neither," the young detective said without removing his eyes from his computer screen.

"I thought you liked egg salad."

"You got to be kidding."

Jennings shrugged, then leaned over and removed the cover of the box. On top of the yellowing file folders were two sandwiches in fresh plastic wrap. "You sure? They're the good ones from that deli around the block."

Gilroy looked up. "Tuna." He continued his data entry.

Jennings grinned and flipped him the sandwich. He then hungrily unwrapped his and began chomping away. For a moment, there was silence between the two men. Only the sound of Gilroy's typing and Jennings's chewing disturbed the white noise from the ventilation system. Suddenly, Gilroy stopped. He leaned back in his chair and gazed over at his partner. "Have you noticed it?"

"Noticed what?"

"Leah—she's been real tense the last week or two."

Jennings set his sandwich aside. "What do you mean?"

"I don't know. Maybe she and Frank are fighting."

"I hadn't noticed."

"You have too."

"Well, it's none of my business. But you know I was sure happy when she got together with him. Frank's a good man. And now she's got a life, besides this place."

"What's wrong with this place?"

"How old are you, Philip?" Jennings asked.

"Almost thirty-three."

"Who's the girlfriend du jour?"

"I'm working on a little redhead in dispatch. So what's it to you?"

"Oh, nothing, just that sooner or later—and the sooner the better—you're going to have to pair up with someone permanent-like—or this job will kill ya. I've seen it happen every time."

Gilroy cleared his throat.

"No, really," Jennings said, "unless you've got something more important waiting for you outside these walls, something to give you perspective and keep you shielded from all the senseless violence that we are up to our knees in every day, by the time you are forty—well you'll either be a drunk, a head case, or selling used cars, cuz you can't hack it anymore."

"Thanks for the sandwich."

"You're welcome. So which file do you want—Rose or Alexander?"

"I'll take Rose for my lunchtime entertainment."

Jennings leaned over and retrieved a thick three-ring binder with the victim's name and case number inked on the spine. "Here," he said, passing it over to Gilroy. "Enjoy."

"Where's the rest of it?"

"One of their records guys will bring the other boxes over in an hour. I'm too old to be packing that much weight."

"Hey, throw your back out and it's an instant disability retirement. Sixty percent, and it's all tax-free."

"Yeah, but then what would I do?"

"Sell used cars?"

Jennings chuckled as his young partner spread open the binder he had been handed. On the inside cover was a pocket containing a dozen eight-by-ten, black-and-white glossy stills of the Wendy Rose murder scene. Gilroy was instantly drawn to these. He pulled them out and examined them closely. Meanwhile, Jennings had finished his sandwich and retrieved the first binder of the Alexander murder. He opened it and also found victim photos.

A solemn minute passed. Both men flipped through the pictures of the dead women without a remark—or wince. Finally, Gilroy shook his head in disgust. "Yours as cut up as mine?" He twisted the picture so that Jennings could see the image. It was of a nude sixteen-year-old girl lying on a bed of pine needles, her throat and abdomen slit wide-open; one breast was neatly severed and resting in the palm of her hand.

Jennings leaned close. "Hmmm." He picked up one of the photos from his case packet and held it beside Gilroy's. While both victims were young women, both stripped of clothing and jewelry, Jennings's appeared less brutalized. The wounds were more precise, similar to Sellinzski's.

"Same guy, ya think?"

Jennings set his photo down and glanced at his case file. "Mine was murdered in '78; yours, '82; and Sellinzski was 1975. It's possible. There's an obvious escalation of violence. That would fit. Say, where was your dump site?"

"Out in the county near Lake Sammamish, on a trail just outside the state park boundary. How 'bout yours?"

"A Dumpster near Renton."

"And Sellinzski was inside Woodland Park Zoo. You'd think the killer would have chosen more remote locations—

Jesus, any one of these places had people crawling over 'em in the daytime. Fat chance of hiding the body for very long."

"Doesn't look like he was trying to hide them." Jennings retrieved his photo. "Look, mine is lying right on top of the trash."

"So what do you make of it?" Gilroy asked.

"The guy's motivation?"

"Yeah."

Jennings shrugged. "That's Leah's department."

Gilroy stroked his chin. "But why would he have left them out, almost in the open? It's like he wanted them to be found, and quickly."

"Perhaps, perhaps not."

"You don't think it's weird?"

"It's not that, Phil. Why this guy did what he did is only one piece of the puzzle. And not necessarily the most important one. Over the years, I've seen a lot of investigations go south because the dicks handling the case got so fixated on trying to figure out what was ticking inside the suspect's head that they'd waste days coming up with psychobabble theories to explain the unexplainable while the obvious was overlooked. I'll tell you, if there's one thing I know for certain, and it's from over thirty years on this job . . ."

"What's that?"

"Stick with simple explanations—the simplest are always the right ones."

"I still think it's weird."

Jennings sighed. "We better get started on the time line. Leah will want that first."

"I've already started," Gilroy replied. "Bakerman is all entered. At least, what we know up to now. Why don't you read off all the witness names and dates you got there, and I'll crunch it with what I got here?"

Jennings drew a deep breath and began.

16

Curious squirrels lifted their heads and watched as Leah Harris paused on the front steps of the park administration building. The offices were housed in a modest, cedar-shake bungalow directly behind Monkey Island, a quarter mile north of the children's petting zoo.

Sergeant Harris had left Milkovich to guard the scene and wait for Jane Fenton's arrival while she alerted the zoo management to their presence. She had walked the short distance, oblivious to her surroundings, her mind solely focused on the significance of their find. She and Milkovich had yet to confirm that this was Sellinzski's ring, but the Seattle detective felt certain that it was. How long it had been lying there was now a critical element they needed to establish. Because of this, Harris's first call had been to her lab tech. Fenton was particularly skilled at dating evidence using soil stratification. The principle was similar to tree rings: an object's date of abandonment, or placement, could be judged by examining the associated ground it had been found in or on. Fenton was the best in the department with this technique.

Harris's eyes roamed for a moment. Unlike the barnyard area, this part of the zoo was nearly deserted on a weekday.

Only a scattering of retirees on park benches and ambling loiterers populated the area. Nearby, a passenger van with tinted windows caught Harris's attention. In the midafternoon light, she could see the faint outline of steel wire mesh reinforcing every pane. Harris craned farther. Printed in neat black letters on the driver's door were the abrupt government markings KING COUNTY CORRECTIONS AND DETENTION—FOR OFFICIAL USE ONLY.

What are they doing here? Harris wondered. She shrugged the thought away and proceeded through the double doors into a warmly lit reception area. It was deserted except for an elderly volunteer seated behind a heavy pine counter, her attention buried in a thick romance novel.

Harris came forward; simultaneously the gray-haired woman looked up. "May I help you, ma'am?" She had a Canadian lilt.

Harris smiled. "Is the park superintendent here?"

The lady eyed her for a moment, then replied, "I'm sorry; Mr. Frandsen left about an hour ago. Is there someone else who might be of assistance to you? Perhaps his deputy, Mrs. Petrokôw?"

"That will work."

"Might I say who is inquiring?"

Harris fished into a coat pocket and withdrew her credentials. "Tell her Sergeant Harris, Seattle PD."

The volunteer's eyes widened as they focused on the gold detective's shield. Instantly, she fumbled for the telephone and pressed an extension. Harris stepped back from the counter and waited as the receptionist carried on a short conversation, then replaced the receiver. "Please have a seat, Sergeant. Mrs. Petrokôw will be out shortly."

Harris nodded a thank-you and backed away. Instead of settling into one of the several Craftsman-style chairs that formed a semicircle around a matching coffee table, she remained standing. Thoughts of the new find, the growing number of cases, and the looming deadline had now nudged her sense of urgency a notch above her usual hyperactive state. She swiveled on her heels and absently stepped over to a large wall display of local seashells. Reaching out, she fingered the smooth, oblong casement of a long-dead razor clam. The feel of the shell sparked a forgotten memory.

It had been a cool summer night. A dozen Girl Scouts sat around a beach fire, giggling, gossiping, and teasing one another. Parents had withdrawn to a nearby travel trailer to play cards, leaving the troop of almost teens the freedom to broach subjects unsuitable for their chaperones' ears. Leah had mainly listened. Talk of boys left her both insecure and jealous. At twelve years old, she was ruefully aware of the lowly rung she occupied within her group's hierarchy of looks. "You'll be a late bloomer," her mother had routinely reassured. But her muddy blond hair and pencil-thin figure had left Leah little doubt that her mother was not being particularly honest.

Her parents had divorced when she was ten. An only child, she had witnessed the disintegration without an ally. Not that it had been all that discernible. Her parents had quietly withdrawn from each other over a period of a year—one stutter step at a time. And as with the sands of an hourglass, one day, the last grain slipped through and tumbled onto the pile of grievances. It was over—her father had simply failed to come home.

"He won't again," her mother had explained. "It's best this way."

There had been no fights, no heated exchanges, no broken dishes, simply a reasoned, unemotional break—a business arrangement. To this day, Leah's mother had remained silent about the actual causes. It was a taboo subject whenever they visited with one another. As for her father, he had remarried. Relocated to San Jose, raised another woman's children as his own. And although he and Leah spoke on a monthly basis, their conversations rarely had much depth.

She sighed as the sound of her cell phone jolted her drifting thoughts. She snatched the device from her coat and activated it. "Harris."

"Hey, boss." It was Gilroy. "Got your voice mail. I musta been on the horn to someone else when you tried me. So, you think it's Sellinzski's ring?"

Harris stepped to a far corner and replied, "That's what my gut tells me. But we'll know more in an hour."

"How the hell did it get there?"

"Good question," Harris said. "All sorts of possibilities, none of which I really like. It looks to be in too good condition to have been sitting out here for very long, and since Bakerman's been on ice for the last decade . . ."

"Uh-oh," Gilroy breathed.

"Do you have the time line done?"

"Just about."

"Anything?"

"Nothing that excludes Bakerman."

"What about his employment record? How'd he make a living?"

"Mostly janitor stuff in hospitals, but in 'eighty-one, he got hired by Metro to drive a bus and kept that job right up until he went to Monroe in 'ninety-three."

"Even with all the DUIs and jail time?"

"Hey, boss, they got a strong union . . ."

Harris didn't laugh. She said, "While we're waiting for Jane, go ahead and run every name mentioned in each of the three murders and see what pops up. Maybe one of them is now serving time somewhere for a similar type crime.

Spokane PD got lucky just last month on one of their old cold cases. Maybe we'll get lucky too."

"You mean," Gilroy chuckled, "our brilliant investigative work might uncover a heretofore unsuspected suspect."

"Save it for the press. . . . Anyway," Harris continued, her tone relaxing, "running everyone will at least get us current addresses—if they're still alive. Odds are, we'll need to reinterview some of them soon."

"What else?"

"Put the grabbus on Eckler. I smell something fishy."

"You got an address or phone number?"

"On my desk. And if you can't find him, call his attorney, Stuart Malconni. Part of the deal for him talking and walking was he'd be available to us twenty-four-seven. Oh, and another thing. Have Ed call the department of licensing. Get them to do a hand check of their old motor vehicle records. I want a list of every car, truck, or van ever registered to Clifford Bakerman and, for that matter, to Eckler, too."

"Eckler?"

"Yeah, you heard me, Eckler."

"You don't think—?"

"Just do it," Harris said. A moment later, a side door marked NO ADMITTANCE opened, and a woman about Harris's own age, and wearing a park uniform, stepped out. Their eyes met.

17

Linda Reese breezed down the cubicle-lined government hallway on a familiar path to her brother's office. She was fifteen years younger than the prosecuting attorney, but even at forty could still turn much younger heads with her surgically enhanced figure, flowing red hair, and piercing blue eyes—all characteristics she accented with tight-fitting skirts and low-cut blouses. Reese was a commercial real estate agent and had made a small fortune during the dot-com bubble—she had also managed to keep it. Her most noticeable quality, though, was that she was used to getting her own way. Thus, when Reese entered the anteroom to Collins's office, she simply surged past the administrative assistant and burst in. The assistant quickly trailed. Collins glanced up from behind a pile of unread court documents and waved her off. "It's okay."

The assistant nodded, then added, "Sergeant Harris called again. She still sounds pretty hot. Says she needs to talk with you, and right away."

"I'll bet," Collins sighed. "Keep holding my calls and close the door on your way out." The assistant complied as Reese approached her brother's desk. She was his de facto campaign manager, and though she preferred to stay in the background, she pulled all the important strings.

Collins waited for the door to shut. As it clicked closed he said, "So what did you find out about tonight? Who's the moderator?"

"Deejah Mohannah," his sister replied. "She's a little slow, but that's okay. I know for a fact that she hates Bernhardt. A few years back, they were on the school board together. Heard they were always screaming at each other."

"She's pretty liberal."

"So will we be." Reese paused and set her briefcase and purse down on a nearby straight-backed chair. She withdrew a legal file and began perusing several pages. Waving them, she said, "I've got the demographics on the show for the past three years. We just target our responses to these groups, come up with a couple of sound bites, and we're home free. Unless of course you're planning some more grandstanding that you're not telling me about."

Collins shrugged noncommittally.

Reese crossed her arms. "Richard?"

"I didn't have time to tell you about Bakerman. Besides, it wasn't a publicity stunt. I was just doing my job."

Reese nodded suspiciously, then straightened.

"Now what?"

"Nothing, I was just thinking. What you just said. That's how we'll play you tonight. 'Richard C. Collins, the man who, despite malicious accusations, lies, and false rumors, ignores it all and just does his job'—I like that."

Collins rolled his eyes, but a moment later a wistful look creased his face.

"Now what's wrong?"

"Nothing."

"Bullshit, I know that look." Reese shifted on her feet and glared at her charge. "What's the matter? That crap from

Bernhardt isn't getting to you, is it? Christ, you've seen ten times worse. You'll eat him alive tonight."

Collins shook his head and said, "I'm just pissed about something else, that's all."

"Jesus Christ—what?" Reese leaned close. As she did, she caught sight of the old Polaroid snapshot Patrick Dellhanney had left only hours earlier. It now rested at the center of the prosecutor's desk. "Hey, what's that?" As the words left her mouth, a smile spread across her face. "Damn, is that you?" She giggled and reached for the image. Collins grabbed for it also, but his sister was quicker. Her prize in hand, she stepped back from the desk to avoid her brother's grasp.

"Give it back," he protested.

She ignored him and said, "God, I was only eleven when you came back from Vietnam. I don't ever remember seeing you in uniform." She smirked and added, "You were quite the Rambo. Look at those abs. Who's the other guy? He's really cute."

"Linda!"

"No, really," Reese teased. "Tell me first or—"

Collins gritted his teeth and muttered, "His name was Mickey Dellhanney."

"Was?"

Collins nodded grimly. "He was killed in a motorcycle accident a year after we got back from our tour over there. It was his older brother who got me on with the PD when I came back home."

Reese stepped forward and Collins made a successful grab for the photo. Suddenly his mind slipped back thirty years to the moment the camera shutter had clicked. He shuddered. The image had captured forever a pair of soldiers standing proudly in bloodstained jungle fatigues, ammunition bandoliers slung from their shoulders, M16s at their sides. The young marines were exhausted, but exhilarated by the battle's end. They posed confidently above a Vietcong bunker. In one of the soldier's hands was a large knife. It had blood upon it. The marine was using the blade to point towards the underground entry he had just emerged from. He was alive and the reprieve of that moment was clearly etched on his young, dirt-smudged face.

A finger snapped. "Earth to Richard?"

Collins glanced up, his trance broken. He blinked several times and set the photo down. Reese shuddered. A look of profound guilt was now on her brother's face. Suddenly Collins swallowed hard and in a shaking voice said, "Linda, I need to borrow some money—no questions asked."

18

"Well?"

"Give me another minute."

"Sorry," Harris said to Jane Fenton. The lab tech was kneeling near the graduation ring, holding a flashlight at an oblique angle in a purposeful effort to cast shadows on the surrounding ground cover. Both detectives were above Fenton, leaning on the rock adjacent the trail, anxiously awaiting a verdict. Harris turned to Milkovich. "So, I told the woman we might be out here for a couple of hours. But we'd be real low-key about it."

"And?"

"She just shrugged her shoulders and went back to her office. No big, I guess." The Seattle detective drew her coat tight. "God, it's getting cold out here." She shivered for emphasis, and went on. "By the way, did you know they use jail inmates to do groundskeeping? There's a crew wandering around here right now."

Before Milkovich could reply, Fenton flicked her flashlight off and rolled to her feet. "Hey, Frank, give me a measurement off the old monument there."

She waited for Milkovich to play out the steel tape to a point where she could grab it, and extended it down to the small piece of jewelry. "Got it." Moments later she was scribbling the numbers in her notebook. That done, she stepped gingerly about the area, peeling back the offshoots of bushes and tree limbs as she passed in a spiraling arc that grew larger with each lap. Finally, Fenton halted at the base of the slope directly below the pair.

"Hand me one of those little envelopes."

Milkovich complied.

Fenton then returned to her starting point and knelt. "Are you thinking this might be a dump site, maybe used more than once?"

"It's a thought," Harris replied.

"I could get the ground radar boys out here, and do this entire grove."

"You think there's a possibility?"

Fenton drew a deep breath. "I doubt it, especially around here. The soil stratifications are undisturbed. Of course, just to play it safe, I'd have some cadaver dogs go over the area. You never know."

Harris looked skyward. "It'll be dark before long. Let's think about doing it tomorrow. So, what about the ring? How long?"

Fenton didn't reply. Instead, she withdrew a pencil from the inside of her smock, and used it to hook the piece of jewelry. Lifting it with extreme care, she brought the object close to her eyes, studied it for a moment, then let it slide off the writing instrument and into the envelope. She folded the flap tight.

"Well?"

Fenton struggled to her feet. "God, I'm getting old." She then looked to Harris and switched to a clinical tone. "Put me on the stand and I'd have to say a month—maybe a little more, maybe less."

"Son of a bitch," Harris groaned.

"By the way," Fenton went on, "there's an inscription inside the loop. I think it says 'To Cindy Jo, Love Mom.'"

Instantly, Harris's hand dived for her cell phone. A frenzied second later she was punching in her office number. Milkovich looked on, a worried look creasing his face.

"It's me," Harris blurted.

"What's up?" It was Gilroy.

"Any luck getting hold of Eckler?"

"No answers with the numbers you gave me," Gilroy replied.

"His address, it's in Ballard, right?"

"Yeah, you're only about ten minutes away. What's the matter?"

"Get a uniform on his apartment. In fact, arrest his ass if he's anywhere around. I'm heading there now."

"Arrest him for what?" Gilroy asked.

"I'll worry about that later. Just hook 'im."

"You find something else?"

"The ring here, it's Sellinzski's all right, but the kicker is that Jane thinks it's only been laying around for a couple of weeks, maybe a month at the most. Guess what?"

"Not Bakerman."

"Yep, no way he could have dropped it here."

"But Eckler?"

"That's what I'm thinking." Harris groaned and smacked her forehead with the butt of her free hand. "Oh, man, we may have let the real killer go."

19

Roy Stoddard drew a last drag from his cigarette and gazed southwestward from the empty loading dock towards the dark gray clouds gathering on the horizon. "Goddamn rain," he mumbled to himself and flicked his finished smoke down to the puddle-pocked alley that traversed the back side of the evidence warehouse. Both he and Fenton had concluded by noon that Sellinzski's biological samples were long gone. However, all the other physical evidence was missing too. That didn't sit right. A random cross-check by Jane, just prior to her being called to the zoo scene, had revealed that evidence from numerous other sex crimes from that era was also missing. All that was left of a paper trail ended suddenly during Patrick Dellhanney's tenure as commander of the evidence section.

Stoddard stuck his hand into his jacket pocket and withdrew the cell phone Fenton had left with him to stay in touch. He punched in a now familiar number. There was one ring and "Yeah?"

"Listen, you lazy cocksucker," Stoddard growled. "Come clean or I'm going to come over and kick your retired ass from here to Tacoma. I don't want to hear any more bullshit."

"Whoa, slow down, ass wipe," Dellhanney replied from his home handset. "I've told it to ya straight, so get off my fuckin' back or I'll see to it you don't have a fuckin' job come tomorrow."

"Oh," Stoddard shouted. "Just like you did with Eddy, huh? Well, just try it. You think you got something on me? Hell, I've got a few things in my back pocket I doubt you'd want out in the daylight."

Dellhanney sighed. "Christ, Roy, are you still carrying Merlock's torch? Get over it."

Stoddard shifted on his feet and in a calmer tone said, "Why'd ya have to spill your guts? He had a wife and kids to support. He lost everything because of you. What ever happened to covering for a pal?"

There was silence from the other end.

"Well?"

More silence.

Finally, Dellhanney said in a guilt-tinged voice, "I had to. I owed people."

"You fuckin' son of a bitch," Stoddard seethed. In disgust, he disconnected and kicked at a discarded soda can. The sound of it skipping off the old concrete cobblestones echoed among the surrounding walls. He was about to turn and reenter the building when George, the evidence clerk, poked his head through the open roll-up door.

"That lying bastard," Stoddard grumbled. "He still won't come clean."

George stepped out. "So what you going to do, Roy?"

"Dunno, George."

"You're taking this kinda personal—what gives?"

Stoddard shifted on his feet. "How long have you worked here?"

"Twenty-six years next May."

"You like it?"

The Asian man cocked his head. It was an odd inquiry. Throughout his career with the Seattle Police Department, he had had only superficial contact with the surly man before him. And always, it had been abrupt and condescending. Suspicious, George replied slowly and cautiously. "I like it. . . . It's a good job. In fact, it's a real good job."

Stoddard pulled out another cigarette and lit up. He inhaled, then let the smoke go in a series of short exhalations. "I hate this goddamn place."

The seasoned officer drew another puff and continued. "This department is loaded with backstabbing, good-for-nothing butt kissers. And the new people they're hiring—Christ, think about it. Some five-foot-nothing broad is going to be a real big help when you're taking on a bar full of longshoremen getting their snootful on skid road."

George leaned up against the doorjamb, intrigued by Stoddard's candor. He asked, "If you hate it so much, why do you continue to work here?"

Stoddard took another drag off his cigarette as a wry grin creased his face. "Cuz, Georgie, being a cop is the only thing I know." He chuckled and added, "If I had to do real work, I'd be sleeping in an alley under cardboard inside of a week."

The warehouseman began to smile.

"I hate this job so much, I love it."

"You're a funny man."

"Shit, I sure don't try to be, but—ah, hell, think about it."

"About what?"

"Being a cop."

"I'm not a cop."

"Ah, you're almost a cop. Christ, you've worked around us bastards for twenty-plus years. Some of it's got to have rubbed off."

The Asian looked blank.

Stoddard shrugged and gazed back up to the sky. "Gonna start raining in a couple of minutes."

George shifted his stare and nodded in agreement. There was a long silence. Finally, the warehouseman, sensing the conversation had dead-ended, glanced at his watch and began to ease back into the building. With his eyes still averted skyward Stoddard mumbled, "This is the last time he screws with me."

George froze.

Stoddard turned to face the warehouseman as the first few drops of the pending downpour spattered his backside. "People think I'm a pretty big asshole who doesn't give a shit about anything, but I've got my principles. I'm sure someone threw everything out, just to cover their ass—and it's got to be Dellhanney."

The clerk blushed and looked about. He quickly said, "What was she like, I mean, the victim? I've spent the better part of my life handling all these things." His hand swept inward, towards the rows of rack and shelving. "It might as well all be rummage from a garage sale. Down here, you never see the faces of the victims; you never know the rest of the story. This stuff doesn't talk; it's all just silent proof."

Stoddard thought for a moment as he eyed the much shorter man. He replied, "Hell, most of the time, you don't want to know."

"But this girl, who was she?"

"Who knows?"

"She was killed in 1975, right?"

"Yeah," Stoddard sighed. "Hell, in 1975 I already had three years on the force, and was heading for my first divorce."

"How come? Your wife didn't like the hours you had to work?"

Stoddard flashed a lecherous grin. "Too many chippies for one guy to handle."

"Huh?"

"Girls, chicks, you know. Christ, back then, we all had a trapline of waitresses and—well, you know."

"Ah." George winked with sudden understanding.

"Hell, that's the way it was—and you never had to pay for a friggin' cup of coffee either. Life was good. None of this political correctness bullshit."

The Asian politely nodded.

Suddenly, there was a gust of wind. It brought with it the squall. Rain began pelting every surface, the drops ricocheting off the roofs and walls like spent bullets. Stoddard stepped to the shelter of the doorway, turned, and faced the storm. With his eyes fixed on a distant point, he went on. "There was this cute little gal I had just started seeing on the side. She worked at the same place as the one in this case— Donna Pearson was her name. God, she was hot—twenty-one, 'bout five foot two, and built like a brick house." A lewd grin formed on Stoddard's lips. "I was the only car out working the Fremont sector the night before the attack. With no one else around, I thought, what the hell? and decided to slip up to Wallingford and get a quick one. Who was to notice? 'Cept as I drove by Donna's place—lights off—to check it out, there she was on her front porch with her pal from work. They were arguing over something."

"What about?"

"Who the hell knows? And I wasn't about to get mixed up in a cat fight, so I did an about face and headed back to where I was supposed to be. Two days later, when I came to work, I found out that this other gal had been attacked— damnedest thing."

"You tell the dicks?"

Stoddard remained silent.

"You didn't, huh?"

"How could I? I had already been caught there once by the shift supervisor. Twice and I would have been canned. I had to keep mum. Besides, I'm sure Donna told 'em about it. She had to have been interviewed, being a coworker and all."

"So she never told you what they were arguing about?"

"Naw, never had the chance. I broke the relationship off right then and there, and put as much distance between her and me as possible. You can see the position I was in."

George digested Roy's words, then said, "It's a shame about the evidence. Like I said, maybe Sergeant Harris will be able to come up with new leads."

Stoddard shrugged.

"Is there anything else I can do for you? I got to get back to work."

"Yeah," Stoddard suddenly said. "You can tell me what the fuck happened to all the shit I've been looking for. You know more than you're saying, I can tell."

20

Carl Eckler's basement residence was located across the street from Saint Alphonso's Catholic Church, four miles due west from the Woodland Park Zoo. The small apartment building, built in the late forties, had replaced the original shotgun shacks that had belonged to Seattle's first wave of immigrants, hardscrabble Scandinavian loggers and fishermen. Their quiet and unassuming manner still laced the city's personality—a perfect fit for the region's melancholy weather.

Harris's Ford Taurus eased in behind an occupied patrol car, its blue strobes rotating lazily. Unconcerned about the now pelting rain, she bolted out of the driver's seat and dashed towards the other vehicle. The young officer inside, observing her in his rearview mirror, reluctantly got out of his car.

"Kill those goddamn lights," she shouted above the downpour.

A look of bewilderment flashed across the rookie's face, but like a boot camp recruit, he lurched back inside and did as told. By the time he had straightened to apologize, Harris had crossed over to the sidewalk and sought shelter beneath the entrance awning. Milkovich was already there, having pulled in behind her in his car and made directly for the dry spot.

On the drive over, he had checked in with his office. There were no messages, even though it was nearing the time Chief Logan had indicated he would call for him. That caused concern. He didn't want to be too far out of position to respond immediately. Further, he knew his assistance to Leah at this point had been minimal, but the possibility that Sellinzski's real killer had been set free would inevitably cause condemnation from above. To Milkovich's way of thinking, quickly building a solid relationship with his new superior would be Leah's best defense if and when the inevitable finger-pointing commenced.

Harris reached Milkovich's side. She dusted off the raindrops from her coat and waited sternly for the patrol officer to join them.

He did, with trepidation.

"What did dispatch tell you?" Harris challenged as he joined them under cover.

The officer gulped. "Contact a Mr. Eckler?"

"And?"

"Sit on him until you got here. And if he wasn't here, sit on the place."

"With your lights on?"

He shrugged sheepishly.

"Look, in the future," Harris said sternly, "when someone tells you to sit on a place, it means be inconspicuous. Christ, if it weren't for the rain, we'd already have a crowd. And Eckler—he's the kind of people with an aversion to the color blue. One look at a set of strobes and it's U-turn time." Harris paused, drew a deep breath, and smiled forgivingly. "Keep that in mind, okay?"

The rookie nodded understanding.

"Okay, so what's happening here?"

He glanced nervously about and said officiously, "According to the landlord's wife, Eckler showed up here yesterday about five and gave notice he was vacating immediately. He was later observed removing possessions in the evening. He didn't have much; the place comes furnished. He subsequently spent an hour this morning scrubbing the place. He was supposed to turn in his key and do a damage inspection this afternoon, but he's been a no-show so far."

"Did you check the unit out?"

"I knocked on the door."

"And?"

"There was no answer, of course."

"What did you see?"

"What do you mean?"

Harris sighed. "Were the drapes open or closed? Did you peek in? Were there any signs of occupancy? Were there . . ." She stopped. Gauging by the young man's blank expression, she knew he had done none of the above.

Milkovich now spoke, although his tone was pedagogical. He understood Leah's growing impatience—her focus was on catching a killer. He, on the other hand, was little more than an observer with no reputation on the line. He could afford to be calm.

"Officer Allen, right?" Milkovich said. He had observed the man's name tag. "How long have you been solo?"

"Three weeks."

"You like it?"

"Love it, sir."

"Let me tell you something I've learned over the years."

"What's that, sir?"

"First, knock that *sir* stuff off."

Allen nodded. His rigid posture eased. Milkovich waited

a moment, then continued. "There is one thing about this business that never changes."

"What's that, sir?"

Milkovich winced, but went on. "It's like this: you never know what you are getting into. A barking-dog call, in a blink of an eye, can turn into a home invasion robbery; a car stopped for a broken taillight can become a shoot-out. You have to always be ready for the unexpected. In fact, look for it." Milkovich paused and purposely drew a deep breath through his nostrils. "Smell anything?"

The officer cocked his head.

"Go ahead; take a whiff."

The young man obeyed.

"Well?"

He shrugged his shoulders.

Harris interceded. "What is it, Frank?"

Milkovich raised a finger, then addressed the rookie. "Which is Eckler's unit?"

The officer pointed to his left towards a covered flight of stairs that led to the sub-ground-floor units. "His is the first door at the bottom."

"So that window well there belongs to his apartment?"

Allen nodded.

"Frank?"

Milkovich momentarily ignored Harris's entreaty. He continued. "Do me a favor; grab the landlord and a key, and meet us down there, okay?"

"Sure." Allen snapped to attention. He executed a crisp echelon right, quickly disappearing through the main entrance.

"Frank?"

Without further explanation, Milkovich grabbed Leah's arm and led her along the covered walkway to the side of the small complex. They then continued down the eight steps that accessed the daylight basement dwellings. Here, they were met by a garbage can toppling with trash, and an unattended cleaning cart. Both were adjacent to Eckler's unit. Milkovich stopped in front of the large bin and studied the contents. He then turned to Leah. "You smell it?"

She curled her nose and nodded. "Now I do. God, it smells like a dozen cats peed into that garbage can."

"Actually, it's a combination of ether and ammonia."

Harris stepped closer as Milkovich pointed to several pieces of unmarked brown glassware resting atop the trash. Leaning down, she was about to touch the objects, when she suddenly retracted her hand and straightened. "Son of a bitch. You think Eckler was cooking meth here?"

"Could be. See those emptied cold capsules in the dust bunnies? Throw in some lithium flashlight batteries and voilà, you got shake-and-bake methamphetamine, à la the Nazi method."

Harris sidestepped the cleaning cart and slipped up to the unit's large picture window. It started two feet left of the front door. Peering through a crack in the drawn curtains, she attempted to determine what else might wait for them inside. After a moment of shifting from side to side, she pulled back. "I can't make out much. Looks like someone's been cleaning in there. The furniture has all been pushed aside."

Suddenly, the sound of approaching footsteps echoed off the concrete. Both investigators alerted, but immediately relaxed as they caught sight of Officer Allen's shiny new shoes atop the stairwell. They were followed by two other pairs—one male, one female. Both moved slowly. Harris and Milkovich waited as the elderly property owners eased downward, their hands tightly gripping the wrought iron handrail. When eyes met, the eighty-year-old man was first to speak. "You detectives?" he grunted.

Leah stepped forward and extended her hand. "Sergeant Harris," she said graciously. "And this is Lieutenant Milkovich."

He cautiously took Harris's proffered hand. "What in heaven's name is going on here? I just got back from the grocery store and saw the prowler car out front. What gives?"

"This is Carl Eckler's apartment, right? Do you have any idea where he might be right now?"

The landlord withheld a reply and turned to his wife. In an irritated tone he said, "I told you, Miriam, that boy was up to no good, what with all those late-night comings and goings. Why I ever let them talk me into renting to him and his kid—"

"Kid?" Harris spoke up. "What kid?"

"His son," the elderly man retorted. "A teenage juvenile delinquent, that's what he is."

"Jason's a nice boy," the wife offered.

The man glared at his wife.

She acquiesced.

He returned to the detectives. "His place is still a mess inside and it stinks like a fish market."

Milkovich winked at Harris. That last bit of information confirmed his suspicion about the drug manufacturing.

Leah nodded her understanding and continued, "Your wife told Officer Allen that Eckler was supposed to be here this afternoon but hasn't showed yet. Is that right?"

"Uh-huh."

"Did he leave any kind of forwarding address, someplace you could send him his mail?"

"Nope, and I wouldn't take the time even if he did."

The landlord's wife spoke up. "Carl and his son Jason were always nice to me. Two Sundays ago, they both helped me with my flower beds."

"Aw, Miriam," the old man scowled, "they were just using you."

"Tell me about this Jason," Harris asked. "You said that this was Eckler's son? Where'd he come from?"

The landlord folded his arms tight. "Why I ever let him move in . . ."

Meanwhile his wife perked up. She said, "Jason just showed up a couple of days after we rented to his father."

"How old is he?" Milkovich asked.

"Eighteen," the landlord growled. "Carl said he had been living with some aunt in Oregon. When he heard his dad had made parole, the kid just up and thumbed his way to here."

Harris looked to Officer Allen. "Do me a favor. Go out to your car and put it over in the church parking lot, out of direct view. Stay there and keep an eye on the entrance to this place. You see anyone matching Eckler's description heading our way, give me a yelp on car-to-car." Harris paused and parted her coat. She produced a small portable police radio. Clicking it on, she adjusted the frequency and volume. "Use TAC-three."

"TAC-three," Allen replied smartly. "Got it." He then turned and took the stairs two at a time, his footfalls quickly fading.

"You want to go inside and look around?" the landlord offered.

Harris glanced at Milkovich. "What's the new protocol on mini-meth-labs?"

He sighed. "You don't want to know. Hazmat team only and probably a twenty-four-hour response—if we're lucky."

Harris frowned. "That's not going to work."

"Those are the rules."

The old man suddenly sensed a problem larger than a dirty apartment. "Hey, what're you two talking about?"

He was ignored for the moment.

"What about a cursory walk-through?" Harris suggested.

"Legal, I suppose," Milkovich replied. "But there's plenty of probable cause sitting right out here. After working drugs as long as I did, you never forget this smell. That alone would get us paper. I could whip out a telephonic warrant in half an hour."

Harris thought for a moment and said, "Let's not waste the time. It's Eckler I want. Let's just get some drug dicks down here and let them worry about this mess."

A look of motherly concern now etched the face of the landlord's wife. She asked, "Did Carl do something wrong?"

Harris turned. "We're not sure, ma'am."

The older woman thought for a moment and said, "If you really need to find him, you might try our pastor across the street. He might know where Carl is. The boy's a steady churchgoer. Even told me he used to be an altar boy."

Harris raised a brow.

"Of course, his girlfriend might know, too . . ."

"Girlfriend?"

"Her name is Nancy something. She's a cocktail server at one of those nice restaurants on the ship canal. Maxie's, maybe? The one right there by the locks."

"She's trash too," her husband sniped.

Harris glanced questioningly at Milkovich.

"I'd try the priest first," he replied to her gaze. "I'll paw through the garbage."

Harris wrinkled her nose. "Works for me."

"And toss me your phone. I'll give Jerry Cummins in Narcotics a call. He'll see the big picture and work with us on this."

Harris agreed, then escorted the owners back to their unit, directing them to stay put until other officers contacted them.

Meanwhile, daylight was fading—but not the rain.

21

"Want a soda?" Detective Gilroy asked, rising from his desk and stretching. His eyes and backside ached from hours of poring over the voluminous records of the cold cases. "I'm buying."

Detective Jennings looked up and yawned. He rolled his neck from side to side and replied, "Sure." He pushed himself away from his desk and added, "So, what do you think?"

"About these?"

"Yeah."

"I think I'm ready for glasses. God, how did you ever do police work without computers and word processors? If I have to go through another old, handwritten case report, I'm going to file a disability claim for ruining my twenty-twenty vision."

Jennings chuckled. "At least my guy had nice printing." He raised a sample page.

Gilroy bent towards his partner, then straightened without comment. "You see anything worth following up on?"

"Not at the moment."

"Me neither," Gilroy sighed. He was about to start for the Coke machine in the hallway when his telephone rang.

"Now what?" he muttered, and reached for the handset. "Homicide, Detective Gilroy." It was the deputy medical examiner returning his call. "Oh, hey, Dr. Reid." He eased back into his chair while his free hand began shuffling through the piles of strewn documents in search of the packet of Sellinzski photos. "Have you had a chance to look at the picture I left word about, the one with the fresh incision? I think it was number nineteen."

Jennings looked up. "Who ya talking to?"

"Medical examiner," Gilroy mouthed back. He then said into the mouthpiece, "Oh, yeah, I understand. It's been busy here too. . . . Yeah . . . yeah . . . no rush, when you can get to it . . . sure . . . thanks."

He hung up.

Jennings set his report down. "What the heck was that about?"

Gilroy located the photo pack and withdrew the one in question. "Here, you take a look." He passed it over. "See?"

The older detective took possession of the picture and studied it. He soon nodded.

Gilroy continued. "The autopsy report says nothing about the new incision."

"Lee me see."

Gilroy shuffled through more paper as Jennings continued staring at the image. His eyes did not linger on the victim's face. With two daughters of his own, it was too easy to imagine the worst. He set the picture aside and said, "Refresh my memory; how soon did she die after the attack?"

"Several months."

"Judging by how everything has knitted, it sure seems longer than that."

Gilroy passed over the new photocopy of the original hand-typed document.

Jennings leafed through it, but suddenly stopped.

"See something?"

"Royal manual—probably a model eighty-one."

"Huh?"

Jennings leaned back and grinned. "This is long before your time—back in the Stone Age—but we use to make IDs based solely on the uniqueness of typed characters. It was almost like fingerprints. See, every model of typewriter came with a set of keys that, with use, wore out in differing patterns. Moreover, the strikers would become clogged with ribbon residue, and that further individualized the appearance of the text."

"I remember reading something about that."

"Where, medieval history class?"

Gilroy grinned.

"Anyway, with manuals, because everybody's fingers pressed down with differing amounts of pressure, you could make the machine and the person who typed it. There was a whole science to it . . . but it's a lost art now," Jennings lamented.

Gilroy leaned back in his chair and said, "I still don't know how you guys did police work without computers."

Jennings began a retort, but stopped before the words could leave his lips. His attention had been drawn to the last three pages of the file. Several times, he flipped them back and forth, studying not the content of the narrative but the type itself. Gilroy waited impatiently, his fingers wrapped around the back of his head, his eyes glued to his elder.

Seconds ticked by. Finally, Gilroy could wait no longer. "So, what the heck is it?"

A slight, knowing smirk spread across Jennings's face.

"Come on, what gives?"

"I think," he said slowly, "I can answer why there's no mention of that incision." Jennings now beamed with visible pride. He never missed an opportunity to demonstrate to his young partner the lessons absorbed long ago.

Gilroy leaned forward.

"It's elementary, my dear Detective Gilroy. The report has been altered."

"Altered?"

"Yeah, Phil. A different person typed the second-to-last page and on a different machine. Same model, though."

Gilroy grabbed for the report.

"Look at 'em. See what I mean?"

The young detective plumped back into his seat and did as told.

"Check it out," Jennings said. "On page forty-seven, the letter e and the letter p both have thick loops? And the ws are weak? Now go to the next page. Look at the difference."

Gilroy studied the contrast.

"Now go to the last page; the es and ps are back to looking like those on page forty-seven."

Gilroy allowed the last page to fall open.

"See, what did I tell you?"

He nodded with understanding.

"I'm not a betting man," Jennings went on. "But you know what, I would bet dollars to donuts that that's not the original page forty-eight there in that report. Someone has altered it and shortly after the fact—maybe deleted something. What do you think?"

22

"Answer your damn phone," Jane Fenton muttered to herself. She hit REDIAL again, then plunked down onto her worktable stool inside the cluttered main room of the Seattle Police Department crime laboratory. A moment later, Harris's voice mail activated. Fenton groaned and hung up. She looked over to the nearby microscope she had been peering through moments before. Sellinzski's class ring lay beneath the lenses.

Like Harris, Fenton had immediately focused in on how and why the ring had found its way back to a thirty-year-old crime scene. It made no sense to her either. And despite spending an hour peering at the object and pondering this puzzle, she had found no logical reason. Her time, however, was not misspent. She had made a discovery.

Fenton retrieved her handset and punched in a new number. It rang once. She said, "Hey, Phil, it's Jane. Have you heard from Leah? Her cell phone has been busy for the last ten minutes. I keep getting bumped to her voice mail."

Gilroy replied, "She just called me on a hard line. Said she's at a church across the street from Eckler's apartment."

"Did they get him?"

"Who?"

"Eckler," Fenton said.

"Naw, looks like he's flown the coop. But get this, the boss and Mr. IA-man found what's left of a small meth lab. It was probably his. By the way, she's got an address for our nun."

"Where?"

"Right in town. Ed's on his way to the place now. It's on Queen Anne Hill." Gilroy paused, then asked, "So, what do you have?"

Fenton drew a deep breath, then blurted excitedly, "There's a partial print on the ring."

Gilroy's bored tone instantly vaporized. "You're kidding me. Can you lift it?"

"Maybe," Fenton replied. "But better yet, I've got some fresh skin flakes in the rim of the setting. They've got to have come from the last person to handle it."

"Oh, man!" Gilroy yelped. "How soon can you type the DNA and put it through the database?"

"Technically, less than a day, but the state crime lab is so backed up, we might have to wait months."

"That's bullshit."

Fenton agreed. "Maybe if Leah could get Captain Varna to get the chief to make a few phone calls, we could get cuts in the line, but even if that happens, we're still talking weeks. Damn budget cuts—"

The sound of an opening door caused Fenton to pause. She twisted in her seat and through the connecting door caught sight of Roy Stoddard entering the adjacent room. In his arms, he was carrying a tattered cardboard box marked EVIDENCE. It was overflowing with fading documents. He glanced Fenton's way and with a sly grin whooped, "That bastard Dellhanney forgot to shred this one."

23

Frank Milkovich twisted away from Detective Jerry Cummins as the sound of Leah Harris descending the steps to Carl Eckler's apartment caught his attention. Harris's hand trailed a collapsed umbrella. It was dripping wet.

"Over here," he called out. The pair of men were in the shadows, twenty paces beyond the still untouched garbage can.

Harris brushed by the refuse and stopped. "Hey," she said. "I thought you were going to go through this?"

"That wouldn't be a good idea." Cummins spoke up. He was a tall, athletic man of thirty-five. Part Irish, part Sioux, he wore a broad smile and radiated an easygoing, ironic manner—necessary traits for work in the twilight world of drugs. He eyed Harris and added, "In fact, you probably shouldn't stand too close. The stuff's all carcinogenic."

Harris stepped back.

Continuing, Cummins said, "We're in luck. The moon suit boys can be here in about an hour to do the evidence recovery."

Harris nodded and moved closer to her colleagues. She turned to Milkovich and said, "No luck on Eckler's whereabouts, but I did get a line on the nun that may have given

Sellinzski the holy card. She's retired but still lives in the city. I've got Jennings looking her up right now."

Milkovich shifted on his feet. "Jane's been trying to get a hold of you. She just got through to me. Sorry, I had your phone tied up talking to a couple other boys in Narcotics."

Harris raised a brow.

He grinned. "She thinks she can lift a partial print off the ring, and—get this—she also has DNA material present—skin flakes."

Harris jutted her hand. "My phone—now!"

Milkovich's arm came up. Just short of surrendering the device, he said, "Before you call, listen to what Jer just told me about your boy Carl. I think you'll be interested."

Harris's hand came down slowly. "What about him?"

Cummins stepped close and cleared his throat. "His name used to come up a lot at our countywide drug task force meetings. Always with tangential links to one clandestine lab or another. He's a cooker. Give 'im a chemistry set, and you get meth, LSD, ecstasy, you name it. Word was, he was trying to go straight. I didn't buy it. And you know, I thought we finally had him the other day. That possession pop, what with the points from his burglary raps and a few other things, he was looking at a ten-year gig, which would have suited me just fine. But now Frank tells me that he got sprung in exchange for some info. Was this place included in the deal?"

"I'm not sure what was traded. That was between Collins and Eckler's attorney, Stuart Malconni."

Cummins grimaced. "Malconni—shit."

"What's the problem?"

"Just talk, that's all."

"Like, what?"

"Scuttlebutt."

Harris frowned. She knew what was coming. Typical

narc dribble. Cummins didn't disappoint her either. He said, "Look, Sarge, in my little doper world, talk is cheap. Everyone informs on everyone else. Most of it's all bullshit. But over time, the haze begins to take a shape and you can recognize trends. The problem is that it's all hearsay and rumor."

"So what about Malconni? Give me some facts."

Cummins sighed. "That's hard to do. He's dirty, that's all. Of course, maybe it's just that he's always the first attorney to jump up and defend a dirtbag, but I've heard it dozens of times he's got his fingers in the drug pie."

Harris looked to Milkovich. She appeared indifferent to the information. "Phone, please."

"You don't think it's odd?" Cummins pressed.

Harris turned back. "You know, I really don't give a shit about dope. The scene's yours. I've got a murder suspect–slash–material witness to find."

Cummins's jaw stiffened.

"She's just funning ya, Jer," Milkovich was quick to add. He was lying. Leah's brusqueness when working a case was a side to her personality he didn't like witnessing firsthand. He knew she didn't mean to be that way, but as her focus narrowed, the sharp edges of her ego surfaced. Of course, that very trait had been her life jacket at the inception of her career. Seventeen years prior, and fresh out of college, she had been recruited onto the force as one of the first fully commissioned female officers. From the very start, she found herself the target of sexist behavior from her male coworkers. Used condoms had been routinely stuffed into her locker, and defective ammunition purposely issued during firearms qualifications. Then there were the unwelcome shoulder rubs as well as a constant barrage of lame remarks. Some of the men were just trying to be funny—a side effect of their uneasiness. Others were simply ignorant assholes,

enjoying their little exercises in territorial markings. Whatever the obstacle, Leah had pushed her way through it, ignoring the worst and giving back whatever had come her
way. But times had changed. Despite lingering traces of the
old days, women now made up a third of the force, and the
likelihood that by the end of the decade there would be a female police chief in Seattle was now accepted without question.

There was an awkward silence.

Harris glared at Milkovich, nostrils flared. However, her
features softened as she realized the Narcotics detective did
not share her sense of urgency. "Sorry," she sighed. Harris
tempered her next words with a collegial tone. "Tell ya
what, if you turn up anything when you go through the trash,
would you please give me a call?"

Cummins's response was an unenthusiastic, "Okay,
Sarge."

Milkovich's pager suddenly beeped. Startled, he tossed
Harris the cell phone and yanked the device from his belt.
He drew it close to his face, but his arm quickly drooped.

"Ya gotta go?" Harris said, interpreting Milkovich's reluctant demeanor.

Milkovich nodded, looked towards the continuing downpour, and turned up his collar. "It's the chief. I'll call ya
when I clear there." Without further comment, he proceeded
to the stairs, stopping only once to make a playful try for
Harris's paisley umbrella. Moments later, he was back in his
car and twisting the ignition key. He was about to place the
transmission into drive when he glanced sideways. Through
the rain-streaked windows, he could see Leah beneath the
awning, speaking into her cell phone, her free hand waving
wildly. She had followed him up to that point to avoid remaining awkwardly alone with Cummins. But that wasn't
what got his attention. Rather, she was backlit by a bright se-

curity light which silhouetted her slender figure. He stared longingly.

Milkovich slumped. The chances of a quiet evening with Leah, no matter how late it got started, were now down to zero.

24

Linda Reese strode back into her brother's office and clicked her purse open. "Here," she said, pulling out a sealed business envelope. "Sorry I'm late getting back. Traffic was murder out there."

Collins reached up, but before he could grasp it, his sister yanked it away. She stepped back. "Okay, brother dear." Her tone was serious. "What's this all about?" She waved the packet.

Richard Collins feigned a yawn. "It's not a big deal. I'll pay you back at the end of the month."

Reese eyed her brother. Despite his efforts to appear blasé, it was easy for her to see otherwise. The wastebasket to his right was toppling with crumpled papers—it had been empty only two hours prior. His tie was undone, his shirt-sleeves were rolled up, but more telling, she caught the slight whiff of alcohol tainting his breath. She was about to comment when she glanced at her brother's desk clock. "Oh, Christ," she blurted. "Look what time it is."

Collins remained still, his right hand extended. He said in a quiet tone, "Linda, the envelope, please . . ."

His sister thought for a moment, wrinkled her nose, then

flipped the money his way. She changed the subject. "So, did you polish up what we worked on this afternoon?"

Collins slid the envelope beneath his dog-eared legal pad and nodded. Despite his apparent agitation, he had managed to draft a position and a response to Bernhardt's allegations, in addition to a dozen witty, spontaneous remarks.

"We got to get our butts in gear," Reese continued. "We should have been at the TV studio by now. And God, we've got to do something with your hair."

"What's wrong with my hair?"

"I told you to get it cut. Why didn't you?"

"I've been busy."

Reese drew a calming breath. "I've got some spray gel in my purse. We can try that."

Collins reached up and patted his short locks. He frowned. "The wet weather kinda curls everything up, doesn't it?"

"God, you look like a crazed Russian poet, but I can fix it. Come on, we got to go. I've got to make sure our people get seated right—close to the aisles, and next to the audience mikes. And I've got to get them their questions."

Collins rolled his eyes.

"Now, you remember what you're going to say if Bernhardt starts dancing out statistics?"

"The numbers are high," Collins replied mantralike, "because these people then qualify for diversion into a state-paid drug treatment program."

"Don't use the word *people*. They're *individuals,* okay? And better add the word *successful* before *drug treatment.*"

"How do we know that?"

"We don't, but don't you see, we'll box Bernhardt in. He's on the record all over the place advocating these types of deferrals. Remember that quote from two weeks ago? He said something like even the worst treatment program was better than prison. Throw that back at him. Hell, better yet, bait 'im to it. Then take his knees off when he bites. It'll be beautiful. Now lean forward."

Collins complied and his sister primped his hair. "There, that's better."

The attorney reached up again.

"Leave it alone," she scolded. "Come on, we can take my car. We'll get there faster if I drive."

"I'll drive myself. I've got an errand to run afterwards."

"Tonight? Oh, no, you don't. You're supposed to be at Senator Danielson's birthday party afterwards at the Rainier Club. And don't forget about the Lions Club breakfast tomorrow. Which speech are you going to use?"

"The same one I always use."

"Good, it's simple, on message, and plays well to that crowd."

Collins frowned.

"Focus, Richard—we need focus. What in the hell is the matter with you? For God's sake, would you tell me what this is all about?"

The prosecutor didn't reply. Legal pad and envelope in hand, he rose, walked to a corner closet, and retrieved his trench coat. Draping it over his arm, he turned and strode past his sister. "I'll follow, and I promise I'll keep up."

Reese was about to protest, but decided against it. Instead, she reached into her purse once more and pulled out a small container of breath mints. "Here," she said, tossing them to her brother. "Use 'em."

25

"Hey, Bakerman," the jail guard growled. "Get your ass out from under those covers and hand me your dinner tray. You know the rules."

There was no response.

The guard placed a heavy foot inside the single-bed cell. It was one of a dozen within the segregation unit used to house high-risk prisoners. He glanced down. On the floor, next to the bed where Bakerman now lay facing the wall, was a plastic food tray heaped with corned beef hash, Jell-O, and two biscuits. All were untouched.

The guard's ire grew. "Get the fuck outta bed now, or I'll write you up."

There was still no response.

"Ah, for crying out loud. That's it—you can kiss commissary and TV good-bye for a week."

The guard reached up to his shoulder mike and keyed it with his thumb. "Hey, Jimmy," he said, tilting his head for a better transmission. "This new guy, Bakerman, he's playing possum with me. Get down here and give me a hand. I think he needs a trip to the little ol' behavior-modification room."

"On my way," the radio crackled.

The guard stepped cautiously in. His years of experience

had left him well schooled in the tricks an inmate might play, especially new arrivals, whose psychological instability was normally at its peak. In this transition period, it was common for an inmate to lash out, sometimes with deadly effect. Much damage could be done with only the sharpened end of a toothbrush or discarded pencil nub.

The officer drew a deep breath. "Okay, Bakerman, one last chance. Get your ass up outta bed and hand me your tray or—"

In the hallway beyond, the guard could hear approaching footsteps, their rushed pace identifying them as his backup.

"I guess we're going to have to do it the hard way."

He reached down to his equipment belt and unsnapped a small pouch. From inside, he withdrew a fresh pair of heavy-duty latex gloves and began slipping them on. He did so in an exaggerated manner so that Bakerman would have no doubt about what was to follow.

The footsteps stopped. A second guard peered in at the motionless body. "What's his problem?"

The first guard turned and replied, "The old fart doesn't want to cooperate."

The second guard leaned farther in. "You sure he's not sick or something? He's not moving."

"He's faking it. Better get your gloves on. He's been in the joint for the past ten years. Who knows what kinda shit been stuck up his ass."

The second guard eased past his coworker and carefully stepped to the foot of the wall-mounted bed. He then positioned himself so that he had room to dodge any kicks. He slowly reached down, then gave a quick nudge to a partially exposed shoe tip. "Hey, you, ya gotta get up."

Nothing.

He tried once more.

Still nothing.

Finally, he grabbed hold of the blanket and gave it a hard tug. What it revealed caused the first guard to shriek, "Oh, my God, his face is blue! He's not breathing."

26

Detective Ed Jennings eased down the rain-soaked residential street on Queen Anne Hill, scanning the house numbers and wondering if the address he had been provided was correct. It seemed odd to him, as he passed another large, turn-of-the-century home possessing a million-dollar view of downtown Seattle, that a retired nun would be living in one of the city's premier uptown neighborhoods. He slowed further, signaled, and turned into the driveway of an impressive Tudor. Its profile seemed strangely familiar. The dwelling was centered on two city lots, and its manicured grounds were surrounded by a shoulder-high wrought iron fence. Stopping, Jennings rolled down his window, reached out, and pressed an intercom button. He waited as drops fell through the opening and spattered his shoulder. Several moments later, "Hello out there." It was a mature woman's voice, gracious in tone.

The investigator leaned outward. "Detective Jennings," he shouted over the torrent. "We spoke half an hour ago."

"You made good time, Detective. Pull right in. I'll be at the front door."

There was a buzz, and the gate began rolling clear. When it stopped, Jennings slipped the car back into gear and proceeded onto the short circular way, stopping, as directed, at the well-lit entrance to the home. Ahead of him was a solitary vehicle, a new Volvo sedan. Exiting, he made a dash for the covered porch, skipping up the three steps in one hop. Before he could reach for the antique brass knocker, the large door parted, and before him stood a diminutive but buoyant older woman.

"Good evening, Detective," she said. There was a sparkle in her eyes, he noticed.

"Sister Cecilia?" Jennings's voice was tentative. His image of the seventy-two-year-old nun he was supposed to meet little resembled the lady before him. She was dressed in a bright nylon jogging suit and tennis shoes, with a pink sweatband wrapped about her short gray hair. She appeared to have been recently exercising.

The nun nodded and smiled. "Nasty evening, isn't it? Please come in and get out of the rain."

Jennings stepped through the threshold onto the marbled foyer. "Thanks for seeing me on such short notice. I hope I am not interrupting anything?"

"Oh, no, nothing important," she breezily replied. "There is a reception I'm heading off to in a while, but I like to be fashionably late."

Jennings smiled. "I'll be as brief as I can."

"We can use the study," Sister Cecilia offered. "There's a nice fire going in there." She turned and led the Seattle detective down the polished hallway a short distance to a large walnut-paneled room. It was filled with comfortable chairs, Victorian side tables, and bookshelves lined with old editions and family photos. As promised, a large propane-fed blaze roared in the hearth. Jennings was immediately drawn to its warming flames.

"Would you like some tea or coffee? My housekeeper is gone for the week, but I'm certain I can find my way to the kitchen and prepare a cup or two." Sister Cecilia then chuckled and added, "But you better not want anything else. I'm afraid the cupboards are a bit bare. I'm not much of a shopper."

"No, thank you," Jennings replied as his eyes swept the area. His thoughts were still in dissonance over the woman's apparent wealth versus her religious calling. Stalling, he said, "You have a beautiful home."

"My grandfather built it," the nun said as she nestled into a nearby chair. "He made his fortune during the Klondike gold rush."

Jennings cocked his head. "It that right? Did he hit pay dirt in the Yukon?"

"Oh, no, he never left Seattle. He owned a hardware store down by the docks. I suspect he charged a pretty penny for every shovel and pickax he sold, because by the time the rush was over, he was a wealthy man. Not bad for an Irish immigrant who came to America with only the clothes on his back."

Jennings stepped away from the fire and took a seat opposite the older woman. "Sounds like you have an interesting family."

Sister Cecilia smirked. "Oh, we've had a few black sheep."

Jennings glanced about once more and sighed. "You really do have a nice home here."

The nun nodded graciously and replied, "I can tell by the look on your face, you are wondering how a retired nun would be living in such grandeur."

The investigator raised a brow. She was reading his mind. It made him uneasy. Shifting in his seat, he replied, "It's really none of my business."

"It's okay, Detective. Most people meeting me for the first time are surprised to learn that not all nuns are garbed in black and spending their days cloistered from the world. I was with a teaching and nursing order. Besides the time I spent here in Seattle, I spent many years working in Central America. I truly loved it. And I truly loved being a nun. But as fate would have it, my father worded his will so that this home could not be sold or given to charity until my passing. He wanted to make sure I would always have a place to live. Granted, it's is a bit much in this day and age, but when I do pass, the church will benefit. I have seen to that."

"You have no other family?"

"Oh, I do." She pointed to the mantel. There, among several other photographs, was a brass-framed image of two smiling young adults. "My nephew and niece," Sister Cecilia said. "But they have their own trust funds. Besides, neither of them is really interested in living in this drafty old place. I suspect they're embarrassed by its size."

"My wife would sure love this place," Jennings commented. He then straightened. "That's it—that's where I've seen your place before." He looked to Sister Cecilia. "Last month, the Sunday pictorial, your home was featured, wasn't it?"

The nun gave a self-conscious nod.

"I knew it; I knew I had seen your face before." Jennings glanced about once more, marveling at the handsome woodwork and high ceilings. He was also thinking about how best to begin.

Sister Cecilia preempted him. "So, Detective Jennings, what is it that you would like to know? You mentioned wanting information on a former pupil of mine. Which one?"

Jennings reached into his breast pocket and withdrew a small spiral notebook. He flipped it open and glanced at his scribbling. "We're currently investigating an old homicide from 1975. The victim, we think, was a student of yours, when she was in the sixth grade." Jennings looked up. "Her name was Cindy Jo—"

"Sellinzski," Sister Cecilia murmured. The sparkle in the woman's eyes instantly faded.

"Then you did know her?" Jennings said.

She nodded grimly.

Jennings hurriedly returned to his breast pocket this time withdrawing a folded piece of paper. He straightened it, and handed the woman a photocopy of the holy card found in Eckler's glove box. There was a slight tremble in the nun's hand as she took the image and drew it close for study.

"You recognize it?"

There was a moment of silence.

"Take your time."

More silence. Then Sister Cecilia sighed longingly, "One of my favorites, the Blessed Virgin at Fátima. This was a special card. You had to earn this one."

"Would you have given one to Sellinzski? We checked the records; she was in your class in 1968."

"She was a good student," Sister Cecilia replied. "A real dear. You know, her father died that year, killed in a commercial fishing accident. And unfortunately, her mother took to the bottle. . . . I felt so sorry for her."

"Is there any chance you can recall specifically that you gave her a card like this one?"

"Oh, dear. That would be difficult. It was such a long time ago."

"I guess it would be," Jennings empathized. He added, "I'd have a hard time recalling what I had for lunch yesterday."

The nun let go a nervous chuckle, then grew pensive. "I became quite close to her during those years, and even when she entered high school, she'd drop by from time to time just to chat. I was like a favorite aunt."

"It must have been a shock to learn she had been killed."

"Devastating."

Suddenly, the emotions of the moment caused her eyes to cloud.

Jennings shot up and grabbed for a nearby box of tissues. "Here," he said. "Take a couple."

She did.

Resuming his seat, the Seattle detective delayed his questioning until Sister Cecilia had regained her composure. "Dear me," she said through a sniffle. "It was such a tragedy."

"Are you all right?"

She bobbed her head. "I'm fine. I just remember her lying there in a coma all those months."

"You visited her after the attack?"

The nun wiped her eyes once more and set the tissue aside. Her demeanor grew stoic. "Why, yes, I did. Is that important?"

"I'm not sure at this point. We've just reopened the investigation."

A grim look flashed across the nun's face. "Oh, dear," she mumbled to herself. "You have?"

Jennings nodded. "In fact, we have a suspect in custody."

"Who?"

"A fellow by the name of Clifford Bakerman." Jennings paused and reached into a second pocket. From it, he produced a faxed copy of the suspect's recent booking photo. He unfolded the sheet and passed it over. "Any chance you've heard the name or remember the face?"

Sister Cecilia snatched the image and studied it intently.

"I know it's a long shot," he went on. "But you never know."

Seconds ticked by. Then slowly, she handed the picture back. "Sorry," she murmured. "He doesn't look familiar."

"It was worth a try," Jennings said convincingly. Meanwhile, his years of experience were telling him that the woman's body language was out of sync with her words. *Why?* he wondered. However, he continued the conversation as though nothing were amiss. "Anyway, back to the card. You said it was special. How many of these might you have handed out in the course of your career, specifically with your name stamped on back?"

Sister Cecilia drew a deep breath. "Oh, my, I really couldn't say."

"Do you remember where they came from?"

"That I can tell you. My brother, God rest his soul, would give me a new set every Christmas as a gift. He knew how I loved to reward my students with these more expensive cards rather than our standard issue. Not that they weren't satisfactory."

"How many were in a set?"

"Several dozen, usually. But may I ask a question?"

"Certainly."

"Why all this interest in the card?"

"It's a long story, but we have information that our suspect took it from the victim the night of the attack."

The nun shuddered and said, "I see; that explains it. You need to establish the nexus between the card, the killer, and Cindy Jo."

"Why yes, very good."

Sister Cecilia forced a smile. "I'm a big Perry Mason fan."

Now it was Jennings's turn to chuckle. "So am I. . . . Anyway, is there a chance you would have a record of which students got this particular card, and when?"

The nun thought for a moment, then shook her head no. "I'm afraid those records would be long gone . . . sorry."

"Well, it was worth a try. By the way, you mentioned visiting Cindy Jo after the assault. Where was that?"

Sister Cecilia tensed again. She replied slowly, "It was a Catholic nursing home on the Eastside, run by our order, but it's no longer operating. It shut down years ago."

"I see, but what was the name of it?"

"Sisters of Mercy."

"Any idea where the records for that place may have ended up?"

Sister Cecilia shook her head no.

"What about people who worked there? You must have known some of them."

"Indeed, but I'm afraid they've all passed. And quite frankly, when Cindy Jo died, I volunteered to go to Panama, to a school there, and unfortunately lost touch with a lot of my former coworkers."

"Hmmm. A couple more questions, if you don't mind."

"Certainly."

"While you were visiting Cindy Jo, were there others doing the same thing? And if so, can you remember who they might have been?"

"Oh, my," the nun sighed. She thought for a moment, then said tentatively, "I vaguely remember one young woman being there occasionally. Perhaps a classmate. I don't know. I'm sorry; I'm getting old."

"It's understandable," Jennings replied. "Unfortunately, I've really got my work cut out for me on this one."

"How is that, Detective?"

"Well, Sister, it's like this. Every case I work, I focus on all the minor loose ends and bit players. Ninety-nine percent of the time they turn out to be insignificant. But I have to track them all down."

"You do?"

"Yep, you just never know."

Jennings began to rise. "You've been a big help, Sister. I don't want to keep you tied up. I know you have an engagement, so I'll get out of your way. But if you don't mind, cases like this have a way of dredging up many oddball facts. I'm sure I'll be needing to talk to you at some later date. Perhaps even tomorrow."

Sister Cecilia also rose. "By all means," she said. "Feel free to call anytime. Except not before ten a.m. I'm something of a night owl."

Jennings nodded and said, "Terrible tragedy, young beautiful girl and all."

Sister Cecilia nodded grimly and mumbled, "Sometimes it's hard to understand God's will."

"That it is, Sister." He reached out and patted the nun's hand. He sighed and added, " I hate to admit it."

"What, Detective?"

Jennings shifted on his feet. "I'm a religious man, Sister. I go to church every week and pray daily. But I've worked this job for over thirty years, twenty of them in Homicide. I've seen a lot. And despite all my beliefs about God's will, and his love for all of us, there are times when there is only one explanation I can come up with for such undeserved misfortune."

"And what is that, Detective Jennings?"

"It is simply your turn to die."

27

Leah Harris had every intention of heading back downtown. However, she had been prevented from departing Eckler's apartment by Detective Cummins's supervisor, a lieutenant who had wandered on the scene just as she was trying to leave. "I need a written statement before you clear," he'd commanded. Then under his breath, "Goddamn Homicide dicks, they think their shit doesn't stink."

Despite the urge to flip the man off, with a new chief at the helm, Leah was uncertain whether she'd be backed on the decision to ignore a direct order. With teeth gnashing, she had returned to her Taurus and yanked out a clipboard. In a few minutes, she had scribbled out a rough draft, read it, tossed it, and restarted anew. Half an hour later, she submitted the handwritten document to the lieutenant as several vans marked DEPARTMENT OF ECOLOGY wheeled to the curb.

Not wanting to get further involved, Harris made a quick dash for her car and departed. Six blocks later, she spotted a 7-Eleven store and decided to stop. She pulled in and parked in a corner, away from the busy front door. She purchased a large cup of black coffee inside and returned to her vehicle. She restarted the motor for the heat, then leaned back and quietly sipped her brew. However, a moment later, she bolted forward, realizing that she had forgotten to try Collins one last time. Despite their differences, he needed to know that Sellinzski's DNA samples were likely long gone. Further, finding the ring spun the whole case sideways. She glanced at her watch. "Damn." It was too late now.

The Seattle detective settled in her seat and refocused. A new checklist was needed, but Harris knew it was best to get her team together to brainstorm the next steps. The synergy from her partners had proved fruitful on countless other occasions.

Harris took a few more sips, and departed the minimarket parking lot. She proceeded south on Fifteenth Northwest, but as she neared Market Street, she spotted a small commercial sign labeled MAXIE'S. Below the wording was a directional arrow pointing west to the ship canal locks. In spite of the heavy traffic clogging the wet arterial, Harris whipped across three lanes and made the turn.

Change of plans—Eckler's girlfriend had now drifted into Harris's sights.

28

The elevator door slid open. Silence greeted Frank Milkovich as he stepped out onto the twelfth floor of the Seattle Police Department administrative building. Rows of workstations and cubicles were now deserted, their overhead lights dimmed. Ahead, even the executive suites appeared to have been emptied, save one. A glow still came from behind the door marked CHIEF OF POLICE. Milkovich gulped. It was a Pavlovian response. In his entire life, no good had ever come from a trip to the headmaster.

He approached slowly, listening for any telltale clue that might allay his suspicions. His stomach knotted. Reaching the entry, he drew a deep breath and gently tapped on the doorjamb.

"Come in," a voice called out.

Milkovich recognized it as Logan's. He drew another deep breath and slipped through the opening into the brightly lit corner office.

"Good evening, Frank," the chief said, looking up. He was dressed in a crisp new uniform. Neither a thread nor a hair on his head was out of place. He rose from behind his desk and came around to greet him. "Sorry I had to put you off for so long. I just couldn't get away from my last meeting."

Milkovich took the extended hand and felt the firmness of his grip. Up close for the first time, he was surprised at the man's youth. Logan was obviously younger than he, with the physique of a person who enjoyed exercise. This was further confirmed by a framed picture on the nearby sideboard. It was a portrait of his wife and two adolescent children hugging their father—an apparent finisher in a recent Boston Marathon. "Your family?" Milkovich asked, nodding towards the photo.

The chief beamed proudly. "That's my wife, Tricia, and our twins, Erin and Kelly. They'll be thirteen in a month—a handful."

Milkovich smiled, but as he did, he caught sight of his personnel file resting open atop a stack of others. It was centered on the chief's desk. He groaned inwardly.

"Have a seat," Logan offered. There was a small round conference table in the center of the room. Both men took a place there.

"I just heard from Dellhanney," the chief began. "He's late, but that's okay; it'll give us a few minutes to chat. I'm trying to meet with all the senior staff, lieutenants and above, by the end of next month. I want to make some changes around here, move some people around, cut some deadwood. I want to get this organization moving again—"

Milkovich nodded with feigned enthusiasm. This was his fifth CEO in two decades. All started out wanting to do the same thing.

"—and we need to become more efficient and more responsive to the needs of the citizens we serve. And I need staff people who share this vision and are willing to look fresh at the ways we do things, to root out the barriers that have been built up over the years. So, tell me, Frank, if you were chief for a day, what would you like to see changed?"

Milkovich shifted uncomfortably in his seat. He suddenly realized that he was in a job interview. He cleared his throat. The rest of his career might hinge on this answer. "Ah—"

"Take your time, Frank. By the way, what do you think of Captain Varna as a possible deputy chief, or Ken Yamamoto? I hear both of them are real hard chargers. Ever work with either of them?"

"Some."

"So what do you think? They got the *cajones* to run a division?"

Milkovich glanced back at the photo and purposely ignored the question. "How do your wife and girls like Seattle?"

Logan frowned. "They're still in Philly. It's taking us forever to sell the old place."

"You must miss them."

"I do, terribly. In fact, I'm catching a red-eye in a couple of hours to spend a long weekend with them. With a little luck, though, I'll have them moved out here by Thanksgiving."

"You're a fortunate man."

A sly grin crept over Logan's face. "So are you, Lieutenant Milkovich. I've been reading your file. Says you've been wounded twice in the line of duty and nearly killed when a suspect rammed your car."

"I rammed him."

"Oh—well, it also says you had the most narcotics arrests four years running starting in 'ninety-two. On top of that, you've received dozens of citations and awards. So, how'd you end up in IA?"

"I pissed off the wrong people."

Logan chuckled and leaned forward on his elbows. "You don't like IA, do you? I've already heard you want out."

"It's a living."

"But the word is, you do an excellent job. The line respects you. To me, that says everything."

Milkovich shrugged. "I guess I'm old-fashioned."

"How so?"

Milkovich looked directly into the chief's eyes and said, "Someone gives me an assignment, I do my best, whether I like the assignment or not. It's that simple."

Logan returned the gaze. "That's commendable, but given a choice right now between staying in IA or getting a field assignment, what would you choose?"

Milkovich shrugged. "I'll do whatever you need me to do."

Silence followed. Then slowly, Logan leaned forward in his seat, his chin resting on his fingertips. "I'll level with you, Frank. I think you're just the man I need. You see, in this new administration, Internal Affairs isn't going to be the bastard child of the department anymore. In this day and age, it's critical this function be proactive and, seen by both the employees and the public as unbiased, fair and able to treat confidential information discreetly. It's the cornerstone"—Milkovich's heart sank—"of a new breed of police agency. And a man like you is just who I need overseeing this vital operation."

Milkovich nodded weakly.

Logan went on. "But I'm going to make a few changes in the chain of command. You will no longer be reporting to Major Campbell. You will be reporting directly to me. Will that work for you?"

Milkovich drew a deep breath. "No chance for a transfer?"

"Look, Frank, I'll make a deal with you. And take the

weekend to think it over. If you stick with IA and give me a solid year, well, this time next October, if you still really want out, you can pick where you want to go. How's that sound?"

Before Milkovich could answer, the sound of a distant elevator door swooshing open turned both men's heads.

"That must be Dellhanney," the chief said.

29

"It's got to be here," Roy Stoddard kept mumbling to himself as he painstakingly examined each yellowing document, hoping to find a "destruct" order or some other incriminating piece of paper with Dellhanney's name on it.

Jane Fenton ignored him. She was content to let him pursue his fixation, even though, in her opinion, it contributed nothing to the case they were working on. At least it kept him occupied and out of her business. Unfortunately, he was nearing the bottom of the box and she could tell his agitation level was on the rise. She glanced up from her work space to where he was seated on a stool twenty feet away. "How's it going?" she asked halfheartedly.

Stoddard twisted in his seat and replied in a depressed tone, "Doesn't look like the son of a bitch is here—I'm almost to the bottom."

"Hey, where'd that box come from, anyway?"

Stoddard smirked. "George had it stashed behind a locker in the men's room."

"He had it squirreled away?"

"Yep, you shoulda seen the look on his face when I came out with it. You would have thought I had stolen his life savings."

"You sure?"

"Yeah, I'm sure," Stoddard replied. Without thinking, he reached into his breast pocket for a cigarette.

"Don't you dare!" Jane Fenton shrieked. "I'm about to fume the ring. Christ, you'll set off the smoke alarms, and I'll never get this done."

Stoddard lowered his hand. "I'll be in the men's room for a while." He rose and departed, leaving Fenton to continue her work.

Before preparing the ring for printing, Fenton had spent the past half hour poring over it with a microscope, carefully removing the small flecks of skin cells that had become lodged in the crevices of the setting. Fenton assumed they were recent deposits. This excited her. A simple DNA test could positively identify the last person who had held the ring, at least by inference.

The fingerprint was different. Because the band was narrow and fitted for a female, there was little flat area for an impression to be left—it would be a partial at best. Further, there would be no telling which of the individual's ten digits left the mark—all fingers were unique in their whorls and ridges. Lastly, an educated guess had to be made as to which part of the finger made the mark. Here, experience and deductive reasoning were important. Unlike achieving certainty with DNA, making a positive ID from a partial print was more art than science—a long shot at best. With the advent of computerized scanning and matching devices, though, the odds had greatly improved. While a DNA test itself now only took two hours to complete, with the current backlog the wait might be months. Prints, on the other hand, could be digitized and compared by AFIS, the Automated Fingerprint Identification System, in a matter of minutes. And Fenton could complete entire process without leaving the lab.

Lifting the door to the foot-square Plexiglas box she had

constructed herself, Fenton carefully looped the light gauge wire attached to the ring onto an interior clip. The ring could now dangle freely in the box, like a wind chime. She fumbled through a drawer and found a box of aluminum foil. From the package, she measured out six inches and ripped the segment free. With deft hands, she quickly folded the sheet into a small watertight tray, the size of a coaster.

Setting it aside, Fenton rose and walked over to her coffeepot. An old brew still simmered within. She grabbed an extra cup and filled it halfway. Returning to her work space, she took a whiff of the cup's contents, grimaced, and set the container beside a warming plate set to 130 degrees Fahrenheit inside her makeshift testing device. Fenton then returned to her foil tray.

From an overhead shelf the lab technician reached for a quart-sized plastic bottle, hand-marked "Super Glue." She undid the top and squirted a tablespoon of the clear liquid into the aluminum receptacle, then placed it on the heating element. Then she carefully closed up the box, making it airtight.

Fenton glanced at the wall clock. It would take one to two hours for the glue to vaporize, mingle with the molecules of liquid in the coffee mug, and mix with the amino acids, sodium, glucose, and other chemicals deposited by the human contact. The reaction would produce a sticky white outline wherever a ridge from the latent was present. Once that occurred, and if there was sufficient detail for identification, Fenton would photograph the results, all the while hoping the image she gleaned was from a fingertip already recorded during a criminal booking, government employment check, or military induction. The AFIS system now had nationwide access to tens of millions of print cards. With a little luck, a needle in this haystack would soon fall out.

30

Milkovich remained seated as Patrick Dellhanney entered the chief's office with a swift, cocksure stride. For a brief moment, he and Milkovich exchanged glares and silent animosity. Logan jumped into the void. "Have a seat, Captain."

"Thanks," Dellhanney responded gruffly. Turning to Milkovich, he sniped, "So, Milky, I hear you made lieutenant last year. Well, I'll be. Guess they'll promote anybody nowadays."

The short, flush-faced man chortled.

Milkovich remained silent, letting his set jaw provide a reply.

Dellhanney next looked about. "Spent a lot of years around here," he said philosophically. "Worked with a lot of good men. We sure had a handle on things—and we took care of our own. Cops were family. Not this bullshit I see happening today."

Logan nodded graciously.

Dellhanney's head whipped back to Milkovich. "Hey, what's this I hear about you shacking up with some sergeant? How'd that happen?"

Milkovich remained stone-faced.

Dellhanney grinned. "Ah, that's my boy. But you know

something, Milky? Despite our differences, there were always two things I could count on from you. One, you'd back me, or any one of the other guys, when the crap got deep out on the street—no matter what. Cop's a cop, period."

Milkovich raised a curious brow. "What was two?"

Dellhanney's grin widened. "You dumb shit, you never lied. Even if it meant you took it in the ass for standing tall."

Milkovich remained unfazed. He leaned back in his chair, glanced at the chief, then returned to Dellhanney. "So, Pat, what brings your fat ass down here?"

The retired officer settled into the offered seat with a plump. He drew a breath and replied, "I've got a beef with one of your boys."

"Which one?" the chief asked.

Dellhanney raised his hands. "Whoa, not so fast. There's a little complication that we need to discuss first."

"What kind of complication?" Milkovich asked suspiciously.

The chief nodded a wary agreement.

Dellhanney rubbed the back of his thick neck and gazed at the numerous college diplomas featured on the far wall. "You know," he said, "when I came on back in 'sixty-five, I don't think our ol' chief even made it through high school."

Neither Logan or Milkovich commented.

There was a long pause; then Dellhanney clenched his hands, sighed, and leaned forward. In a surprisingly humble voice, he said, "Look, it's like this. My last wife screwed me outta half my pension, and most of my investments have gone south. Shit, they're even foreclosing on my house. I got this real estate deal cooking with some Jap investors that will get me outta hock, but any bad PR, like my name on the front page, and I can kiss my ass good-bye—*comprende?*"

The chief suddenly spoke up—it was obvious he was

growing impatient. "You said you had a beef with an employee. What's the employee's name?"

"Roy Stoddard."

The chief glanced at Milkovich with an questioning eye.

"He's a civilian," Milkovich replied. "Works evidence. Was a cop for twenty-plus years, then was disabled in the line of duty—a car crash." Milkovich smirked at Dellhanney. He said, "In fact, I think it was you, Pat, who hired him back. You were in charge of the evidence section back then, weren't you?"

Dellhanney nodded.

"Funny, I thought you and Roy used to be drinking buddies?"

Dellhanney didn't respond. But Milkovich detected a slight look of guilt on the man and a nervousness he had not seen before. Suddenly, the pieces came together: Dellhanney, Stoddard, and the missing evidence. He chuckled.

"What's so fuckin' funny?"

"Roy's leaning on you, isn't he?"

"The fuckin' asshole. The statute of limitations expired years ago. Besides, we didn't do anything wrong."

"Statute of limitations?"

Milkovich shifted towards his new boss. "I think Patrick here wants to cut a deal with us."

The chief looked to the retired captain. "A deal for what?"

"Information for anonymity," Milkovich continued.

Dellhanney grinned. "I always knew you were the smart one, Milky." He looked to the chief. "So, whatdaya say?"

Logan went rigid. "You tell me what you know, whatever that might be; then we talk deal."

Dellhanney glared at the younger man. In an ominous tone he quietly said, "That's not how we're going to play this game."

The chief's eyes narrowed. "The hell we're not. I hold all the cards."

"Think so? Tell 'im, Milky—tell 'im how things really work around this place."

"Are you threatening me?" Logan said, rising to the challenge. His own tone was now threatening. Milkovich noted the change. *The guy's no willow whip,* he thought. Another wrong word from Dellhanney, and Milkovich was certain he'd be refereeing a knockdown fight right in the middle of the Seattle police chief's office. His opinion of Logan began to change.

"Look," Dellhanney said, retreating. "You're the new guy on the block. The last thing you, or the mayor, needs is a public scandal. There are still people on the payroll here that know about this. Even one or two in the prosecutor's office. We do it my way, or I'll have to go straight to the press and blow the whistle. My fingers may be a little soiled, but the first pig to that trough always gets to call the spin."

The chief thought for a moment and cocked his head. "What do you think, Lieutenant?"

Milkovich continued to eye Dellhanney. "So, Patrick, how high up did it go?"

The old cop remained tight-lipped.

Milkovich rubbed his jaw for a moment and said, "Take the deal. He's probably already got things squared on the other end, anyway."

Logan glanced at his watch, and Milkovich assumed his flight time was nearing. A moment later the chief said, "Okay, we'll keep you out of this, unless there's something still prosecutable with your name on it. Is that good enough?"

"Works for me." The old captain grinned.

"So what's the story?"

Dellhanney drew a deep breath, and began.

31

"Second night she hasn't shown up yet," the bartender shouted above the din of the loud, midweek crowd.

"What's that?" Leah Harris shouted back. She was sandwiched between several servers trying to fill orders at the trendy watering hole. Noise and laughter filled the air, and although only the width of an elaborate mahogany bar separated her from the bartender, neither could make out much of what the other was saying.

Harris tried again, but she was waved off. "Hang on a sec."

The bartender spun and proceeded to prepare a batch of martinis, one tequila straight up, and several tankards of local ale. He performed the task with the deftness and flair of a skilled juggler. Though impatient, Harris looked on without interrupting. It gave her a chance to study the man. He looked to be about thirty, tall and slender, with a bleach-blond buzz cut. He was dressed in tight-fitting jeans and a white polo shirt with a small Starbucks Coffee logo embroidered on the left breast.

"Okay," he said, returning his attention to the Seattle detective. He leaned close. "You were looking for Nancy, right?"

Harris nodded. "Nancy Doyle. I understand she works here."

The bartender suddenly eyed Harris suspiciously. "Who's looking for her?"

Harris unsnapped her purse. "I am." She flipped out her department ID without further explanation.

The bartender groaned. "It's that dumb shit Eckler again, isn't it?"

"What do you mean?"

Another server arrived.

"Hang on."

The bartender filled the order. In the meantime, Harris turned and gazed out at the crowd of young executives and professional types surrounding every raised table. They all appeared well-heeled, although that had been obvious to Harris before entering. Passing through the choked parking lot, she had observed row after row of late model BMWs and Porsches.

"Hey?"

She turned back.

"So why do you want to talk to Nancy?"

Harris didn't reply. She allowed her silence to speak for itself.

He blinked, thought for a moment, and said, "She called in sick yesterday, and I haven't heard from her since." He glanced at his watch. "She's supposed to work tonight, but she's been a no-show so far."

"When was she supposed to be here?"

"Five."

"Anyone try calling her?"

The bartender sighed. "Look at this place. This is the first break I've had since starting my shift."

"Who's the manager? Maybe I could talk to him or her?"

"You're looking at him. I run the bar."

"Okay, then how about a phone number or address? I'll make the call and find out what's going on."

"Nobody has been answering."

"Then, you did try?"

"Look, I don't want to get anybody in trouble. I run a bar. What people do outside of here is none of my business."

Harris edged to within a foot of the bartender's face. "It might be *my* business if there's a little meth dealing going on around here—maybe in the rest rooms, or out in the back parking lot?"

Another server arrived. "I need five dry ones, all shaken—hold the olives on two."

The bartender ignored the young woman. He reached for a pad of paper and scribbled a telephone number on it. "Here," he said, passing it to Harris. "That's Nancy's, but like I said, I've tried."

"Where's she live?"

He shrugged. "Around here somewhere, I guess."

"You don't have a street address?"

"I'd have to go look it up in the office."

"I'll need it."

"It's going to be a few minutes. Christ, look around here."

"So tell me about Eckler."

The bartender frowned.

The server elbowed in. "Come on, Kyle, I got thirsty people."

He pulled away from Harris without further comment and resumed his duties. A second bartender slipped into the work space, causing him to stop what he was doing. He turned the order over, wiped his hands with a bar rag, and shouted out to Harris, "Come on, follow me."

32

Philip Gilroy felt abandoned. He was all alone in the squad room, his eyesight blurred from staring at his computer screen and piles of old documents. He was hungry. A soda and Snickers bar an hour previous had done little to soothe the rumblings in his stomach. He leaned back in his chair and knotted his hands behind his back. He had completed the time line and the data entry of facts from the three old homicides. Nothing new had been gleaned, despite his additional visits to various Internet databases. Bakerman was still a good suspect, worth working until he was eliminated. However, Gilroy wondered what Harris would turn up when she found Eckler. The whole situation seemed odd. Something didn't feel right, and despite his rearranging the known particulars into various scenarios, no logical explanation was forthcoming. Like everyone else, he was bothered most by the newfound ring. How could it have got there? But more importantly, why? Gilroy was about to let his eyes close for a moment when his telephone rang. He shot forward and snatched up the receiver. "Homicide, Gilroy speaking."

"Hey, Phil."

It was the 911 dispatcher he had eyes on dating. She

worked in the department's emergency communications center, in the basement of the building.

Gilroy shifted gears. "Hi, Deb, what's up? How's your night so far?"

"I have a call holding, some woman who wants to talk to a detective about a homicide case. Are you in, or should I put it to Sergeant Harris's voice mail?"

"Victim, suspect, or nutcase?"

"Wouldn't say, but she sounded legit. And the full moon isn't till next week."

"Put her through, I guess," Gilroy said.

"Will do."

"Hey, wait a second."

"What?"

"You doing anything Friday night?"

Deb reminded him, "We're on a recorded line."

"I'll keep it clean."

"You're going to get me in trouble."

"Okay—what time is your lunch break, then?"

"Eight thirty."

"Wanna split a sandwich?"

"You better take the call."

"Pastrami or turkey?"

"Phil—"

Gilroy sighed. "All right, put the lady through."

"She's all yours—and make it roast beef."

There was a series of clicks, then, "Hello, hello—?"

"Homicide, Detective Gilroy speaking."

"I'm sorry; what was your name again?" It was a polite female voice with an educated manner.

"Detective Gilroy," he repeated.

"Very good, Detective. I'm not interrupting anything, am I?"

"No, not at all." Gilroy leaned back in his chair. "What can I do for you?"

"I believe my husband has some information that may be helpful to you on one of your cases. . . ."

Gilroy flinched. Calls like this came often. His recent favorite had been a screwball who showed up at their office certain he could illuminate a dead person's aura using smoke from a Navajo herbal concoction. Sergeant Harris had been in a generous mood that day. She had allowed the man to do a brief demonstration. Traces of the loaded-diaper-like odor still lingered in the squad room air.

With hesitation, Gilroy asked, "Which case are we talking about?"

"My husband and I were just watching the news on television, and they showed a photo of the fellow you have in custody right now. They said he was being held in connection with the killing of a girl back in 1975."

"Okay?"

"My husband didn't want me to call—he doesn't like to get involved in things—but he suddenly mentioned to me that he was working the same shift with that girl, the one at the fast-food place, where she was last seen."

Gilroy jerked upright. He snatched a legal pad and pen. With the telephone receiver pinned between his shoulder and ear, he eagerly said, "I didn't get your name."

"It's Lynn Felder. My husband is Russell Felder."

The name instantly rang a bell. With his free hand, Gilroy grabbed for the first volume of the Sellinzski file and opened it to the witness list. Running his finger down the names, he quickly found what he was looking for. "Your husband was the night manager at Dick's, right?"

"I guess so."

"Jeez, thanks for calling. You've just saved me a lot of

time. My boss was wanting me to find your husband. We definitely need to talk to him. Where do you live?"

"Just north of the city limits in Shoreline."

Gilroy glanced at the wall clock. "I'd like to talk to him in person. Is it too late for me to come out tonight? I could be there in less than a hour."

"That would be fine."

"I'm on my way."

Gilroy started to rise.

"Detective."

"Yes?" He stopped midway.

"Aren't you interested in why I decided to call?"

Gilroy sank back down.

"It was the photo they showed on the newscast. He's sure it's him."

"Who, Bakerman?"

"Yes, my husband never forgets a face. The gentleman was a regular at the burger joint he worked at while he was going to college."

33

"Look, Eckler was always hanging around here," Kyle, the bartender, said in the quiet of the restaurant's office. It was located in the basement of the building amid stacks of canned food and liquor. "Cuz of Nancy and—"

"Drugs?"

"Like I said, I don't know anything about that."

Harris subtly scoffed.

"Hey, it's the truth—the man was in love."

"What do you mean?"

"Him and Nancy. Hell, if I had been in prison for three years and, well, you know, hadn't been with my girlfriend for that long, shit, I'd be hovering around her too."

"Nancy—she and Eckler were hooked up before he went to prison?"

"Yeah, I guess they've been together for a while. They met at AA. Nancy's been clean for years, but Carl, I guess he's her life's project. Although actually, Carl's a pretty cool guy. He came with Nancy to a company party a coupla weeks ago and had us all rolling on the ground with his prison stories. Of course, we were all shit-faced at the time. Except Carl. He doesn't drink."

"So what does he do here, when he's *hanging*?"

"Sips iced tea and talks to ex-dot-commers. That's all."

Harris was tempted to comment, but decided to skip it. Instead, she said, "Tell me about Doyle. How long has she been working here?"

"Forever. Long before my time. It's a good gig. The clientele has bucks, and even if she's getting a little old, she still knows how to shake it for the big tips."

"What's her address?"

"Oh, yeah, you wanted that."

Kyle reached over and grabbed a Rolodex. He spun through the names and stopped at the desired entry. "Here you go, forty-one fifty-eight Latona Avenue."

Harris scribbled the information down, then looked up. "Anything else you can tell me about Eckler?"

The bartender shrugged. "Hey, I gotta get back upstairs. Wednesday is ladies' night. Say, you want one on the house?"

"No, thanks."

"Never say I didn't ask." He rose.

Harris followed, trailing Kyle back through the maze of boxes, up the stairs, and through the door marked EMPLOY-EES ONLY. It was adjacent to the women's rest room.

"Appreciate the help," Harris said, and she handed the bartender a business card and requested he call her if he heard from Doyle anytime soon. He palmed it and said he would, although Harris was certain he wouldn't. Odds were he was getting a kickback from Eckler on any business transacted on the premises.

For a moment, Harris stood there. The noise from the bar beyond filtered her way, but it was quiet enough in this area to hold a conversation. Leaning up against the wall, she fumbled for her cell phone. The address Kyle had given her was back up by the zoo, ten blocks south of the parking lot where she had first met up with Frank at noon. If Eckler was there, Harris reasoned, he'd probably jackrabbit if she tried a solo knock-and-talk. It'd be best to have at least one person on the back door, and two on the corners. Harris found her phone and pulled it out. "Oh, man," she groaned. The device had powered off while in her pocket. She quickly pressed the ON button, and two seconds later the voice mail indicator was flashing. She dialed in and waited. Moments later, the recordings began to play.

"Message one. 'Hey, Leah, I just wrapped it up with the nun. Boy, what a house. I'll tell you about it later. Anyway, we're probably not going to get a positive ID on the card. She remembers it, but passed out dozens of them over the years, so it could have been Sellinzski's or it could've come from somewhere else. Funny thing, though, she seemed kinda hinkey about me being there. I may have been reading her wrong, but I got a feeling in the ol' stomach that she knows more than she's letting on. By the way, she actually visited our victim in the nursing home after the attack. How 'bout that? Speaking of feelings in my stomach, I'm going to stop off at my place and get a bite to eat. Give me a call there—bye.' *Beep*. Message received at seven ten p.m.

"Message two. 'Hi, boss. I got a lead on the Dick's manager. He lives in Shoreline. . . . I'm heading out there right now. Give me a call.' *Beep*. Message received at seven thirty-three p.m.

"Message three. 'Darn it, Leah, would you turn your phone on?'" It was Jane. The words were followed by a labored sigh and " 'Like I told you before when you called, I'll have the print on the ring ready to go in about an hour. Call me, okay?' *Beep*. Message received at seven forty-one p.m. End of messages. *Beep*."

Harris was about to enter Fenton's number when she felt a slight tap on her shoulder. She spun.

"Hey, Sergeant Harris."

She was now standing face-to-face with a smiling Tessla Quinn.

34

"And that's the story," Patrick Dellhanney said, summing up. He leaned back in his chair. "I was just following orders—that's all there was to it."

"So, again," Chief Logan asked, "how many cases do you think were lost?"

"Forty or fifty, maybe a few more. I don't remember exactly. Look, things were tight then, just like they are now. My brother-in-law was up for reelection on the city council. I owed him a favor or two, so I suggested using jail inmates to do the maintenance and cleaning in city-owned facilities. It was a good idea. It saved taxpayers thousands of dollars and the voters loved it."

Chief Logan folded his hands and leaned forward. "I guess I don't understand. This sounds perfectly legit, except the part about destroying the evidence. Why'd you have do that?"

Dellhanney was about to answer when Milkovich interceded. The Internal Affairs lieutenant glared at the retired captain and said, "Probably because his brother-in-law took credit for the plan. Played it up big-time. Isn't that right?" Dellhanney nodded. "And about a month later, the freezer in the evidence warehouse goes TU and probably because of one of the inmates."

Dellhanney nodded again.

"What are you driving at?" the chief asked.

Milkovich turned to him and replied, "They had to cover it up. How would it have looked to the voters that the councilman's brilliant idea had resulted in fifty rape victims' losing any chance of ever seeing their attacker behind bars? The press would've eaten them alive."

"And how!" Dellhanney added.

Logan shook his head in disgust as Dellhanney continued. "When I talked to the assistant chief and he talked to the chief, they thought it best we just quietly sweep this thing under the rug. After all, my brother-in-law was a real supporter of the department. We couldn't afford to lose that. That's why we tossed everything and doctored the records to make it look like the stuff had been lost or destroyed years prior with no connection to the inmate workers."

Logan straightened. "I see."

"Hey, like I said, I was just following orders. I got nothing out of it."

Milkovich narrowed his eyes. "You made captain."

Dellhanney offered no rebuttal.

Logan drew a deep breath and said, "You're sure about the names of everyone else involved?"

Dellhanney folded his arms. "Do you think I'd be here if I wasn't? Now, would you get Stoddard off my back? The bastard's been calling me every hour. If I lose this deal, I swear, I'll sue you all for defamation."

Logan glanced again at his watch, then to Milkovich. "I do have to get going. Will you get a hold of Officer Stoddard and tell him to cool his jets? Tell him that there is now an official internal investigation being initiated, and he needs to let us handle it from here."

Milkovich nodded, looked at Dellhanney, and rolled his eyes. "Using jail trustees to do the maintenance at the evidence warehouse—I can't believe it. . . . So, what do you think actually happened?"

"Shit, one of them numb nuts must've flipped a breaker when he was dusting around the power box. That's all I can think. Hell, if any of the clerks had been doing their job, and not worrying about playing the ponies, none of this would have happened. That freezer sat for nearly a week without anyone noticing it was warming up."

Milkovich stroked his chin. "You don't think it might have been done on purpose?"

"Huh?"

Logan perked.

"You heard me."

"Where are you going with this, Frank?" the chief asked.

"Just thinking out loud, sir."

"Tell me."

Milkovich shrugged. "Well, just suppose an inmate had flipped the breaker on purpose, maybe someone whose semen sample was inside?"

"My God," Logan mouthed. "Is there any way of knowing who might have been assigned there?"

Milkovich glanced at Dellhanney. He got no reply.

"Would the jail have kept those records?" Logan pressed.

"Perhaps," Milkovich said. "But I wouldn't count on it. I'll check it out, though. You never know."

Logan rose. He was clearly agitated. He stepped back around to his desk and said, "I don't mean to pressure you, Frank, but you need to get started on this immediately. First thing tomorrow, start the interviews with the people the captain has named. My God, if there is even a slight possibility that what you just said is true . . ."

"One problem," Milkovich said. "Our labor contract requires me to give a seventy-two-hour notification prior to questioning anyone. That is, of course, if you are planning disciplinary action against anyone should there be findings."

Logan thought for a moment as he shuffled the folders on his desk into two stacks—Milkovich's personnel file was still on top. Finally he said, "I may regret this, but my gut tells me that the truth is more important right now than trying to punish anyone for something that happened some fifteen-odd years ago."

Milkovich turned back to Dellhanney. "One last question. Why in the world is Roy so hot about this? I don't get it."

Dellhanney started up from his chair. "Remember Eddy Merlock?"

"Vaguely," Milkovich replied.

"He was Roy's first partner."

"So?"

"Stoddard's got it up his butt that I'm somehow responsible for the jerk having eaten his gun a few years back. The dumb shit got canned after beating the crap out of his wife. Put her in a hospital for a month."

"What caused him to do that?"

"She was sleeping around."

"I still don't get it."

A wry glint sparkled Dellhanney's eye.

"Well?"

Dellhanney sighed. "Let's just say I owed Mrs. Merlock more than I did Eddy—and leave it at that. . . . Anything else? I got to get going."

Milkovich leaned back in his chair. "I'll probably need to ask you some more questions as I get into this. What's a good number to reach you at?"

"I'm in the book," Dellhanney grumped. He straightened

his tie, retrieved his hat, and swaggered out the office door without a further word.

As his footsteps faded, Logan picked up his raincoat and briefcase. "Frank, I hate to dump you with this, but I have to—"

"Go catch your flight," he cut him off. "I'll call you tomorrow when I have more information."

Logan hesitated.

"Go—see your kids, damn it. They're a hell of a lot more important than anything else around this place. Go on."

The chief locked up and he and Milkovich rode the elevator together down to the third floor. Milkovich exited, leaving Logan to continue to the parking garage. As the door began to close, the chief jammed his foot into the opening. "You trust Dellhanney?" he asked.

Milkovich mulled the question for only a moment, smirked, and replied, "Not for a single second."

35

"The weather is miserable," Harris agreed as she stood impatiently in the hallway of Maxie's. For the past couple of minutes, her conversation with Quinn had remained on a superficial level, each aware of the potential breach of ethics if either spoke specifically about the Bakerman case—though both wanted to.

"I was born and raised here," the young attorney continued. "So I'm used to it. In fact, I love a dark, gloomy day, and the more drizzle, the better."

Harris chuckled. "I grew up here too, but I hate it."

"Ever thought of moving?"

"A couple of times. I like San Diego, but all that sunshine, that could get to be depressing too."

Several patrons passed by, forcing the pair of women to sidestep closer to the wall.

"The place is packed. Are you here with someone?"

"I'm working," Harris replied.

"Oh."

There was an awkward silence. Their eyes wandered, both women unsure of how to proceed from this point. For her part, Harris was well aware of the benefits of nurturing a friendly relationship with the defense. Cross-examinations were less brutal. But more important, once a line of communication had developed, body language and offhand remarks, if properly interpreted, served both parties, and the interests of justice. Harris was first to fill the void. "You did a good job this morning," she said. "You caught Collins off guard."

An immodest grin spread across Quinn's face. "I did okay."

"It won't happen again."

"I still have a few tricks."

"I bet you do." Harris smirked. "So, how about you, are you here with someone?"

Quinn's face soured.

Harris laughed. "I know that expression. Someone from the office, right?"

"God, how could you tell?"

"Experience. Think of how many more lousy dates I've been on than you."

"It's not a date, " Quinn protested.

"Tell that to Mr. Right . . ."

There was another pause. A moment later Paul Anders popped around the corner, heading towards the men's room. "Hey," he said nearing the two women, "I was wondering what was taking you so long." He stopped, extended his hand. "Hi, I'm Paul. You must be a friend of Tess's."

Quinn gave Harris a sideways glance. The detective withheld judgment. She took Anders's hand and gave it a polite shake.

"Paul, this is Sergeant Harris."

His eyes lit up. "You're the detective on our case. Cool, nice to meet you." Their hands unclasped. "Can I buy you a glass of wine—sparkling water? I've got some questions I'd love to ask you, if you have the time."

"Paul, Sergeant Harris is on duty right now."

A look of befuddlement creased the young attorney's face. "Here? The Bakerman case? How come? I knew it—I knew it all along."

"Knew what?" Quinn asked.

He turned to Harris. "You can't find it, right? That's why you're working the OT. Come on, you can admit it."

"Paul . . ."

Harris didn't reply. Instead, she looked to Quinn and gave her an affirming wink that caused Quinn to break up laughing.

"Hey, what's so funny?"

Neither female answered. Instead, Harris reached into her coat and pulled out a business card. "Here," she said to Quinn. "Call me if you want to try a little quid pro quo. I've got to go."

Quinn nodded and took the card.

36

"He's stabilized for now," the emergency room doctor said to the waiting corrections officer. They were a few feet apart, a glass wall away from where Clifford Bakerman now lay unconscious but breathing normally, his body wired to multiple monitors and IVs.

"Another couple of minutes, and—"

The officer nodded, then asked, "What should I tell my sergeant?"

The doctor thought for a moment. "He's not going anywhere, if that's what you mean. I want to keep him here in ER for another hour for observation, then move him to a room for the night. You'll need to arrange security."

"That's my sergeant's problem. I get off in twenty minutes."

The doctor winced. He had dealt with this particular jail employee before, and each time, he had been exasperated by the fellow's abrasive, uncooperative manner. "Would you mind," he sighed, "at least calling and getting the ball rolling?"

"What's the hurry? Looks like that old fart isn't going to be hoofing it soon."

The doctor cocked a sharp eye.

"Okay, okay," the officer relented. He tipped his head to

the radio mike hooked to his epaulet and keyed it. His voice would be transmitted from where he stood within the Harborview Medical Center emergency room to the King County Jail, located six blocks away across Interstate 5. "Hey, Vern, you got your ears on?"

The radio crackled static.

"Vern?"

More static.

"Can't get out?" the doctor asked.

"It's all your instruments causing interference. I'll have to use the phone."

The doctor pointed to the nurse's station. "You can use one of those."

"All right," the jailer relented, "I'll see what I can do." He turned and ambled towards the oval counter space. Several staff members sat about it chatting. It was early in the evening for them—a quiet time. However, as each hour ticked closer to midnight, the volume of mangled bodies—crushed in drunken car wrecks or wounded in domestic assaults—increased exponentially. Soon, every gurney, observation room, and surgical area would be filled with the hurt and near-dying. Harborview was the primary trauma center for all of Western Washington, and so adept were the nurses and doctors in dealing with violent injuries that the military sent their medical personnel there to observe the facility in action—and get a feel for combat conditions.

The doctor turned and was immediately met by a young female lab technician. She was dressed in surgical garb. "Here are the preliminary workups on Bakerman."

He took hold of the offered clipboard and scanned the results. Soon, a look of puzzlement appeared on his face.

"I thought you'd find these odd."

He looked up. "Everything is normal except—"

The lab tech nodded.

The doctor scratched the nape of his neck. "Are you sure about these?"

"I can run them again if you like."

"Why don't you? This doesn't add up."

The tech nodded, received her clipboard back, and departed. The doctor started on his way again, but soon halted when he heard a loud bang followed by a heated male voice. He whirled around to see what the commotion was about. It was the jailer, now red-faced and huffing loudly. He had thrown the telephone receiver down with such force that nearby employees feared he had split the device in two.

The doctor closed the distance as the disgruntled jailer slumped and drew a deep breath.

"Hey, what's the matter here?" the doctor called out.

There was no immediate reply; however, one of the senior nurses began to chuckle. "Seems he drew the overtime."

"I had plans," the jailer griped.

"Yeah, right," another nurse commented to her colleague. Both were out of earshot. "A date with a fifth of vodka."

"So what'd your sergeant say?" the doctor asked.

The jailer looked up. Through gnashed teeth he replied, "Everyone is tied up, so I'm stuck here till the next shift change."

"When's that?"

"Twenty-three hundred."

The doctor frowned. He would have preferred having a new guard. This one's grumbling would continue up to the moment he was relieved. To reduce the tension, he said, "Why don't you go down to the cafeteria and get yourself a cup of coffee? We can keep an eye on Bakerman. It'll be at least a day before he's ambulatory."

The guard grunted and trudged off without further comment.

The time was 2015.

37

"You did great," Linda Reese exclaimed. She was lying. In reality, she was appalled by her brother's uncharacteristically poor performance.

"I thought so too," the moderator, Deejah Mohannah, agreed. She, too, was lying, but politely. "I appreciate your taking the time to appear on my show tonight. I thought it all went very well."

Collins forced a weak smile, but then caught sight of his opponent weaving his way towards him through the thick crowd of audience members now gathering on stage.

Reese elbowed Collins.

He extended his hand as Bernhardt closed the distance.

"No hard feelings."

"Of course not," Collins replied. It was also a lie. But then, he knew Bernhardt's spontaneous show of magnanimity was pure fabrication as well. Print reporters were still nearby, and scribbling.

"Just a couple more days to go, eh?"

"I'll be glad when it's over," Bernhardt chirped confidently.

"So will I."

"I'll bet your staff will, too." This was a subtle dig.

Collins was well aware that half his employees were in Bernhardt's camp. A new prosecutor meant new job opportunities. Senior staff holding the top slots in the current organization would likely be axed whether they were competent or not.

"Excuse me."

It was an AP photographer.

"Can I get the two of you shaking hands again?"

Bernhardt puffed up. "Sure." He turned back to Collins. "You don't mind, do you?"

Collins hesitated.

Reese nudged him again.

He gritted his teeth. His veneer was peeling, although only his sister was picking up the cues. She leaned close. "Damn it, don't go south now."

Collins nodded, and forced a smile.

"Great," the photographer said. "Now, if I can get the two of you to take one step to your right."

"Here?" Bernhardt eagerly responded as the house lights went up.

"Perfect. Now you, Mr. Collins. Right next to him . . . ah, Mr. Collins?"

The incumbent didn't hear him. His attention had suddenly shifted offstage to the rear of the studio, where his eyes made contact with his next appointment. His jaw stiffened.

"Ah, Mr. Collins?"

The prosecutor refocused his attention and edged closer to Bernhardt.

"That's good. I should be able to get both of you with your campaign posters framed in the background. Okay, now, just like before. A nice smile . . . ah, a little more this way . . . now hold it."

The camera clicked.

"Once more, if you don't mind."

Neither man responded. Both were locked eye to eye, no longer capable of containing the months of bad blood, rumor, and political hyperbole.

The grip between them tightened.

Suddenly, Collins reeled a resistant Bernhardt close. In a low tone he said, "You're a lying sack of shit. I hope you do win, so I can watch you fall flat on your ass trying to run the place."

Bernhardt's smile did not waver. "If I were you, I'd start packing right now. I've got your ass whipped."

Collins let go right as the AP man clicked. Reese was horrified. "Do another."

The photographer didn't reply.

"Christ almighty," Reese blurted.

Bernhardt's smile widened as Reese latched on to her brother's arm and yanked him away, quickly putting a dozen steps between Bernhardt and the inner circle. Reaching an unoccupied corner, she turned and glared like a schoolmarm at her undisciplined student. "God, where have your brains gone to? I've never seen you like this. What the hell is the matter? Is it about the money I gave you—what?"

Collins stepped beyond the fringe of the stage and into the shadows. Reese followed. When they were out of sight, he slowly parted his coat and pulled out the photo he had shown his sibling earlier in the day. With agitated hands, he passed it over to his sister. She gave it a cursory glance. "So, enough of the histrionics. What the hell does that picture have to do with anything?" She glanced back up and in the dim light, she saw an expression on her brother she hadn't seen before. It startled her. She whispered, "Richard, are you ill?"

"Yeah, I am . . . I'm sick to death of all this political crap."

Reese folded her arms. "What are you talking about? Is it me? Christ, I know I can be a bitch at times, and I've been pushing you hard for weeks. Maybe if you just had some rest, you'd feel better. In fact, go home now, and get some sleep. I'll go to the reception and send your apologies. I'll tell them you picked up a flu bug or something. And tomorrow, I'll come by first thing and pick you up for the Lions Club speech. We'll go together. How does that sound?"

Collins didn't respond.

"Richard—?"

Suddenly, he mumbled, "I killed them—all of them."

Reese's eyes widened. "Killed who? What's this all about?"

"They weren't even teenagers."

A look of horror appeared on Reese's face. "Richard, what are you saying?"

He suddenly began rubbing his hands as though he was trying to wash away a nagging stain.

Reese whirled around, fearful other eyes might see this. No one was watching. Turning back, she pushed her brother farther into the recesses of the backstage until they were in near total darkness. Frantically, she clicked her fingers in front of her brother's face. "Snap out of it, Richard. Goddamn it, get a hold of yourself. You're talking crazy. Are you having some sort of flashback? Jesus, you're scaring the shit out of me."

Collins suddenly straightened. Color returned to his face. He drew a deep breath and said, "I did terrible tonight, didn't I?"

Reese hesitated, then nodded affirmation.

"I'm sorry," he sighed. "I know how hard you have been working for me. I don't deserve your help."

"Richard, what were you just talking about? Was it something in Vietnam? What happened—what's with the picture?"

He drew another deep breath and let it go slowly. "You can't see the blood; there was too much dirt caked on me."

"What do you mean?"

Collins slumped against a storage locker and replied, "When that was snapped, I had just crawled out of a VC tunnel. It was a huge complex, and it was supposed to be empty, cleared hours earlier. It was so quiet and dark down there. I just reacted instinctively—I thought they were regulars." Collins's voice cracked.

Reese flinched.

There was a long silence.

Suddenly, a side curtain parted and a man's head poked through. It was Patrick Dellhanney. "There you are," he wheezed. He stepped inward as Reese whirled about. "Oh, I see you have company."

Collins stiffened. A moment later, he glanced to a nearby exit and motioned his intention. Dellhanney understood. He tipped his head and withdrew.

Reese turned to her brother and blurted, "Who the hell was that?"

Collins didn't reply. Instead, he suddenly brushed by his sister and made a beeline for the egress.

"Wait, Richard!"

His pace only quickened.

38

Jane Fenton leaned close to her now open fuming box. With a magnifying glass, she studied the partial fingerprint detail clearly outlined by the process she had initiated. A smile spread across her face. The primary whorl was tilted in such a manner that a left-handed finger likely deposited it. She was willing to bet it came from a forefinger, as this would be the most natural way a person would have last handled the object.

"This is good," she said, delighted.

Straightening, she looked over to her partner's unoccupied work space. A half hour earlier, Roy had returned from his smoke more angry than she had ever seen him. From what she'd been able to decipher before he bolted right back out the door, he had been cornered in the hallway by Lieutenant Milkovich and ordered to stay away from Dellhanney. Further, he was to turn over all the material he had obtained relating to the malfunctioning evidence freezer. Stoddard had screamed cover-up, but to no avail. The only thing that slowed him on his way back out of the lab was a telephone message Jane had received while he was in the rest room. The female caller had specifically asked for Roy and been disappointed he was not available. Reluctantly, she had left a return number and asked Jane to forward the information. Jane did as Roy rushed by on his way to drown his sorrows. He paused only to grab the slip of paper, then shoved it unread into his shirt pocket.

Fenton now traded her looking glass for her digital camera. Activating it, she double-checked the internal time-and-date stamp, then tried various angles and distances to get the best shot. After several attempts, she was satisfied, and she snapped three pictures. These would only be used if she accidentally smudged the impression while removing it from the box.

That done, she set the camera aside and with tweezers carefully reached in and removed the ring from where it was still hanging freely on the slim wire. Slowly, she lifted the piece of jewelry off the hook, backed it out, and gently set it onto a sheet of gray matte paper. Retrieving her camera, she again studied the possible angles, choosing one after several dry runs. In rapid succession, she obtained a dozen images of the exposed fingerprint, then rose from her stool and walked over to her desk. Here, she docked the camera, and waited impatiently as her computer downloaded the shots and sent them to a photo-editing program. While waiting, she reached for her telephone and dialed a familiar number.

It rang twice.

"Harris."

"So where you at now?" Jane asked.

There was a brief pause followed by a chomping and slurping sound. "Sorry, you caught me in the middle of my fishwich."

"Besides eating, whatcha doin'?"

Harris's reply was succinct. "Freezing."

"Huh?"

"I'm sitting on a house. It's supposed to be Eckler's girlfriend's place. I'm waiting for backup to do a knock-and-talk—you got a print yet?"

"Yeah, that's why I'm calling. I'm almost there. It's a good partial. I make it to be a left forefinger. I'll do a quick classification and feed it to AFIS—who knows?"

There was another slurp.

"Fishwich, huh?" Fenton laughed. "Where'd you get it? Sounds kinda good right now."

"Kid Valley."

"Jeez, they're the best."

"Last bite—hang on a sec."

Fenton waited, then changed subjects. "Is Frank still hovering?"

"He doesn't hover."

"He does too."

"Well, if he does, I like it." Harris's voice held a defensive note.

"Yeah, right."

"Well, he's not here right now. The new chief called him in a couple hours ago. I think he's going to be up to his neck in an internal for the rest of the week."

"You sound relieved. Come on, come clean with me. We're buds. What's going on between you and him? The both of you are so tight-lipped about everything. God, it drives a gossip like me crazy."

"Nothing is going on."

"Leah—"

"Absolutely nothing."

"Liar."

"I'm going to hang up," Leah warned.

"No, you're not. There's a problem, and you're going to let me help you with it."

"There is no problem."

"Oh yeah, there is. I could tell this afternoon when I was

with you at the zoo. God, you two guys are just like teenagers—it's so obvious."

"What do you mean?"

"The looks . . . I've been divorced a couple of times. Believe me, I know all about the looks."

"I swear there's nothing wrong."

"Come on, what happened? Did you have a fight or something?"

Harris sighed.

"Ah, I can feel it—we're getting close. Spit it out, and set yourself free," Fenton said.

"We're just not getting to spend much time together. . . . You know how busy I've been. Thank God Frank has a day job and can work his schedule around mine. If he wasn't in IA, we'd never see one another."

"Oh, come on, there's got to be more."

"There is," Harris admitted.

"Now we're getting somewhere."

"I don't want to talk about it. Besides, I think that's my backup down the street. I got to go."

"I'm not going to drop this. You deserve to have a life outside of this office, and I'm going to make sure you don't screw up this opportunity."

"Don't you dare say anything to him."

"I have my ways."

"Jane!"

"Hey, my pictures are ready to edit. I'll call you back as soon as I have anything. By the way, do you still want the cadaver dogs at the zoo tomorrow?"

"Probably should."

"Agreed—talk to ya later." Fenton hung up before Harris could resume her protest.

Setting the phone down, Fenton glanced at her computer screen. Thumbnails of the pictures were now arrayed in their order of capture. Fenton fumbled for her reading glasses and donned them. Leaning close, she studied each image, settling on the second to last. "There's a winner," she mumbled.

With her mouse in hand, she clicked several times, bringing the selected photo to the forefront. She enlarged it, rotated the angle, and saved it as a file, naming it zoo_ring_1.bmp. Then she sent the image to her laser printer. Seconds later the picture was spooling out. She grabbed it and returned to her workbench, laying it flat before her.

Using a jeweler's magnifying glass mounted on a black metal holder, she quickly noted the unique details of the ridges and whorls, finding half a dozen points for identification. She noted these on a separate sheet of paper. With growing smugness, she rose again, and returned to her computer. From this terminal, she could access AFIS. She first converted the picture to the proper format, accomplished in less than a minute. Her last step was now to log on, but as she made the final mouse click, a banner message scrolled across her screen: AFIS WILL BE DOWN FOR ROUTINE MAINTENANCE FROM 1900 WEDNESDAY TO 0700 THURSDAY MORNING.

"Son of a bitch."

The time was 2050.

39

"Mr. Felder?"

The nervous, middle-aged man nodded.

"Thank you for contacting us."

Detective Gilroy brushed off the raindrops from his coat and followed the average-built fellow inside an older, split-level home. It was located on a narrow waterfront lot where Puget Sound gently lapped against a low bulkhead. It was an unassuming residence, but a moneyed location, close to town, yet situated so that one could step out a back door to the rocky beach beyond and watch seals and otters playing in the tangled kelp beds.

"Love that salt-air smell," Gilroy commented as he was led up the entry stairs to the main living level.

"We do too," Felder replied.

"It's what sold us on the place," a third voice remarked.

Gilroy looked up. Leaning over the half wall was a woman in her forties, slimly built, with a scholarly look to her face. Her glasses were out of style, her hair was simply pulled back, but her eyes sparkled with a book-smart impishness.

Felder continued, "This is my wife, Lynn. She's the one who called you."

Gilroy reached the last riser. "Nice to meet you."

She came around and shook his free hand. "Would you like a cup of coffee? Tea, perhaps? It's already made."

"No, thank you," Gilroy replied. He then noticed another individual sitting on the couch to his right. He was a man about Felder's age, also with a professional look, but dressed in casual clothes—pressed jeans and a sweater. He set the magazine he was perusing aside and rose to his feet.

"Oh, excuse me," Mrs. Felder said, seeing Gilroy's inquiring look. "This is our next-door neighbor, Ray Addams. He was just leaving."

Addams extended a hand and said, "Wish I could stay. This all sounds very interesting. Lynn and Russ were just filling me in. Unfortunately, still have work to do for tomorrow. I'm in the middle of a tough civil trial."

"You're an attorney?" Gilroy asked as he shook hands.

He nodded and said, "Nice to meet you, Detective. Good luck on your case." He then slipped by Gilroy and exited through the front door.

Meanwhile, Felder turned to his spouse. "Shall we use the kitchen table?" he asked.

"I guess. Is that okay, Detective?"

Gilroy looked about and shrugged. The coffee table, end tables, and every space on the multiple bookcases bracketing the fireplace were filled with medical texts and journals. Even the kitchen table had a stack of scholarly tomes.

Lynn Felder slipped over and hastily removed them. "Sorry the place is such a mess," she apologized. She placed the books on the stove. "I'm afraid neither one of us is much of a housekeeper. Work keeps us pretty busy."

Gilroy nodded as though he understood—he didn't. He had driven to the area expecting to find an aging fast-food manager, but instead, he was face-to-face with a pair of seemingly unpretentious scholarly types. Something didn't fit. He started cautiously. "So, Mr. Felder, twenty-eight years ago you were flipping burgers at Dick's. What do you do now?"

"Actually, it's Dr. Felder. I teach pulmonary medicine at the university."

Gilroy summoned an impressed smile.

"And my wife is a senior researcher at the cancer institute."

"Two doctors, huh?"

They nodded with satisfaction.

"Please have a chair, Detective," Lynn Felder offered. "Russell has been pacing the floor ever since we saw the news story this evening. I'm dying to hear more about this."

Her husband stiffened. "I've already told you, dear, it's not a big deal."

"Then why are you acting so funny?"

He didn't reply.

Gilroy took the seat he was offered and waited for the Felders to take theirs. As they settled in, he opened a folder he had brought along, and withdrew a pen from inside his coat. He leafed through a couple of pages, then leaned back in his chair. "Tell me, Dr. Felder, how long did you work at Dick's?"

"Too long," he groaned. "My cholesterol level never recovered."

Gilroy chuckled for effect.

"Actually, I got the job there when I was a senior in high school—I went to Roosevelt—and I kept it through four years of undergraduate work. In fact, this whole tragedy with Cindy Jo happened a couple of weeks before I quit to begin medical school."

"So about five years, huh?"

"About. It was a great job. I got all the free food I could eat. Of course I haven't had a hamburger since."

"You have, too," Lynn Felder sniped. "He's lying; he'll sneak a burger whenever I'm not looking."

The doctor rolled his eyes.

"Tell me about Cindy Jo Sellinzski," Gilroy said, keeping the conversation focused. "Were you the one who hired her?"

"Oh, no," Felder said as he leaned back in his chair and crossed his arms. "The owner did all the hiring. But she got assigned to my crew from the start. I think it was sometime in April of 1975. I remember that because I had just bought a very used VW microbus, and I was showing it to some friends when she came to work for the first day."

"Did you get to know her well?"

"Kind of. She was friendly, a great worker. She learned quickly and was never late. During the slack time, we'd talk a lot. She wanted to know about college and how it would be, what classes to take, how much studying, those kind of things."

Gilroy scribbled a note, then asked, "Did she talk about her personal life?"

Felder thought for a moment and replied, "Not that I recall specifically. She seemed pretty squared away, though— and mature for her age."

"What about Bakerman? Your wife said on the phone that you recognized him, even after all these years. Tell me about that."

The doctor gritted his teeth. "I had several run-ins with the jerk. That's why I remember him."

Gilroy straightened. "You did?"

"Yep, he hung around the drive-in a lot. He'd show up after school got out, order a cup of coffee, and sit on one of the picnic tables, leering at the young girls that might happen by. After we started getting complaints, the boss told me, if he showed up while I was on duty, to go out and let him know he wasn't welcome on our property."

"Did you?"

"Oh, yes, a couple of times."

Gilroy scribbled more notes. Without looking up he said, "So, what happened after you confronted him?"

"Not much—he'd disappear for a few weeks but always wandered back. One night, I came from behind the grill and there he was at the order counter, talking to Cindy Jo."

"What did you do?"

"I called the cops."

Gilroy raised a brow.

"Something wrong, Detective?" Lynn Felder asked. "You look puzzled."

"I am. There's no mention of any of this in the original report." Gilroy looked to Russell Felder. "Did any officers actually come out?"

The doctor leaned forward. "Why, yes. That summer, I must have called three, maybe four times."

"And officers always came?"

"Sure, right away."

"What'd they do with Bakerman?"

Felder let go a long, pensive sigh. "Back then, we didn't know much about pedophiles."

"How do you mean?"

"Well, when I was growing up, people didn't talk about those things. And the police either weren't interested or had no understanding of the problem. Child molesters were rarely dealt with as they are nowadays. The police would just shoosh him away and that was about it."

Gilroy thought for a moment, then nodded in agreement. He mumbled, "That's probably why there's no record of the police contacts. That's probably it. . . ." He jotted another note and asked, "Okay, tell me about the night Cindy Jo was abducted. According to the report, you were working and perhaps the last person we know of to have seen her alive. Was Bakerman still hanging around in that time frame?"

"You know," Dr. Felder said slowly, "I hadn't seen him for a while. I think the last time I called the cops on him was around the end of July. Of course, I started passing out free burgers and coffee to any of the officers who came by, so after that, they were always dropping in to check on us. That probably kept Bakerman off for good."

"Was there anything unusual about that night? How about anyone else that might have caught your attention?"

"Not that I remember. I do recall it was warm. We were in the middle of an August heat wave, and things got real hot back by the grill."

"Were there other employees on duty?"

"Oh, boy, I couldn't remember all their names. I would think they would be in your report."

"They are, but I thought maybe one of them would have stuck out in your mind for some reason. Now, what about other people, regular patrons, delivery people, friends of your coworkers? Any of them hit you the wrong way?"

"What do you mean?"

"You know, acted suspicious."

"Wait a second," Lynn Felder interrupted. "I thought this Bakerman fellow was responsible for the murder."

Dr. Felder glanced at his spouse. She ignored him. She said, "Why all the questions about other people? Bakerman's guilty, isn't he?"

"Perhaps," Gilroy responded. "Perhaps not."

A confused look showed on Russell Felder's face.

Gilroy went on. "Look, I have to ask you this next question because it is not adequately recorded in the report."

Felder suddenly blushed. "Now I understand. You want to know, where was I at the time Cindy Jo was abducted?"

Gilroy clasped his hands together. "Please," he said. "I'm not trying to imply anything. Bakerman certainly profiles out as the perfect suspect. And we have circumstantial and hearsay evidence that points to him, but there are a few loose ends that could dump the entire case."

Both Felders nodded slowly.

"However," Gilroy reassured, "what you've told me so far is great stuff. The fact that you can actually place Sellinzski and Bakerman together within weeks of her demise is critical, but I do need to know specifically where you were after you closed the restaurant. If this ever goes to trial, the defense will build reasonable doubt in the jury by implying you could have been the one actually responsible, even though that's ridiculous—right?"

The doctor gulped and turned a bright red.

"So where were you, Russell?" Lynn Felder demanded. Her tone made everyone nervous until she gave a teasing wink and a gentle elbow to her husband's midsection.

Felder ignored his wife. He leaned farther forward. "Remember that microbus I told you about?"

"Uh-huh."

"That night, I couldn't get it started—dead battery."

"What time was that?"

"Twelve thirty, maybe a few minutes later."

"So what'd you do?"

"Actually," Felder said, "I was in luck. A police car came through the lot just about that time and offered a jump start, except my VW had the old six-volt system, so it wouldn't work. Instead, he gave me a lift to my place, over by the zoo. A couple of us premed types had rented a place close to where those new soccer fields now are."

"Was anyone home when you got there?"

"I'm afraid not. The guys all had out-of-state summer

jobs. I had the whole place to myself until school started again in September."

"So you don't have an alibi," Lynn Felder gibed. She winked again at Gilroy.

The doctor's head whipped around. "Damn it, would you cut that out?"

"Whoa, Dr. Felder," Gilroy said. "This is all just for the record. I certainly don't think you had anything to do with Sellinzski's death. Besides, I've got the watch bill from that night, so I can probably find the officer who gave you the ride."

Felder straightened. "That won't be necessary. I know who it is. He used to hang around the drive-in all the time. In fact, he was always hitting on the girls. Even Cindy Jo, I think."

"Who was that?"

"Why, the attorney that was on TV. You know, the county prosecutor, Richard Collins."

The time was 2125.

40

The lockdown rooms were already occupied with a new crop of mentals, their screams and wall-pounding ignored by the medical staff as they hurried to perform other duties. Bakerman's gurney was wheeled through this area without stopping. His guard trudged behind, his own agitation rising. He had yet to receive confirmation he would be relieved anytime soon.

The orderly continued down the long sterile hallway and entered an awaiting elevator. The guard followed, watching his charge. Bakerman seemed to be resting peacefully, his eyes closed. Color was back in his cheeks, and his breathing was regular. His recovery from what had been diagnosed as a severe insulin reaction was expected to take only a few days.

The guard looked over to the orderly. He was a man about his own age, Hispanic, with short-cropped, black hair speckled with gray.

The doors closed.

"Been working here long?"

"No."

They began their ascent to an eighth-floor ward.

"Looks like you're busy."

He nodded.

The guard glanced at Bakerman again. "Hey, buddy. Can you hear me? If you can, listen up. Try anything funny and I'll blow your fuckin' brains out. You got that?" The guard chuckled.

The orderly's eyes widened.

The officer turned to him. "Just setting the ground rules. I once had a young punk who tried to make a run for it outta here, IV lines and all. Shit, I nearly broke my leg chasing that asshole down the emergency exit."

"I doubt he'll be going far."

"You never know about these old bastards."

The guard then bent close to Bakerman's ear. "You hear me, gramps? No funny business. At least not until someone else comes on duty." He straightened and chuckled again.

"When's the next officer coming in?"

"Better be less than an hour. My feet are killing me. Hey, where we going anyhow?"

"A regular room."

"Well, damn, at least I'll have a TV to watch."

The elevator slowed to a stop. When the doors opened, the orderly dutifully pushed the gurney out and proceeded towards a nearby nursing station. It was occupied by two staff members. The older one rose. "I take it that's Bakerman?" she said. "ER gave us a heads up he'd be coming here." She gave the patient a once-over. "He looks pretty tame. There shouldn't be a problem."

"What room do you want him in?"

"We'll use twenty-six. That wing is empty right now." She eyed the guard. "So we won't be scaring off any visitors."

The guard leaned on the counter. "Hey, you got any coffee around here?"

"I suppose we can find you a cup. Want anything in it?"

"Yeah, a couple shots of whiskey."

The nurse sighed as the guard turned and followed the cart down yet another long hallway. They came to a T; here, the orderly went to the left. The second nurse trailed them. When they reached the private room, she assisted the orderly in moving Bakerman from the gurney to the hospital bed. In the process, the patient stirred. His eyes opened. "Where—?"

"Harborview," the nurse replied. "Now, just relax, Mr. Bakerman. You're all right."

"But—?"

"Don't worry; we'll be taking good care of you. Now, we're going to slide you over onto your bed. Just let us do it, okay?"

He gave a weak nod.

"Ready? On three. One . . . two . . . and . . ."

In a fluid motion, the two hospital workers slid their patient onto the bed, then wrapped him up in several layers of thin cotton blankets.

"There," the nurse said. "All comfy and cozy."

Bakerman blinked, but suddenly caught sight of the guard. For a moment, they glared at one another; then the inmate's eyes glazed, and he seemed to sink back into semiconsciousness.

The nurse straightened. "Chances are, he'll sleep the rest of the night."

The orderly pulled the gurney away from the bed and departed. Both the nurse and the guard stepped back. She drew a curtain, blocking direct sight of the bed. "He's all yours."

The guard nodded and settled into the solitary easy chair, his hands fumbling with a television remote control.

"Keep it low. He needs to sleep."

"Yeah, right."

The nurse shook her head and stepped out—her bright

smile disintegrating. She made her way back to the station where the first nurse still remained.

"Something wrong?"

"What the hell are those jerks down in ER thinking?"

"What's the matter?"

"Don't you know who that guy is?"

"No."

"He's a serial killer. I saw it on TV. Jesus Christ, and we've got him up here with only one stinking, half-wit guard. God, I hate this place. I'm calling my union rep."

The time was 2133.

41

"Collins, huh?" Leah Harris replied into her cell phone. She was still parked in the shadows, half a block down from the darkened residence of Eckler's girlfriend. Her backup had been delayed. An in-progress domestic assault—a young man stabbing his father during a fight over drug use—had temporarily diverted all nearby units.

"Yeah, that's what Felder said, " Philip Gilroy reiterated. "Small world."

"That son of a bitch," Harris sighed. "He should have told me that."

"Does it make a difference?"

"It could—big-time. . . . Damn this case." Harris fumed for another moment, then refocused. "So, what kind of witness will Felder make?"

"Perfect. Get this: he's an MD slash college professor, and his wife is, too."

"Did you get a statement?"

"In writing." Gilroy laughed. "Hey, you wanna know what was funny, though?"

"What?"

"For a moment, his wife had me thinking that she thought her hubby might be the killer."

"From what you told me," Harris deadpanned, "he could be."

The line went silent.

"Hypothetically speaking," Harris quickly added. "But what's to say he didn't slip right back out of his house after Collins dropped him off? Any good defense attorney is going to point that out."

Gilroy suddenly chuckled. "Wouldn't that be something?"

"What, the doctor?"

"Yeah."

"It's a long shot, but we better do a little further checking on him. See, I'm sure Sellinzski knew, or was acquainted with, her killer. Run down everyone in that category; what's left at the end of the day will be our guy. . . . By the way, how come it was his wife that called, and not him?"

Gilroy snickered and said, "He claimed he was going to tomorrow. He was just too upset to do it right away. Said he felt responsible for Sellinzski's death. That he should have been giving her a ride home that late at night. Seeing it in the news today rekindled the guilt."

"You buy it?"

"Maybe—say, what about this Eckler guy? What's your gut feeling on him?"

"I think he's skipped town, that's what I think. There's been no sign of life here since I arrived. I got a bad feeling this place is going to be a water net, too."

"Hmmm. So, what do you want me to do from here?"

Harris thought for a moment and said, "Head this way. If no one is home, we'll call it a night. It's getting late. Tomorrow, first thing, say about eight, I want to lay everything out on our conference table and brainstorm what we have. Plus, we'll need to cut a material-witness warrant for Eckler and probably his girlfriend."

"What about Collins?"

"He's my fish to fry. When we're done recapping, I'm going to head over to his office and break his door down if I have to. He'd better have some pretty good answers to the questions I'm going to ask."

"You don't actually think he had anything to do with this?"

Harris thought for a moment. As she did, she massaged her stiff neck. Finally, she said, "It's funny about people and how you can misjudge their motivations."

"What do you mean?"

"In court this morning, when I was sitting on the hot seat and Collins was leading me to his finale, there were tears welling up in his eyes. I thought, God, what an actor. But you know what, now I'm thinking the tears might have been real."

"You sound tired."

"I am. Hey, I got to go. Ed just pulled in and it looks like he's got a couple of uniforms in tow. This should just take a couple of minutes. Tell ya what, I'll call if I need ya. If you don't hear from me, go ahead and head home, but be in the office by eight sharp."

"Oh, man!" Gilroy suddenly shrieked.

"Now what?"

"Nothing. I just gotta call dispatch."

"Something wrong?"

"Just some personal business."

"The blonde or the redhead?"

Gilroy didn't reply.

Harris pushed the END button and set her phone aside. She rolled down her window as Ed Jennings edged up. He was crouching, keeping his profile low. Leaning inward, he asked, "Which one is it, boss?"

"Second from the last, on the left."

Jennings craned his neck. All the other homes in this mixture of run-down working-class houses and student rentals were lit up, all except Doyle's. Not a light showed from any of the windows.

"Been like that since I got here," Harris continued. "There's an alley running in back. Have one of the guys plant themselves there. You and I will do the front door, and we'll have the other uniform cover us from the bottom of the steps. I doubt if anyone is home, but let's not take any chances."

"You have your gun?"

Harris leaned over to her glove box and flicked it open. From inside, she withdrew her Glock forty-caliber semiautomatic. She pulled the action back to confirm there was a round seated in the firing chamber, then slipped the weapon into her waistband at the small of her back. Next, she opened her purse and pulled out a pair of handcuffs and a small canister of pepper spray. These she slipped into her coat pockets. "Okay, I'm ready. You got your portable with you?"

Jennings nodded.

"Set it on TAC-five. Have the others guys do the same."

Jennings complied and slipped back to where the two backup officers had parked, out of sight around the block. He filled them in and returned with one. Harris was exiting when her eyes fell on the man. It was the same rookie she had chewed out only hours before. *Oh, great*, she thought. *He's going to be real eager to cover my ass.* She forced a smile. "Hey, we meet again."

The young man nervously scanned the area through the now misting rain. "What have we got this time, ma'am?" The eagerness in his voice told Harris that she hadn't made a permanent enemy.

"Looking for the same guy as last time."

He nodded with understanding.

Harris turned to Jennings. "Who's on back door?"

"MacRae."

"Good, he knows what he's doing."

In silence, the trio closed the distance to Doyle's narrow two-story residence, pausing when they reached the weathered concrete steps that led up from the sidewalk to a short walkway and a flight of rotting wooden stairs. All were damp and mossy.

"Check in with MacRae," Harris said in a hushed tone.

Jennings keyed the mike and whispered, "Are you set?"

"I'm in tight," MacRae replied.

"Anything moving?" Jennings asked.

"Nope. By the way, there's a carport back here, but it's empty."

"Right, we're going to try now."

Jennings looked to Harris. Although the nearby streetlights illuminated much of the adjacent area, several large fir trees caused deep shadows to fall on the path they were to take. The front door was indistinct from where they stood.

Harris took the lead and began the ascent. Jennings trailed, his gun already drawn but held covertly behind his back. The rookie hastily unsnapped his holster and followed.

When they reached the porch steps, Harris signaled him to remain at this position while she and Jennings proceeded. Slowly, they both continued upward, their ears straining for any telltale sign that someone might still be inside. Only the drizzle dripping down the broken gutters and the creaking of footsteps on the old wood textured the night air. When they reached the top, Jennings eased right, Harris left, until they were positioned on either side of the front door. For several seconds, they stood there, quietly assessing the sights, sounds, and smells. Then Harris looked questioningly to her partner.

"Be my guest," he mouthed in reply.

Harris nodded and commenced a solid knock, but her second rap caused the wooden entry to slip its latch and part. "Oh, shit," Harris breathed. She whipped her eyes towards the older detective. "It's open."

"Oh, great—try knocking again, I guess."

Harris thought for a moment. "What the hell." She did, this time harder, but there was still no response

Jennings straightened. "Hey, son," he called down, "toss your flashlight up here."

The officer pitched the device to Harris's outstretched hand while Jennings brought his portable radio up and keyed the mike again. "No sign of anybody, but now we've got an open door."

"Roger that. I'll sit tight."

Jennings looked to Harris. "So what do you want to do now?"

She didn't respond. Instead, she took the flashlight she had been flipped and, with her toe, pushed the door until it was wide-open. "Seattle Police," she called out. "Is there anyone home?"

Silence.

Leaning on the jamb, Harris illuminated the front room, sweeping the area with the powerful beam. All was still and appeared normal, though several half-filled boxes lay about, seemingly abandoned in the middle of being packed with personal items.

"Looks like someone is moving out," Jennings offered. "Shall we give it a further look-see?"

"Is that legal?" the rookie spoke up.

Harris turned. "What do you think?"

The young officer shrugged.

Harris glanced at Jennings. He winked back. Returning to the officer, she said, "That's a good question. If we were to simply walk in, anything we found of a criminal nature probably couldn't be used in a court of law. However . . ."

The detective sergeant's demeanor suddenly grew grim. She looked upward and continued wistfully, "I suspect all present will note the concern on my face regarding the possible disappearance of Nancy Doyle. Her boss has reported her missing. Therefore, as part of our community caretaking responsibility, it would be prudent to do a cursory walk-through of her home in order to ascertain that she is not here. This is a welfare check. After all, she might be inside and in need of medical care."

Jennings chuckled. "Boss, you've got more ways to get inside a house than a pack of termites."

"Skip it."

Harris instructed the young officer to remain where he was while she and Jennings entered. Jennings in turn told MacRae they were going inside and to continue his watch of the back door. Cautiously, the two detectives entered, eyeing everything in their path, switching on lights as they went. In five minutes they had completed their task, even the basement, its spidery dampness causing Harris to shudder.

Jennings then radioed MacRae. "We're coming out your way."

Two clicks confirmed that the message had been received. And as the detectives emerged through the rear door, MacRae was there to meet them. "So?" he asked.

Harris sighed. "Looks like she got interrupted as she was packing to clear out."

"What do you mean?"

"All her newer clothes are stacked on her bed, jewelry and toiletries in a shoe box. My guess is that she was right in the middle of grabbing just the essentials and getting the hell out of here."

"With Eckler?"

"Probably."

"So what are we going to do now?" Jennings asked.

Harris folded her arms and kicked at a chunk of moss. "We'll need a search warrant to really toss the place, but that shouldn't be hard to get. In fact, I'd bet the drug dicks will want to give this place a once-over. There's enough of a tie between the apartment and here to get paper."

"That's step one," the senior detective mused. "What about two through two hundred?"

"God, I don't know," Harris groaned. "I'm getting tired. Maybe we have a uniform sit on the place tonight, and we do the search tomorrow."

"Don't quit for my sake," Jennings offered. "I can stick around."

Harris smiled. "Thanks," she said, then added, "Tell ya what, I'll get a hold of the drug dicks and see if they can head over here right now. It'll take 'em ten minutes to amend their warrant on Eckler's place to include this location. Then we can tag along when they rip the place apart."

Jennings thought for a moment and nodded agreement.

42

Harris clicked off her phone and leaned back in her car seat. While the recent surge of adrenaline from the search had recharged her body, it was a temporary fix. Already, the intoxicating effect was waning as the muscles in the nape of her neck resumed throbbing. She reached back and massaged them more while thoughts of the case churned in her brain. The images were loud and disjointed, like a school yard at recess. Having an eyewitness who actually saw Bakerman and Sellinzski interacting weeks prior to the attack was a big plus, but a defense attorney could rip wide holes in that identification. A thirty-year-old recollection without physical proof left too much room for doubt. Further, Dr. Felder's own lack of an alibi, however improbable his involvement, was fodder for the opposition. It created reasonable doubt. Enough so that even if Harris was siting on the jury, she could not in good conscience vote to convict. *And what about Collins?* Harris pondered. He was another wild card she couldn't figure.

Harris yawned and sank deeper into her seat. She was about to close her eyes and give them a brief rest when abruptly her passenger door began to open. Instinctively, her hand whipped to her waistband and the semiautomatic still lodged there. However, before she could grab hold, a familiar profile began to ease in. "God, Frank," Harris blurted. "What are you trying to do, give me a heart attack?"

Milkovich settled into the seat beside Harris. He had a bothered look on his face. "Hi," was all he said.

Harris twisted so that the back of her head rested on her window. She could sense something wrong but was unsure what. She therefore avoided a direct inquiry and instead asked, "How'd you know I was here?"

"Hey," Milkovich replied with a hint of sarcasm, "I'm a cop. I called dispatch, and guess what? They actually gave out your location to me."

Harris nodded. "I guess that was a dumb question." She changed subjects. "How'd your meeting go with the chief?"

"Okay, I guess."

Harris crossed her arms. "Well, what happened?"

Milkovich shrugged. "Not much."

"Frank—"

"Leah—"

Silence.

Milkovich fidgeted in his seat. Finally, he reached out and touched Harris's hand. "God, you're freezing." Instinctively, he wrapped his palms around hers and gave a gentle squeeze.

She felt his warmth.

Slowly their eyes met, and without another word, both leaned towards each other until their lips touched. Instantly, their bond renewed, and for a brief moment, all thoughts and worries of the day faded. For nearly a minute, they remained locked until the awkward position they had assumed forced them both to pull back.

"I'm sorry," Harris gushed.

Milkovich feigned surprise. "For what?"

"You know for what, for putting you off this afternoon, and being a shit to your pal Jerry."

A slight smile formed on Milkovich's lips. "It's no big."

"You liar," Harris exclaimed. She reached over and lovingly swatted his knee. "I embarrassed you, and earlier when you wanted to talk, I ignored you. That's not right."

Milkovich shifted in his seat and said, "Christ, Leah, I understand. You're right in the middle of a homicide investigation. Besides, I got my own quirks you have to put up with."

Harris nodded, but tentatively.

"Really, I do understand."

Harris suddenly leaned back over, gave Milkovich a quick kiss, then resettled into her seat. "So, tell me, what's the new chief like? More deadwood?"

"I kinda liked him."

"You're kidding."

"No, and before I had a chance to resign from IA, he sweet-talked me into doing at least another year."

Harris's eyes brightened. "Hey, that's great."

Milkovich cocked his head. "Wait a second—why in the world would you want me to stay in IA? You know how much I hate it."

Harris glanced away.

"Come on, what gives?"

"Nothing." She looked back.

"Now I know you're lying."

Harris's lower lip began to twitch.

More silence.

Milkovich suddenly thumped his forehead. "Now I get it. You want me to stay in IA, don't you?"

More silence.

"Come on, would you please say something?"

Harris stammered. "It's . . . well . . ."

"Come on, out with it."

"Ah, damn it, Frank." Harris sat upright. "You don't get it, do you?"

"Get what?" He too straightened. "Jesus, Leah, you've got me so confused. I haven't a clue what you're talking about."

Harris drew a deep breath and said, "Don't you see, Frank? If you opt out of IA and take a field assignment, we'll never see each other again. With my crazy schedule, having you working eight to five made it possible for us to have some semblance of a real relationship. You go back to the field, and it's over. I can see it right now."

"We can work it out."

"Been there, done that. And the burden is always dumped back on me. It's always, 'Hey, Leah, why don't you take the promotion and do admin stuff? Then we could have more time together.' The hell with that. I'll never be a paper shuffler." Harris's face was now red.

Milkovich reared back. "I'd never ask you to give up your job. Never in a million years. I know how much all this means to you. Don't you see I love you for that?"

Harris raised a brow. Her body became less rigid. "You wouldn't—?"

"Of course not," Milkovich said with open arms. "Where in the world did you get an idea like that?"

"And you're going to stay in IA for at least another year?"

Milkovich's arms came down in defeat. "I'm afraid so, but get this: I'm going to be reporting directly to the chief. No more having to run the brass gauntlet."

"I love you," Harris burst out, and she leaped at him. Seconds later, the car windows had fogged.

43

Leah Harris slid back over the console and settled back into her seat. She brushed her hair back and joked, "God, I wish I had a bigger car."

"That's not why I'm here," Milkovich said with a sly smile. He twisted in his seat and reached to the floorboards. "But what the hell—"

Harris cocked her head. "It's not?"

"No," Milkovich replied as he retrieved the radio microphone that had been knocked free from its mount. He set it back in the holder and continued. "Right after I met with the chief, I got a page from Jer. The hazmat team was just wrapping up Eckler's apartment and came across something in the garbage that he thought might be of interest to you."

"Why didn't he just call me?"

Milkovich didn't respond.

"Ah, never mind. What'd they find?"

Milkovich withdrew some papers from his breast pocket and unfolded them. "Hit your dome light."

Harris complied. A moment later, they were bathed in a reddish glow, the standard white bulb having been replaced by one tinted to preserve night vision. She took hold of the documents and studied them. The first page was a photocopy of the front and back of a standard letter envelope. It was easy to tell that it had been crumpled into a ball before being discarded. The image captured all of the crinkles and creases. The envelope was addressed to

> Carl Eckler
> 1445 NW 56th #A2
> Seattle WA 98105

The return was stamped

> Dr. Jacob Vandegrift, Ph.D.
> Assistant Director
> Sex Offender/Substance Abuse Treatment Unit
> Mail Drop 1421
> Monroe State Reformatory
> Monroe, WA 98272

Harris looked up. "Hey, that's the fellow that's been calling me today."

"I knew you'd find this interesting. Look at the next page."

Harris did. It, too, had been crumpled before being discarded. She drew the page close. It said:

> *Dear Carl,*
> *Thank you for placing your confidence in me.*
> *While I am not an expert on substance abuse, as part*
> *of your twelve-step program, your disclosures are an*
> *important part of your recovery. I wish you the best*
> *of luck.*
> *Unfortunately, I was not permitted to follow up on*
> *the information you provided me. As you are well*
> *aware, the prison has become extremely crowded,*

*and anything delaying the release of short-time
prisoners is, to be blunt, overlooked. I cannot tell
you how frustrating this can be. Thus, Mr. Bakerman
will be released as scheduled despite your
suspicions.*

*Good luck on the outside. If you need a reference,
feel free to use my name.*

Sincerely, . . .

Harris let the copy drop. "He did report it. . . ."

"Guess this takes Eckler off the prime suspect list."

"Maybe, maybe not."

Milkovich raised a questioning brow.

"This may sound far-fetched, but perhaps Eckler is
smarter than we think. He still could have framed the whole
thing, like some kind of insurance policy."

Milkovich pondered the thought and said, "Well, he's lost
his touch cooking meth. Jerry field-tested the residue in the
garbage can. Real low quality, like an amateur made it . . ."

Harris barely heard the words. This newest discovery
sent her mind spinning. The different strands had unraveled
yet again. She knew if Eckler was indeed telling the truth,
then Bakerman had to be her man. But the ring? Bakerman
couldn't have put it there, and if Eckler hadn't—then who?
Harris's eyes bored into the night. She now realized there
had to be another player. Someone with his own game to
play? Perhaps connected to Bakerman or Eckler—perhaps
not. A free agent whose agenda was still buried deep in the
past.

Harris sank in her seat, only to straighten as her radio's
alert tone triggered. It pulsed a brief, shrieking pitch through
the interior of her car. Both she and Milkovich instinctively
turned an ear as the 911 dispatcher spat out, "Armed intruder, Fifty-seventh and Kirkwood Place. Caller on cell

phone has fled out the back door. Possible others still inside."

"Ah, shit," Harris groaned. "That's going to suck up all the manpower."

Nearby units began checking in. "Four one from Phinney . . ." "Eight six from Fremont . . ." "Five three, I'm right on top of the place—dispatch, go ahead with the numbers."

The dispatcher came on again. "Responding units, this will be the two-story white house—five seven zero two. . . . Stand by for further."

"Wonder if it's that kid from the earlier assault?" Milkovich theorized. He leaned back in his seat and sighed. "You're right—Cummins and his gang will have to divert to this if it doesn't get resolved quick."

They listened further.

"Responding units," the dispatcher continued in a purposeful tone, "be advised that the suspect is a white male, about twenty years of age, wearing jeans and a black leather jacket. He is armed with a hunting knife. Caller further advises that there are several handguns inside the residence and two other roommates that did not get out."

"Oh, great," Harris groaned.

A patrol supervisor inserted herself into the radio traffic. "We need to set up containment. This is probably our boy. He's methed out, so be careful."

"Roger that, two nine," dispatch said.

Other radios clicked in affirmation.

The patrol supervisor set out strategy. "Five three, take the north end of Kirkwood; eight six, you got the alley; I'll set up south—break, dispatch?"

"Go ahead, two nine."

"I want a K-9 unit out here, and alert any investigative units in the area to respond. I need more bodies."

"Received—also?"

"Go ahead, dispatch."

"Shall I page out SWAT?"

"Stand by, let me get on scene."

Milkovich looked at Harris. "So, what do you want to do?"

She shrugged as someone tapped on the window of her car. Harris turned. It was Jennings. He had been waiting in his car around the corner. She eased her window down.

"So?" the older detective said as he stooped. "Do we respond?"

Harris thought for a moment. "Let's just bag it and go home."

"You sure?"

She nodded and said, "You wanna spend the rest of the night freezing your tush off while a hostage negotiator tries to sweet-talk the kid out?"

"Not really."

"Go home, then. We'll do the house first thing tomorrow."

He agreed and departed. Harris turned. Milkovich was now exiting. "Where ya going?"

"My car."

Harris winked. "What's your hurry, big boy?"

Milkovich eased back down. "What'd ya have in mind?"

She reached over and squeezed a thigh. However, instead of responding in kind, Milkovich looked past her. He deadpanned, "Ed's back."

Harris frowned, twisted, and rolled her window down once more.

"Hey, sorry to interrupt, but I promised my youngest I'd give her a ride to school tomorrow. You mind if I'm a few minutes late?"

"Of course not," Harris sighed. "Take all the time you need."

Jennings smiled and trotted off.

Harris turned back. "Where were we?"

Milkovich was again preparing to exit.

"Hey, you're not going to—?"

"It's almost midnight," he sighed. "Let's both get a good night's sleep and make a date for tomorrow. No matter what happens, we knock off by five and make an evening of it. Promise?"

Harris nodded reluctantly. The homicide detective was certain it would take a miracle for that to ever happen.

44

"I need your phone," the young corrections officer said in a panicked tone. He had replaced Bakerman's original guard at eleven and had just come from the convict's room.

The nurse at the floor station, whom he had been flirting with since his arrival, was slow to react. She asked, "Is there something wrong?"

"Damn it, just give me the phone."

She handed up the receiver from her work space as two other graveyard nurses turned to see what the commotion was about.

"Is there a problem with Bakerman?" the supervising member inquired.

He waved her off and rapidly punched in a familiar number. Snubbed, she turned to her subordinate and said, "Go check on him. Make sure he's okay."

The guard spun and shouted, "Stay right here! No one goes near the room without me." Meanwhile, his free hand had already grabbed for his holstered weapon.

The woman froze.

"It's Gordy," the guard spat into the telephone. "I need the sergeant—get him now!"

"He's tied up."

"Jesus Christ, I don't care what he's doing. I gotta talk to him."

"He's, well . . ."

"Goddamn it, I don't care—get him out of the head. It's an emergency."

"Okay . . ."

The guard's face was now flushed. Sweat dripped from his forehead.

The nursing staff exchanged nervous glances. One inched towards a silent alarm secreted beneath the counter.

"Hurry up. . . . Hurry up," the guard continued into the mouthpiece. He waited anxiously, his eyes darting wildly.

"What the hell's the matter?" the supervising nurse finally demanded.

"It's Bakerman," the guard grunted.

"What's wrong with him?"

He was about to reply, but instead, he stiffened. There was a new voice on the receiver. The guard sucked a deep breath and blurted, "Sarge, we got a really big problem here. . . ."

45

The pair of officers had quietly parked their patrol cars three houses down from where this newest call had emanated. Per procedure, they had entered the neighborhood without lights or sirens and had even doused their headlamps a block away to conceal their approach. It had been a long, tiring night. With the hostage situation still continuing, and all available units still on that scene, these two officers had drawn the short straw and been detailed to answer all the other calls in their sector.

"I got an open door," the lead officer whispered as he cautiously peered around the groomed boxwood at the west corner of the large home. His partner was three paces behind, hunched and waiting for direction.

"What do you want to do?"

The first officer stepped back and straightened. "We wait here for more backup, or we go in. What's your pleasure?"

"I'm ready to go home."

"Me too. With that kid still holed up on Kirkwood, it could be an hour before someone gets shook loose."

The second officer bobbed his head as the first keyed his shoulder mike. He whispered, "Seven one, dispatch?"

"Go ahead, seven one."

"We have an open front door."

The radio waves crackled. "All units, Queen Anne sector, seven one has an open door."

"Like there's anyone within five miles of us right now," the second officer sniped.

The lead officer told dispatch, "We're muting radios and going in—close the air."

"Received, seven one—break, all cars and stations, seven one and six two are initiating a building search. The air is closed for emergency traffic only."

"Shall we?" the lead officer asked his partner.

The second officer tipped his head as both men drew their weapons and began a slow approach to the front door, each step carefully placed to avoid signaling their presence.

At the entry, the pair bracketed the doorjamb and paused to listen for any explanatory sounds—there were none. Only a cold silence met their ears. Keeping cover, the first officer knelt and leaned left to peek into the void, temporarily illuminating it with his flashlight.

He retreated.

"Well?" the second officer mouthed.

The first officer shook his head to indicate he had seen nothing amiss. "Long hallway, staircase at the end. Two doors on the left, one on the right. Everything's open."

"No alarm?"

The first officer reached downward and felt the wood molding. His fingers soon stopped. "Got a contact point. The system must not have been armed." He struggled to his feet. "Ah, the hell with it. Let's just knock and announce. If there's anyone in here who's not supposed to be, with a little luck, they'll just skedaddle out the back way."

The second officer nodded. He reached up, and pounded on the heavy, leaded-glass doorway. "Seattle Police, anyone inside?"

Silence.

"Seattle Police, we're coming in. . . . Is anyone home?"

More silence.

"Well?"

"I guess so."

The first officer stepped in and jogged to his right. The second officer followed but veered the opposite way. Both used their flashlights to sweep their field of view, but saw nothing to concern them.

"I'm hitting the lights."

The first officer flipped several switches. Suddenly, they were bathed in bright light from an overhead chandelier, with wall sconces lining the way.

"That ought to wake the dead."

The second officer chuckled and said in a still-low tone, "Doesn't look like anyone is home. I wonder if there's just something screwy with the phone system. Those damn cordless ones can trigger 911s when their batteries go on the fritz. I had a call like that just a couple of nights ago."

"We still gotta check each room."

The second officer sighed, but kept his gun at the ready. Despite their cynicism, years of training and experience had taught both officers that the most dangerous situations were those that seemed innocuous at first. Barking-dog calls or landlord-tenant disputes were more likely to get you killed than responding to a bank robbery or bar fight.

"Hey, did I ever tell you about the time we were looking for a pipe bomb planted in an abandoned house? Some kids were screwing around with their chemistry sets and decided it'd be fun to blow a place up."

The first officer didn't reply. He had already begun moving towards the first door.

"Musta been half a dozen of us tiptoeing through the old place."

"Ya find anything?"

"Not at first, at least not until I took a break back outside and sat down on a log pile stacked against the garage—you wouldn't believe it."

"Shhhh—I'll go left and you go right."

"One . . . two . . ."

The pair of officers again bracketed the door, then plunged into the dim room, keeping their profiles low and away from backlighting. As before, they listened for any sound, then lit up the space with their flashlights.

"Nice library," the second officer said, straightening while his partner flipped on the room lights. He stepped over to the fireplace and felt the hearth. It was cold to the touch. Meanwhile the first officer stepped about the area.

"So what happened?"

"You mean about the bomb?"

"Yeah."

The second officer chuckled. "I found it."

"How?"

"While I was sitting on that stack of rotting firewood, I looked down towards the ground, and guess what?"

"Just tell the story."

The second officer gazed to his left. "That door must connect to the next room."

"Okay, I give, so what happened?"

He chuckled. "Two inches below my crotch, poking out from a space in the wood was a length of det cord. Son of a bitch, I was sitting right on top of the goddamn thing."

"What'd you do?"

"Wet my pants—Christ, what do you think I did?"

"Whoa, lookee here."

The second officer paused and focused on what his partner had found. The first officer had holstered his pistol and was now bending to the floor beside a leather couch.

"Whatcha got?"

"A remote phone." He straightened and showed off his prize.

"What'd I tell ya? I bet it fell off this arm and activated." He pushed the OFF button and set the handset on an end table. "Come on."

The two exited the way they had entered and moved down to the next room. It too, was large, and like before, they entered with caution, although at a diminished level.

"Nice pool table," the second officer remarked. "Hit the switch—I want to get a better look at it."

The first officer complied; however, when the room was bathed in bright light, both officers froze.

Behind the antique billiard table was a human figure, petite in size, crumpled on the polished hardwood floor. She lay in a pool of blood—her own. The left side of her head was crushed, her brain oozing from the large open wound. The two officers rushed to her side, but it was immediately clear that nothing could be done to save her. Death had been instantaneous. Probably from the bloodied fireplace poker that lay discarded three feet beyond.

46

Harris had slept through the first page; however, the second, coming five minutes later, roused her from a deep sleep. Checking in, Captain Varna had been apologetic. "Sorry, Leah," he had said, "but I'll need you to drop everything and put your team on this. We still have half the department out with that damn barricaded suspect, and we'll have to rotate in some fresh bodies real soon."

In a fog, the homicide detective had slipped out of bed and struggled to her bathroom. It wasn't until she had brushed her teeth and pulled a set of nylon warm-ups over her fatigued body that she did a double take. Instantly, she dived for her telephone and re-called dispatch. After reconfirming the information, Harris sprinted for her car, gathering en route her running shoes, a Gore-Tex jacket, and a baseball cap to cover her disheveled hair.

Twenty minutes later, Leah Harris pulled to the curb across from Sister Cecilia's Queen Anne Hill home. Several patrol cars, blue lights flickering, already kept watch. They blocked the street at either end while several more were parked adjacent to the driveway. An ambulance was inside the gate; its crew and several officers were standing in a somber circle. Harris headed for this group after fishing her department badge from the door pocket. It hung on a chain and, once on, dangled from her neck like an outsize dog tag.

"Hey, Sarge," Officer Liftner said as he caught sight of her. Others in the group stopped talking and turned, too.

Harris closed the distance. "Okay, what do we have?" she said with authority. "All dispatch told me was an elderly female, blunt trauma to the head. Any idea how long ago it happened?"

Officer Bowles stepped forward. He and his partner, Tommy Purello, had been the ones to discover the body. Harris knew them both. They were competent veterans.

"The blood's starting to cake," Bowles started. Purello nodded in agreement. "There's drying on the edges. But she's still lukewarm to the touch." He glanced at his watch. "That was exactly thirty-nine minutes ago."

"Who's all been inside?"

"Just me, Tommy, a medic, and right now one of your dicks with a couple other guys finishing up a sweep of the house. Once we found the body, we stuck with her until we got help."

Harris turned to the medic. "What's your take?"

"Massive blow to the head." He raised his hand to his forehead and fingered his brow. "Right here. Probably from the fireplace poker next to her. Odds are, she was dead before she hit the ground."

"Anything else?"

"My guess," Bowles offered, "she was in the process of calling 911, when the intruder surprised her. She dropped the phone and tried to escape into the adjoining billiard room. She was followed and—"

"Any other obvious wounds, resistance marks, or indication of a sexual assault?"

Purello was next to speak up. Unlike his partner's, his

voice was shaky. The sight of the elderly dead woman was still vivid for him. "N-not that I saw."

"Okay, anything else?"

"Yeah," Bowles replied. "Her hands were clutching a string of rosary beads."

At that moment, Harris caught sight of Ed Jennings arriving. She waved to signal her presence, then turned back to the group. "I want written statements from all of you. Go back to your cars and do them now. I want to know everything you saw, heard, and smelled, from the moment you got here to right now—understand?"

They all nodded in unison.

"And no one leaves, or does anything else, until I say so."

There were further nods.

"And for God's sake, kill all the blue lights; we're starting to draw a crowd."

The men dispersed.

Moments later Ed Jennings reached her side. Unlike Harris, he was neatly dressed in his usual conservative suit, tie, and freshly pressed white shirt. However, his typical unflappable demeanor was missing. "I can't believe it," he grimly said. "I was just talking to her, what, twelve hours ago—you think there's a connection to the Sellinzski case?"

"There's got to be."

"But what?"

Harris thought for a moment but could provide no immediate reply.

Jennings shifted nervously on his feet. "How'd she get it?"

"Crushed skull."

Jennings groaned. "My God, I may have been the last one to have seen her . . ." He bit at his lip and looked about. "Her car's gone. Anyone check the garage to see if it's in there?"

"Haven't got that far."

Jennings drew a deep breath and let it go slowly. It steadied his nerves. His focus sharpened, and his game face began to form. "Okay, how'd the call come in?"

"On 911, open line. The number was punched in, but the dispatcher heard nothing. The line went dead right afterward."

"Have you been inside?"

"No. Phil's doing a sweep of the place right now with a couple of uniforms. When he comes out, we'll put together a plan."

"I hear they're still out with that kid on Kirkwood."

"Yeah," Harris replied. "Now aren't you glad we slipped out of there when we did? At least we got a couple hours of sleep."

Jennings remained doleful.

"What's the matter?"

"My daughter. She's going to be mad at me for a week because I didn't drive her to school this morning." He sighed and twisted his neck in a circle. He and Harris both knew there was another long day ahead.

47

Philip Gilroy emerged from the front door of the large home with two officers in tow. All were somber. Seeing Harris and Jennings nearby, he headed in their direction.

"Lovely morning," he quipped.

Harris skipped all pleasantries. "How's it look?"

"No sign of any intrusion—exterior doors are all dead-bolted from the inside. Same with the windows. Whoever did it had to have come right in the front door."

"Was her car in the garage?" Jennings pursued. "There was a new Volvo parked out front when I was here last night."

Gilroy shook his head no.

"First thing, Ed," Harris said, turning to him.

"Do an all-cars-registered-to," he said knowingly. "And get an APB out."

"You're reading my mind."

He finally smiled.

Harris turned back to Gilroy. "Speak to me."

He brushed his unshowered hair back and said, "The place is as clean as a whistle except for the library. An end table is askew. The victim or the perp musta knocked into it. There's a fresh scuff mark on the hardwood floor."

"Was her bed slept in?"

"Doesn't look like it." Harris returned to Jennings. "When you left that voice mail for me last night, you mentioned you thought she wasn't fully disclosing. Any second thoughts on that?"

Jennings wrinkled his brow and replied, "Sorry, I can't put a finger on it. I just sensed it, especially when I was talking about Sellinzski being in the nursing home. By the way, she did say she was going to some sort of reception after I left."

"Where?"

Jennings shrugged. "Sorry—I didn't ask."

Harris folded her arms. After a moment's contemplation she said, "First thing, I'll scratch out a search warrant. Ed, you see about the Volvo. Phil, you work the neighbors. As soon as Purello and Bowles have their statements done, post one at the front door and one at the gate. We'll let all the other units go except for a couple to handle the street. No sense attracting any more attention than we need to. The press will be on us soon enough. Once we've got signed paper, we'll go back in and scour the place."

"What are we looking for?"

Harris turned slowly about. She looked at the still open front door, the small crowd beyond the iron fence, milling about in overcoats and pajamas, and lastly the ambulance crew preparing to depart—empty-handed. In a muted tone she simply replied, "The reason Sister Cecilia had to die."

48

Frank Milkovich rolled over and groaned. A loud static now filled his bedroom from a clock radio set to trigger at six forty-five. Reaching out, he fumbled with the appliance until he managed to silence the noise. Straightening, he yawned, flipped on a light, and stared wearily ahead.

His plan for the day was to visit the evidence warehouse to get a visual sense of the layout, then look up Stoddard and get his input now that he'd had time to cool down. Further, Patrick Dellhanney had mentioned a number of names. Two were still employed with the department. They would also have to be interviewed in depth.

Another thought came to mind as he stretched. Perhaps within the bowels of the King County Jail, records might still exist of the work crews. And while there were no indications that the freezer had been purposely sabotaged, a list of those inmates who had worked at the facility might prove interesting.

Milkovich eased out of bed and ambled to his kitchen. He activated his coffeemaker, then turned to the thirteen-inch television set resting on the bar separating the cooking area from the adjacent living space. With his remote control, he turned it on and flicked through the channels until he came to a local station with a newscast. It was just beginning. He stepped over to his refrigerator and withdrew a carton of milk, then pulled out a bowl from the cupboard. He retrieved the box of Cheerios left out from the previous day's use and was about to pour some, when the lead story immediately caught his attention.

"Seattle Police still surround a Greenlake area home, where an eighteen-year-old man allegedly burst into the residence at eleven last night and took an occupant hostage. For more on the story, KOMO reporter Julie Kwan is live at the scene."

Milkovich set the box of Cheerios down.

"That's right, Jim," the reporter replied. "It's now been ten hours since Jason Eckler, the man police have identified as the suspect in this case, broke into the home of several college students and proceeded to take one hostage. The other members of the residence were able to flee out the back door."

"What the—?" Milkovich's eyes were now glued to the set.

The camera cut from the reporter and zoomed in on a darkened home beyond the police barrier. "Authorities here say that Eckler is wanted in connection with a reported assault on his father that occurred last evening some ten blocks away. It appears he fled from there on foot, and when police units attempted to take him into custody, he managed to elude them and enter uninvited into this house. Since then it has been a standoff, though I am told that police have had several telephone conversations with the young man. He has refused, however, to surrender or let his hostage go."

The news anchor inquired, "Do we know what condition the suspect's father is in?"

The camera refocused on the reporter. She frowned. "That's part of this whole sad story, Jim. According to the young man's girlfriend, Eckler's father came to her house last night, and an argument broke out over drugs. That's when the son allegedly attacked his father. The girlfriend called 911, but before police had arrived, both men had fled. Mr. Eckler Senior is evidently also wanted by police on drug charges."

"That is an unfortunate situation. What about the other neighbors in the area?"

The reporter nodded knowingly. "Early on, police went door-to-door along this entire street and evacuated anyone who was present. From that point, no one has been allowed back in. Red Cross put many of them up for the night in local motels, but at this point, I am sure most of them are ready to come home."

"Have you spoken with any police officials there at the scene? Have they said what their plan may be?"

The reported nodded again. "Officials here are being very tight-lipped about what they are planning. They are obviously afraid the suspect may have a radio or television on to monitor what is happening outside. However, I have seen numerous SWAT team members taking positions close in. I have also seen several of these officers carrying what appear to be sniper type rifles."

"I understand that it is the policy of the Seattle Police Department to continue to negotiate until every last effort has been made, and that shooting a suspect with a hostage is only done as the very last resort."

"That's right, Jim. In fact, that has been the one thing that I have been constantly told by officials here, that they will give the order to fire only when it is clear that the hostage is in immediate mortal danger. They say that even if it takes all day and another night, they will stay on scene here, and try for a peaceful resolution of this matter."

"Looks like it could be a long day out there."

"That it does, Jim. . . . Reporting live from Greenlake, Julie Kwan, KOMO TV News."

"Eckler?" Milkovich murmured as the anchor fixed his gaze on another TelePrompTer and said, "We'll be keeping you updated on this story as it continues to unfold—meanwhile, on Queen Anne Hill, we have more breaking news. For that, we go to our Jennifer Rogers."

The television image shifted to a shivering blond female clutching a mike. Meanwhile, in the background, the dawn light revealed several police officers stringing yellow crime scene tape.

"That's right, Jim," the reporter started. "Things are very unclear at this moment and police are being tight-lipped here, too, but it appears that the body of an elderly female was found earlier this morning inside the large residence down this street where you can see all the activity."

The camera zoomed in and showed a number of plain-clothes detectives huddled near the porch. Milkovich leaned close. "Leah?"

"From what we have learned from neighbors, the home belongs to one of Seattle's founding families and an heir still resides here. We are uncertain whether this is our victim or not. In speaking briefly with a detective sergeant, she would only confirm that the woman was clearly a victim of foul play. No motive or other details were given at this time."

"Do we know who discovered the body?"

"Apparently police did when they responded to a 911 call originating from this home."

"Thanks, Jennifer. I'm sure you'll being staying right on top of this story for the rest of the day."

The blond reporter nodded and the scene returned to the newsroom.

Milkovich was no longer paying attention. He had already stepped around the kitchen counter and had his hand on a wall-mounted telephone. The number he was punching in was well memorized. As the call was connecting, another news story began. Milkovich, with his eyes turned away and ear pressed hard against the receiver, missed it.

"In what has been a very busy night for Seattle Police, reports are now coming in of an escaped King County Jail prisoner who was being treated at Harborview Medical Center. For more on this story we go to . . ."

The time was 0711.

49

The still-idling vehicle had come to rest sideways on a residential sidewalk after jumping the curb and skidding along a grassy strip. Chunks of muddy sod encrusted the wheel wells. Miraculously, the older-model Dodge had missed a long series of parked cars, mailboxes, and shrubs lining the length of the erratic path. Neighbors had yet to stir; however, the vehicle had barely settled in when a passing patrol car happened on scene. It stopped just short of the first skid mark, and a veteran officer wearily emerged and ambled over. He reached out, grabbed the door handle of the car, and pulled hard. Immediately, he caught the strong odor of alcohol permeating the stale, interior air.

"Ah, shit," he muttered as he recognized the driver. The gray-haired cop leaned in and gave the slumped, semi-conscious man a shove with his nightstick. "Goddamn it, Roy, wake up. If that new sergeant finds you here, he'll have your ass arrested. The little punk is already bucking for lieutenant."

The officer jabbed Roy again. The lab tech stirred, and a bloodshot eye peeked open.

"Damn it," the officer urged, "move it. He'll be pulling up any minute."

Another eye popped open. Stoddard groaned.

"Come on—oh, shit, give me that bottle."

Confused but gaining awareness, Stoddard looked about. Suddenly he realized his former squad mate was referring to the near empty fifth of bourbon still clutched in his right hand. He obediently surrendered it. The officer stepped back from Roy's vehicle and tossed the glass container into the bushes. He then surveyed the lack of damage to the tech's personal car. "Jesus, you're a lucky son of a bitch."

Stoddard straightened. His head was clearing. "Did someone call this in?"

"No, at least not yet. I was just heading to the barn when I saw you here."

"Got a smoke?"

"Christ, there's no time. There's a rookie sergeant rolling this way. You okay to drive?"

Stoddard nodded.

"Then get your ass outta here."

Stoddard slowly placed his hand on the steering wheel and looked about.

"Goddamn it, just back it out."

The tech nodded again. He reached down and placed the transmission into reverse. Twisted in his seat, he began easing his way towards the pavement. His colleague assisted, giving him hand signals. Moments later, Stoddard's car bounced onto the street and swerved into the lane. Roy gave a quick wave, put the transmission into drive, and proceeded down the block, disappearing around the first corner he came to. As his taillights faded, the officer turned, and froze. From the other end of the street, a second patrol car appeared. It pulled in behind his, and a young sergeant eagerly exited. "Whatcha got?" he called out.

The veteran shrugged. "Looks like a drunk lost it. See the tire tracks?"

The sergeant eyed the fresh marks, then looked up. "Any sign of the car that did this?"

"Not a one."

The sergeant looked suspiciously about until his gaze fell on a scrap of paper near a deep rut. He bent down and retrieved it. "Hmmm," he mumbled. "It's dry. This must've come out of the vehicle that did this." He handed the slip of paper over to his subordinate. "There's a phone number and a woman's name—Donna, I think it says. Try the number and give the third degree to whoever answers. Damn drunks. I'd love to nail the bastard who's responsible for this."

The veteran took the note, nodded submissively, and slipped it into his jacket. When his supervisor turned and headed back to his car, he balled it up and was about to toss it when he reconsidered. There was a chance the sergeant would follow up to see if he made the call. If he didn't and was found out, it would be three days off without pay. Begrudgingly he shoved the note back in his pocket. He'd make the call when he got back to the precinct, then pencil-whip a report to cover Roy's ass. He knew Stoddard would have done the same for him.

50

"Damn it, Richard," Linda Reese muttered beneath her breath. "Answer the door." The prosecutor's sister was standing, arms knotted, on the porch of her brother's Magnolia Bluff home. Though the houses were modest in size, this older neighborhood of the Foursquare and Norman-style residences were a favorite for the city's established professionals who preferred homes with patina to the suburban faux mansions crowding the suburban hills beyond.

Reese glanced at her watch. "God, we're going to be late." This time, she pounded on the entrance. That attracted the attention of a retired neighbor retrieving his morning newspaper. The man crossed over the dividing flower bed and investigated the fuss.

"G'morning, may I help you?"

Reese did an about-face.

"Oh, it's you," the man said. "You're Richard's sister, aren't you?"

"Yes," Reese snapped.

"I don't think he's around."

Panic welled up in her voice. "What do you mean?"

"When he comes home every night, he turns his porch light on. Done that for years—but it's been off all night."

Reese raised an inquiring brow.

He grinned. "Got a weak bladder." He then pointed to his home next door. "My bathroom is right there."

Reese observed that there was a milk glass window in a direct line of sight from where she stood. "You're certain?"

"Rich is as regular as I am," he chuckled. "In fact, the only people who have been by in the past twenty-four hours were his housecleaners. They do his place every Wednesday and Friday."

Reese fumed for a moment, then suddenly started digging into her purse. The neighbor looked on with curiosity. "Damn it," she mumbled. "I know he gave me one." She pulled out a tarnished brass key and inserted it into the lock. With a gentle twist and shove, the door gave way. Reese stepped in, followed closely by the uninvited old man. However, even to an untrained eye, it was immediately apparent that no one had set foot inside the residence since the housekeepers had departed. The nap on the thick carpet pile was undisturbed from a recent vacuuming. Reese proceeded anyway, hopeful for a clue to her brother's whereabouts.

"Anyone home?" she called out. "Yoo-hoo, Richard?"

There was no reply.

Reese scooted from room to room making certain they were unoccupied, lastly reaching the upper areas and the master bedroom. Like on the floors below, everything had been dusted clean, fresh towels laid out, and the bed turned down. There was no sign that anyone had disturbed the home since the maid service had completed their work.

"Like I told you," the neighbor repeated, "he never came home last night."

Reese slumped. A rush of horrific scenarios flashed through her mind. She shuddered, then glanced at her watch and frowned. She realized if she didn't leave now, there would be no one to speak at the Lions Club breakfast. But then what? Her brother could be anywhere, and worse, in any shape. Rapidly, her mind formulated a checklist. First things first, take care of the speaking commitment. Breeze in, send his apologies, and give a ten-minute talk. Second, work the phone. Someone had to know where he might be. And last, if he didn't turn up, she'd drive to the family cabin on Whidbey Island on the outside chance he had fled there. She hated the place, but she knew it always gave him peace of mind.

51

Jane Fenton trudged wearily into her work space, set her purse and bag lunch down, and stepped over to her coffeemaker. She had overslept. In a well-practiced ritual, she dumped out the old grinds into the trash, then rinsed out the carafe in the laboratory sink amid the dirty test tubes and beakers. That done, she refilled the container with clean water and scooped out new grounds. She pressed START. As the coffee percolated, she removed her coat and took a seat at her desk. Booting up her computer, she leaned back and waited.

The lab tech had seen the latest news and checked in with Harris, and both decided it would be best if she ran the partial fingerprint through AFIS on the outside chance a suspect identification could be had. Whatever the results, she was planning to depart for the new crime scene as soon as she had completed that task.

Fenton was alone now. The other techs either had not arrived yet or were already deployed at other crime scenes. The entire floor was empty except for her and the brewing coffee. The dripping seemed especially loud, although the aroma was soothing to Fenton's corroded sense of smell. She reached into her sack and pulled out a banana. Peeling it halfway, she took a bite as her monitor lit up. "Here we go," she mumbled. She typed in her password.

As promised, the Automated Fingerprint Identification System was back on-line. With several mouse clicks, the laboratory technician sent the previously prepared image file to the department's mainframe. It would take a minimum of five minutes for the data to be crunched, so Fenton rose and poured a cup of coffee. She then ambled over to the adjoining room and looked at the box of old records Roy had found. Suddenly, a sense of injustice touched her. *How many cases,* she wondered, *never had a chance of being solved? How many women were still fearful their attacker might be just beyond the next door, the next turn in the hallway, the next stall in a public rest room?* Decades had passed, but Fenton was sure that that kind of fear never fully dissipated. It was like a scar from a burn. It might fade, but the mark was there until the day you died.

She turned away as her computer *ding*ed.

Now what?

Thinking the quick electronic return was due to an entry error, Fenton was slow to return to her seat. She sighed, took another sip of her coffee. However, as she drew close, she was surprised to see the flashing red warning icon indicating possible matches. A surge of adrenaline rushed through her body. She leaped for her keyboard and pressed ENTER. Immediately, a long list of candidates scrolled down the screen, causing her initial excitement to fade. She had entered a partial print, with less than the necessary six points for legal identification. Thus, the database had culled from the electronic stacks all the potential matches. She groaned. The list was nearly five thousand names long, and not sorted alphabetically.

There was another problem. An AFIS match was only step one. The computer provided likely suspects; it was then up to the technician to obtain a copy of the original finger-print cards used in the submission and visually confirm a match. AFIS provided probability, but only the trained human eye could insure the two were from the same hand. Because of this, there were usually delays. The FBI retained copies of all the print cards, but high nationwide demand meant long queues, even in exigent cases. The other source for a card was the originating agency. But before Fenton went down that road, she needed to cut the list to a manageable size. She did this by narrowing the parameters. Hence, she initiated a new search, only using the names before her. First, she struck all females and deceased entries. The processing took only seconds. One sip of coffee later, there were now only three thousand names to wade through.

"Hmmm," Fenton mumbled. "Let's get rid of DOC actives." These were individuals currently incarcerated, and therefore logically unable to have placed the ring at the zoo.

A moment later the list was reduced by two hundred more names.

Fenton leaned back in her chair. *What else?* She finished her first cup of coffee, then placed her hand back on her keyboard. *How about only persons with previous criminal records?* It seemed unlikely to her that anyone involved in this case could have gone for thirty years without an arrest for something—even littering. She tapped in the instruction. Again, there was a short wait, but to her dismay, her screen flashed NO RECORDS FOUND.

"You got to be kidding me."

If there was a match in the AFIS database, the originating card had come, not from an arrest, but rather from a routine, noncriminal printing. *It's can't be Bakerman's or Eckler's,* Fenton suddenly realized. *There is a third player.*

Fenton quickly cut and pasted the long list into an E-mail file and sent it to Gilroy's desk. When he returned, he would be able to compare all the names in the old case files with what she had sent. It was a shot in the dark, but occasionally, the arrow found its mark. A person appearing on both rosters would have a lot of explaining to do.

52

Frank Milkovich leaned on a wall just outside the assistant jail administrator's office. The door before him was shut tight, but he could hear the gist of a heated exchange going on inside. This went on for several minutes until suddenly the door popped open and several red-faced jail guards exited. Their slumped posture and panicked looks told Milkovich that they were the ones responsible for Bakerman's unexcused absence, a turn of events he had discerned from his police scanner while en route to this location. He waited for the pair to pass, then advanced through the doorjamb.

"You must be Lieutenant Milkovich," the assistant jail administrator said, looking up. "Reception said you wanted to talk to me." The manager was red-faced too, but from anger, not shame. He was a beefy man, barrel-chested with thick arms and jowls. It was obvious by his steely-eyed stare and gruff voice that his primary duty was to enforce the rules, whether violated by an employee or an inmate. He continued, "I suppose you are here about Bakerman. That fuckin' hospital sure screwed up." Milkovich shrugged as the jail executive went on. "I take it you're the lead on our missing boy, huh?"

Milkovich shook his head no.

"You're not?" The administrator cocked a suspicious brow.

"No, I'm IA."

"Wait a second; you've got no—"

"Whoa," Milkovich said, raising his hands. "I'm not here to headhunt. I just need some information."

The administrator leaned back in his chair and eyed Milkovich. Slowly he said, "What kind of information?"

"Just a couple of questions answered."

"About the escape?"

Milkovich shrugged noncommittally.

The administrator stroked his chin. Suddenly a flash of recognition lit his eyes. He wrapped his hands behind his head and said, "Frank Milkovich . . . say, didn't you use to be in Narcotics?"

"A long time ago."

The administrator's stiff facade eased. "I remember you from, what, ten or fifteen years ago. I was a shift lieutenant then. Christ, you used to bring in a whole carload of dirtbags every friggin' night. Pissed us all off, having to book all them goddamn assholes."

Milkovich cracked a smile.

"You're in IA now, huh? Who'd ya fuck with?"

The smile faded.

"Hey, no offense," the administrator hurriedly said. "I know how shit rolls downhill." He unknotted his hands and shifted forward. "Look, what do you need to know? I'll try to help you if I can."

"Appreciate it," Milkovich replied. He thought for a moment and asked, "How long have you been working here?"

"Forever."

"No, really, how many years?"

"Started in 1980. Right after I got out of the navy."

"Around 1985, were you aware of inmates doing maintenance for city facilities? Did you ever transport them, or keep an eye on the work parties?"

"What's that got to do with anything?"

"Long story."

Suspicion returned to the administrator's demeanor. He said cautiously, "We've been doing that for years. There some kind of problem?"

"Years?"

"Sure, we've got crews out cleaning roads and parks all the time. We keep it discreet, dress 'em in street clothes so they look like city workers, but they're out there all the time. Saves taxpayers thousands of dollars."

"What about working at a police department facility— say, like, the evidence warehouse?"

A twinkle came to the administrator's eye.

"Does that mean yes?"

There was a long pause.

"Well?"

"Hey, I wasn't involved. Back then, I was the low guy on the totem pole. I just heard the rumors, that's all."

"What kind of rumors?"

The administrator shifted in his seat.

"Well?"

He sighed. "All I remember is a couple of guys got fired over it, that's all."

"Guards?"

"Yeah."

"Over what?"

The administrator drew a deep breath. "It was like this: the savvy inmates knew a few bucks would get you on the crew. Once you were on it and working outside, you could hook up with a pal while the guards weren't looking. These guys'd load up with dope to peddle when they came back in at the end of the day. Some of our more entrepreneurial types made a small fortune, even after the kickbacks." The man paused. "Hey, you wanna know something funny?"

"What?"

"Odds are, the dirtbags you were arresting at night back then were back to dealing drugs the next day, if they got on a crew."

Milkovich didn't laugh.

"It is kinda ironic."

Milkovich remained stone-faced. "Did you hear anything about our evidence warehouse—any problems there?"

"Not that I'm aware of. We had crews there for maybe a few months, and then they stopped using us. That's all I know."

"Are there any records from that time?"

"You got to be kidding. Everything got shredded years ago. We're on a seven-year destruction cycle." The administrator impatiently shuffled some papers. Looking up, he asked, "Anything else?"

"Yeah, can you tell me if Clifford Bakerman had had his blood drawn for DNA typing, like the court ordered yesterday?"

The administrator shrugged. "I'd have to check."

"Would you?"

The administrator picked up his telephone and dialed in a three-digit number. A moment passed, then: "Yeah, it's me. Did you get the DNA blood draw done on Bakerman yesterday? Right . . . uh-huh . . . I'll hold."

The administrator stared blankly ahead, the receiver tight to his ear. A moment later, "I see . . . right . . . thanks." He hung up and sighed. "They tried once, but he was feeling too ill after lunch, and they decided to bag it until today. Guess they're too late, huh?"

Milkovich nodded gravely.

53

Harris looked on as a member of the Medical Examiner's Office plunged a liver stick—a meat-thermometer-like device—into the uncovered abdomen of Sister Cecilia. The nun remained as she had been found, lying on the hardwood floor. The blood had caked and lividity, the gravity-induced migration of interior fluids, had set in. It caused her upside to turn a stark white while below, at the lowest points, the skin was bruiselike and purple.

A photographer had already snapped dozens of shots and was now in the adjoining room, along with a video cameraman recording the scene before Harris's team began its search for less obvious evidence. That process would begin once the body's position was measured and triangulated for future reference. Meanwhile, Jennings had disappeared upstairs and Gilroy was working on next of kin. Immediate family needed to be notified and interviewed as soon as possible.

News of Bakerman's disappearance had only recently reached Harris. Details had been fuzzy and, ironically, her first reaction had been one of relief. With Bakerman on the lam, there would be no court hearing the next day. But more importantly, his escape seemed an admission of guilt. But then, Harris wondered, could he also be responsible for Sister Cecilia's death? On the surface that seemed improbable. He had neither the means nor the opportunity—or did he? Determining the nun's exact time of death had become critical.

"So?" Harris impatiently asked.

"Just another second," the medical tech replied. He reached down and withdrew the probe. He noted the temperature, then set it aside. Stepping back, he pulled off his bloodstained gloves and tossed them into the garbage bag recently set up to prevent contamination of the scene. All gloves, booties, and coffee cups would go into it.

He reached into a breast pocket and pulled out a small reference book. He consulted it, then looked up. "You think the temperature in here has been constant since she was killed?"

Harris dipped her head in assent and added, "The thermostat on the wall was set to sixty-eight degrees."

"What time did the 911 call come in?"

"Oh, four thirty."

He looked at his reference again, then placed it back in his pocket. "Textbook," the tech smugly said, "except for the 911 call. She couldn't have made it. She died at oh two hundred, plus or minus half an hour."

Harris nodded a grim acknowledgment. She had already noted that disparity. With lividity already set, she knew Sister Cecilia had to have been dead hours before the emergency call had been received in the 911 center. Unfortunately, that didn't make any sense. But from the moment she had entered the residence, warning bells had sounded. There was no sign of forced entry and nothing of value apparently taken, even though some drawers showed vague indications that they'd been rifled. That pointed to a killer known to the victim. Further, the opportune use of the fireplace poker suggested to Harris that the killing had not been premeditated. Or had it? Harris knew inferences made in this manner were always double-edged. A smart killer wanting to throw off police would kill just like this, making it look like a crime of passion rather than an execution.

The sounds of approaching footsteps broke the Seattle detective's concentration. She turned to the doorway. It was Jennings.

"Any luck?" she asked.

He groaned. "It'll take a year to go through all the stuff around here. And the attic is packed to the ceiling with old boxes." He grimly surveyed the scene and sighed. Despite the hundreds of mutilated corpses he had viewed over the years, Sister Cecilia's breached his wall of detachment. He shook his head in disgust. "What kind of person would do a thing like this?"

Harris refocused her senior detective. "Did you see any sign of a scuffle anywhere else?"

Jennings shook his head no. "Nothing. Except for that little bit in the library, the rest of the place is spotless."

Harris's cell phone rang for the seemingly hundredth time. She pulled it from her coat pocket. "Harris?"

"It's Purello. I'm on the east barricade."

"Whatcha need?"

"I got a lady here, says she's a niece of the victim. What do you want me to do with her?"

"Hang on a sec." Harris stepped into the hallway and covered the phone's mouthpiece. She called out, "Hey, Phil?"

From a distant room came a muffled, "Yeah, boss?"

"We got a relative out front. Go check it out."

A moment later, Gilroy's rapid footsteps were echoing off the old-growth floors.

Harris returned to Jennings. "C'mon."

She led the older detective in a wide arc around the billiard table and passed into the library. The photographers were finishing. Harris paused and waited for the last shots to be taken. She then directed the men to begin the upper levels. They departed as Jennings pointed out the cordless telephone to Harris. She knelt down for a closer look. It had been returned to the spot where Officer Bowles indicated he had originally found it for the requisite photos and sketches. When she looked back up, she saw that Jennings's eyes were sweeping the room, and a look of concern clouded his face.

"Something wrong?"

"Something's different."

Harris alerted. "What?"

"Darn it, I wish I wasn't getting so old. There's something different about this room, but I'm not sure what."

Harris rose and joined the scrutiny, allowing her subordinate time to collate his fragmented remembrances. Finally, Jennings shook his head in disgust. "It will come to me, probably tonight when I'm trying to fall asleep." Giving up, he circled about until he abruptly refocused on the fireplace mantel. "What the—?" He carefully stepped over the phone and past the leather chair he had sat in the previous evening, his attention focused on the brick hearth. Leaning close, he eyed the top surface. "Hey, boss, there were two pictures, in brass frames, sitting up here last night. One's gone now."

"You sure?"

He nodded. "You can see where it sat. There's a faint dust outline from it."

Harris rushed to Jennings's side. She didn't have a moment to ponder the potential clue when her cell phone rang yet again. Wearily, she stepped back and activated the device. "Yeah?"

"It's Phil. You better come out here—and quick."

The time was 0814.

54

The African-American patrol officer eased her prowler car up to the plastic clown holding the drive-through menu.

"Welcome to Burger King. May I take your order?"

The officer scanned the reader board. "Hmmm . . . how 'bout a sausage-egg muffin and a large coffee."

"That'll be two eighty-nine at the second window."

The officer rolled forward, falling in line behind two other vehicles. As she came to a stop, she leaned over to retrieve her purse from the passenger floorboard. Straightening, she began fishing through the leather bag, trying to find the proper change. Meanwhile, her mobile data unit—a center-console-mounted laptop with a wireless connection to the dispatch center—beeped a low-level alert. She paused her search and glanced down at the LED display.

The line moved.

Reflexively, the officer's head bobbed back up, diverting her attention back to the queue. She didn't want to delay other patrons. A mild panic set in. She still hadn't found enough quarters and dimes to cover her order.

The line moved once more.

Dumping her purse on the adjacent seat, she rummaged through the pile of gum wrappers, makeup containers, and old receipts, finding at last a crumpled five-dollar bill. She snatched it up just as it was her turn to pay.

Taking her food, the officer exited the lane and eased out into the expansive mall parking lot and adjoining park-and-ride bus station. The commuter slots had long since been taken—rush hour was nearly over—and now the perimeter of the retail lot was filling with mall employee vehicles. The officer headed to a corner to park and enjoy a few minutes of quiet before the next call would inevitably come. This time and day of the week were normally quiet, the few details shared among several squad members. This morning, however, due to the ongoing hostage situation, she was the lone patrol car in this area. The rest of her colleagues had been diverted to the Greenlake scene to relieve the graveyard shift.

Backing into a parking spot bracketed by other cars, she left the engine idling as she removed the lid to her coffee and took a careful sip. "Ah," she sighed and took one more before setting the container into her cup holder. Next came her sausage muffin. She was about to unwrap it when her eyes returned to the mobile data terminal and the message still awaiting a confirmation receipt. Dutifully, she speed-read the bulletin—a stolen-attempt-to-locate—and was about to clear the screen when she looked up.

Her eyes squinted. "What the—?"

Squarely in front of her, across the aisle, was an unoccupied green late-model Volvo S70, matching the one in the alert.

The officer set her breakfast aside and leaned forward. "Mary . . . Adam . . . Victor?" Excited, she glanced back down to the computer. The first three letters were a match.

Thoughts of breakfast vanished. She popped her door and quickly exited, moving close enough to read the plate in its entirety. A moment later, she keyed her radio mike. Sister Cecilia's car was no longer missing.

55

Leah Harris crossed the front doorway of the stately home into the bright morning sunlight. She paused and squinted. The rain was long gone, but the grass and pavement glistened with dampness.

"Hey, Sarge," Officer Bowles said. He was guarding the doorway and, as instructed, keeping a log of every person who entered and exited the house. "Did ya hear it on the radio?"

Harris turned. "Hear what?"

"Eight four spotted the Volvo you were looking for. It's parked over at the Northgate Mall."

"When?" And in rapid succession, "Who found it? Was it abandoned? Is there anything in plain view?"

Bowles shrugged unknowingly.

Harris's hand dived for her cell phone, and in a moment she was connected to the dispatch center. "This is Detective Sergeant Harris. What's the status on the Volvo we put out a while ago? . . . uh-huh . . . okay . . . are you sure? Right. Okay, tell whoever is on scene to not let anyone near the car till I get there, okay? . . . Right, don't touch anything."

Harris gazed intently to the street. Beyond the barricades dozens of people milled about, officers mingling with waiting reporters and camera crews. She spotted the backs of Gilroy and Officer Purello amid the group and tried to make out the individual he had called about. Unfortunately, Harris was too far away to identify her.

"Sergeant?" dispatch said.

"I'm still here," Harris replied, returning her attention to the call.

"Officer Stevens requests an ETA to her location."

"Ah, Jesus Christ," Harris groaned. "Just tell her I'll be there as soon as possible."

"Right, I'll relay."

The line went silent again. Harris lifted her gaze back to the street. This time, she spotted her junior detective waving. She squinted again.

"Sergeant? Sergeant Harris?" dispatch asked.

"Yeah?" was Harris's distracted reply. Her eyes were now glued to the person standing between Purello and Gilroy.

"Any further instructions?"

Harris tightened her grip on her cell phone. "Yeah, one of my lab techs, Jane Fenton, is supposed to be en route to this scene. Page or call her and have her divert to Stevens's location."

The dispatcher acknowledged the instructions and hung up. Meanwhile, Leah Harris had already begun a jog towards Sister Cecilia's relation. TV cameras captured her urgent pace. As she closed the distance, she could see tears rolling down the young woman's cheeks. The women's eyes met as Harris skidded to a stop.

Grimly, Gilroy said, "I think you already know Tessla Quinn."

56

Harris took Tessla Quinn by the arm and escorted her through the barricade and away from the eager reporters. Once out of earshot, she slowed and searched her pockets for a Kleenex. She came up empty-handed. Detective Gilroy, who was trailing, took note and hand-signaled to Leah that he'd find some. He hurried off.

"I don't understand," Quinn moaned between sniffles. "How could this have happened? Who could have done such a thing?"

Leah Harris didn't reply. Instead, she gave the shorter woman a reassuring hug and let her cry on her shoulder for a few moments. She then stepped back and, in an empathetic tone, tried to soothe the attorney's nerves. Despite the show of compassion, dozens of questions were rapidly forming in Harris's mind.

A minute passed.

Gilroy hustled back with a box of tissues and gave it to Leah. She withdrew several and passed them to Quinn, who nodded gratefully and dabbed her eyes. The sobbing slowed.

"I need to ask some questions," Harris said, broaching the inevitable.

Quinn nodded after a moment. "I understand, but please, can you tell me what happened first?"

Harris didn't answer immediately. She was at the crossroads of an odd paradox. A possible relative of the victim was representing a possible suspect for the murder. What she said could affect this and the Sellinzski case. Harris began cautiously, although sensitive to Quinn's needs.

"At this point, we really don't know much ourselves," Harris said. She glanced about and continued. "It doesn't appear to be a robbery, and there's no sign of a forced entry."

"How did she die?"

Again, Harris hesitated. She didn't want to be graphic. Yet from experience, she had found it best to fully disclose, except when the victim was a child and the person receiving the news was the mother. In that situation, toning down the circumstances was the only humane thing to do.

"I can take it," Quinn pressed.

"I'm sure you can"—Harris sadly smiled—"but first, tell me—you're Sister Cecilia's niece, right?"

Quinn dipped her head. "Aunt Maggie was my dad's sister."

"Maggie?"

Quinn cracked a forlorn smile. "It is confusing. Margaret Quinn was my aunt's birth name. When she became a nun, she took the name Cecilia Thomas. She's gone by that ever since."

Harris rolled her eyes.

"Something wrong?" Quinn asked.

"I don't believe it."

"Believe what, boss?" Gilroy said.

Harris ignored her subordinate and kept her focus on Quinn. "Yesterday, in court, the holy card that linked your client to the victim?"

"Yes?"

"The name on back was your aunt's."

Quinn's mouth dropped open. "Y-you're kidding me."

Harris's grave look assured her she was not.

"But—"

"On top of all that," Harris went on, "your client, Mr. Bakerman, took a powder earlier this morning."

"What do you mean?"

"He escaped. From what I was told, he got sick last night around dinnertime and was taken to the ER at Harborview. Later on, he somehow gave his guard the slip."

"My God, the holy card—him—Aunt Maggie—could he have—?"

"Good question. But if he did, I've got two better ones— how and why?"

Quinn sagged.

Harris's tone became urgent. "Look, we've just found your aunt's car at Northgate. It was abandoned in the mall parking lot. I've got to head over there right now. Can I get you to come along with me, so we can talk?"

Quinn gazed longingly towards her relation's home.

Harris recognized the look. "I'm sorry, but I can't let you in just yet. It will probably be hours."

"I know," Quinn replied. She drew a deep breath and wiped her eyes once more. "I want to help. Whatever you need. Where's your car? I'll be happy to go with you."

57

Instead of entering the freeway on-ramp that would have taken him southbound towards the evidence warehouse, Frank Milkovich changed lanes at the last moment and veered back onto the city street. He proceeded underneath the interstate and quickly braked. Here, he encountered a forward contingent of searchers. Several officers on both sides of the street were rousting homeless men camped out in the deep concrete recesses of the overpass. Milkovich recognized several of the officers. He rolled his window down and shouted, "Hey, where's the CP?"

One of the officers straightened and pointed up the hill. "The hospital's employee parking lot. Take a right, two blocks up."

Milkovich waved an acknowledgment and accelerated.

As he approached the epicenter of the search, he began noticing more elements of the hunt: a K-9 team was making a track down an alley, while a mixture of King County deputies and Seattle police officers were stationed on the corners for containment. Ahead, beyond the long row of empty patrol cars, was a command bus. Around it, several K-9 units waiting to be dispatched and extra officers milled about, joking and jostling one another as though it were a football tailgate party. Coffee and donuts were in abundance.

Milkovich double-parked and wove his way to the latter group and the inner circle of supervisors. Line officers parted like the Red Sea, in advance of his arrival. "He's IA," he heard one whisper to another.

"Hey, Frank," a captain called out. He moved away from his subordinates. "Whatcha doing up here?"

Milkovich stepped up to the friendly-faced precinct commander and glanced about. "Looks like you have everybody working today."

The captain grinned. "It's been some night around here, huh? I bet we've already blown the new chief's overtime budget. Hey, you want a cup of coffee or anything? The hospital just brought all this stuff." He pointed to a folding table covered with food items.

Milkovich ignored the offer. "What's the bottom line on this Bakerman guy? Where do you think he's at?"

The captain scratched his head. "Good question. What's your interest?"

"Don't worry; it's got nothing to do with anyone here."

The captain nodded understanding. He recapped. "We had a good dog track from the bed he was in to a stairwell at the end of the wing. From there, it's obvious he went straight down to the lobby and right out the front entrance to the sidewalk."

"Nobody saw him?"

The captain shook his head discouragingly. "He blended in. That time of night, there're a lot of oddballs floating around here waiting for their buddies to be stitched."

Milkovich nodded knowingly. "Okay, so then what happened?"

"About a block west, our best dog lost the scent."

"You think he could have been picked up by someone?"

"Possible."

"Taxi?"

"Nope, already checked the records."

"Then how in the world did he walk out of here in one of those hospital nightgowns? He would have froze his ass off."

"He didn't."

Milkovich raised a brow.

"He had his street clothes."

"What?"

"You heard me. The jail never got around to changing him. He was still in the civvies he wore from prison when he was brought over to the ER. They took 'em off when he got here, but put them all in a bag and sent them with him to his room."

"You got to be kidding."

"I wish I was. It looks like all he had to do was get up from the bed while the guard was out making time with the nurses, change, and simply tiptoe out."

"Christ, he could be anywhere."

The captain scratched the top of his bald head again and nodded agreement.

The time was 0859.

58

Harris and Quinn were nearing the Northgate shopping mall. Between Queen Anne and here, the Seattle detective had untangled the victim's family tree and determined there was not a person on the planet who might have had a motive to kill the nun other than Bakerman—whatever his motive might be? However, moments after that had been established, Quinn grew uneasy.

"What's wrong?" Harris asked.

"Just a thought," the young attorney replied. Her tears had dried, her composure was returning. "Aunt Maggie was pretty rabidly antiabortionist. I guess you'd expect that from a Catholic nun, but then of course my dad was, too."

Harris turned to her. "How rabid?"

"Oh, she didn't blow up clinics or anything like that, but she was very outspoken in church circles. She was a recent chair of the diocese's right-to-life committee."

"Did she ever get any death threats?"

Quinn thought for a moment and said, "If she had, she never mentioned it. And to be honest, I stayed away from the whole topic anyway. Our views were pretty much a hundred and eighty degrees apart."

Harris nodded as she navigated the Seattle traffic. Her

police radio, set to scan, was active on numerous channels. Simultaneous conversations flickered back and forth between a dozen officers, all at unrelated scenes. To the untrained ear, it was as unintelligible as Mandarin to a Westerner, but despite an otherwise oblivious appearance, Harris found it second nature to monitor what was being said.

She suddenly cocked an ear.

"What's going on?" Quinn asked.

Harris waved her off as the radio blurted, "We've got a woman up here that says she's a friend of the suspect. She wants to try talking to him. Do you want her up there?"

The airwaves crackled.

"Ah, eight nine . . . bring her over to my position. . . . We'll try putting her on the telephone and try talking the kid out."

"Roger, I'll walk her down now. Break . . . dispatch, did you get anything back on the ID check?"

"Stand by," the dispatcher replied. "NCIC is slow this morning."

"So am I."

That comment was followed by a series of agreeing clicks from other officers who had been on station all night.

"God, they're still at it," Harris mumbled under her breath.

Quinn leaned forward, trying to decipher the staccato communications. She looked up questioningly.

Harris explained. "Some methed-out kid has been shacked up all night in a house with a hostage. We've been trying to get him out ever since."

Quinn suddenly straightened. "How do you do it?"

"Do what?"

She spread her hands. "This? I mean, one moment you're dealing with a thirty-year-old homicide case, then my aunt's murder, and at the same time, there's another death just waiting to happen. . . . How do you do it?"

Harris was about to reply when the radio crackled again. "Eight nine, are you clear for traffic?"

"Oh, those poor suckers," Harris said with a smirk.

"Now what's the matter?"

"Looks like the girlfriend has a warrant out for her arrest."

"Go ahead for eight nine." It was another officer, out of earshot of the woman in question.

"Be advised that there is a stop-and-detain order from this office on your subject."

"Right, stand by."

There was a moment of silence. Harris decelerated, signaled, and turned into the mall parking lot. Ahead at the far corner sat the telltale white evidence van that indicated Jane Fenton was already on scene.

The radio traffic resumed. An officer asked, "Confirm the name again?"

"Copy . . . last of Doyle, first of Nancy, middle R, with a DOB of ten-twelve of 'sixty-two."

"Received . . . ah, we're going to go ahead and see if the woman can get the kid to come out. We'll worry about the warrant later—break."

"Go ahead."

"The scene commander wants to know what the stop-and-detain is for, and who issued it?"

"Stand by." A moment later, "It was issued by Sergeant Harris in Homicide. I'll be contacting immediately . . ."

The dispatcher didn't have to. Leah Harris's hand was already wrapped around her cell phone—the direct number to the communications center had already started to ring.

59

Ed Jennings had supervised the removal of Sister Cecilia's body. The billiard room floor now lay bare except for the pool of dried blood. He stared at it as he thought.

The missing picture bothered him. The whole case bothered him. In his twenty years of hunting killers, he had never seen a more odd setup. None of the pieces went together. In fact, most contradicted one another. He shook his head in disgust, then turned to go out to the barricades. He had flipped a coin with Gilroy and lost. It meant he had to go on camera for the press and, per Harris's instructions, release just enough information for them to pack up their bags and move on to the next carcass. He was already late, but he still hesitated. *What am I going to say?* his mind repeated, like a looped message.

Suddenly, a voice interrupted his thoughts. "Where the hell is everyone?" It was Roy Stoddard. He was standing in the hallway, equipment cases in both hands. Jennings flinched as he caught a whiff of the evidence tech's sour, fermented odor.

The veteran detective averted his nose and answered, "Phil's around here somewhere, and the boss is over at the other scene."

"What other scene?"

"Victim's car was found at Northgate."

"Oh."

"Didn't you get the pages?"

Stoddard shrugged. "I was busy."

"I bet you were," Jennings mumbled beneath his breath. He then said, "Hey, isn't that my stuff?"

"Yeah, I snagged these from your trunk. I came in my own car."

Jennings sighed. "Look, this is a real screwball case. My gut says we're not going to find a print in this place that will be worth anything, but we still need to do the dusting. Why don't you get started on that? Do this room, then the library next door. Oh, and hey, there's a fireplace poker over there—see it?"

Stoddard leaned inward. "Yeah?"

"That's probably the murder weapon. Leah doesn't want it field-tested. So wrap it up real careful-like so Jane can examine it back at HQ. But first, there's a cordless telephone on the floor in the next room. Check it out. The victim's prints better be on it, or—"

"Or what?"

"Just check it out, okay? I got a date with the bloodsuckers out there. I'll be back when I'm done. Shouldn't be more than a couple of minutes."

Stoddard sniggered.

"Now what's the matter?"

"You let that rookie dick outflip you again?"

"Just get to work."

Stoddard gave a toothy grin and proceeded to set the cases down, open them, and remove the necessary equipment. Jennings grimly strode past, his pace slow and deliberate, as though he were heading to his own execution.

60

Jane Fenton was leaning into the trunk of the Volvo as Harris's Ford Taurus eased into a parking spot several rows over. Yellow crime scene tape had been strung by Officer Stevens, blocking entry to the area. Meanwhile, the officer was prowling the perimeter, keeping curious shoppers at bay. She soon spotted the Seattle detective and Quinn on foot, and headed their direction. She reached for the warning strip and lifted it head-high to allow both women to pass.

"Good job IDing the car," Harris said as she bent under.

The officer grinned.

Harris then instructed the young attorney to wait at the perimeter. A look of protest formed on Quinn's face, but she complied. Meanwhile, Fenton, hearing the approaching steps, twisted up and around.

"Who's that?" the lab tech asked as Harris reached her side. Fenton's eyes were on Quinn.

"The victim's niece."

"Why's she here?"

"I'll explain later."

Fenton shrugged acceptance. "By the way, did you get my voice mail?"

Harris shook her head no.

"The partial print on the ring."

"What about it?"

"It's not Bakerman's or Eckler's."

Harris didn't react.

"You're not surprised?"

"Frankly, no. What about near hits?"

"None with a criminal record."

That news caused Harris's eyes to widen. "You're kidding me."

"Nope, we got three thousand noncriminal names to plow through; of course, even then, our boy may not be in the pile. The best I could do was five ID points."

Harris kicked a pebble and watched it ricochet off a nearby tire. "God, there's just too many loose ends. . . . So what do we have here?"

"Car's clean as a whistle except for the trunk. There's a couple of full grocery bags in there. Other than that, it was unlocked. Key's still in the ignition. Even the coin holder is nearly full."

"Groceries?"

"Yeah, standard stuff—fruit, veggies, a loaf of bread—I haven't had a chance to take a closer look."

"What about prints?"

"Everything's been wiped clean."

"Fibers—hair?"

"Maybe, but it'll take time."

Harris suddenly gazed about and mouthed, "Why here?"

The huge parking lot was now a beehive of activity. It was three-quarters full with a constant flow of cars coming and going.

"Needle in a haystack," Fenton suggested.

Harris nodded agreement. "And that cements it for me. We're not dealing with some run-of-the-mill burglar. Whoever did this is cool under fire."

Fenton nodded agreement as Harris suddenly brushed past her and bent into the still open trunk. Fenton followed. "Whatcha looking for?"

Both were careful not to touch anything.

"You see a receipt in any of the bags?"

The lab tech surveyed her side of the trunk. "Here ya go." She reached into the nearest paper sack and withdrew a sales slip. Both woman straightened.

"What time does it show these were bought?"

Fenton scrolled down the tape. "Jeez, after midnight, at twelve thirty-seven this morning."

"That's how he did it," Harris mumbled to herself.

"Did what?"

"How our killer got into the house without breaking the door down. He must have been waiting for her outside. That's got to be it. He probably surprised her just as she was unlocking the front door and going in. That's why the groceries are still in the trunk. She never had a chance to unload them."

At that moment, Officer Stevens called out to Harris and Fenton. "Hey, it just came over the radio; they finally talked that kid out of the house. He's in custody. So's the woman you put the warrant out on."

The time was 0951.

61

With the hostage situation finally resolved, Harris was able to obtain a squad of officers to go store to store, contacting employees to determine if any of the early arrivals had seen a person associated with the abandoned Volvo. Polaroid photos were taken to aid in their recollection. Meanwhile, Harris had Stevens run every license plate in the vicinity to obtain names and addresses of the owners for further follow-up. That done, she arranged for another officer to give Quinn a ride back to her car, with a promise to stay in contact should there be further developments. All this had been accomplished at a rapid pace. And while evidence at this scene still needed to be collected and processed, and witnesses identified and interviewed, this was for others to do. Finding Carl Eckler was still an imperative. Loose ends like him had a habit of unraveling the best of cases. Harris knew she needed to quickly get face-to-face with Eckler's girlfriend and convince her to cooperate. The longer she sat unattended, the more likely she might develop second thoughts.

Per Harris's request, Doyle was taken to the North Precinct and sequestered in an interview room to await the detective sergeant's arrival. The facility was only a few miles away from the mall. Harris covered the distance in minutes, running a traffic light in the process. Arriving, she wheeled her Taurus into a handicapped slot directly out front and exited in a sprint. Surprisingly, the shift supervisor, a lieutenant, was waiting outside the entrance for her as she bounded up the steps. "She's in holding room three," he said, "but you're probably too late."

Harris's heels ground to a stop. She spun as the lieutenant pointed towards the public parking area, and to a red Mercedes. It had a set of golf clubs in the rear seat.

"Her attorney got here about five minutes ago." The patrol supervisor reached into his shirt pocket and pulled out a business card. He passed it over. Harris snatched it and read the name at the bottom. She groaned loudly. The Mercedes belonged to Stuart Malconni.

"How in the hell did he know she was here?"

"Don't look at me."

Harris hunkered down and proceeded through the doors to the rear of the precinct, where Doyle was being held. A lone officer stood outside one of a series of small, secure rooms. Thick, bulletproof glass provided a view into each.

Harris stopped short and waved for the officer to join her. He did. She asked, "Were you the one who transported Doyle in?"

The officer nodded.

"She say anything?"

The officer shifted on his feet. "Ah, I dunno. She was sobbing mostly. I guess I wasn't paying too much attention."

Exasperation flexed Harris's face. "She didn't say anything? What about when she found out you were bringing her here? She didn't protest?"

The officer shrugged. "She was sobbing, like I said. Like someone wanting to do herself."

"What about her attorney—did he say anything to you?"

"Yeah, he asked for a cup of coffee."

Harris ground her teeth, stepped past the officer, and proceeded to the entry. She knocked.

Inside, both heads turned, and Harris got her first look at Nancy Doyle. The officer was right; she looked suicidal. Deep lines etched her face, her bleached blond hair was matted, and the bags beneath her eyes indicated she hadn't slept soundly for days. Even her clothes looked tired. The tight-fitting jeans and extra-large sweatshirt seemed wilted from multiple days of wear.

Harris cracked the door and with an empathetic tone said to Doyle, "I'm Leah Harris. I'd like to ask you some questions, if that's all right?"

"Perhaps," Malconni said, swiveling on his seat. In contrast to Doyle, her attorney appeared freshly showered and shaved, his dark suit and monogrammed white shirt crisp and sharply creased. "Nice to see you again," he added. "Any luck finding Carl?"

Harris frowned. "I was hoping that you might have heard from him."

"Sorry, I'm afraid he hasn't contacted me since we all talked on Tuesday."

Harris eyed him and launched a missile. "Did you know he's been operating a mini-meth-lab at the address you gave us?"

"It wasn't him," Doyle cried out.

"Nancy!" Malconni commanded. His head whipped back to his client. "Don't say a word unless I tell you."

She meekly nodded.

Malconni returned to Harris. "If you would excuse us, I need a few more minutes here. By the way, what exactly is Ms. Doyle being charged with?"

"She's not charged with anything—yet."

"Then she's free to go?"

"I didn't say that."

"Sergeant," the defense attorney started in a condescending tone, "I'm sure you know the law as well as I do. If there are no charges, we'll excuse ourselves right now."

Harris remained unfazed. "Tell you what, Mr. Malconni. For the record, we'll start with conspiracy to manufacture and distribute methamphetamine—does that work for you?"

Malconni tensed. "That's bullshit."

"Okay, how about obstructing justice?"

The attorney cocked a curious eyebrow.

"But tell ya what—give me Carl, tell me where he's at, and Nancy walks. Think about it—I'll be back in ten minutes." Harris jerked away and shut the door before either Malconni or Doyle could utter another word. She strode by the window without a sideways glance.

"That's sticking it to 'im," the guarding officer marveled.

Harris didn't respond. With hunched shoulders, she double-timed her way to the employee break room at the other end of the hall. Several patrol officers were just departing, which left the entire space to Harris. She found a dollar bill in her coat pocket and purchased a Diet Pepsi, then headed to a well-worn couch. She flopped onto it while simultaneously letting go a loud, pent-up groan.

For a moment, she just lay there, her mind swirling, her eyes staring blankly at the ceiling. It had been only forty-eight hours since she had sat right across from Carl Eckler in Collins's office, and not once had she detected anything odd about him other than the continual nervous twitch of a recovering meth addict. Bakerman was the same way. As ordinary as a longtime neighbor in a blue-collar neighborhood—a bowling buddy, mechanic, or mailman. *How does it go together*? she kept asking herself. *And how did this vortex descend on an elderly nun?*

"Damn," Harris muttered. She rolled up to a sitting position and popped the top on her soda. She took a long drink, then set the can aside. Activating her cell phone, she decided she'd better check for messages. She was now keeping the device off until it was necessary. The battery was getting low—she had forgotten to put it on the charger when she had returned home the previous night. A moment later an automated voice began, "You have six new messages. Would you like to hear number one?"

She pressed the pound key.

"Message one. 'Hey, it's Frank. I'm up at the hospital. Give me a call.' *Beep*. Message received at eight fifty a.m."

Harris pressed delete.

"Message two. 'It's Ed. I took care of the press and that's the last time I do it. I don't care whose turn it is. . . . Anyway, Phil has turned up zippo from the neighbors. Nobody heard or saw anything. He's back with me and we're going to scour the place. Oh, hey, by the way, Roy printed the telephone—nothing usable on it. It's obviously been rubbed clean, but he thinks he knows how the 911 call was made, and I happen to agree with him on this one. We're thinking that the suspect cornered our victim in the library just as she was punching in the number. He grabs the handset before she can hit send, then chases her into the billiard room, where he does her with the poker. Later, when he comes back to wipe his prints off, he accidentally activates the call. I checked with dispatch and had them replay the tape with it amplified. Guess what, you can actually hear a heavy breath right after the dispatcher answers, then what sounds like the phone dropping and footsteps running away. So whatcha think? Give me a call.' *Beep*. Message received at nine twenty a.m."

"Good work," Harris mouthed to herself.

"Message three. 'It's Captain Varna speaking. Your boss,

remember me? Give me a call and update me as soon as possible.' *Beep.* Message received at nine thirty-two a.m."

Harris deleted it.

"Message four. 'It's Frank again. I'm back in my car. The dog track ended about two blocks west of the hospital. They're telling me that's because of the rain and wind last night; the scent probably got dispersed. Which means they don't know if Bakerman stayed on foot or somehow managed to thumb a ride. They're going to put a bunch of guys down into Pioneer Square and toss every wino. I'm going to cruise around down there too. Who knows? Call me when you can.' *Beep.* Message received at nine fifty a.m.

"Message five. 'I'm going to go ahead and impound the Volvo to indoor storage.'" It was Jane. "'It'll be easier to process it that way, but I doubt seriously we'll find anything usable. So for now, I think I'll head back to the Queen Anne house, okay?' *Beep.* Message received ten oh eight a.m.

"Message six. 'It's me again.'" It was Ed Jennings. "'The captain just showed up here looking for you. He couldn't stick around, but told me to tell you to call him A-SAP.' *Beep.* Message received at ten fifteen a.m."

Harris straightened and dialed in her subordinate's number. It rang once.

"Jennings."

"It's Leah." She shifted the cell phone to her other ear.

"You got my message about Varna?" Jennings asked.

"Yep."

"Good, I'm off the hook."

"Anything new?"

"The press finally packed it up, the lousy jerks. They cornered the niece trying to get in her car. They got her on camera crying."

"They're just doing their job," Harris reminded him.

"I don't have to like it."

Harris let go a long sigh.

"Something eating you, boss?"

"Everything. . . . Hey, is Jane there yet?"

"She's in the next room."

"Put her on."

The line went quiet for a moment, then, "Hi, what's up?"

"I have a theoretical question for you."

"Shoot," Jane said.

"The ring."

"Yeah?"

"Any chance the print on it was made thirty years ago? And just not handled since then?"

Fenton thought for a moment. "I see where you are going, but it would be a million-to-one chance for a print to have survived that long. No, I'm sure it's fresh."

"Just thinking."

"Any luck with Doyle?"

"She lawyered up," Harris said.

"That was quick."

"I got here five minutes too late. Malconni must have been watching the news and made some quick calls."

"So, what are you going to do?"

Harris glanced up at a wall clock. "See if I can bluff my way to some answers."

"Good luck."

"You, too."

Harris hung up and powered off. She took another swig from her soda and started for the holding cell as an odd thought flashed through her consciousness. She remembered a saying she was told when she was first promoted to detective and became the first woman in the Homicide unit. The hostile atmosphere was thick, but one old hand had ignored his comrades and graciously taken her under his wing to teach her the ropes. On the first day, he had sat on the edge of her desk, smiled, and said in an oracular tone, "Evidence is evidence. It speaks for itself. If a piece doesn't fit nice and neat, invert it, flip it a hundred and eighty degrees, and view it from the back side. It's like with people—you learn more about their character by seeing their backyard, then by seeing only the front."

Harris paused just before she reached the holding cell. An odd smile creased her lips.

"You forget something?" the guard asked, trying to interpret Harris's demeanor.

"Maybe I have," the Seattle detective mumbled to herself. "Maybe I have."

62

Linda Reese eased her car down the forest-shrouded, dirt driveway that led to the family cabin on Whidbey Island. The refuge was only thirty miles north of Seattle, plus a twenty-minute ferry ride, but was a haven from the congested roads, strip malls, and miles of tract housing that had mushroomed in the Puget Sound basin in the past thirty years. Deer still roamed the thick woods, and clam beds studded the deserted beaches.

Reese tightened her grip on the steering wheel as she approached the last turn. "Damn you, Richard," she muttered. "You better be here." She slowed for the sharp right and braced herself. Sunbeams streamed through the conifers as the branches thinned. The canopy then opened, revealing the residence their grandfather had built in 1939.

"Thank God," she sighed with relief. "You are here." Her brother's vehicle was parked directly in front of the large log structure. A whiff of smoke rose from the chimney. Reese pulled in beside the other car and quickly exited. "Richard?" she called out in the still air.

There was no response.

She shivered. The city clothes she had on did little to insulate her from the cool dampness, and her high heels immediately sank into the thick bed of wet pine needles. Reese groaned. She carefully tiptoed her way to the porch and climbed the hand-hewn stairs.

"Richard?"

Still no response.

She tried the door and found it unlocked.

She entered.

Her next breath filled her nostrils with the pleasant odor of crackling cedar logs in an open hearth. It came from the room beyond.

"Yoo-hoo, Richard?"

More silence.

"Ah, for crying out loud. Where the hell are you?"

Reese continued inside.

Because the cabin was built on high-bank waterfront and faced outward towards the beach, the first room Reese had entered was the kitchen. She quickly passed through it, and into the adjoining great room. She surveyed the area. Except for the fire, everything appeared as though no one had been inside since summer. Surfaces needed dusting, magazines were out-of-date, and sandals, adequate for the warmer months, still lined the floor adjacent to the front door.

"Richard?"

Reese was about to proceed upstairs to the bedrooms when she gazed through the large picture windows and caught sight of her brother hiking up from the beach. He appeared in deep thought. Reese rushed outside. "Hey, Richard," she shouted, her tone a mixture of anger and relief. "For crying out loud, get up here."

The prosecuting attorney squinted, then grimaced. However, he continued on until he reached the base of the stairs that led up to the deck where his sister stood. There he stopped.

Reese leaned over the railing. "Well, are you coming up?"

Collins drew a deep breath and let it go slowly. "Beautiful morning, isn't it?" He gazed back towards the bluff. "I forgot how much I loved this place."

"What'd you do to your hand?" Reese asked, observing fresh bandages around his thumb and forefinger.

"I slipped coming in last night. It was really dark."

"I'm freezing. Would you get up here? We need to talk, but inside."

"I suppose," Collins said with resignation. He reluctantly grabbed hold of the banister and trod upward. Inside, Collins chose to sit on a window seat, while Reese put her back to the fire. She crossed her arms and was about to begin a scolding when her brother suddenly laughed.

"What's so funny?"

"You—out here with that silk suit and nylons."

She looked herself over and shrugged. "So where'd you get the jeans and flannel shirt?"

"I still have some old clothes in the back bedroom." He drew another breath, relishing it. "Don't you love the smell of this place? I've got to start coming back up here more often."

Reese frowned. Even as a child, she had disliked the cabin. Weekends spent here had seemed like an eternity, with no TV, no friends, no shopping center for miles. And the power was always going off for days at a time, leaving as the only night activity candlelit card games next to the crackling fire.

"Okay, Richard, enough is enough. You've had your flipping nervous breakdown. It's time to get back in focus. I covered you at the Lions breakfast this morning, but that's the last time. Tomorrow you have to tape a couple of ads and there's the Press Club dinner at six. On Saturday, you have a League of Woman Voters dinner. Hey, I also got you a twenty-minute slot on KIRO radio."

"When?"

"Tomorrow, eleven a.m."

"But I've got the Bakerman hearing."

Reese smirked. "I guess you haven't heard."

"Heard what?"

"Richard, some people are handed luck on a golden platter. And you are one of them. I know you've been worried about the case, but stop it. He escaped last night. It was all over the news on the drive up here."

"Escaped?"

"Yeah, don't you see the beauty in it? He's as much as admitted guilt. You won. The voters will love you."

Collins's face did not reflect his seemingly good fortune. He slumped and in a brooding tone said, "Big deal."

Reese gritted her teeth. Before she could say anything further, Collins reached forward to where his sport coat lay folded across the back of a wicker chair and parted it. He withdrew the envelope his sister had provided him the previous day and flicked it to her. She missed the catch, but quickly knelt down and retrieved the packet. She could immediately tell it had yet to be opened. She rose, a questioning look on her face.

Collins faked a smile and said, "I'm not going to need it now."

Reese reared back, anticipating the worst. "God, Richard, I'm not sure I want to hear this." Her eyes focused on her brother's wounded hand.

Collins took note and chuckled. "What, you think I—"

"Christ, I don't know what to think."

He rocked back and thought for a moment. He said, "I guess I owe you an explanation. . . . Who would have thought after all these years?"

"Damn it, Richard, would you just give it to me straight?"

Collins sighed. His eyes became distant. "That old Polaroid you saw yesterday, the one with me and Mickey Dellhanney standing on an enemy bunker . . ."

Reese didn't respond.

Collins drew another deep breath and continued in a low tone. "When that was snapped, I thought I had just single-handedly wiped out an entire NVA platoon. I had emptied all my magazines until there were no more screams. . . . God, it was so dark down there. How could I have known?" He closed his eyes and grimaced. "They later counted twenty-two dead." His voice started quivering. "All children . . . all from a nearby village. They had been taken hostage just before we arrived."

Reese gulped, a look of horror on her face.

Collins's eyes reopened. He was near tears. "A couple of the guys . . . they went back down to do the body count. . . . That's when the truth was discovered. . . . I had killed them all, but none were Vietcong or NVA—only children. . . . God, I doubt if any of them were older than ten."

Collins slumped farther and used his shirtsleeve to wipe away a bead of perspiration from his forehead. He said, "Ten minutes after we figured out what had happened, the major showed up. He's the one that made the call to cover the mess up. He ordered the bunker torched, to get rid of the evidence; then he wrote it up making it sound like I was some kind of hero."

Reese spoke up. "But the money—what's that all about?"

Collins buried his face in his hands. Reese could hear his teeth grinding. Without looking up he replied, "When

Mickey and I got back from 'Nam I needed a job, so he got his brother, Pat, to get me on with the PD. He pulled a few strings and I ended up number one on the eligibility list. A year later, Mickey was dead. He planted his motorcycle in a telephone pole. But at some time point before that, he had told Pat all about Chu Lai and what really happened. And ever since the day I entered politics, Dellhanney has held that sword over my head."

Reese straightened. "He's been blackmailing you?"

Collins looked up and shook his head no, but added, "Not in the traditional sense. I mean, this is the first time he's ever asked for money. It was in more subtle ways, like asking to give a pal a break if they got into a legal jam, or helping out on a land use case he or his brother-in-law had a moneyed interest in. I suppose it was unethical to some degree, but once it started, I couldn't stop it. It was like quicksand. The more I squirmed, the deeper I sank. And of course, I kept justifying it by telling myself it was the price I had to pay to do the otherwise good work I had done in the office. That was, until last night. It was that picture; it brought it all back. I just couldn't do it, not an out-and-out bribe to keep him from shouting baby killer to the public."

Collins drew a deep breath and continued. "I've made a lot of mistakes, but that was a line I couldn't cross. Damn it, I've been in public service since 1969, as a soldier, cop, and DA. Even my big ego couldn't justify a cash payment just for the sake of continuing my political career. Besides, if I ended up on the state bench, the stakes would only have risen."

Reese walked over to her brother. She bent down and gave him a loving hug. "I'm proud of you," she whispered. "You're still my hero." A moment later, she let go and straightened. She thought for a moment and said, "So what do you think Dellhanney's going to do?"

Collins looked up and sighed. "I've been thinking about it all morning. But more importantly, what am I going to do?"

"Well?"

A look of serenity descended upon the aging prosecutor. He folded his hands and started to reply. . . .

The time was 1210.

63

"Here's the deal," Stuart Malconni said.

He and Harris were outside the interview room. Nancy Doyle remained within, her head buried in her arms.

"She wants to cooperate, but is afraid that whatever she does, it'll end up causing more grief for either Carl or his son."

Harris nodded, then motioned for the attorney to step farther away from the cell, and the prying ears of the officer standing nearby. They moved a discreet distance and Harris resumed the conversation. "So, what *can* you tell me?"

"The meth lab, it's not Carl's," Malconni replied.

"Then whose is it?"

"I can't answer that."

Harris eyed the attorney and broke a slight smile. "His son's?"

Not a muscle twitched on Malconni's face.

"Hypothetically speaking, then?"

"Hypothetically," Malconni repeated rhetorically. The words were followed by a slight wink.

Harris's smile widened. "Let me take a wild guess. His kid set the lab up while we had dad on ice for the past week?"

"Look, Sergeant Harris," Malconni said, his lawyerly facade temporarily fading, "let me give you a little background. That way you can better appreciate our position."

Harris swept her hand in a wide stroke. "The floor is yours."

Malconni acknowledged with a nod. "I've known Carl and Nancy for a long time. At heart, they're good people, and neither would ever hurt anyone, but they're not the brightest bulbs on the Christmas tree, if you get my drift. They're pretty simple. They've also both had to deal with lifelong substance abuse problems. Nancy's been clean for nearly six years, but Carl, well, he keeps trying. It's a devil that never leaves his shoulder. I know," Malconni sighed, "from personal experience."

Harris alerted.

"Hypothetically speaking," Malconni was quick to add.

Harris eyed the attorney. "Okay, Carl and Nancy are not Ozzie and Harriet. So where is he?"

Malconni threw up his hands. "Nancy doesn't know—honestly, she doesn't. Look, since Carl got arrested on that drug beef last week, she hasn't slept a night. She was convinced he was finally going to clean his act up. Then from out of nowhere, he gets arrested. You need to understand that she's convinced it was a setup by you guys. She'll swear on a stack of Bibles that Carl wasn't using or cooking."

"What did Carl tell you about the meth that we found on him a week ago?"

The attorney pondered the question and asked, "Are we way off the record?"

"As far off as you'd like."

He thought again and said, "It was his kid's. Carl found it in the apartment, took it, then went out for a drive to cool off. Naturally, with his kind of luck, a taillight was burned out on his pickup. And the idiot had left the Baggie of meth in plain view on the passenger seat."

"Good story. I might even buy it if I were on the jury. . . . So, tell me, Mr. Malconni—"

"It's Stuart."

"Okay, Stuart, tell me this. If Carl and Nancy were such a tight couple, why weren't they living together? Isn't it kind of odd they had separate places?"

"Asinine, bureaucratic rules," Malconni said, shaking his head in disgust. "Since Carl was on parole, and Nancy's a convicted felon, too, the state corrections people, in all their wisdom, won't let them share a house. They'd both be associating with known criminals."

Harris cringed, thought a moment, and said, "So, let me take a stab at how this all panned out. Eckler gets sprung on Tuesday, by snitching on Bakerman, and between then and last night, he finds his kid has been using his place to brew a batch of crystal?"

Malconni nodded. "When he told Nancy, she freaked out. Of course Carl was pretty whacked himself. He was already looking at taking a fall for his son, and he knew his parole officer could walk into his apartment at any time, unannounced. One whiff, and Eckler Senior was on his way back to the pen for serious time. Not to mention the trouble Junior would be in. Anyway, he and Nancy spent all Tuesday night cleaning the place up, and they were going to finish up on Wednesday after Carl got off work, but when he came home and saw a cop car out front—blue lights and all—he rabbited."

Harris rolled her eyes.

"Something wrong?"

"No," she replied as the image of the officer sent to sit on Eckler's place flashed briefly in her consciousness. "Keep going. I'm beginning to buy some of this."

"Well, there's not too much else to tell. Carl called Nancy from a pay phone right afterward. Told her to pack a few things, that they needed to get out of the state. Unfortunately, while she's on the phone, Junior calls her from his girlfriend's house. He had seen the cops at the apartment, too. He's higher than a kite and rambling about what he should do. That's when Senior decides to do the parental thing and heads over to the girl's house. You pretty much know what happened from there."

"So where's Carl?"

"Nancy hasn't seen or heard from him since the phone call."

"You're sure of this?"

"Look, Nancy says she drove around half the night looking for him, but she couldn't find anybody who knew where he might have gone to. Then when she heard on the radio about Junior, she went there to see if she could help."

Harris glanced back at the cell. Doyle still had her head buried. The detective thought for a moment, and turned back to Malconni. "Did you hear about the murder on Queen Anne this morning, the elderly woman?"

Malconni nodded cautiously.

"Eckler might be involved."

The attorney straightened. "Impossible."

"A warrant for his arrest is being issued as we speak."

Harris was bluffing.

"I want to see it. What's your probable cause?"

"In due time."

Malconni bit at his lip. "Okay, even if this is so, what does Nancy have to do with any of this?"

"If she has a clue where he is, you know as well as I do, that's enough to keep her here until she talks. She's a material witness."

"You have no evidence she knows anything."

"Maybe, maybe not, but you can't get a writ of habeas corpus heard until tomorrow morning. We have that long to decide. Oh, and by the way, the victim from this morning—were you aware that she was related to one of your associates?"

"Who?"

"Tessla Quinn."

Malconni's jaw dropped. For a moment, he said nothing. Harris could see his mind racing. Finally, resignation slumped his shoulders. He looked to the floor and back to Harris. "Give me a few more minutes. I want to talk some more with her."

The time was 1231.

64

The tail on the liver-colored Labrador retriever began to wag like a metronome set to high speed. "Ya got something, boy?" his K-9 handler asked.

Several officers and a sergeant were standing nearby. The group included Frank Milkovich, who had delayed his trip to the evidence warehouse yet again. Orders or not, the recapture of Bakerman was now the department's number one priority. At least that was how Milkovich was going to justify this diversion and his assistance to Leah, should Chief Logan ask.

All present turned to the activity.

"Ya smell something, huh, Conan?"

The dog suddenly froze and scented the air. His handler froze too after hand signaling the others to remain where they stood. From the side of his mouth he added, "Conan's got it, I think. Just give him another second."

The search party was in a run-down subsection of Pioneer Square. It was lined with cheap hotels, soup kitchens, and grocers making a living selling fortified wine. From this spot, an observer could turn and look eastward, up the steep First Hill slope, past the interstate, to a point twelve blocks away where the other dogs had lost Bakerman's trail.

The Lab broke its point, and began a slow circle, its nose pressed to the pavement.

"Hey, Smitty," one of the officers called out. "Does he have something or not?"

"He's got it; I'm sure of it."

Milkovich stepped back from the group and swept the area with a careful eye. He sensed Bakerman could be in any one of these old, turn-of-the-century brick tenements. For a couple bucks a night, no questions asked, you could get a room the size of a closet and a urine-stained mattress to sleep on.

Conan started forward.

"He's definitely got something," the handler yelled. Moments later, the pace quickened from a lope to a double time as the big canine pulled the group west, causing oncoming pedestrians to step aside.

The procession continued until the dog suddenly stopped, circled back a number of steps, and began sniffing at the entryway of one of the old buildings. Milkovich gazed upward. The sign above read HOPE HOUSE—WASHINGTON STATE DEPT. OF CORRECTIONS.

"He must have gone inside," a trailing officer theorized.

"Or come out," Milkovich said.

The handler reeled in the leash and had the dog sit. He then pulled out an old knotted rag from his back pocket and tossed it to his four-legged partner. The dog chewed at it greedily, his reward for a successful track.

"Good job, Smitty," the sergeant added. He immediately dispatched two of their group to the rear exit, then radioed the command post their location. He next requested direction on how to proceed and was given permission to do a low-key building search.

Milkovich was already stepping through the familiar doorway, ignoring the others. His years in Narcotics had made him a frequent visitor to this location. The men who inhabited the structure were all recent graduates of the state prison system, a few of whom were trying to get their lives back on track. That was the purpose of the halfway house. It provided a secure, semi-drug-free environment, where acclimation to a new life of choices could begin. For some of the residents, it was a turning point in their lives, and they felt compelled to free their consciences of past wrongs. Milkovich had discovered this fountain of information one night when he had been called here to take a statement. One look around and he had realized the potential for more. Thus, over the years, with his discreet, empathetic approach, he had played parish priest on many occasions for those wanting to bare their souls.

"Hey, long time, no see," Murray, the day manager, said as Milkovich crossed the threshold into the lobby. The furnishings were modest, but superior to the neighboring flophouses. "What's all the hubbub about outside?"

Before Milkovich could answer, the sergeant and several of his men burst through the door, sans Conan and his partner. "You got a Bakerman in here someplace?" the sergeant growled.

The manager glanced questioningly at Milkovich, then to the sergeant. "Who?"

"We're looking for a Clifford Bakerman. He's an escapee from County. Our dog just tracked him to here."

Murray reared back.

Meanwhile, out of the corner of his eye, Milkovich caught sight of a number of residents lounging in the adjacent TV room. The commotion now had all their heads turned his way.

The manager recovered. "Did you say Bakerman?"

The sergeant nodded while two officers fanned out, their hands slipping to their holsters.

Snaps popped.

"Jesus," the manager said. "Is that necessary?"

"Bakerman, is he here or not?"

"Hey, come on, I'm on your side. Gimme a sec. Let me check the records. Christ, I just came on duty an hour ago."

Milkovich turned to the sergeant. "Would you guys tone it down?"

The sergeant chafed. He was the one following procedure, not their uninvited companion.

"Let's see," the manager said as he scrolled through a computer-generated list. "Bakerman, ah—" His head bobbed up. "He's not due in till next Wednesday. But I've got some sticky notes the night guy left. Let me see if—" The man leafed though several of them. "Ah, here we go, Clifford Bakerman. Says he showed up here just before midnight last night. Said he'd gotten an early release."

"Which room?" Milkovich asked as he shot a glance towards the sergeant. His side arm was now unsnapped, his hand tightening its grip around the butt of his 9-mm semi-automatic pistol.

The manager gulped. He was a thin, passive man, a social worker, not an enforcer. "The note," he started slowly, "says he was put temporarily into number thirty-one." His eyes drifted to the staircase.

"Let's go," the sergeant barked. He drew his weapon and led the charge up to the third floor. Heavy footfalls echoed throughout the building.

Milkovich remained. He shrugged his shoulders and ambled towards the TV room. Inside, a dozen men sat about on a tattered couch and easy chairs. An old console television was at the center of their semicircle. They were mostly young, at least to Milkovich's eyes. In their late twenties and early thirties. All wore the badges of their recent imprisonment—cheap gang tattoos, defiant eyes, and toned biceps.

Milkovich stopped at the jamb and leaned in. Several of the occupants continued to stare at him, while the majority turned back to the Road Runner cartoon that was flickering on the screen. However, one individual had not flinched since Milkovich had entered the building. He had remained frozen in his chair, his eyes staring straight ahead. Milkovich had noticed him right away, but not by his face. Milkovich couldn't see it. Instead, it was by the strands of balding gray hair, barely visible above the back of an over-stuffed lounger.

"Mr. Bakerman?" Milkovich gently said.

There was no response.

One of the young residents motioned to Milkovich with a circular motion of his hand and a roll of his eyes. "Cuckoo," he whispered.

Milkovich nodded in understanding and slowly stepped his way around the group until he was face-to-face with the older man. He knelt to one knee so that their eyes were level. "Cliff—?"

The man suddenly stirred from a dreamlike state. "Who are you?"

Milkovich smiled. "Mr. Bakerman, I'm afraid you're going to have to come with me back up to the jail."

"Why? This is where I am supposed to be."

"You're a week early," Murray called out from the TV room entrance. He had followed Milkovich to this point, curious about the investigator's actions.

"Why don't you leave the old fart alone," a young resident protested. "You fuckers are all alike. Cut the geezer some slack."

Milkovich ignored the man and turned to the manager. "Would you go up and tell the sergeant I've got Bakerman in custody? Oh, and ask him if I can borrow a pair of cuffs. I might as well run him up to the jail myself."

Milkovich turned back. "Cliff, would you stand up for me?"

At first Bakerman remained unmoved, an Alzheimer's-like confusion etched on his face. However, the older man slowly processed the request and nodded. Using both arms, he leaned forward and, with Milkovich's help, rose to his feet.

"I've got to pat you down."

Bakerman again nodded a slow understanding.

Milkovich proceeded, but found nothing except a couple of old nickels. Otherwise, the pockets were empty.

"Okay, Mr. Bakerman, let's go for a little walk. You think you can make it?"

"I—I guess so."

Milkovich took his arm and led him out of the TV room to the lobby. As he did, he could hear the excited steps of the other officers flying down the stairs. When they reached the last landing, they slowed. Their first glimpse of Bakerman caused them to quickly reholster their weapons. "That's him?" one of the young officers said disparagingly. "Christ, he's going to need an oxygen bottle just to make it to the car."

"Can it," Milkovich ordered. He reached into his pocket and pulled out his keys. "Here," he said, tossing them to the sergeant. "Have one of your boys jog up and get my car."

An officer volunteered and departed. The rest of the men gave Bakerman a once-over, chuckled among themselves; then they too departed. Throughout this, the old con seemed barely aware of his surroundings. He stood slumped at the shoulders, his glazed eyes drifting without purpose.

Milkovich pulled Murray aside and in a low tone said, "Do me a favor."

"Sure."

"Find out from those clowns in the TV room when any of

them first saw him. And call the night manager. Get him out of bed if you have to. I want to know exactly what Bakerman said when he got here and what was he like. And by the way, don't let anyone into his room. We'll need to search it."

"No problem."

"And one more thing."

"Yeah?"

"Ask the night manager if there was any chance Bakerman could have left and come back—you got all that?"

"Sure, Frank, but what are you thinking?"

"Just call me up at the jail when you have the info."

Murray nodded and headed for his desk telephone. Milkovich returned to Bakerman's side. "Come on, Cliff. My car should be outside now."

The older man nodded as Milkovich took his arm and led him through the building's double glass doors.

65

"I got the details on my way out of North Precinct," Leah Harris said into her cell phone. She was nearing the Queen Anne crime scene, having failed to get Nancy Doyle to say anything further. "Nice job on the collar. Did he say anything?"

"Not a word," Milkovich replied from a jail telephone. "The medical staff is checking him out right now. They think he simply woke up last night, was disoriented, maybe due to the drugs, maybe to his screwy mental state, and simply found his way down to Hope House. The staff around here seems to be buying it, hook, line and sinker."

"Do you?"

"I'm not so sure. Everything on the outside says this guy is some old, pathetic fart, but for just a few seconds, right while I was walking him out to my car, I felt it."

"Felt what," Leah chuckled, "his aura?"

"Yeah, right. . . . No, it was his arm."

"Arm?"

"Yeah, he flinched."

Harris slowed for a four-way stop and said, "So?"

"Leah, the guy is in pretty good shape. Despite all outward appearances, he's solid. I bet he can bench-press twice what I can."

"I didn't know you lifted weights."

"I've been meaning to start."

Harris proceeded through the intersection, her interest piqued. In rapid fashion she asked, "What about timing? When did he get there? Anybody see him?"

"Whoa, slow down. Listen, I just got off the phone with the night manager. He swears Bakerman showed up on their doorstep a few minutes before midnight."

"And that's not odd?"

"Guess not," Milkovich replied. "He said nowadays parolees show up at all hours."

"You got to be kidding me. Doesn't anyone from the prison drive them to the halfway house?"

"Not anymore—budget cuts." Milkovich drew a deep breath and continued. "Get this; new releases going to Hope House get a bus schedule and enough fare to make it. Then the prison kicks their butts out the door. That's why these guys show up there at all hours. They get lost, or take a side trip, if you get my drift."

"But," Leah said, her tone becoming serious, "could he have slipped back out? That's the big question."

"The manager doubts it. He said he had to practically carry Bakerman up the stairs to his room."

"What about security? Any there?"

"The back exit is alarmed," Milkovich replied, "and so are the fire escapes, but from what I remember about the place, if the desk guy is using the head or something, anyone can slip in or out the front door unnoticed."

"Oh, great," Harris sighed. "So there's no way to nail down any of this. . . . Hey, what's the odds one of the residents saw him lurking around later on? Maybe, like, between five and six a.m.?"

"Is that when the nun got it?'

"Actually, no. We're looking at about two a.m. But we're pretty certain the killer hung around till four thirty tossing the place, but very carefully. You can hardly tell."

"Hmmm—the only thing the night manager said was that he had gone into the kitchen to make a pot of coffee around seven thirty this morning. When he came back out, Bakerman and a couple other guys were sitting around the TV, watching the news."

Harris thought for a moment and asked, "What about this? When you were close to him, could you tell if he had taken a shower recently?"

Milkovich understood Harris's line of reasoning. Even a clean kill would have left trace evidence on the perpetrator, which would need immediate cleansing. Blowback from the iron poker that split Sister Cecilia's head open would have spattered the perpetrator's hand with a microspeckling of blood.

"Come to think of it," Milkovich replied, "what hair he had was all fluffy like it had been recently washed, and he wasn't ripe like his TV companions." Milkovich thought another moment. "Yeah, I'd say he had taken a shower within the last couple of hours."

"What about his clothes?"

"Already bagged and tagged for you, but I didn't see anything obvious."

"Don't forget his shoes. We might get lucky and find carpet fibers from the Volvo stuck on them." Harris signaled a left turn, then suddenly gnashed her teeth.

"Now what's the matter?"

She looked both ways before she replied, "Everything. It's all so goddamn circumstantial. Even if Bakerman did manage to slip out, and somehow got up to Queen Anne Hill, and killed Sister Cecilia, and drove her car to the mall, why the hell would he have done it in the first place? Christ, Frank, nothing makes sense."

"What about the ring? Anything come of it?"

Harris groaned again. "Jane managed to lift a partial print, but we have something like three thousand names to go through, all of 'em with no criminal record."

"So it wasn't Eckler or Bakerman?"

"Jane doesn't think so."

"Someone else, huh? Any ideas?"

"God, Frank, I don't know. Phil, Ed, me, Jane, and even Roy all have theories, but that's all they are, a bunch of speculative bullshit."

"There still has to be a reason for the ring and the cards and your victim being killed. Hey wait a second—what was the time on that grocery receipt you mentioned?"

"Twelve thirtyish."

"Hmmm . . ."

The phone connection went quiet. Harris slowed her vehicle and wheeled to the curb. She was now three cars back from the barrier tape that still blocked entry to the Queen Anne murder scene. A new officer stood guard eyeing a dwindling crowd of onlookers. All traces of the media were gone. "Thank God," she mumbled to herself.

"What's that?" Milkovich piped back up.

"The TV reporters, they've moved on. . . . Okay, out with it. What are you thinking?"

"The timing," Milkovich offered. "It's really odd."

Harris was confused. She turned the ignition off and settled into her seat. "How so?"

Milkovich replied, "If the perp got into the house like you think, that had to have been no later than one a.m. If your time of death is two, that means a whole hour passed before she was killed . . . .Were there any signs of a struggle on her part? Were her hand's bound? Anything at all?"

"No, I didn't see any marks. . . ." Harris suddenly straightened. "I see what you mean. What were they doing for all of that time? If it was just Sister Cecilia's silence the guy was after, he would have just killed her and got the hell out of there."

"Obviously he was looking for something beyond silence."

Harris found herself nodding in agreement. "But wait a second, Frank. If we plug Bakerman back into the equation, how would he have known where she lived, not to mention how in the hell did he get from Pioneer Square to Queen Anne in less than an hour after he checked into Hope House?"

Milkovich suddenly chuckled.

"What's so funny?"

"Just a thought." His bemused tone continued. "I think I know a way to prove Bakerman was or wasn't there."

Harris jumped forward in her car seat. "How, Frank?"

Milkovich told her.

Harris's reply was instantaneous. "You got to be kidding. It would never hold up in court."

"That's not the point. Bakerman may not be your guy. This might confirm that. Besides, what have we got to lose?"

Harris thought for a moment, rubbed the back of her neck, the same spot that had been sore the previous evening, and sighed, "Ah, hell, let's give it a try."

The time was 1331.

66

Paul Anders stepped solemnly down the corridors of Mendleson, Malconni and Swigartt, LLP. He thought he was alone except for the secretarial staff. All the other attorneys were in court or interviewing their clients in jail. However, as he rounded the corner to the section housing the junior associates, he saw an open door. "Tess?" He quickly closed the distance, stopping abruptly at the entrance to the windowless, inner office.

"Tess?" he gently repeated.

The young female attorney did not respond. Her back was to him; her head slumped in seeming despair.

"Hey, how are you doing?"

Slowly she stirred and swiveled about. It was obvious she had been crying. Her eyes were red and puffy. "Paul," she sniffled, "what are you doing here?"

"Working," he replied. He leaned on the doorjamb and continued. "But what the heck are you doing here? God, I'm so sorry for you. I saw you on TV—your poor aunt. And to top it off, Bakerman. Say, did you hear? He's back in custody. The news said they found him in the halfway house he was supposed to check into next week. Did you know he had gotten sick last night and was taken to Harborview?"

Quinn shook her head no and added, "Not till Sergeant Harris told me this morning."

Anders leaned farther in. "Look, Tess, when I heard about all of this, I figured you'd be in no shape to handle tomorrow's hearing, so I decided to get to work on it so you wouldn't have to worry. And now, given the circumstances, why don't we just go ahead and get a continuance?"

"I don't know . . . ," Quinn sighed. She wiped an eye and continued. "Sergeant Harris let it slip this morning that there is no DNA evidence. It was destroyed years ago."

Anders straightened. "What did I tell you? The heck with the continuance, we'll spring him for sure."

Quinn reached for a tissue and blew her nose. Anders backpedaled, suddenly realizing his exuberance was inappropriate. "Jeez, Tess, is there anything I can do for you, anything at all?"

She drew a deep breath and sighed. "I just needed some quiet time. The phone at my apartment was ringing off the hook. I just needed to be alone for a while."

"Does your brother know yet?"

"I called him. He's flying in tonight."

"Do you need help with the arrangements or anything?"

"Thanks, Paul, but once the word got out to the diocese, it looks like the archbishop himself is going to perform the service. The church is going to take care of everything."

"Okay, well, I'm going to go down to my office and draft a couple of motions. I've been doing some research. I think, with a little work, I can overturn Bakerman's original conviction. It was clearly an illegal search of his house."

Quinn nodded apathetically. Meanwhile, Anders stepped back from the doorway and took several slow steps, but once out of earshot, he double-timed it to his cubicle.

67

Harris keyed the mike on the portable radio. "Are you set, nine one?"

"Affirm. I just gave Conan another whiff of Bakerman's bedsheet. He's loaded for bear."

"Switch over to TAC-five."

"Stand by, switching."

The hand holding the radio drooped as Harris looked outward from the carriage porch of Sister Cecilia's home. Flanking her were Jennings and a skeptical Gilroy. All eyes were focused on a distant patrol car parked three blocks away, at a point where the quiet residential street intersected with Queen Anne Avenue, the main north-south arterial. There, a lone officer and his anxious K-9 partner waited for the signal to begin.

"Ten bucks," Gilroy joked, "says the dog doesn't get anywhere near here." He turned and eyed his colleagues.

"I don't bet," Jennings mumbled.

"You're on," Harris replied. She lifted the radio. "Okay, Smitty, have at it."

"Starting now."

The trio on the porch leaned forward, straining to see the activity. Unfortunately, for nearly a minute, there appeared to be little. The big Lab, now on a twenty-foot tether, seemed to be more interested in the surrounding shrubs and telephone poles than in finding a trail that led their way.

Impatient, Harris reactivated her radio. "Anything, Smitty?"

"Not yet."

Harris bit at her lip.

"It's an interesting theory you have." Jennings spoke up, sensing Harris's misgivings. "Frank tells you that one of the K-9 units had a perfect track from the hospital room to a point about a block west of Harborview, then lost it. And then this dog picked the trail up about a block shy of Hope House. That's at least a mile gap."

Harris nodded and said, "That's what Frank figured. He thinks the only way that could have happened was if Baker-man had gotten a lift."

"Taxi?"

"Already been checked out."

"What about a bus?" Jane Fenton said innocently. She had quietly joined them from inside the house.

"Yeah, right," Gilroy sniped.

Harris didn't comment. Instead, she snapped the radio to her lips. "Smitty?"

"Go ahead, Sarge."

"Take your boy down a block to Kerry Park. See if he'll work back this way on Fourth or Fifth Street."

"Roger, moving down now."

Moments later, the K-9 unit dipped from sight.

"The main bus stop there?" Jennings commented.

Harris nodded again.

"What?" Gilroy said. "You think he rode a bus here to commit this murder? You got to be kidding me. My money is still on Eckler."

"It makes sense," Jennings said, ignoring his coworker.

"A bus," Fenton added. "There's something really sick about that, but brilliant at the same time."

"Especially on a Wednesday night," Harris agreed. "Think about it. There's free shuttles running every ten minutes for the bar crowd—all feeding to and from Pioneer Square. Bakerman could have blended right in. Who would've noticed another drunk look-alike?"

Jane stepped to the forefront. "Come to think of it, Northgate Mall—the park-and-ride, not three hundred yards from where we found the Volvo, all the early-morning commuters. He could have caught a bus back downtown from there."

Gilroy suddenly popped his forehead with the palm of his hand. "Of course," he said, thinking aloud. "He was a bus driver for twelve years. He would have known all the routes."

Harris nodded knowingly.

"Excuse me," Roy said as pushed his way through the gathering. "Time for a smoke." He stepped by without further comment and proceeded to the evidence van Jane had parked on the circular drive. There, he opened the passenger door and pulled out his jacket. He had stowed it there on a previous trip out.

The group looked on as each cycled through their thoughts, anxiously awaiting any radio communication confirming Harris's theory. Nervous chitchat began to fill the void.

"Nice day," Fenton began. "Sure beats yesterday."

Jennings inhaled deeply. "There's something clean-smelling after a hard rain. It's like everything has had a good scrubbing."

"Did you get a nose-hit off of Roy?" Fenton rebuked.

Jennings frowned. "You should have been here when he first walked in."

Gilroy chuckled.

Harris did not join in. Her eyes were focused on an imaginary spot, several blocks below the majestic house, where she could visualize her suspect slipping off a crowded, late-night bus, and walking the rest of the distance to this door.

"Okay, Sarge," Harris's radio crackled, "I'm almost there. We have a lot of civilians in the area. I'm going to have to use a short lead, all right?"

Harris gulped, glanced at her comrades, and lifted the radio to her mouth. "Let 'im go."

"Roger that."

All superfluous conversation ceased as each eyed the other in silent anticipation. Even Roy seemed interested in the results. He blew a couple of smoke rings and looked their way.

"Hey," the radio squawked. "We may have something. Conan is scenting. Ya ought to see his tail go!"

Harris covertly crossed her fingers.

"Yeah, he's got something, all right. I'm beginning a track; we're westbound from the bus stop. Mark my time."

Gilroy reached for his wallet.

"Skip it," Harris said, catching the movement from the corner of her eye. A self-satisfied grin began to grow on her face.

"Still proceeding west . . ."

"Boss," Jennings gushed, "you're a genius."

"It was Frank's idea," Harris demurred. "And hang on; he's not here yet."

"Turning onto Fourth. . . ."

"Come home to Papa," Gilroy jabbered.

"Northbound on Fourth . . . he's riding a rail."

Roy quashed his cigarette on the pavement and ambled toward the group. Meanwhile, Gilroy turned to Harris. "So Bakerman gets here maybe a little before our victim pulls in.

He jumps her and they go inside. What do you think happened next?"

Harris thought for a moment and replied, "I'm wondering that myself. There's no real sign of any struggle. It's as if they met at the front door, went in for a—"

"I'm onto Highland Drive . . . almost to you . . ."

A dog across the street began to bark. He was the first to sense the other canine's looming presence. A moment later, Gilroy cried out, "There he is. God, look at him go. He's on a beeline right for us."

"Maybe I will take that ten bucks," Harris quipped.

As Conan and Smitty reached the edge of the Quinn property, he reeled his four-legged partner in for more control. The canine resisted. His nose was still a millimeter above the concrete sniffing wildly, his eyes were bulging, and he strained hard against his collar. At the driveway's entrance his handler jerked hard and gave the command to hold. With hesitation, the dog finally sat, then glanced back over his shoulders, a sad, *gee, boss, why now?* look on his muzzle.

Smitty called out, "Do you want me to come in any farther?"

"Sure," Harris replied. "Let's see where he heads." Then to her colleagues she said, "Come on, let's get out of the way. He'll probably want through here."

The group stepped off the porch and formed a semicircle to the left.

"Okay, boy," the K-9 officer said. "Have at it."

The Lab leaped forward. However, as he neared the entryway, he suddenly reared back and scented the air.

"Whatcha got, boy?"

The Lab continued to scent.

"Now what?" Harris called out.

"Your suspect," Smitty theorized, "probably came in and out of here a couple of times . . . probably some mixing."

"What about the rest of the track?"

"Dead-on," Smitty gushed. "Once I cleared Kerry Park, there was no hesitation. The scent trail was fresh and undisturbed."

Conan suddenly alerted.

"Ah, here we go. He's got it back."

The Lab's tail began to wag again. He moved forward, but after three steps he paused, sniffed the air again, and without warning diverted ten feet to where Harris and her crew were standing. One by one, Conan nuzzled up to the officers, sniffed, then moved on to the next, until he came to Roy.

"Hey, Stoddard," Gilroy chuckled. "He likes you."

Abruptly, the canine reared back on his haunches and began barking wildly. Smitty pulled hard on the leash, but the dog continued its wild behavior. Roy jumped backward, causing a set of examination gloves he had loosely stowed in a rear pocket to fall to the ground.

"Jesus Christ, Smitty," Stoddard screamed. "Call your mutt off."

He didn't have to; Conan instantly focused on the gloves, ignoring the irate lab tech.

"What is it, boy? The gloves? Is that it?"

His tail whipped the air.

Harris looked to Roy. "What was the last thing you touched with those?"

Stoddard eyed the dog suspiciously and replied, "I just bagged the poker from the billiard room."

Harris turned to the dog handler. "If our suspect had touched that, would his scent have transferred to the gloves when Roy bagged it?"

"Maybe, especially if your suspect handled it within the last twelve hours."

Harris exchanged looks with Jennings and Gilroy, then knelt down and patted the big dog. "If only you could testify in court." She lovingly rubbed his thick neck for a few more moments, then rose and said, "Okay, guys, we know who. Any ideas why?"

There was no reply.

The time was 1456.

68

Frank Milkovich pushed the plastic tray of food away from where he sat, and leaned back. "Not bad," he remarked to the jail sergeant who sat across from him. "My mom use to make pea soup just like it."

The man across from him grinned as though he had been the cook. "We like to try to put a little weight on our boys before we kick 'em back out. Lucky we had some left over from lunch."

The Internal Affairs lieutenant stood, thanked the sergeant for raiding the kitchen on his behalf, and headed to the booking station. As he did, he passed by the glassed-in holding tank. Bakerman and several other new arrestees were waiting their turn to be photographed, printed, and changed into the standard bright orange jail overalls. However, unlike the other, younger men, Bakerman sat silently alone at the opposite end of a long metal bench, unmoving and blankly staring. The old con had been checked out and cleared medically for continued custody; his blood sugar level, oddly, was now stabilized. However, the admitting physician was concerned about several suicidal remarks he had made. Because of this, the doctor had placed a call to Monroe prison and spoken with the psychologist whose name appeared in Bakerman's file. After a brief consultation, the psychologist offered to drive the thirty miles and do the evaluation himself. Milkovich had opted to hang around for the psychologist's arrival on the outside chance he might gain some insight into Bakerman and thus help Leah with her case. This despite two pages from his administrative assistant warning him that Chief Logan had called several times from his home in Philadelphia wanting an update on the freezer situation.

Milkovich strode by the holding tank without pausing or gazing in. He did this on purpose, curious what Bakerman's reaction might be.

"Hey, get me my lawyer," one of the young, unwashed men shouted from within. "I want to see my fuckin' lawyer."

Milkovich continued and noted that despite his seeming disengagement, Bakerman had carefully tracked his passage.

"The shrink here yet?" Milkovich asked as he paused in front of the long counter of the booking station. Several corrections officers were milling about, oblivious to the new prisoners beyond.

"Just got here," one said and pointed to an interview room now occupied by a studious-looking man in his late thirties. "We were just gonna bring Mr. Bakerman over to him."

"Would you hold off a sec?" Milkovich asked. "I'd like to talk to the guy first."

The jailer shrugged and returned his attention back to his coworkers.

Milkovich stepped to the room and leaned through the open door. "Hi—Frank Milkovich, SPD. Do you have a minute?"

The man glanced up from a file he was reviewing. He adjusted his wire-rimmed glasses and nodded. "Have a seat. What can I do for you?"

Milkovich took the offered chair, leaned back, and quickly sized up the man before him. He was thinly built, dressed in a corduroy sport coat and jeans. He needed a haircut; the back of his straight brown hair was ducktailing. However, Milkovich quickly sensed a caring individual, albeit frustrated, perhaps by his inability to effectively influence his patients' mental health. It was a slow-burning frustration common to most prison professionals.

Milkovich affected a smile and asked, "How well do you know Mr. Bakerman?"

"He's been a client of mine for a number of years. Why do you ask?"

"Have you had much interaction with him?"

"Actually, yes."

"And?"

The doctor raised a curious brow. "Are you involved with the Sellinzski homicide, the one in the news yesterday?"

"Sort of—it's a long story."

The psychologist closed his file and said in an irritated tone, "I've been trying to get a hold of the lead investigator on that case. She hasn't returned any of my calls."

Milkovich suddenly remembered the name on the crumpled letter found in Eckler's garbage. He now realized the man in front of him had written it.

"She's been busy," Milkovich quickly apologized.

"I suppose, but I think I can help. You know, we're all part of the same criminal justice system."

Milkovich forced an empathetic nod. He then said, "I can assure you, she wasn't ignoring you on purpose. So what did you want to pass along?"

"Are we off the record?"

"If we need to be."

Doctor Vandegrift swallowed hard; his eyes widened. "The guy is dangerous—real dangerous."

Milkovich's smile faded.

The psychologist drew a deep breath and continued. "Beyond that simpleton demeanor is an obsessive-compulsive sociopath. Now, don't get me wrong, he's not some evil genius. In fact, he's pretty much average in intelligence except for a near savantlike ability to focus on trivia."

"How so?"

The younger man rolled his eyes. "He can list for you all the presidents of the United States, their wedding dates, and their wives' maiden names. Or how about all the Roman Catholic popes, starting with Saint Paul?"

"He'd do well on *Jeopardy,*" Milkovich grimly quipped.

"It's not funny."

"I'm not trying to be. . . . What else is he obsessive about?"

"Many things . . . oh, genealogy is one of his favorites. He'd spend months tracking down supposed lost ancestors. He's convinced he's descended from Prussian princes."

Milkovich raised a brow. "How'd he do the research?"

"Letter writing, books, newspapers, and now the Internet. The prison library has limited Web access for inmates to use for harmless diversions like that."

Milkovich leaned back in his chair and stroked his chin. "This is all very interesting, Doctor, but a moment ago I sensed you were real troubled at the prospect of Bakerman on the loose. Why?"

The psychologist shifted in his seat.

"Well?"

"I have no proof."

"Of what?"

He sighed. "I've dealt with hundreds of convicted sex offenders, molesters, rapists, sadists, exhibitionists. Like Bakerman, the majority weren't all that bright, and all of them had significant substance abuse issues. That made them sloppy in their crimes. But Bakerman—sometimes I think he's from another planet. His obsessive focus is yogi-like. He can control his body as if he were a machine—have you seen his medical records?"

Milkovich shook his head no.

"Well, he's been diagnosed with practically everything in the book, but I'm willing to bet most of it is bunk. The symptoms he fabricates, except the diabetes. That's how he gets sympathy—and victims."

"What about this suicide thing?"

"It's BS. He just wants to talk to me, play some more games." The doctor's eyes narrowed. "Listen, Bakerman has killed. I'm certain of it. When Carl disclosed to me the information in that journal, it all fit—the perfect profile."

"What about Eckler? Why did he come to you?"

The doctor was slow to reply. He looked into Milkovich's eyes. "We're still off the record, right?"

Milkovich dipped his head.

The doctor thought for another moment and said, "I was treating him for sexual dysfunction. All the years of drug use had left him impotent. I had helped him with the problem—and his twelve-step program. I guess he felt an obligation to tell me of his discovery."

"And you sent it up your chain of command?"

"One link up and it was promptly ignored. It's the state's damn budget problems and the stupid bureaucracy. Bakerman was a short-timer. They needed his bed for newcomers. The fact that we might be releasing a serial killer made no difference. Rules are rules and damn the consequences."

Milkovich shifted topics. "The nun that was murdered this morning—we think he is somehow responsible. Do you have any idea why he would have chosen a victim like this?"

"How was she killed?"

"Blow to the head, probably with a fireplace poker."

"That doesn't make sense."

"How come?"

"Too quick. Guys like this want to take their time. You know, like a cat with a mouse. He gets his jollies from the fear the victims emit, not the actual coup de grâce." The psychologist suddenly paused and reflected.

"What's the matter now?"

"I was just thinking," the psychologist replied. "If you had to put me on the stand as an expert witness to testify about the likelihood of Bakerman being the perpetrator of a murder like that, well, I'd have to say no—sorry. Not his style."

"I think, in a sense, it was an accident. I think that Bakerman knew the nun, that he originally went to her house not to kill her but to get something."

"What?"

"I don't know. What do you think?"

The younger man shrugged unknowingly, but then muttered, "Accident, hmmm? Well, he definitely is capable of killing, I am certain of that. His regard for human life, other than his own, is nil."

"So tell me, though, do you have any proof of any of what you just told me, anything that can be used in court? He's due back there tomorrow at nine, and unless we can come up with some hard evidence, by nine fifteen there's a chance he could be a free man."

"But the escape, can't he be held for that?"

Milkovich frowned. "I seriously doubt any charges would be filed. At this point, we can't show any intent. He simply walked out of his unguarded hospital room and was later found in a DOC facility. Escape? Technically, he was already back in custody when I found him at Hope House."

"What about the DNA from the old case? The news said he'd be held when that was produced in court."

"It's long gone," Milkovich bluntly replied. "So's probably all the other DNA evidence from other potential victims of that time period."

The doctor sagged. "Oh dear, what are you going to do?"

Milkovich had no ready reply.

69

"Stay on the red line," the jail guard growled. "That's rule one around here."

The exhausted young man emerged from the holding tank. It was his turn to be booked. He stepped cautiously towards the marking, paused, and in a dazed tone pleaded, "I gotta have a cigarette."

"Sorry, kid, no smoking. That's rule number two. Now get your ass in gear."

The slightly-built teen wavered, and caught himself on the doorjamb. Meanwhile, Frank Milkovich had just stepped out of the interview room. Their eyes met.

"Pick it up, Eckler," the senior guard at the counter bellowed. "We don't have all day. You can sleep it off when we get your prints done."

Milkovich stopped. He looked over at the paunchy officer. "Is that the kid from—?"

"Yep. The little turd that knifed his dad and—"

"Yeah, I heard. . . . You mind if I talk to him too?"

The guard glanced at a wall clock. "It's near break time. Why not? Use the room next to the doc's."

Milkovich reversed his track and entered the adjacent room. He took the far seat and waited. Moments later, Jason

Eckler was brought to him. "Take a load off," he said to the trembling youth. Eckler teetered, then plopped into the offered chair. The metal door clanged shut. Startled, the new inmate shot a fearful glance backward.

"That's why they call it the slammer," Milkovich said in a reassuring tone.

The young man turned back. "You a lawyer?"

"Cop, actually."

"I ain't saying shit."

"You've been advised of your Miranda rights, haven't you?"

"Yeah?"

"Then you know you don't have to."

"So what the fuck am I doing in here with you? I just want to crash."

Milkovich nodded knowingly, then said, "You realize you're in a lot of trouble right now."

"Big fuckin' deal."

"It will be in a couple of days when you figure out you'll be twenty-five, maybe thirty years old before you're walking free again."

Jason sagged.

"You ever been arrested before?"

Without looking up, Eckler replied, "I know what it's like. My ol' man did lots of time in the joint."

"You mean Carl?"

His head bobbed back up. "Yeah, you know him?"

Milkovich didn't answer. In observing Eckler Junior, he noted that the young man appeared to be well fed, his clothes were relatively clean, and he lacked the crude tattooing that so many longtime meth users possessed. In short, he talked tough, but the veteran investigator saw right through it.

"Look, I'm not here about your case. I'm working something else. In fact, I'm kinda interested in that old guy who is in the tank with you."

"What about him?"

"He say anything?"

Jason grimaced. "He's a fuckin' pervert."

"How so?"

"Shit, ever since they tossed him in with us, all he's been doing is staring at me and lickin' his chops."

Milkovich leaned back in his chair and chuckled the irony. "I think he knows your dad—you two must look alike."

The kid gave an uncommitted shrug.

"Speaking of your dad, do you know where he might have gone after—?"

"Oh, man," Eckler sighed. "Now I get it. You're here about the shit in his apartment?"

"You want to tell me about it?"

"Aw, fuck, that's how this all got started."

"How so?"

"I ain't saying."

"Let me take a guess, then, okay?"

There was no reply.

Milkovich thought for a moment and said, "The way I see it, you found one of your dad's old cookbooks and decided to try to mix a batch of meth for you and your pals."

Eckler's eyes jittered. "Maybe—maybe not."

Milkovich leaned forward. In a forceful tone he said, "Look, son, I really don't give a rip about the meth or the assault or anything that happened afterward. I just need to find your dad and you can go a long ways in helping your, and his, situation by telling me where he might be holing up."

Eckler's head began to droop. "I just wanna go to . . ."

"Come on, tell me."

It fell farther. "I—I don't . . ."

Milkovich reached over to shake him, but it was too late. There was a dull thud as Jason Eckler's head hit the table. He was fast asleep.

70

"Heads up, the captain is back," a portable radio crackled. The officer guarding the front entrance to Sister Cecilia's home stiffened. Harris groaned. She was on her cell phone, just inside the doorway.

"Something the matter?" Frank Milkovich asked over their connection. He was now in his car, nearing the evidence warehouse. Traffic was heavy.

"Brass alert," Harris replied. "I gotta go."

"But what do you think about the shrink's profile?"

"I couldn't agree more—it's great backfill—but we still need the Rosetta stone. We don't have anywhere near enough for an arrest warrant."

Harris peeked out the doorway, saw her supervisor nearing the front gate, and ducked back in before she could be seen. In a hurry she said, "Call me back in a bit; we're planning on heading to the barn soon, ordering pizza, and chalkboarding the two cases. You want pepperoni or Canadian bacon?"

Milkovich sighed longingly.

"Jesus, Frank. Did you really think we'd have a quiet evening tonight?"

"Pepperoni."

Harris disconnected. She adjusted her ball cap in a feeble effort to look more presentable and stepped back outside. The officer standing watch, sensing the pending confrontation, meandered out of earshot.

"Hey, Cap," Leah cheerfully intoned as the husky-framed man, dressed in a dark business suit, neared the porch. "What brings you this way?"

"Cut the crap, Harris," Captain Varna snapped. "Damn it, I ought to be chewing you out, but right now I'm just a messenger boy."

Harris looked skyward, her face flush with innocence.

The captain continued. "You know, if you'd answer my messages once in a while, maybe I could help you. That is my job, you know."

"I'm—"

"Skip it," Varna gruffly interrupted. "Look, about an hour ago, I got a call from the PA's office. Collins has yanked himself from the Sellinzski case, and his chief deputy, Ted Wallace, is handling it from here on out. He wants to see you, like, yesterday. He's scrambling to put something together for tomorrow's hearing. He's afraid, after all is said and done, Bakerman will walk. On top of that, now I'm hearing rumors you think Bakerman is somehow responsible for this murder. What gives?"

"Collins yanked himself? Why?"

"Wallace wouldn't say, but he sounded pretty POed. Especially when I told him we didn't have the DNA sample."

"How'd you know?"

Varna scowled and looked about. "Some of your subordinates do return phone calls." His head swung back. "And what's this I hear about Milkovich poking into this? Christ, whatever happened to the chain of command around here?"

Varna was now red-faced.

Harris sighed. "You want the long story or just the executive summary?"

"Neither. Look, Leah, you wouldn't be out here free-agenting it unless I had a hell of a lot of faith in your ability to produce results. I still have that faith, and I'm not about to start second-guessing you now. Just stay in touch, so I can cover your, and my, ass—especially with a new chief in town."

Harris nodded obediently. This was the third time in the last six months she had been given this lecture—she was certain it would not be her last. And judging by Captain Varna's exasperated brow, he was certain of this, too.

"I don't suppose you have Wallace's direct number?"

Varna parted his coat and pulled out a scrap of paper. "Here," he said, handing it over. "I figured you'd need these. That's his office line, cell phone, and home phone."

Harris gratefully accepted the information. Then in a peacekeeping effort, she offered, "Hey, boss, do you want a quick tour?"

Captain Varna shook his head no. "Just solve the damn thing." He did an about-face and marched back the way he had come, leaving Harris all alone on the porch.

The sun was setting behind a band of clouds; daylight was fading, and the shadows were growing long. Only a few hours remained to solidify her suppositions. Harris felt a chill. She shivered and pulled her collar up. With her cell phone still in her hand, she started to dial Wallace's number, but stopped midway. "Ah, man," she groaned. The low-battery signal was flashing. A moment later, the phone powered itself off. In quiet despair, she slumped against the doorjamb and felt her confidence wane. Suddenly the only thought that filled her mind was the unthinkable prospect that the debt owed Cindy Jo Sellinzski, and now Sister Cecilia, would likely go unpaid.

71

Frank Milkovich popped his car door and stepped out onto the old concrete pavement surrounding the evidence warehouse. It had been years since any repairs had been made to the surface, and wherever it had been worn raw, the original hoof-scarred bricks showed through.

While en route, Milkovich had returned Chief Logan's call at his East Coast residence. His wife had answered. They were just sitting down to their first family dinner in months, and the irritation in her voice from the disruption was evident. He left a quick message and hung up, relieved at not yet having to explain the day's events directly to his new boss.

Milkovich straightened as the sound of approaching footsteps caused him to turn around. It was George, the evidence clerk. He wore the happy smile of a man completing another day's work. In one hand, he held his empty lunch pail, in the other, a folded newspaper. He was humming a quiet tune, but this, and his smile, vanished the moment he caught sight of the Internal Affairs lieutenant.

"Hi, George," Milkovich called out in a friendly tone. "I was just coming to see you."

The clerk took one last step and froze.

Milkovich affected a casual demeanor. He leaned forward, resting his elbows on the top of his car as though he were about to exchange pleasantries with a neighbor. "Nice day, huh?"

The clerk remained where he stood, twenty feet from Milkovich. He was clearly trembling. Milkovich took note. While he had grown used to having fellow employees become nervous or hostile the moment he turned his focus on them, George's reaction seemed over-the-top. Was it because of the documents Roy had turned up, Dellhanney, or something he should have anticipated? Milkovich proceeded cautiously. "Something wrong?"

George's reply was a slow, mortified headshake.

Milkovich thought for another moment. He had known the man in front of him for many years, at least on a casual basis. During his days in Narcotics, he had placed hundreds of items of evidence in his custody and never once had he seen his cheerful smile break.

The clerk drew a calming breath. He moved closer and in a wavering voice said, "Is there anything I can do for you, sir?"

"Actually there is," Milkovich replied as he continued to study the man. "We need to talk."

George stiffened. "Are you ordering me?"

Milkovich was not surprised by the answer. In fact, it was a standard reply by a rank-and-file member. He responded in turn with a vague, "Maybe yes, maybe no."

A confused look formed on the Asian man's face.

"You see," Milkovich continued in a measured tone, "I had a little meeting with your former boss last night, good ol' Captain Dellhanney."

George's eyes widened. He stuttered, "H-how's he doing?"

"Oh, just fine, George, just fine." Milkovich shifted on

his feet, but retained his laid-back facade. "He told me, and the new chief, a funny story 'bout some, shall we say, screwups from a few years back, and unfortunately, your name came up in the mix."

George's pail dropped.

"You want to tell me about it?"

"I—I'm not sure what you mean."

Milkovich straightened. It was time for his bad-cop routine. His eyes bored into the much shorter man and he growled, "Don't give me that crap." Milkovich then stepped around the back of his car and confronted the warehouseman. "Look, I don't have time to play games, and if you want your union rep, well, you can kiss my sweet ass. I don't have time for that either. I need answers, not bullshit."

George took it all in, gulped, and slowly knelt to retrieve his lunch box. As he rose, he grimly muttered, "He'll kill me if he finds out."

"Who?"

"You know."

"Dellhanney?"

The clerk nodded.

Milkovich paused. The conversation had immediately vectored into an area that might bear fruit. He was certain George had not been involved in the original incident. He was an outsider who would never have been included. More likely, he had been intimidated into assisting in the cover-up. Yet Milkovich sensed that this was not what the clerk meant.

Milkovich probed further. "Dellhanney's a jerk, but he's not about to cause you any harm. In fact, he's the one who came to us and spilled the whole story about the jail inmates and the freezer."

"And you believed him?"

"Perhaps, but now that the cards are on the table, there's no reason for him to be coming after you for talking."

George's lack of response told Milkovich there was definitely more to the story. He continued eye contact to gain a clue—but none was forthcoming. He tried a different tack. "Tell me, George, back in 'eighty-five, were you working any of the days when they brought the jail inmates in here to clean up?"

He nodded slowly.

"Was anyone watching them, guards or someone?"

He nodded again.

"Closely?"

He shrugged.

"Yes or no?"

"Kind of."

"Damn it, yes or no."

A guilty look flashed across George's face. Milkovich caught it and suddenly understood its meaning. He said, "The jail inmates had nothing to do with the freezer heating up, did they?"

George lowered his head. In a remorseful voice he replied, "I couldn't afford to lose my job. I still can't."

Suddenly, the detective's stiff posture slackened, and he said, "Just tell me the truth, and odds are your name will get deleted from my final report."

George looked back up, a glimmer of hope returning. "No, Lieutenant, the jail workers never got near the freezers. It was all my fault."

Milkovich raised a brow.

"See, late one Friday, after I had been working in there, I didn't double-check to make sure the door was closed properly. Over the weekend, the door swung open and warmed everything up. I caught the problem when I came back to work on Monday, but by then—well, everything had thawed and was ruined."

"And you knew Dellhanney would've fired you?"

George nodded. "I had a wife and four kids to feed. What was I to do?"

"So what exactly did happen?"

"I went over to the breaker board," the clerk replied, "way over at the other end of the warehouse where the jail crew had been the week before, and threw a switch to make it look like that caused the malfunction. When I reported the problem a few days later, well, everyone naturally assumed, you know, one of those guys had done it."

Milkovich gazed skyward, a bemused look on his face. It vanished a moment later as a new thought crossed his mind.

The warehouseman was confused by Milkovich's sudden change of expression. "Excuse me, Lieutenant, is there something wrong? I'm telling you how it really happened."

"I know you are," the Internal Affairs lieutenant replied. "But I've got the feeling there's a little more to it, isn't there?"

"How do you mean?"

Milkovich shifted on his feet again. "Yesterday—Roy— the old records he found. Did he find them, or did you *let* him find them?"

George wilted.

"Look," Milkovich said, "I know how things used to work around here. Stashing paperwork you were ordered to shred was just insurance. Might keep your butt out of the wringer when the time came."

With a slight dip of his head, George confirmed Milkovich's supposition. The only question that now remained was why he did what he did, and it took Milkovich only a moment more to realize that the answer to that question could only be Dellhanney. In an understanding tone, he said, "Was the captain leaning on you, maybe to forget everything about the incident and back up whatever he told us?"

George drew a deep breath. "I just don't want no trouble. Understand, Lieutenant? I never have. I like my job; I got four more years before I retire. I just don't want no trouble."

Milkovich nodded. "Look, so far, your name is not in my report. So talk to me."

The warehouseman gulped.

"Come on."

George processed.

Milkovich grew stern.

"Okay, okay." He paused, gulped again, and said, "When Sergeant Harris phoned down the request for that girl's bio-evidence Tuesday afternoon, I panicked. I was so scared; I knew there was going to be a big problem. So I called the captain at home cuz he was the one who ordered me to throw everything out. I just didn't know what to do. See, I was hoping that maybe he could handle it. The captain still knows his way around the department."

Milkovich grimaced.

"Anyway, he was real upset. Guess he's been on hard times. Said that of all things, he didn't need this kinda crap happening right now. He said he had some kind of business deal cooking and any bad press with his name involved would bankrupt him."

"Did he threaten you to keep quiet?"

"At first—well, you know how he is. But then, he offered to make my silence worth my while."

"How much?"

The clerk swallowed hard and replied, "Ten thousand."

That raised Milkovich's brow. He said, "If he was so broke, where in the hell was he going to come up with that kind of cash?"

George shrugged unknowingly.

"Okay—so what did you tell him?"

"I was scared, Lieutenant. Honest, I was."

"You agreed, then?"

The evidence clerk nodded, but added, "That night, I didn't sleep a wink. I knew it was wrong, but what was I supposed to do? I was the one who screwed up. It was all my fault in the first place."

"Have you talked to Dellhanney since?"

George shook his head no.

"So you've seen no money."

He repeated the gesture.

"All right," Milkovich said. He sensed the clerk was now telling the whole truth. "Let's move on. You had second thoughts, right? That's why you *let* Roy find the destruct records you've kept all these years."

"Yes . . ," George admitted with a sigh. "I couldn't just give them to him. The captain would have found out, and well, you know what he would do."

Milkovich didn't respond. He looked skyward and for a couple of seconds his thoughts drifted. It would be a pleasant, clear evening, he sensed. Perhaps a bit cool, but the kind of night when the stars would shine and the moon's reflection would shimmer off the waters of Puget Sound. He wished he and Leah could share the moment, but he knew it was not to be. He drew a deep breath and looked back to the clerk. "Get outta here," he barked. "Go home; be with your family."

"But am I—?"

"In trouble?" Milkovich interrupted. He thought for a moment and replied in a world-weary tone, "Christ, George, I wouldn't have a clue how to spell your last name. So why would I want to put it in a report?"

72

It was rush hour again, and the heavy traffic from Queen Anne Hill to the center of downtown tripled the time it would normally have taken Leah Harris to drive the short distance. She headed directly for her assigned parking stall beneath police headquarters, left her car, and proceeded to walk the four blocks to the King County Courthouse.

Throughout the journey, Harris had continued to re-sort the evidence, systematically flipping items back and forth in her mind, testing the fit in untried ways. "There has to be a reason," she kept mumbling, mantralike, while her fingers nervously tapped the steering wheel, waiting for each red light to turn green. Fatigue, unfortunately, was beginning to dull her thinking, and the hoped-for paradigm shift seemed stuck in an unending cycle of discarded theories. Thus, with her mind so absorbed, it wasn't until she had left the confines of the parking garage and stepped out onto the crowded city sidewalk that she suddenly became self-conscious about her appearance.

Still in the jogging suit she donned at five a.m., and with not a trace of makeup on, she was horrified to see her reflection in the first shop window she passed, a jewelry store. She stepped back. "My God," she mouthed. Slowly, her hand rose upward and fingered the deep lines that now visited her sleep-deprived face. Worse, in a sea of business suits and wool coats, Harris's clothing now seemed acutely out of place. Panic—the ugly-duckling feelings from distant years—welled up. She felt naked, and she suddenly imagined scornful eyes casting glances her way. Harris shuddered and struggled to override this flood of pent-up insecurity. *Why now? Why, in God's name, now?* But then, an odd thought washed ashore. Her mental tremors ceased. She turned away from the ring-laden display and whispered, "I wonder . . . ?"

A surge of adrenaline crackled through her body. With renewed vigor and focus, she darted her way along the sidewalk, passing everyone. Five minutes later, she had cleared through the security check at the courthouse and was exiting the elevator on the eighth floor, excited to discuss her revelation with Ted Wallace, Collins's chief criminal deputy. This case was solvable, she now knew. She just needed more time. Unfortunately, as she neared the PA's familiar office, Harris was dismayed to see that he was not alone. His open door revealed two men, in chairs just inside. They turned as Harris approached. She recognized neither, although both looked polished and professional.

The two men rose to greet her.

"Oh, there you are," Wallace said. He remained behind his desk. "I tried to call you, but—anyway, I'd like you to meet Dr. Felder, and his attorney, Ray Addams. They requested to meet with you personally, to clear up a few things."

Harris eyed the pair as both extended their hands in greeting. *Felder?* Her mind raced. *Felder—the burger flipper.* She took his nervous hand while glancing back at Wallace.

He shrugged innocently.

Harris then shook Addams's hand. Caught off guard, she fumbled for words. "Clear up some things? I don't understand."

"Maybe I can help," Addams said in a confident tone.

Harris was about to retrieve an extra chair, but before she could, Addams lurched for one and placed it kitty-corner to his own. She ignored him for a moment, her eyes intent on Felder. A bead of sweat had already formed on his pale brow. He looked away, unable to meet her stare.

"Sergeant?" Addams said.

She turned back.

"Have a seat. I'm sure you've had a long day. I can tell that just by looking at you."

A self-conscious moment flashed. However, Felder's curious presence quickly negated the feeling. As Harris settled in, Addams directed his attention back to Wallace. "Like I was telling you, Ted, before my client speaks, we need to establish some ground rules."

"Look, Ray," the deputy PA replied, "I know virtually nothing about this case. Richard dumped it on me about three hours ago. I wouldn't have a clue what to say yes or no to."

"What kind of ground rules?" Harris said, asserting herself. "Give me a for instance." She had quickly moved to the edge of her seat.

Addams paused and glanced at his client.

Felder dipped his head.

"Okay," Addams continued. "For instance, everything said in this room stays here."

Harris raised a questioning brow.

"Really, Ray," Wallace broke in. "This is a criminal case, not some civil lawsuit. I can't agree to that."

Harris noticed Felder wince. She turned to Addams and said, "Dr. Felder is an important witness in the Sellinzski case. He was likely the last person to have seen her alive. Further, he can put Sellinzski together with our suspect. Why in the world would he not want to be open about what he knows?"

"I want to be," Felder protested.

Addams raised a hand to his client. "I'll do the talking for now, Russell. Just be patient."

The doctor chafed.

Confusion appeared on Wallace's face. "With what Leah just said, it would seem Dr. Felder is going to be pretty high profile, no matter what. Why the need for anonymity?"

"Perhaps I misspoke," Addams backpedaled. "We're not talking about what is already on the record. It's, well—" He paused, thought for a moment, and said, "This is hard to characterize without inadvertently divulging the essence of our purpose here."

"Maybe I can help," Harris said in a quiet yet commanding tone.

Since the moment she had entered the room, her thoughts had focused on why here, why now? What had happened to have caused this seemingly successful physician to be quaking in his shoes? It made no sense unless . . .

"What do you mean?" Addams was quick to respond.

Leah leaned forward, her eyes cemented on Felder. Time was running out. She knew she had to take a chance; she had no other choice. Yet this was not some wild stab in the dark. It was an educated guess, the distillation of all that had transpired in the last two days, coupled with the insight only minutes before revealed.

"Well?" Addams pressed.

Leah smiled and said, "Let me offer you one of my own hypotheticals. . . ."

The Seattle detective was now certain that the man sitting to her left, the former fast-food manager, now professor of pulmonary medicine at the University of Washington, was the third party she had been searching for. Dr. Felder had to be the ring man.

73

"Not bad," Gilroy remarked as he flipped the gnawed pizza crust into the empty delivery carton in front of him. "Where'd it come from?"

"New place around the block." Jennings anxiously glanced at the wall clock, then to the remaining unopened boxes. "Where do you think everyone is? Leah had me order enough for an army, and now it's all getting cold."

"I got dibs on the leftovers. Love this stuff for breakfast."

"You got to be kidding," Jennings said. He grabbed his stomach and groaned for effect.

"No, really, pizza is the perfect breakfast food."

Jennings set his piece down. "That reminds me." He opened his desk drawer and withdrew a plastic container of Tums. "Want some?"

Gilroy waved him off. Jennings shrugged, twisted open the lid, and fished out two tablets. Meanwhile, Gilroy wiped his hands on a paper towel and began thumbing through a fresh stack of papers.

"Whatcha got there?"

"Jane e-mailed me a list of potential hits on the partial print she made. I printed it out."

"Looks like a telephone directory."

"Yeah," Gilroy sighed. "I hope I can export the file she sent and get it into our database. If not, it'll take days for one of the secretaries to do all the data entry."

A quiet moment passed; then Jennings asked in a philosophical tone, "So what do you think about the case?"

"Which one?"

"Take your pick."

Gilroy leaned back in his chair and folded his hands behind his head. He thought for a moment and said, "Without any DNA or a confession, we'll never get a jury to convict Bakerman, or anyone for that matter."

"For Sellinzski."

"Of course."

"What about for Sister Cecilia?"

"I don't know. What do you think?"

Jennings didn't reply. Instead, he inserted the antacid tablets into his mouth and began grinding them up with his molars.

"Jesus, Ed, you sound like you're crushing a load of rocks."

The older man grinned and swallowed, washing down the remnants with his soda.

"So?" Gilroy pressed.

"So, what?"

"Cecilia, aka Margaret Quinn," he continued.

Jennings said, "I think the boss is right; Bakerman has got to be good for it."

"What's the motive, then?"

"It has to be something to do with the missing picture. That's the simple explanation. And for my money, it ties the whole setup together, nice and neat."

"Hey, someone is coming," Gilroy interrupted. He shifted around and a moment later Roy entered the room, a scowl contorting his face. In his arms, he carried a box of miscellaneous items he had gathered from the Quinn home. They had been taken as potential evidence. Among the minutiae were old telephone bills, letters, an appointment calendar, and several family photographs. With a thud, he dropped the box on a neighboring desk, and took an empty seat.

"Pizza?" Gilroy offered.

"Fuckin' son of a bitch," Roy groused.

Gilroy and Jennings traded looks.

"Goddamn, fuckin' son of a bitch . . ."

"Hey, Roy," Jennings intervened. "What the heck's the matter?"

Stoddard's jaw tightened. He looked angrily about the squad room and pronounced, "I hate this goddamn fuckin' place. This is the fuckin'est place on the planet."

"Catch you smoking again?" Gilroy sniped.

Stoddard lowered his fiery eyes on the young detective. "You wait, sunshine. Someday you'll see what I mean."

"Ah, come on, Roy," Jennings tried again. "What's eating you?"

"Fuckin' Dellhanney."

"What about him?"

"I just heard it on the way up here. The asshole keeled over today sometime after lunch—goddamn heart attack."

"How is he?"

"Fuckin' dead before his head hit the ground. Goddamn it, and I had the bastard. He was finally going to pay for what he did to Merlock."

Jennings and Gilroy traded looks again.

"Ahh," Roy waxed, "I should've known he'd figure a way to slime out of this one." The evidence tech drew a deep breath, shook his head in disgust, and reached for the six-pack of soda. He selected a root beer.

Meanwhile, Gilroy rose and stepped over to the box Roy

had delivered. He stuck his hand in and pulled out a photograph of the extended Quinn clan. The colors had faded; Tessla appeared to be only a toddler at the time it was snapped, her younger brother not yet born. It was a Christmas scene. Everyone crowded around a richly trimmed tree: Tessla's parents, Sister Cecilia, and an assortment of relatives and friends.

"Hey," Gilroy said. "Take a look at this." He passed the picture over to his partner while Roy continued to stew.

Jennings grasped the eight-by-ten and studied it. "Nice looking family, and well connected too. That's ol' Mayor Blackwell and his wife next to our victim, and on the other side the last King County coroner before we changed to a medical examiner system. I forget his name, but he was a character." Jennings passed the picture back.

"Hey, let me see," Roy asked. His temper had subsided.

Gilroy passed it along.

Like Jennings, Roy studied the picture. Suddenly he said, "Doc Hagerty. That's who it is." He handed it back to Gilroy, who set it aside and resumed shuffling through his pile of documents. A questioning look had formed on his face. Meanwhile Stoddard changed subjects. "Hey, Ed, how's your kids doing?"

Jennings beamed. "Great. Joey got his engineering degree last June and is working at Boeing. Andy's engaged and Suzy is expecting her second."

"What about your youngest?"

"Jillian? Oh, she's a pistol. I was supposed to drive her to school today, but—well, we got kinda tied up. You ought to see the E-mail she sent me."

"She a junior or senior now?"

"Senior."

"Hmmm, just like that Sellinzski kid."

Jennings's face clouded. "Yeah, just like Cindy Jo Sellinzski."

Gilroy straightened. He now had Sellinzski's autopsy report back in hand. He was about to open it, but was distracted when Jennings reached over and withdrew Sister Cecilia's appointment book from the evidence box and began perusing a random page. Gilroy leaned towards the older detective. "Anything interesting?"

Jennings shrugged and flipped the page. "She was a pretty busy old gal. A lot of charity work . . . wait a second."

Gilroy perked. He set the autopsy report aside.

"Look at this," Jennings continued. "She had an interview with a *Seattle Times* reporter last August. That had to have been when . . . hey, Phil, quick, go to their Web site."

He shrugged and turned to his keyboard. "What am I looking for?"

"Do a search in their archive for Sister Cecilia Thomas."

Gilroy complied. He opened his browser and after several mouse clicks said, "Is this what you're looking for— 'The Quinn Family Home,' from September first?"

"Yep, print it out."

As Gilroy did, Jennings jumped from his seat and stepped quickly to the network printer. In the meantime, Stoddard leaned down and picked up the autopsy report. Straightening, he opened it and absently thumbed through the contents.

A moment later, the *Seattle Times* article spewed out. Jennings grabbed it and scanned the contents. "My, God," he groaned. "It's got her street address and her family history. That's how Bakerman would've found her. It's all here in print. And with a darn map to boot."

Stoddard ignored Jennings. However, a moment later he looked up and said, "Hey, did you see this?" He flipped the autopsy report around. On the first page, embossed at the top center, was the letterhead:

> Office of King County Coroner
> Dr. Sean P. Hagerty, MD, Coroner
> Courthouse Building
> Seattle, Washington 98104

"Small world, huh?"

"Hey, let me see that," Frank Milkovich said. He had just entered the squad room.

The time was 1812.

74

"Okay, Dr. Felder," Harris said, her facade skeptical. "Let me get this straight. . . ."

In the past twenty minutes, Leah Harris had listened quietly to the story Felder had to tell. It sounded credible, but Harris was cautious in accepting it at face value. There were certain details that seemed too pat. She wanted to probe further, to study his reaction to purposeful doubt. In her experience, normal people made bad liars. In fact, given a little time and subtle persuasion, most people wanted to rid their souls of guilt. Living a lie was worse than the consequences of disclosure.

". . . So you noticed, after Cindy Jo had left for the night, that she had forgotten her high school ring."

"That's right," Felder replied. "She always took it off at cleanup time, when we had to scrub up the grill."

"And you found it lying in the soap dish, right?"

"Correct. We had a three-tub washrack in back, for cleaning up the dirty pots and pans."

"And you picked it up for safekeeping?"

Felder nodded a yes.

Harris shifted in her chair and, from the corner of her eye, attempted to judge Wallace's reaction to Felder's responses.

He remained stone-faced, although he had been jotting down occasional notes.

"All right," Harris continued. "I guess the first question that comes to mind is, why didn't you return the ring to her mother after she had been attacked?"

Felder blushed. "I should have. . . . I don't know; I was so shook up by the events. To be honest, I forgot I even had it."

"Okay . . ." The response was shaded with doubt.

"Sergeant Harris." It was Addams. "Look, I've known Russell for years. He's as honest as they come. If he says he forgot about the ring, it's the truth."

In response, Harris slyly suggested, "Will he take a lie detector test?" She had been waiting for the right moment to pop that particular question.

"And what good would that do?"

Harris didn't reply. Her attention was focused on Felder, and his reaction to her request.

The physician looked frantically towards his counsel.

Harris smiled.

Addams smiled back. He said, "I'm not sure what would be gained by a lie detector test. You said yourself that Russell is an essential witness in your case. Suppose he were to fail the test, for God knows what reason. That fact would be subject to discovery by the defense. You'd therefore be handing them all they need to impeach your own witness."

"Perhaps," Harris replied. She was well aware of that legal trap and, actually, had no intention of going through with her request. Felder's level of discomfort was all the answer she needed. She thought for a moment and shifted focus. "Let's move on a bit. There's another point I'm curious about."

"And what might that be?" Addams said.

Harris ignored him and locked eyes with his client. "Dr. Felder, you say you kept this ring for all these years and then suddenly, last August, on the anniversary of Cindy Jo's attack, you suddenly decide to, as you say, return it to the scene of the crime."

Felder's head bobbed in acknowledgment. "That's correct. Actually, I had been going through a box of old things from my college days, trying to clean out the garage, and I came across it. It was mixed in with other memorabilia."

"When exactly was that?"

"Fourth of July weekend. I remember it well."

"But why take it back to the scene?"

Felder sighed. "Frankly, Sergeant, I've carried a lot of guilt over her death."

"How so?"

"If my van hadn't had a dead battery that night, I would have driven her home after work."

"Did you do that often?"

Felder blushed again. "W-well, no, not every night, but I was concerned about her walking alone. Besides, her place was on the way to mine."

Harris nodded. She said, "So you simply tossed the ring into the leaves where she was attacked and went on your merry way."

Felder shrugged. "Look, I know it sounds a little weird, but it seemed the right thing to do at the time. Then yesterday, when I saw on the news that you had arrested a suspect, I thought, oh God, you'll probably have a team go over the crime scene again and find the ring I had left there . . . I panicked. Don't you see, I knew there was a possibility that there might be trace evidence on it left by me. Or that I had been seen in the area. The next thing you know, I'd be under arrest for Cindy Jo's murder. . . . Don't you see? Don't you see what could have happened?"

Wallace cleared his throat. "I have a question."

All turned his way.

"Yes, sir?"

"How'd you know where the actual crime scene was, especially after all these years?"

The physician's hands began to tremble. He gulped and said, "I—I had been there before."

"Really?"

Now it was Addams's turn to glance questioningly at his client.

Felder nodded slowly.

"How many times?" Harris pressed.

He shrugged.

"Twice, half a dozen, perhaps a dozen times?"

"Oh, no, not that many times." He paused and wiped his forehead with his hand. "It's like I said; I felt responsible for her death and since I never knew where she was buried, this was her grave site for me. Over the years, I felt compelled to visit and apologize to her . . . . Is there something wrong with that?"

Silence followed. However, as Harris shifted in her seat, readying a new round of questions, Wallace's telephone rang. "Excuse me for a moment," and he picked up the receiver.

Eyes drifted as the PA responded to the call. He said, "Who did you say you were—oh, from the *Times*? You want what? My reaction? To what?" Wallace then listened, his features hardening as the seconds ticked by. "I'm sorry; I can't confirm or deny that. You'll have to speak directly to him. . . . I know, but I can't comment right now—and that's not my comment, understand." He hung up and groaned, "Christ almighty. I don't believe this."

Harris was first speak up. "Something wrong?"

Wallace sagged. "The press caught wind of a rumor that Collins is pulling out of the race and resigning from the PA's office. I'm sorry, Leah, but we're going to have to cut this short. I've got serious damage control to handle."

"What about tomorrow's hearing?"

Wallace threw his hands up. "I'll try for a continuance, but right now, I've got to figure out what's going on." He turned to his other visitors. "Thank you, Dr. Felder, for coming up here and volunteering the information. I'm sure that Sergeant Harris will want to get a written statement from you and check out a few things. As far as keeping the information confidential, we'll do our best, but I can't guarantee it."

Felder seemed relieved. He said, "I just wanted you to hear my side of the story before the police came knocking on my door and putting me in cuffs for something I didn't do."

"Understood. Now if you will excuse me—"

All rose and rapidly shook hands. Addams and Felder then left. However, Harris lingered. As the pair's footsteps faded she asked Wallace, "So what do you think?"

The deputy PA rolled his eyes. "I think I'm going to have a hell of a day tomorrow. Christ, if that reporter is right, Collins is going to announce that the reason he is withdrawing is because someone tried to blackmail him yesterday using an allegation from his past."

"Why would he resign over that?"

Wallace slumped back into his chair. "Evidently, it has something do with his war record. Lying about a medal or something. Beats me, I don't know. It's all ancient history. But what I do know is that his office is going to be a madhouse tomorrow. With Collins pulling out, and Bernhardt a shoo-in, hell, half of us are going to be out of work by the end of next month. God, what a system. I sure hope I can find my old résumé around here someplace."

The attorney began fumbling through his drawer as

Harris looked on in disgust. Moments later, she slipped away without saying a further word—her mood free-falling to its darkest depths. It continued as she trudged back to her office. Arriving, she said little, choosing instead to pace the squad room like a caged tiger while her colleagues glumly rehashed the cases. Unfortunately, their newest information— Milkovich's resolution of the freezer matter, the dog track, Felder's ring story—while clearing up many questions, only added to the pile of circumstantial evidence against Bakerman. A pile that could be easily explained away by any competent defense attorney. They needed more, the glue that bound both cases and victims to an aging diabetic.

"What about the King County victim," Gilroy suggested, "Wendy Rose? We should know tomorrow if they have any DNA evidence."

"It'll take weeks to get that processed," Jennings replied. "Meanwhile, Bakerman walks."

"The state still has to do a blood draw on him. Maybe we'll get lucky and get a hit when it's fed into the database."

"Always the optimist," Jennings sighed.

Milkovich glanced at Leah. "Would you sit down?"

She flashed dagger eyes at him and continued her gait.

"Let her be, Frank," Jennings said. "She does her best thinking when she's like this."

Gilroy glanced at the wall clock. "Less than fourteen more hours till court."

The room fell silent. They all knew time had run out.

75

"All rise," the bailiff announced. "The Superior Court of King County, Department Twenty-one, is now in session, the Honorable Helen Stromberg presiding."

The jammed spectators rose to their feet in unison as the short magistrate emerged from her chambers and walked briskly to the bench. "Be seated," she said en route.

At the prosecutor's table, Leah Harris resumed her place beside Deputy PA Ted Wallace. He had been doodling on a legal pad, ignoring the several binders of notes in front of him. It was clear to Harris his mind was elsewhere. A front-page story on Collins's pending withdrawal from the election had made the headlines in the morning paper. The mob of reporters now present were waiting impatiently for this hearing to conclude so they could corner him for his comments. Bakerman was yesterday's news.

To Harris's left, at the defense table, a somber Tessla Quinn was joined by an animated Paul Anders. She gazed straight ahead, while he nervously reread his notes and fumbled with his law books. Next to him was Clifford Bakerman. He was dressed in a bright orange jail uniform and sat silently, an expression of kindly befuddlement on his face. Directly behind their table, among the contingent of press, was Stuart Malconni. He looked on with paternal apprehension. Meanwhile, in the back row, Phil Gilroy, Ed Jennings, and Frank Milkovich sat discreetly in a corner, observing those ahead and exchanging whispered comments.

"Who's Joe College over there?" Gilroy murmured as the judge settled in.

"I think that's Quinn's brother," Milkovich replied from the side of his mouth. "And that woman over there, next to what's her name from KING-TV, that's Collins's sister, Linda Reese."

Gilroy nodded and said to Ed, "See that guy, fifth row to the left."

"Uh-huh."

"Guess who that is."

Jennings shrugged.

"Dr. Felder, and that's his wife next to him."

Milkovich leaned close. "Any idea who that woman, sixth row, second from the right, is? Felder keeps looking at her like he knows her."

The lady Milkovich was referring to looked to be about fifty. She was on the plump side, but dressed neatly in inexpensive clothes.

"Which one?" Gilroy asked.

"There." Milkovich pointed. "He's staring at her again."

Gilroy leaned forward, then turned questioningly to his partner.

"Beats me," Jennings replied.

Judge Stromberg glanced up and slowly surveyed the courtroom. Her eyes settled on Tessla Quinn. She gave a compassionate nod and said, "Ms. Quinn, due to your personal circumstances, will you be needing more time? The court is willing to delay this matter until Monday—your call."

Quinn rose. "That will not be necessary, Your Honor. My personal situation should not infringe on Mr. Bakerman's freedom. If it pleases the court, my associate, Mr. Anders, is prepared to proceed in my place."

"Very well," Stromberg replied. She shifted to her left. "Mr. Wallace?"

He rose slowly.

"I understand Mr. Collins is unavailable this morning. However, I believe the ball is in your court. Please proceed."

Harris hunkered down, a sense of doom weighing heavily upon her shoulders.

Wallace cleared his throat.

The court hushed.

"Your Honor," he started, "if it pleases the court, let me take a moment to review why we are here today."

"Where's the DNA?" Anders groused.

Quinn kneed him.

Stromberg straightened. Her eyes bore down on the young defense attorney.

He flushed at the unspoken reprimand.

Looking back, her point made, she said, "Go ahead, Mr. Wallace."

The deputy PA drew a deep breath and began. "If you recall, Your Honor, on Wednesday, the state was here because there was probable cause to believe the gentleman to my left, Mr. Bakerman, was responsible for the heinous rape-murder of Cindy Jo Sellinzski. The crime occurred some thirty years prior."

The judge nodded.

"We were led to believe this was so, because a third party, a Mr. Carl Eckler, had provided us with certain circumstantial information linking Mr. Bakerman to this case. In good faith, Mr. Collins filed charges and requested that Mr. Bakerman be held without bail. You stayed this request until this morning, at which time you directed the prosecution to present before you the physical evidence, specifically DNA samples, gleaned from the Sellinzski homicide."

"That is correct, Mr. Wallace. So really, the only question in need of an answer this morning is whether or not your samples exist."

The prosecutor drew a labored breath. "To be honest, Your Honor . . ."

Stromberg leaned forward. "Mr. Wallace, I understand you have had little time to prepare; however, I just need a simple yes or no answer to this one question."

Wallace's face clouded. "Your Honor, there is no one in this courtroom who wants justice for Cindy Jo Sellinzski more than I. But justice takes time and due to the circumstances, I think it would be fair for the court to grant the prosecution a continuance. At least a few more days."

Anders leaped from his chair. "Objection!" he cried. "The internal turmoils of the prosecutor's office are not the problem of this court. Besides, the question concerns the custody of evidence by the police, not their representatives."

"Your Honor," Wallace quickly rebutted, "I had planned on calling witnesses to testify that the evidence culled at the scene of Cindy Jo's attack was missing, but for a good reason. And that—"

"Save it," Judge Stromberg interrupted.

The reporters raised their heads. They caught the first whiff of a new scandal.

"Correct me if I am wrong," Stromberg continued. "But did you just say that the samples are missing?"

Wallace bowed his head. "Yes, Your Honor."

"I see—how missing?"

"Your Honor," Harris said, rising to her feet.

"Yes, Sergeant?"

"There is currently an internal investigation into this situation. A mechanical failure some fifteen years ago may have rendered the biological evidence from this case unusable. However—"

"Fifteen years ago? I see." Sarcasm now laced Stromberg's tone. "And your department has only discovered this in the past forty-eight hours? I hate to ask how many other cases may have been affected by this *mechanical* failure." Harris began to reply, but Judge Stromberg waved her off. "That is not a matter for this court. I want to stay focused. One more time, for the record, Mr. Wallace. The samples Mr. Collins promised, are they available?"

The deputy PA sighed, turned to Harris, and without looking at the judge said, "I am sorry—but no."

The courtroom fell silent.

The judge's brow furrowed. "You understand, Mr. Wallace, that I have no other choice but to deny you motion for a continuance. Further, because of Mr. Collins's haste in filing the charges against Mr. Bakerman without confirming the existence of his evidence, it leaves me no other choice but to dismiss this case with prejudice. Hence, your office may not in the future refile against the defendant for this crime. Next time, don't be in such a hurry."

"But, Your Honor," Wallace protested. "The state can still build a case."

"Mr. Collins should have thought about that before he rushed ahead. I am sorry, but the law is clear in this area."

Wallace slumped.

A murmur erupted in the room.

"Order," Stromberg shouted. "Let's have order here." Her gavel came down hard. Silence followed.

"That's better."

A slight smile cracked Bakerman's face. Only Harris caught it.

In the void, Anders rose to his feet. "Your Honor."

The judge looked down to him. "Yes, Mr. Anders."

"First, I would like to thank the court for its decision. Obviously my client and I are glad to see justice done, to see the innocent protected from the state's malicious, misguided prosecution—"

"Objection."

"Sustained. Mr. Anders, I've got a full calendar for the rest of the day. Please make your point quickly, and save the salt for some other open wound."

Anders dipped his head in deference and continued. "There are two other matters I would like to bring before the court before we are adjourned."

"And what might they be?"

"First, if it pleases the court, Mr. Bakerman has a medical condition that necessitated hospitalization on Wednesday evening. Subsequently, due to this condition and the medications he was placed on—and further, the negligence of the on-duty corrections and nursing staff—he thought he was supposed to be elsewhere and proceeded to that location—Hope House, in Pioneer Square. What I—"

"Your Honor," Wallace said, cutting Anders off. "I believe what defense counsel would like to know is if the state intends to file escape charges against their client."

"Why, yes," Anders said.

"I have reviewed the matter," Wallace replied, "and feel that the circumstances do not warrant such an action. Especially in light of the fact that Mr. Bakerman has only five more days left on his original sentence. That alone raises reasonable doubt, even for me."

Anders nodded happily.

Harris plunked back down in her seat, barely able to control her disgust.

"Very well," Judge Stromberg said. "And what was the other issue?"

"Your Honor," Anders started. "We believe Mr. Bakerman has been the subject of a grave miscarriage of justice."

"How so?"

"I am preparing documents at this time to show that Mr. Bakerman's original conviction for child molestation is tainted, and in fact, he is innocent of the crime."

The courtroom stilled.

The judge cocked her head with interest.

Harris elbowed Wallace.

Tessla Quinn remained silent, her unemotional gaze still directed straight ahead.

Anders turned, reached for a legal document, and resumed. "Your Honor, may I approach the bench?"

"You may."

Anders passed a duplicate to Wallace and came forward.

"And this is?" Stromberg asked as she took possession of the paperwork.

"A motion, Your Honor, to stay any blood draws upon Mr. Bakerman for the purposes of DNA typing, as required by law prior to his release from prison as a convicted sex offender."

"Mr. Wallace?"

"A moment please." He speed-read the paperwork.

The judge nodded and also commenced study of the motion. When she had read the two-page argument, she looked up and waited for Wallace to do the same. A moment later he did. She asked, "Would you like a brief recess to consider this, Mr. Wallace?"

"No," he replied. "I think it's reasonable."

Leah Harris snatched the document from Wallace's hand.

"Then you understand what Mr. Anders is requesting, that I stay the mandated DNA typing until he can present in court his case showing that Mr. Bakerman was falsely convicted?"

"Yes, I do."

"Further, any evidence currently in police hands cannot be tested for Mr. Bakerman's DNA until a ruling has been made on his underlying conviction."

Wallace nodded as Harris let go of the motion. Her face was now scarlet.

"He's got us," Wallace whispered from the side of his mouth.

"Very well then," Stromberg proceeded. "Based upon the new information contained in the defense motion, I am granting a ninety-day stay of the required testing. Further, I am ordering custody officers to return Mr. Bakerman to the jail, get him changed into civilian clothes as quickly as possible, and provide transportation to Hope House, where he is to remain until this new matter is resolved."

"Thank you, Your Honor," Anders said with glee. He reached over and shook Bakerman's hand as the judge hammered her gavel to end the session.

76

Leah Harris sat, arms crossed, staring blankly ahead. A look of defeat hung heavily across her face and shoulders. The courtroom was now empty, the last of the spectators having filed out five minutes before, leaving the slumped Seattle detective alone. Captain Varna had already paged twice requesting an immediate in-person briefing, but she was in no hurry to comply. Harris was in shock at the turn of events. Further, the image of Bakerman's gloating last look as he began his journey to freedom refused to fade from her mind's eye. "Damn him," she muttered under her breath. "Damn everyone. . . ."

"Excuse me," a female voice suddenly called out from behind. Startled, Harris twisted. She had been so centered on her own thoughts that she hadn't noticed the courtroom doors slip open. "May I speak with you for a moment?"

Harris rose from her seat, a questioning look on her face. The matronly looking woman came forward. "I'm sorry to disturb you." She stopped at the first row of seats and set her handbag down. "They told me outside that you were the detective in charge of Cindy Jo's case."

Harris's gaze deepened.

"My name is Donna Fasco." She smiled. "But you may know me by my maiden name. It was Pearson."

The name rang a bell for Harris, but she was still uncertain.

"I guess I'm too late, but I tried to get a hold of an officer I used to know and he never returned my call. Then I had this bizarre message on my answering machine yesterday about some accident. I didn't know what to do, so I took the morning off and decided to come down here and—"

"Wait a second," Harris interrupted. "Donna Pearson. Of course, you worked at Dick's with Cindy Jo."

The woman nodded and added, "I see that jerk, Russ Felder, was here for the hearing, too."

Harris raised a brow.

"I was sitting behind you," Pearson explained. "Six rows back, across the aisle from my old burger boss."

Harris instinctively sensed a possible lead. "What do you mean by *jerk*?"

Pearson laughed. "Ya got a few minutes?"

Harris nodded and leaned back on the prosecutor's table as Pearson sat down on the pewlike bench. She glanced about and remarked, "I've never been in a courtroom until today. And I never thought I'd be in one because of Cindy Jo. I gave up hoping for that years ago."

"So, what brings you down here today? Curiosity?"

Pearson suddenly blushed and looked away. The reaction caught Harris by surprise, but it instantly told her much. She had seen the look many times over the years. In a soft sensitive tone, the Seattle detective asked, "Is there something you want to tell me, maybe something that never made it into the original police report?"

Pearson resumed eye contact and nodded. In a guilty tone, she said, "I needed the job. He would have fired me if I had told anyone. Especially after—"

"After what?"

"You know, the attack."

"Wait a second," Harris blurted. "Let's back up a second and start from the beginning. You think Felder killed Cindy Jo?"

"Oh, no, not that. The man's a little weenie. No, his MO was groping the young female employees in the back room and hitting on them for dates. Most had sense enough to keep their distance, but not Cindy Jo. She actually fell for his BS and started going out with him."

Gears clicked in Harris's head.

"There's more."

"How so?"

Pearson sighed. "I guess they call it date rape now. In my day, it was just being too afraid to say no. The night before the attack, Cindy Jo stopped at my house on the way home from work. She wanted to talk. I remember it clearly. It was a hot night and I was sitting out on the porch tying to cool off."

Harris gripped the edge of the table and leaned forward. "Go on."

Pearson drew a deep breath and said, "It ended up in a fight. I told her she should break it off; he was no good; he was just using her."

"How so?"

Pearson sneered. "You know what I mean. . . . Anyway, Cindy Jo became defensive and, well, she ended up storming off and that's about it. Next thing I know, she's in that nursing home, in a coma and nearly dead."

Harris nodded empathetically. This was interesting information, but unfortunately not a smoking gun. She shifted about and asked, "Did you ever visit her while she was there?"

"Sure, a few times, early on, but . . . well, after a couple of months, my car broke down, and you know how it is."

"I do, and I appreciate your coming to me on this. It fills

some of the gaps." Harris glanced at her watch and reached for her purse. She opened it and withdrew a business card. "If you think of anything else, please give me a call. Unfortunately, I've got to get going. I've got a boss who needs to see me right away. "

Pearson straightened. "Oh, wait. There's more."

Harris's hand stopped.

"Actually, the reason I tried calling, then decided just to come here today was because of him, that Bakerman guy."

Confusion flexed Harris's face. "What about Bakerman?"

"I'm sure it's him."

"You mean at Dick's?"

"Huh? No, at the nursing home. When I saw his face on TV the other night, even after all these years, I'm sure it was him in Cindy Jo's room. It was the last time that I visited; he was there. I walked right in on him."

"Bakerman, you're sure?"

"Yep. He was dressed as an orderly. And when I came into Cindy Jo's room, there he was, hovering real close to the bed. He scared me. He had this really weird look on his face. And he was holding a pillow, like—well, I'll never forget it."

"He worked there?" Harris's mind started racing.

Pearson nodded. "A nun told me that. She came in right after he left. She said he was supposed to be in there, fixing a lamp or something."

Harris sprang to her feet. She gathered up her coat and briefcase and headed for the exit, Donna Pearson in tow. There was still a slim chance to get Cindy Jo's killer, but the method Harris was considering violated every rule in the book.

The time was 1015.

77

"Good evening," the night manager said as he looked up from his newspaper. "Can I help you?"

Tessla Quinn cautiously advanced through the lobby of Hope House to the reception counter. Two residents, leaning on the doorjamb to the TV room, turned and followed her every step.

"I'm Clifford Bakerman's attorney," Quinn said as she arrived at the counter. "He called me about an hour ago, said he wanted to see me."

There was a giggle from the pair.

"Knock it off, you two," the night manger growled.

One shrugged and mumbled under his breath, "Why the hell do I always get the fags with the ponytails?"

His companion snickered.

Quinn blushed.

"Get lost," the night manager ordered.

They reluctantly complied, ambling into the adjoining space. A second later, one of them could be heard saying, "Hey, Bakerman, your cute little piece of ass is here."

The night manager sighed. "Sorry, ma'am. Most of these boys have been in the joint for a long time. It takes a while to acclimate to the outside world."

Unfazed, Quinn nodded, then turned to wait for her client—still wondering the purpose of the call.

After court in the morning, she had spent most of the day working out funeral arrangements for her aunt. She had returned to her office in the late afternoon only to put things in order since she would be taking the next week off. Bakerman's call had come at seven p.m., as she was readying to leave for home. She had tried to postpone the visit, but he had been so adamant she relented. She made one more phone call after his, then departed the deserted office.

Clifford Bakerman soon emerged from the TV room wearing a broad smile. "There she is," he called out with glee. "My little guardian angel."

Quinn forced a smile.

"You can talk here," the night manager offered. "I need to go check on the kitchen cleanup crew."

Quinn glanced at him, wishing he would stay, but he had already turned and was heading towards the side door.

Bakerman closed the distance and extended his hand. "Miss Quinn, I never got a chance to thank you or your partner this morning. Things moved so fast."

Quinn took it. It was icy cold.

"I just had to tell you in person how grateful I am."

She let go.

"Really, you've made me the happiest man in the world."

"I'm glad for you," Quinn weakly offered.

"Oh, boy." Bakerman glowed. "I just can't believe it."

Quinn nodded. "If that's all you wanted to see me about, I unfortunately do need to go. My aunt's funeral is tomorrow and I—"

Bakerman's expression dimmed. "You have my deepest sympathies," he said. Then he added in a quiet voice, "That's actually the reason I called."

"What do you mean?" Quinn's uneasiness grew.

Bakerman reached into his shirt pocket and withdrew a package of cigarettes. He glanced up at the NO SMOKING sign and then to the young attorney. "You mind?" he said. "I hate to admit it, but I've already started back up with these. Boy, they're a tough habit to lick. Even after all these years."

Quinn raised a questioning brow.

"We'll need to step out back. That's where they let us smoke around here, out back in the alley."

"What about my aunt?"

"It's what I want to tell you. See, it's kind of tricky, legal-wise; that's why I wanted to talk to you before I go gabbing to the cops. Come on, we can talk about it out back."

Bakerman started for the hallway that led to the rear of the building. Quinn trailed, her apprehension growing with each step.

Two turns later, down a dim corridor, they came to the back door. It was clearly marked EMERGENCY EXIT ONLY—AN ALARM WILL SOUND WHEN OPENED.

Quinn looked to her client. He now wore an odd smile. "No problem," he said, and he reached up and grabbed an alligator clip that was lodged in a crack in the wall. He took it and used the metal clamp to pinch off an exposed wire. "An old cell mate back at the joint told me 'bout this little trick. Don't worry; the guys out front know all about it."

"But Mr. Bakerman—"

He pushed on the bar. "Some rules were simply meant to be bent." He chuckled. "Come on."

No warning sounded.

Bakerman held the door for Quinn to pass through, then followed out a few steps into the deserted alley. He lit up, using only one hand to twist the match out and pass it across the strike board. "Ah," he sighed. "Freedom at last."

Quinn turned, crossed her arms, and faced him. They

were now three feet from each other, and both bathed in the stark glare of a small overhead floodlight. It made their faces ghostly pale.

"Mr. Bakerman?"

There was no response. He puffed away, his eyes fixed upon her as though he were studying a work of art.

"Mr. Bakerman?"

"We have the same nose," he suddenly remarked.

"Huh?"

He smiled.

Unnerved, Quinn took a step back.

"Watch out for that pothole back there." He drew a quick puff and flicked the barely smoked butt beyond the perimeter of the light. It fell silently, somewhere in the darkness beyond.

Quinn froze. "I think we need to go back in," she said.

"Don't be scared."

"I'm not."

It was a lie.

"Look, Tessla—oh, you don't mind if I call you that—it's a pretty name—you're my attorney, right?"

She slowly nodded her head.

"That means anything I say to you is confidential."

"Yes . . . of course. But to be honest, Mr. Bakerman, I plan on removing myself from the case. I just don't think I can represent you right now."

"I understand, but you're still my attorney now? I mean right this very moment?"

"Yes, Mr. Bakerman," Quinn sighed. "I'm still your attorney until the court releases me."

"Good, so now, even if I were to admit to you that I had committed a crime, you could never testify against me, nor could the cops use the information you might tell them to arrest me. Isn't that right? Even if you told them everything you knew."

"Yes, Mr. Bakerman, but what is this all about? Quite frankly, you're making me nervous."

"Why do you say that? I would never hurt you." A sly smile broke on the old con's face. "You ever wonder who your real parents were?"

Quinn reared back. "What the hell are you talking about? I thought you wanted to talk to me about your case."

"Oh, I do, but that's not important right now. Let's talk about your parents—your real parents. They never told you, did they?"

"Told me what?"

Bakerman sighed. "You're adopted."

"That's not possible."

"It is, Tessla."

"But—"

"And to think I almost . . ." Bakerman grew somber, his tone a sad octave. "Thirty years ago, I got a job as an orderly in a maternity clinic. Do you know what kind of clinic it was?"

Quinn slowly shook her head.

"It was for unwed mothers. . . . I cleaned and scrubbed the floors, and did most of the handiwork."

"Mr. Bakerman," Quinn said with a tremor in her voice, "why are you telling me this?"

He thought for a moment, looked down the alley as though he had heard something, then said, "What does 'dismissed with prejudice' mean?"

"Y-you mean your charges?"

"Yes."

Quinn gazed nervously about.

"Well?"

"You're freaking me out. I'm going back inside." She took a side step.

"No, wait," Bakerman pleaded. "I need to tell you."

"Tell me what?"

"You need to know."

"Jesus Christ, Mr. Bakerman. What?"

The old con straightened. "In your veins—your blood—you're descended from a long line of Prussian princes."

"I'm Irish," Quinn retorted.

"You don't understand, do you?"

"Mr. Bakerman, I can assure you I am not adopted, I mean—"

"You were," Bakerman insisted. "And I've tried a lifetime to find you." He paused, as his gaze became distant. "I didn't mean to hurt her. I've never meant to hurt anyone. They just never understood—ever. Can't you see it's not my fault? If only . . ."

A look of horror suddenly rippled across Quinn's face as the realization of Bakerman's innuendoes finally took hold. "My God," she mouthed. "It's not possible—Cindy Jo Sellinzski, you—me?"

He nodded his head slowly as his right hand slid towards his back pocket.

"Don't move, Bakerman!" a new voice commanded from beyond the floodlight's perimeter. Heads whipped about as Leah Harris, gun drawn, stepped from the shadows. "I hate to break this to you, Cliff, but she's not your daughter."

Quinn's eyes flashed back and forth, confusion now replacing fear. "What is going on here?"

"She's wrong," Bakerman cried out to Tessla. "You are my flesh and blood. I saw you only moments after you were taken from Cindy Jo's womb and given over to Sister Cecilia. She told me her brother was adopting you. Now here you are, twenty-six years later. "

Harris stepped closer, her eyes fixed on the jugular of the older man. It had not begun to twitch—she had time to play her hand. She said, "What blood type are you, Mr. Bakerman?"

He thought for a moment. "I dunno."

"Your medical records say you're a type A-negative." Harris flashed a glance at Quinn. "You're an O-positive, right?"

She nodded with hesitation. "But how would you know that?"

Harris ignored the question and continued with the old con. "Cindy Jo's type was also A-negative. That makes it biologically impossible for you to be closely related."

A sense of relief washed over Quinn. "God," she breathed. "I—"

"She is my daughter!" Bakerman boomed. "She has to be! Even if Sister Cecilia wouldn't admit it, the look on her face the other night said everything."

"Sad to say, she was wrong," Harris replied. Then quickly to Quinn, "You are adopted, but he is not your father. Your mother was already pregnant when he attacked her. Unfortunately, your aunt and parents didn't know that. They believed you were the product of a rape, and buried that secret from you and the rest of the world. They even went so far as to have all the records altered so there was no trace of your true origin."

"It's not true," Bakerman screamed. "It's all a lie."

"Who is my father?"

Before Harris could answer, she caught sight of Bakerman's jugular beginning to pulse. A second later, Dr. Jekyll–like, his whole demeanor transformed. His eyes dilated, a bead of sweat formed on his brow, and his jaw was now set—fight-ready. Suddenly he laughed, his tone crazed as his hand slipped imperceptibly rearward. "You can't prove anything. In fact, you'll never be able to pin anything on me. Everything I've said up till now is useless to you." He gazed at Quinn. "Isn't that right, counselor? No one has read me my rights."

"Doesn't matter," Harris calmly retorted. Then she called out, "Ya got it, Frank?"

The second detective emerged from the dark. In his hand, he carried a small plastic Baggie, a single cigarette butt the only contents. He raised it. "We got your DNA, ya bastard. We're at a dead end with Sellinzski, but do the names Wendy Rose or Julie Alexander mean anything to you?"

Quinn twisted to see what Milkovich was holding. At that very moment, Bakerman leaped forward, grabbed her, and thrust a small paring knife to her neck.

"Don't!" Harris screamed. Her finger rode her Glock's trigger, but it did not flex.

Bakerman lurched back, his hostage firmly in his grasp. "No guns," he shouted.

Quinn's eyes widened in horror at the feel of the slim piece of steel pressed hard against her own throbbing carotid artery.

"Don't come any closer."

"The jig's up, Bakerman. Let her go. Maybe I'm wrong; maybe she is your daughter."

A slight trickle of blood began to roll from Quinn's neck. His eyes flashed wildly.

"The knife, put it down."

"No, you throw me your car keys."

"You won't get far."

"I wouldn't count on that."

Harris stepped closer.

"Stay where you are."

"Let's make a deal."

"No deal, just give me the keys."

"Trade me for her."

"Hold it, Leah," Milkovich shouted.

"Stay out of this, Frank. It's the only way."

"For God's sake—"

"What do you say, Bakerman?" Harris continued. "I'm a better hostage. Cops don't care about civilians, but they do care about other cops. So what if she gets it? We just come to work the next day and do the paperwork. But take me, and I'll be your ticket out of here."

"Leah—"

Harris ignored Milkovich. She let her right hand slump, then released her weapon. It fell and bounced onto the pavement.

"Kick it to me."

Harris halfheartedly complied. It only went a couple of feet.

Bakerman glanced at Milkovich. "Do the same."

"Fuck you."

The blade pressed harder.

Quinn shrieked.

"Frank," Harris shouted. "Do it. It's the only way."

"No, Leah. Look at his eyes. He's loving this. He'll take us all."

"Frank—"

Milkovich stepped forward into the bright arena. "Look," he spat. "Here's the deal. I'm going to pull my gun out and point it right at your fuckin' face. But I won't pull the trigger. That'd be against department policy. You make the trade, let Quinn go. When she is over by me, I'll call one of the boys to bring Leah's car around to the end of the alley and then have everyone clear out—deal?"

Bakerman's eyes locked with Milkovich's. Seconds ticked as a tense silence crackled the air. Suddenly the old con flinched. "You're capable," he mumbled. "Okay, deal."

Milkovich nodded and slowly pulled his 9-mm from its holster—a round already seated in the firing chamber.

Harris drew a deep breath. "I'm coming forward. Lower the knife."

Bakerman eased up.

She took three steps and turned, her arms limp to her side. "Your move."

Using Harris as a shield, Bakerman moved in. At the last moment, he shoved Quinn away. She tumbled to the ground as he wrapped his beefy arm around Harris's shoulders and swiftly placed the blade at her throat. "All right, your move."

Milkovich pulled a cell phone from his coat and activated it using only his left hand. His right hand kept a steady aim. "It's me," he said into the receiver. "Bring Leah's car down to the end of the block and leave it there with the keys in it. I'll explain later. . . . Yeah, right . . . and call it a night . . . right . . . okay."

He put the phone away.

"Anyone tries to follow me," Bakerman warned, "and you won't like what you find."

Milkovich didn't reply. His eyes and thoughts were on Leah. She was standing stoically only moments away from probable death. There was no doubt in Milkovich's mind that she would be killed before she ever reached the end of the alley. She would only be excess baggage on a chance flight for freedom.

More seconds passed. Only glances were exchanged. Finally, Milkovich said, "The car should be there. Now it's your move."

Bakerman nodded and took one last look at Quinn. "They're lying. I can tell. You really are my beautiful daughter." That said, he slowly began stepping backward, with

Harris tight in his grasp. "Remember," he called out. "No tricks or—"

Milkovich suddenly laughed.

Bakerman paused. "What's so funny?"

"Department policy."

"What do you mean?"

"The book says I'm supposed to negotiate with all hostage takers. Continue to talk to the bitter end."

"So?"

"Well, Mr. Bakerman, when it comes to Leah . . ."

"Yeah?"

"I don't negotiate."

The slack on Milkovich's trigger vanished.

A solitary round split the night air, echoing off the lonely brick walls. It was simultaneously followed by the thud of a collapsing human body.

78

"Can I have the rest of your fries?"

"Huh?" Leah Harris feigned deafness. "You'll have to talk into my other ear. Some idiot nearly blew this one off."

"I said, can I—"

"You big jerk—I heard you the first time." Harris fished the requested fries out of the bottom of her take-out bag and passed them over to Milkovich. She then leaned back in her seat and gazed out the windshield at the teeming parking lot of Dick's Drive-in. "God," she sighed. "We're going have to spend the whole weekend doing paperwork."

Milkovich chomped on the last of the fries and nodded in agreement. "At least we get to do it together."

Harris sighed again.

"Now what's the matter?"

"Oh, nothing. I just wish we had known about Sellinzski being pregnant and having a baby earlier on. Things would have been so much easier."

"Thank God Donna Pearson finally came forward."

"Funny how things turn out. Poor Tessla Quinn, she's going to have some real issues to deal with."

"So will the good doctor. However, I think it will work out. She's one put-together young gal," Milkovich said.

"Did you catch Collins's mea culpa in the afternoon paper, admitting to taking the medals he didn't earn?"

"I kinda respect him for going public, especially with Dellhanney dead. He didn't have to. There were no other witnesses left."

"I suppose you're right."

Suddenly Harris's cell phone began to ring.

"Ah, Christ," she groaned. "Now what?"

She activated the device. "Hello?"

Milkovich shifted her way.

"Are you sure? Okay . . . yeah . . . lucky SOB." Harris rolled her eyes. "Yeah, I'll tell him."

She hung up, a look of disgust on her face. "Bakerman is already out of surgery and is in satisfactory condition. Christ, you almost missed him. The bullet only nicked his temple."

Milkovich shrugged.

Harris punched him in the shoulder. "That was my neck on the line, pal. Phil and Ed were already in position at the end of the alley. You should have waited. Christ, you're the lousiest goddamn shot in the department."

Milkovich didn't reply.

"Well, you should have. . . ."

There was a moment of silence; then Milkovich turned to Harris and said, "He was going to kill you. One more step . . . I could see it in his eyes."

The glare in Harris's eyes faded. She reached up and touched her neck, right at the spot where Bakerman's blade had rested. She shuddered, then leaned over and planted a wet kiss on Milkovich's surprised lips. "I owe you," she blurted as she pulled away.

Milkovich nodded halfheartedly.

"Jesus, what's the matter now?"

"The way things are going, we'll never get a chance to be alone."

Harris reached over and took his hand. "I don't know; this is kinda nice."

Milkovich nodded and said slowly, "I've been thinking, Leah."

"About what?"

"Us." Harris let go, but Milkovich snatched her hand back. "Not so fast."

"Frank, where are you going with this?"

Milkovich shifted nervously in his seat.

"You're not breaking up with me, are you?"

"Is that what you want?"

"My God, no."

"Me neither."

Harris sighed with relief.

"Let's get married."

Leah Harris's mouth fell open. For a moment, she was speechless, unable to stutter a response.

"Well?"

"I—I . . ."

"If you don't want to, just say so. I'll understand."

Harris gulped.

"If you want to think about it . . ."

Suddenly, Harris leaped at Milkovich and smothered him with open arms. With him firmly in her grasp, she snuggled close and whispered into his ear, "Mrs. Milkovich, hmmm? That sounds really weird." Still keeping him close, she let go with one hand and fumbled for her pager—deactivated it—reached for her cell phone—powered it off—then leaned lip-locked for the two police band radios and disabled them. For the next few hours, the night would be all theirs.

Double Bluff
Michael A. Hawley

In a twenty-four-hour time frame, a Seattle police investigator and an Internal Affairs investigator team up to uncover a conspiracy of blood and brotherhood...

If they can survive the day.

"A roller coaster of a read."
—Steve Martini

0-451-41047-5

Available wherever books are sold, or to Order Call: 1-800-788-6262

ONYX

A KISS GONE BAD

Jeff Abbott

"A BREAKTHROUGH NOVEL."
—*New York Times* bestselling author Sharyn McCrumb

"Rocks big time...pure, white-knuckle suspense. I read it in one sitting."
—*New York Times* bestselling author Harlan Coben

A death rocks the Gulf Coast town of Port Leo, Texas. Was it suicide, fueled by a family tragedy? Or did an obsessed killer use the dead man as a pawn in a twisted game? Beach-bum-turned judge Whit Mosley must risk everything to find out.

"Exciting, shrewd and beautifully crafted...A book worth including on any year's best list."
—*Chicago Tribune*

0-451-41010-6

Available wherever books are sold, or
to order call: 1-800-788-6262

S425/Abbott

SECOND WATCH
By Lowen Clausen

Katherine Murphy is new to Seattle's Second Watch and the Ballard Avenue beat. Her partner, Grace Stevens, grew up in the small Scandinavian neighborhood and introduces Katherine to its rhythms, its people, and its dangers.

When the body of a young boy is found in a trash compactor, Katherine and Grace are the first officers at the haunting crime scene. With only one clue to carry them, they take on a risky undercover assignment to search for the killer. But it may already be too late for them to save another child in desperate need of protection.

0-451-20819-6

Available wherever books are sold, or
to order call: 1-800-788-6262